ASSASSIN'S MAGIC

ASSASSIN'S MAGIC
BOOK ONE

EVERLY FROST

Frost, Everly
Assassin's Magic

Cover design by Claire Holt with Luminescence Covers
www.luminescencecovers.com

For information on reproducing sections of this book or sales of this book,
go to
www.EverlyFrost.com
everlyfrost@gmail.com

*This book is human created. Artificial intelligence was not used to generate
text for this book.

DISCOVER THE EVER REALMS

Seven series. One world.

Suggested Reading Order:

Bright Wicked
Storm Princess
Assassin's Magic
Soul Bitten Shifter
Supernatural Legacy
Dark Magic Shifters
Kingdom of Betrayal

For everyone who brings light into the world.

CHAPTER ONE

$\mathcal{R}$ain drips down my face and back as I brace beneath the weight of the wooden log that rests across my shoulders.

I've stood like this for nearly two hours, unmoving, my feet planted on the courtyard at the center of the Assassin's Legion, and now the muscles in my arms and legs are screaming.

Three paces to my right, the only candidate left standing with me is Slade Baines.

The strain on his body is beginning to show, raindrops mingling with the sweat on his bare chest, the strands of his dark hair falling across his eyes.

We're located in a place that shouldn't exist—that doesn't exist on any map except to those who know its location. Outside these walls, a city of people go about their everyday lives in Boston, sipping lattes, worrying about paying bills, and rushing to work or school.

That life isn't for me.

Death is in my blood. It isn't a choice. I have to finish my mother's work. I have to become an assassin. The first step in my plan is to be trained as a Novice. The second step is to become a fully qualified assassin—what the assassins call a "Superior."

So far, I've made it inside these walls, but for the Master Assassin to agree to train me, I have to pass this test of endurance.

Master Gareth pauses in front of me, his eyes cold and gray. He whispers into the rain, "You will never amount to anything, Hunter Cassidy."

I blink rapidly as water drips into my eyes and plasters my hair to my back. I'm nearly naked, ordered to strip down to my sports bra and underpants. Slade, too, is wearing barely anything. It's intended to make us feel powerless, to get inside our heads and make the test of endurance harder.

Tremors rack my body while my temperature runs hot and cold in turns. No matter how much I want to give up, I remind myself: *I have to do this. I have to finish what Mom started.*

The other candidates are all men. Their mocking expressions tell me they thought they would outlast me—that I wouldn't be strong enough to hold out this long—but over the course of the afternoon, all of them except Slade fell before me.

The plank of wood is square and four inches thick. Sharp, iron nails protrude from its lower side, positioned to impale our shoulders if we don't hold it high enough.

It grows heavier and heavier. I know I can't hold on much longer. But if I fall before Slade, I'll be out. It won't matter that I held on longer than most of the men. I'm a woman. A different standard applies to me. Master Gareth will never agree to train me unless I beat all of them.

I grit my teeth and hold on.

I can't break before Slade does.

As if he senses my self-doubt, Master Gareth leans closer, a gleam in his eyes. All Superiors can use magic, but the energy I sense around him is something else: layered and deep, with levels of darkness I've never felt before.

"No woman has ever been allowed to train in my Legion," he says. "You will not be the first."

I meet his eyes, allowing the slightest glare to enter mine. What he won't admit is that I'm not the first woman to step foot inside these walls. Mom was the first. He didn't train her, though; he isn't lying about that. The Master before him trained her. But Master Gareth trained *with* my mother and it must worry him that I've suddenly appeared on his doorstep and asked to become an assassin like her.

There are three Factions of assassins in the United States: the Legion here in Boston, Massachusetts, the Horde in Austin, Texas, and the Dominion in Portland, Oregon. Each Faction has one intake of Novices each year and candidates must be twenty years old to be considered. Not younger and not older. This is my one and only shot.

Master Gareth straightens and his robes drag, sodden with rain, across the stone courtyard as he paces around me.

I sense him pause at my back, no doubt studying the tattoo that decorates my shoulder. It's an intricate design—one my mother created for me. I had it inked into my skin the day after she died. The day all her plans failed.

I draw on her memory to keep me standing, the memory of her last words giving me strength: *Just because you're born into darkness doesn't mean you can't overcome it.*

Words I've lived by since the day she died.

Half of the trainees gloat at the way Gareth is speaking to me. The other half… look me up and down in a way that makes me shudder. Many of them have an air of entitlement about them.

I never met any of them before today, but I've already memorized their faces and names. The big guy in the middle is Lutz Logan, the smaller guy beside him is Brandon Baker, and the blond guy is Rowan Robertson. The others all seem to have figured out that if they want to survive, they're going to have to do what Lutz says.

I'll need to watch my back at all times.

Gareth shouts from behind me. "You are nothing, woman! You will be nothing!" He leans right in behind me and rants into my ear. "You are worth nothing."

Movement to my right makes me glance in that direction. Slade glares at the ground, his teeth gritted, his palms still pressing upward, but his fingers curl slightly as if he wants to form fists.

He shifts a little so his gaze can meet mine. His eyes are slightly wide-set, a pale blue color but rimmed in a darker gray that looks almost black, making them appear crisp and piercing. Dark brown hair with a wave in it frames his face while his strong chin is indented with a slight cleft. There is nothing soft about his face, not even his lips, which are perfectly formed and pursed in an unforgiving line.

Anger swirls in his face and I'm surprised when he casts his rage in the Master's direction.

I don't allow myself to imagine that Gareth's taunts have made Slade angry—that he could be furious on my behalf. I block it all out, focusing on a point on the muddy courtyard, on a single mossy stone embedded in the ground with all the others.

The court is cobbled stone, but the rain has kicked up dust and debris. The Master may be powerful and strong—the strongest assassin in the Eastern United States—but nature is always stronger. He can't control the rain. Even here in what we call an Assassin's Realm, nature breaks through.

Each Realm is a place that sits right on top of a humanmade landmark. In the Legion's case, its Realm rests on top of the Boston Common. Ancient magic allows the buildings inside the Realm to coexist in the same space as the park. There could be a person walking through the exact location where I'm standing right now and I wouldn't know it—and neither would they.

Another half an hour passes and my shoulders sag. My head droops. My legs wobble. My arms shake.

Slade isn't faring any better. If only we weren't trying to beat each other. Doesn't he know that he doesn't have to prove himself anymore? He's in. He'll be trained. He doesn't have to beat me.

He seems to have the same thought at that moment, his gaze flashing to me. His forearms are shaking just as hard as mine. He takes a deep breath, exhales out through his mouth, and steps forward, tipping his hands backward to allow the plank to drop safely to the ground behind him.

It thuds to the stone, an impact that is met with silence.

He's a step in front of me, so I can't see his expression, but his arms lower in agonizingly slow increments, the muscles in his back tensing and rippling. It's the flow of blood to his fingers that will hurt. I don't want to think about it. All I know is that I have to hold on long enough that it's clear I held on the longest.

Master Gareth takes up position two paces in front of me, staring at me, waiting. His expression tells me that he wants me to fail, no matter what I do. No matter how long I hold up this damn piece of wood.

Mom warned me about him many times. *Don't believe anything he says. Don't accept any favors from him. And above all, never contradict him.*

I hold on for another five minutes, counting out each second within my mind. Seconds closer to relief. Then I step out from under the plank the same way Slade did, trying not to scream as it slides from my numb fingers and the weight lifts.

I don't take it easy. I drop my hands to my sides, letting the blood rush to my fingertips in an excruciating wave.

Slade raises his eyebrows at me, a look of amazement on his

face. I guess he's surprised that I would welcome the pain so readily.

I squeeze my eyes closed. There is no pain that compares to watching my mother die.

There is no pain like standing in front of her killer and not being able to avenge her.

The burning sensation in my arms will be over soon and in the meantime, I refuse to make a sound.

When I open my eyes, I find Master Gareth pacing between Slade and me, tracing a figure eight around and between us.

He stops in front of me and says, "It was a tie."

I blink at him. It clearly wasn't, but I can't say anything.

He repeats, louder, as if he thinks I didn't hear him. "It was a tie."

I grit my teeth. He wants me to contradict him, but I won't say a word. If I want to stay, I have to accept everything he says and everything he does, no matter what.

He can't see Slade's face, but I can. Slade remains with his back to me, but his head and shoulders are turned in the Master's direction. A deep furrow forms in his brow, making the contours of his face even harsher than before.

He opens his mouth, but his eyes meet mine—just in time.

I give him the smallest shake of my head. I don't want him to say anything.

My gesture causes the crease in his brow to deepen, but he doesn't voice whatever he was about to say.

Master Gareth remains staring at me as he says, "The ranking order is as follows: Slade Baines, Lutz Logan, Brandon Baker, Rowan Robertson..." He continues listing out names until he gets to the end and then he spits with disgust, "And Hunter Cassidy."

Despite the fact that Gareth is trying to demean me in the eyes of the other trainees by putting me last, he's done me a favor. My low ranking means I'm not a threat to their egos.

Unlike Slade. Lutz has been sizing him up for the last forty minutes, no doubt trying to figure out when he might be able to slide a knife between Slade's ribs.

I might be ranked last, but I'm in.

Now the real challenge begins: Doing what Mom couldn't.

And maybe... I'll avenge her at the same time.

CHAPTER TWO

One of the nearby Superiors steps up and shouts, "Gather into line, Novices!"

Three Superiors have been standing at the edge of the courtyard, guarding the endurance test. In the early part of the test, several candidates dropped out and one of the Superiors took them away.

Like Master Gareth, the Superiors are all large, imposing men, although not all of them are brutish in appearance. It takes all kinds to make a good assassin. Some of the best appear completely harmless.

I stay where I am, since the Superior who shouted is pretty much pointing to my current position. I take the chance while the other trainees join me to wring out my ponytail, slicking any loose strands behind my ears.

Twelve of us have made it through.

As the other candidates form a rough line out to either side of me, Slade takes a quick step back to stand on my right while Lutz angles in to stand at my left, his gaze dragging over my body.

The rain is only a drizzle now, but his gaze follows the water droplets that travel all the way from my shoulders down my thighs. He's also stripped down to his underwear and his near-nakedness leaves nothing to the imagination.

I've met plenty of Lutz's type in my life. Mom used to make deals with dangerous men for various reasons, although more frequently, she killed them.

I hide a smile at the knowledge that she already taught me everything she knew. The trick for me will be pretending that I don't know any of it yet.

Lutz Logan doesn't take his eyes off my breasts as he towers next to me, raising his voice loud enough for everyone to hear. "Looks like we have a new plaything, boys."

I respond immediately by turning and stepping right into him, forcing him to look higher than my chest. I tip my head back to maintain eye contact and show him that I'm not afraid.

My voice is even and low. "Try anything and I will rip your balls off with my fingernails."

The barest hint of surprise flickers across his face, but he quickly hides it. I guess he expected me to cower in fear of his brutishness.

He shrugs it off. "If you say so, sweetheart."

I adjust my focus to the Superior who ordered us into line. His next order is aimed at me. "Step back in line, Novice."

As I obey, I sense Slade watching me from my other side, but I also catch the slight lift of his head as he looks over the top of me at Lutz. Slade's expression is deadpan, no hint of anything that could be construed as a challenge or dislike, only a calm assessment.

He and Lutz are the same height and build, the only difference being that the trial proved Lutz's muscles are all for show, whereas Slade's are...

I quickly fixate on the pebbles again.

Functional doesn't seem adequate to describe Slade's powerful physique.

Master Gareth takes up position beside the Superior who ordered me to step back, but the Master remains silent, allowing the Superior to take charge.

"I am Superior Ridley. I will teach you combat, weaponry, and survival skills." He indicates the other two Superiors as he speaks, confirming my suspicion that they will be teaching us. "This is Superior Fallon, who will teach you how to use assassin's magic, and that is Superior Lincoln, who will teach you about poisons."

Ridley steps back while Lincoln assesses us. Lincoln is as tall and imposing as Ridley but is more leanly built. As the poisons teacher, his talent will be for killing by deception rather than brute strength.

"Your fight to survive starts now," Lincoln says. "From this moment on, you will follow the Assassin's Code."

He pauses to make sure he has our attention. "The first rule: Assassins don't kill each other. Any Superior or Novice who breaks this rule forfeits their life. Every assassin in this Legion will come after you if you break this rule. The only time you lay hands on each other will be in training. Is that understood?"

Lutz lets out a laugh beside me. "What if we want to have a little fun, sir?"

Lincoln steps up to Lutz, a dangerous air settling around him. He speaks quietly, but threat hangs on every word. "Do you think you're here to have fun, Novice?"

Lutz's grin quickly disappears. "No, sir."

"Correct, Novice. You're here because pain is going to be your friend. Fatigue will be your friend. *Insecurity* will be your friend. Some of you will embrace it..."

Lincoln glances at me, as if he thinks I'm one of the few who will welcome pain with a smile on my face.

He quickly adjusts his focus, saying, "Others will be sent home."

He steps back and Ridley takes over again. "For the

remainder of the day, you will get settled into your dorm and be supplied with new clothing. After that, dinner. Tomorrow morning, you will arrive back in this courtyard at five A.M. without exception." He eyes each of us as if he expects us to disobey him already. "Now follow me to your dorm."

Master Gareth interrupts for the first time, holding up his hand. "I will take them today, Ridley."

Ridley appears surprised but gives a quick nod, stepping aside for the Master. "Of course, Master Gareth."

Gareth strides away across the courtyard and the Superiors quickly hustle us after him. I follow on Slade's heels, sticking close to him since he's the only Novice who hasn't ogled my breasts yet. And because of the look on his face when Master Gareth was taunting me.

It would be foolish of me to trust Slade, but of all the men in this group, he is my safest bet.

We travel across the courtyard and along the wide footpath between buildings. Far off to my right, a building that resembles a cathedral rises up above the others.

The Cathedral is where Master Gareth's personal quarters are located. It's the place I need to infiltrate. If it were as easy as sneaking in there, I would have done it already, but the Cathedral is covered in deadly protective spells. Only Superiors are allowed to enter. Anyone else can expect to meet their death as soon as they attempt to step through the doors.

We finally reach a building made of two levels with an outer staircase up one side and a balcony at the front of each level. A group of men gathers on the balcony of the first level to watch us pass.

Mom once described this place to me and the hierarchy that exists in everything here. In terms of where we sleep, the new Superiors are located on the first floor of this building; and the Novices—us—sleep at the top.

I reach the top of the stairs and shuffle myself closest to the wall and farthest away from the balcony railing, where I'm less conspicuous.

Master Gareth swings the wide doors open to reveal a dormitory with a service elevator on the left and twelve beds at intervals on the right. They aren't much more than rollaway cots. A tall, narrow locker stands beside each, along with a small shelf bearing a lamp.

A single blanket has been folded at the base of each bed. It's summer in Boston right now, but winters are bitterly cold and I don't see any heating. No doubt only the highest-ranked Novices will get extra blankets. Everything is about status here.

Given that there are twelve of us and twelve beds, it means that I'll be sleeping in here with the men. After the looks they gave me earlier, this is not exactly a safe situation for me.

I sense someone's eyes on me. Turning slightly, avoiding any big moves, I swallow a sigh of disgust to find Lutz Logan staring at my backside. The others won't make a move without his say-so. It doesn't matter what Superior Lincoln says about keeping our hands to ourselves—Lutz is the one I have to worry about.

Well, it's bad that I'll have to sleep with my eyes open, but at least I'll have a bed.

I turn back to the room to find Master Gareth suddenly grinning at me. He isn't old. In fact, I know his exact age is forty. But he carries himself in a way that is distant and aloof. He is tall, broad-shouldered, clothed in a dark gray robe over a shirt and pants that are also gray. Somehow, the absence of color serves to accentuate his cold eyes and chiseled features rather than diminish them.

The fact that he's smiling right now makes me shudder. Nothing good could make this guy happy.

I brace for whatever's coming next.

As Ridley joins him, Gareth says, "Superior Ridley, please ask the janitorial staff to remove one of the beds. The lowest-ranked Novice will sleep on the floor until she improves her rank."

Ridley's forehead creases. Even he seems to think this is a bit tough. But he doesn't object. "Yes, Master Gareth."

I totally jinxed myself. There is no bed for me after all.

I tell myself: *It's okay, Hunter. Sleeping on the floor means you're right beside the door with your back to the wall.* It's not a terrible place to be. I'll have a quick getaway if I need it and I only have to watch for what's in front of me.

Ridley leaves the room and after several long and painfully quiet minutes, he returns with two men, both of whom are wearing janitorial uniforms. The janitors swoop toward the nearest cot, roll up the thin mattress, fold the cot in half, and roll it into the service elevator. They don't pay much attention to me or the other Novices.

The service staff were once Novices who made it through to the end of training but failed to become Superiors. They're given the choice between returning to the world outside or staying on as staff. Personally, I'd prefer to leave.

Master Gareth clasps his hands in front of him as the Novices crowd around. "Now, you will choose your beds in order of rank. Slade Baines first."

Slade eyes the bed closest to the door. That's the one I would pick. It has the quickest and easiest escape route if something goes wrong. It's potentially the coldest location, though, especially if the wind whistles through the gap under the door. Still, I'd rather be cold than caught in a trap.

He pauses, a thoughtful crease forming on his forehead. He takes on a respectful tone as he asks, "May I clarify, Master Gareth, that I can pick any bed?"

Gareth gives him an indulgent smile. "You may."

Slade doesn't miss a beat. "Then I choose Hunter's bed."

Silence falls over the room.

Uh, what? I didn't hear that right.

Master Gareth splutters, the Superiors appear startled, and I'm pretty sure my jaw hits the ground.

Slade moves swiftly to my side, taller than I thought now that he's standing so close to me, closer even than when we waited in line. I stand at five-foot-nine, so I can hold my own around tall guys, but Slade is a full head taller.

Up close, he smells like cinnamon, all earthy and warm. After the rain and sweat of the endurance test, it's unexpectedly pleasant and more than a little distracting.

He lowers his voice, speaking in a rapid murmur. "Pick one and do it fast."

I stare at him in confusion. Share a bed with him?

There's barely room for one person to lie on those rollaway cots, let alone two. Let alone… the sharing part. I fixate on the curve of his shoulders, where his skin is still damp with rain, adjusting my gaze to the faint wash of bristles across his jaw and up to his eyes, searching for answers in his open gaze.

Why is he doing this?

Does he see me as a threat, so he wants to keep me close? Or maybe he's just like the other men and thinks he can take advantage of me?

It surprises me to realize that I don't want him to be that guy. After the way he glared at Master Gareth earlier, I want to believe my instincts: that Slade has a conscience.

I don't have time to think through his possible motives or the consequences of accepting his current course of action. The only thought that keeps everything in perspective is that I can always return to the floor if I don't like where this is going.

I point at the bed closest to the door that Slade was studying before. "That one."

Slade remains at my side, keeping himself positioned between me and Master Gareth—an oddly protective gesture— as he inclines his head and says to Gareth, "That's our bed."

Gareth's smile slips and his eyes resemble cold stone, but at the last moment, he grins at Slade. It's like watching a wolf draw its lips back over its teeth.

There is no humor in his expression as he says, "Very well. If you want her all to yourself, that is your right as the highest-ranking candidate. She sleeps with you."

With a sharp incline of his head, Gareth barks at Ridley, "Oversee the remainder. I'll be in my quarters." He turns on his heel and stomps from the room. I guess he thought this would turn out differently and now there's no fun in sticking around.

Ridley calls out to Lutz Logan to choose next. Unsurprisingly, he picks the bed at the back of the room, farthest from Slade. The others follow one by one.

My heart rate increases as Slade remains resolutely by my side, his big arm close enough to brush mine every time he inhales. I think I might be drowning in the warm scent of cinnamon and it's progressed past a little distracting to very distracting, but I can't move away from him without drawing attention.

I now have time to question Slade's motives for wanting me in the same bed. My acceptance of it was instinctive before, but my distrust resurfaces.

Trust has never come easily to me. Mom taught me to trust no one.

I need to make it clear to Slade that I will defend myself if he tries anything.

When Ridley's back is turned, I turn to Slade, saying quietly, "If you touch me—"

"I know. I heard what you said to Lutz." His voice remains low and even. Calm. Surprisingly honest. "I will keep my hands, and every other part of me, to myself. I have no intention of disrespecting you."

His choice of words and his serious tone takes the wind out of my rage.

He continues. "I realize you don't have to believe me, but I could use some friendly eyes watching my back. Code or no code, we're both targets. I'd like to stay alive and I think you would too."

I quietly exhale. So his decision was tactical.

Superior Ridley would be proud. It's true that I need an ally among the Novices.

But can I trust Slade?

It could all be a ploy. He's smart. He won't underestimate my determination to excel during our training. He could pretend to be my friend right up until the end and then stake me in the back.

But if it means a higher chance of getting into the Cathedral, it's a chance I'm willing to take.

CHAPTER THREE

Superior Ridley ushers us from the dorm and shows us the showers in the next building.

Again, there are different facilities for the Novices and the new Superiors, but, as I expected, no separation for men and women. One look inside the communal shower room tells me I'm going to have to figure out an alternative way to stay clean.

Stand in the rain, perhaps?

After that, we wait in line for our new clothing. We had to give up everything we were wearing when we first arrived, so I brought nothing of value with me, not even my favorite pair of boots. All of my belongings are safely tucked away in storage.

We'll train for seven months before we have the chance to become Superiors. The first four months will be spent in the Realm. Then they'll send us out on reconnaissance missions for two months, and in the final month, we'll be given our first missions.

If we pass all of those tests, we'll become Superiors. That's when I'll be able to infiltrate the Cathedral. I plan to be out of here immediately after that.

Slade leaves my side for the first time since visiting the

dorm. As the highest-ranking candidate, he goes first into the fitting room and emerges with his arms full of clothing. It's hard to see what he's been given since it's folded in his arms—shirts, pants, underwear, probably. Everything is navy blue except the boots he carries, which are black.

He slows as he passes me, quickly assessing my current status. Nobody has come near me since he went inside. He gives me a quick nod, which I return, before he heads to the bathroom to change.

I continue to wait for my turn. I'll have to get used to being last, but it has its advantages. For starters, there's nobody glaring daggers at my back.

To my surprise, it's Superior Ridley who greets me inside the fitting room. I expected one of the lower staff to serve us.

Without any prompting, he explains, "I will teach you about weaponry, but that includes apparel. What you wear can save your life. That means it has to match your physique and how you use your body to fight."

His forehead creases as he contemplates me, but not in an angry way, more in a sort of perplexed what-am-I-going-to-do-with-you way. "We don't have any women's clothing, so I've requested that you're allowed to wear the clothes you arrived in. But only while we get new ones made."

Shoot. Now I regret not wearing my favorite boots.

He hands me my old clothing but asks me to stand still while he takes my measurements. As he wraps the measuring tape around my waist, he says, "Your mother was a hell of an assassin."

I treat his comment with suspicion. I have to treat everything with suspicion, even compliments. What he said about my mother causes me to reassess his age. He could be old enough to have met her. Or he could be pretending to have known her so I'll let down my guard.

"Did you train with her?" I ask.

"She was a Novice in the year after me. Nobody messed with her. But that was mainly because the old Master protected her. You don't have that in your favor."

I swallow, weighing up the wisdom of asking my next question. "What happened between her and Master Gareth?"

That was one thing Mom never talked about: her relationships with the people here before she finished her training.

Ridley gives an unexpected chuckle. "She kicked his butt. Multiple times. She was favored to be the first female Master Assassin. She would have been, if she hadn't disappeared."

Masters change every twenty years. The Assassin's Code sets out exactly how it happens, but essentially, the old Master picks his replacement from the intake of Novices in the nineteenth or twentieth year after he takes over. That's my year or the year before me.

Superior Ridley shrugs. "Six months later, we heard she'd had a child, so that explained why she disappeared."

His tone isn't accusing, just matter-of-fact.

He tells me to turn around so he can measure from the base of my neck to my waist. "You're in a tough year, Hunter. You'll need to make a reputation for yourself quickly or the other trainees will annihilate you."

"They won't touch me, Superior Ridley. Don't worry about that."

"Well, I hope you're right. You've got your mother's looks. I'd hate to see you get messed up in this place."

I grit my teeth. "I'm looking forward to your class, Superior Ridley."

"Good. I'll see you tomorrow morning. Don't eat breakfast before you arrive. You'll just bring it up again."

Sounds like his class will be tough, then. I didn't expect anything less. "Thank you, Superior Ridley."

I pick up my clothing, but before I can leave, he places a firm hand on my shoulder. "Your mom did me a favor once, so… if you need help, let me know."

I look him in the eye and say, "Thanks," but there's no way I'm taking him up on his offer.

I can't owe anyone anything. I can't afford allegiances. I'm already uncertain about Slade Baines. I don't need someone else to worry about.

As fast as I can, I pull on my clothing—faded blue jeans and a marbled gray T-shirt, together with soft ankle boots. The boots are my least favorite ones, but they're comfortable enough. My underwear has mostly dried off now, but my hair is still damp and my long mahogany ponytail quickly flattens my shirt to my back between my shoulder blades.

Because I was the last to be fitted, everyone else has gone to dinner and only Superior Lincoln, the poisons teacher, waits impatiently for me outside the fitting room.

All he says is: "Dinner."

He strides away, expecting me to follow him. I race after him, trying to keep up with his long legs, finding myself hurrying at a half-jog beside him. While Superior Ridley seems to be the oldest of the trainers, Lincoln appears the youngest, probably in his early thirties.

Once again, we pass the Cathedral, but closer this time— close enough that I can sense the spells that have been cast around it. Even the Masters of the other two Factions can't enter without an invitation.

It's frustrating being this close to it and not being able to go inside, but even the space around it is protected by a multitude of magical alarms.

I have to stick to my plan.

We enter the food hall, where Lincoln leaves me with a clipped order. "Find a seat. Dinner will be brought to you."

There are maybe forty men, including the Novices, all seated at tables set out in rows. Master Gareth and the teachers are dining at a table off to the side, separated from the rest.

Silence descends as I hover in the entrance and quickly assess my options. It doesn't help that a bunch of empty spots suddenly fill up before my eyes.

Nobody wants to sit with me.

I get it. They can't afford to be seen fraternizing with the woman who wants to train in the Legion.

Inwardly, I shake my head. Female assassins are more common in the other Factions, especially the Horde. The Legion has always been male-dominated. Which makes my choice to train here that much more unusual.

I feel more confident in my own clothes, so I stride down the middle aisle with my head held high.

Lutz stands up and calls out to me, "Over here, sweetheart. You can sit on my lap."

He makes a crude gesture that indicates exactly what he would do if I sat on his lap.

I smile sweetly and prowl in the direction of his table, veering toward the nearest surface—a very handy table holding a multitude of cutlery from which I sweep up a steak knife.

Swiftly testing its weight and balance in my hand, I ascertain that the handle is heavy and the blade is off-balance to the right, but I can accommodate that.

I don't hide the fact that I have it, holding it in a fighter's grip parallel with my body.

"Ooh, I'm scared," Lutz calls as the silence continues around us. "Careful, little girl, or you might cut yourself."

From the long table at the side of the room, Master Gareth and the three teachers watch me with narrowed eyes but they don't intervene.

I'm free to make my own choices in this place. If that includes cutting off Lutz's crown jewels, then so be it. What the Superiors control are the consequences I'll face afterward.

Only Superior Ridley looks concerned, his forehead puckered as he takes a seat, having arrived moments after I did.

He warned me about getting messed up and I'm already throwing his advice to the wind.

Lutz is smart enough to look wary when I continue to advance toward him.

His gaze flicks to the knife and my grip on it. We haven't had combat class yet to size each other up for our existing skills, but I'm pretty sure I appear confident about my aim and abilities right now.

Only seven paces away from him, I prepare to pitch the knife right between his legs, anticipating the satisfying *thud* it's going to make when it impales his chair.

I'm ready for the retaliation that will follow.

CHAPTER FOUR

Slade steps into my path.

My focus on Lutz must have been so intense that I didn't see Slade nearby and I'm suddenly kicking myself for losing awareness of my closer surroundings.

Now he blocks my view, commanding my attention and forcing my focus to shift to him.

I jolt to a stop. He's wearing the navy clothing he was given—supple pants and a shirt that stretches over his chest and biceps, accentuating his muscles. The color enhances his eyes, making them appear an even more striking blue. The angles of his face are still unforgiving but deliberately relaxed, as if he realizes that any sudden movements on his part will send my reflexes into fight mode.

His eyes meet mine, his voice a murmured warning. "You worked harder than anyone else to get here, Hunter. Don't throw it away."

My knuckles turn white around my weapon. "I will slash the smile right off Lutz Logan's face."

Slade suddenly grins, an action that chases away the shadows from his eyes and transforms his face from harsh to…

mesmerizing. Nobody has the right to have lips that curve so tantalizingly.

Somebody definitely needs to outlaw that.

I'm glued to the spot as he says, "One day. Not today."

My eyes narrow and my forehead creases as I shake myself out of the force of his smile and its disarming effect. For the first time, I wonder what has caused Slade to choose an assassin's life. Lutz's reasons are obvious—he's an open book who loves power over others—but Slade has already exhibited more calm and control than I'd expect from a Novice.

I suppress a shiver as I realize that could make Slade more dangerous.

He's hiding his true self, *controlling* his true self. I'm not sure how afraid I should be of who he is underneath the mask he wears.

He gestures to the table he rose from. "There's a spare seat here if you want it."

The table he indicates is populated with last year's Novices— the men who are the new Superiors. I recognize some of them from this afternoon when they watched us from the balcony. There are only four of them, so if the intake was twelve, that means eight candidates didn't make it through the training last year.

The seat Slade gestures at will place my back to Lutz, which isn't great, but the hierarchy here should prevent Lutz from coming over—he is lower-ranked than the new Superiors sitting at this table and they won't tolerate any aggressive gestures.

I give Slade a short nod and lower my arm, but I don't give up my weapon.

To my surprise, as I move to sit down, all of the Superiors at this table stand up. At first, I think it's because they're going to leave and I bury a sigh.

Well, at least I'll have a place to eat, even if they all disappear on me.

Then they resume their seats. *Um...?*

It's like watching something from an old-fashioned movie where the guys stand up for the girl to sit down. I'm speechless for the second time today. But none of them seems condescending about it, giving me quick nods of welcome, so I decide to relax and go with it.

"Thank you," I say, not really sure whom I'm thanking or for what.

The guy to my right gives me a pleasant smile. He has light brown hair and eyes a similar pale blue shade to Slade's, but the contours of his face aren't anywhere near as stern. "Welcome, Hunter. I'm Thomas. Slade told us you held out for two and a half hours during the endurance test today."

I place the steak knife carefully on the table, avoiding any sudden moves with it. These men are not like Lutz, who laughs at my anger. They will take any hostility on my part seriously.

Slade clears his throat as he takes a seat on my other side. "The record used to be two hours. I came here intending to beat it and set a new record of my own."

He shrugs dismissively and his expression is calm. I don't get any sense that he resents me for beating him, but his ambition would explain why he held on so long this afternoon.

Still, I'm suddenly wary. My mother set the previous record of two hours. It's internal knowledge. A new Novice like Slade wouldn't know about it unless he had contacts here.

"How did you know about the record?" I ask Slade.

Thomas speaks, making me swivel away from Slade to the right. "I told Slade about it," he says. "We're cousins."

Just then, staff members appear from the kitchens, pushing food trolleys laden with plates. There's one trolley for each table, so the food quickly reaches us. Thomas leans back to allow a staff member to reach between us and place a plate of mouth-watering deliciousness in front of me.

I didn't realize how hungry I was until this moment.

As I begin to eat, I ask carefully, "So the business runs in the family?" Many assassins come from a long line of family members who are part of the trade. People out there in the world suspect that we exist, but most think we're a myth, a story. The ones who know we're real either have a family member who is an assassin, or they're seeking our services.

"Our grandmother was an assassin," Slade responds, taking a bite of his meal.

"Grand*mother*," I say before I can stop myself. I glance with surprise from him to his cousin and then to the other men around the table. "That would explain why you aren't freaked out by me."

The guy opposite me leans forward, putting his fork down. He has dark brown hair and eyes the color of a forest: deep green flecked with woody tones. He's leaner than Thomas. Even sitting down, I have the impression he could move quickly but chooses to keep an even pace.

"Women often make the best assassins." He gestures to his colleagues. "If a male target sees us coming, he runs for the hills. But if he sees *you*, he wants to date you, not run away from you." A sudden grin breaks across his face. "And I use the word 'date' as a euphemism."

I hide my smile. "Thank you for putting it so politely."

He acknowledges my thanks with a tilt of his head. "I'm Matthew."

"Pleased to meet you, Matthew."

As we eat, the other two men introduce themselves. Each of them is descended from assassins, both male and female.

Thomas asks, "What made you choose the Legion, Hunter?" It sounds like a casual question, but I sense how curious he must be, given that the Legion is notoriously inhospitable to female candidates.

I answer his question with a question, unable to keep the challenge from my voice. "You think I should have joined the Horde?"

He shrugs, an apology reflected in the regretful curve of his broad shoulders. "They're much kinder to their female candidates."

"Wasn't your grandmother here in the Legion?"

"Actually, no," Slade says from my other side. "She trained with the Horde."

Thomas says, "There's only ever been one female here, as far as we know. They called her 'the Glass Fox.'"

"And she was the best," I snap. "With all due respect to your grandmother, I want to be the best. The Legion will make me stronger."

I push away the memory of the expression in my mother's eyes before she died, begging me never to come here.

Find another way, she said.

But there is no other way. Master Gareth controls an object called the Clave. It's the key to a truly dangerous weapon and the most unbelievable part is… he thinks the Clave is just a relic.

He doesn't know it's a key or that it can locate the weapon he has spent his whole life trying to find. I have to keep it that way. I can't let him discover the Clave's true purpose. I have to steal it and take it as far away from him as possible.

Mom died trying to protect the Clave and I won't let her death be in vain.

Thomas is quiet beside me. I stare at my plate, not eating, suddenly regretting my declaration. I was too forceful. The new Superiors welcomed me to their table and now I've responded with anger.

When I look up, I discover that I have a clear line of sight to

Master Gareth. I didn't notice him staring at me before because I was busy eating and paying attention to the people nearer to me. His cold gaze settles on me. His eyes narrow and he pauses in the middle of lifting his fork now that he realizes I'm staring back.

He would kill to know what I know. In fact, he *has*.

I turn to Thomas. "I apologize. Your question caught me off guard. I realize it must seem strange—or even reckless—that I've chosen to train with the Legion."

His lips curve into a smile. "No offense taken. You wouldn't survive here for two seconds without the fire you just showed us." He gestures to the other Superiors. "We can't help you or Slade much, but we can make meal times less painful for you both. This is our table and you're welcome to eat at it."

"Thank you." My gratitude sounds small. "You're not worried about what others will say?"

Thomas's smile broadens. "We're Superiors now. We have the rest of the year to build reputations for ourselves and then we can go out into the world and accept our own clients."

Only a limited number of Superiors stay in the Realm permanently. Those are the Master, the teaching staff, and the Superiors whom the Master trusts the most or wants around for some reason. New Superiors are required to stay in the Realm for their first year, but the rest are expected to make a living for themselves. Ultimately, though, we always belong to the Legion, which means that Master Gareth can call us back anytime he wants.

Matthew leans forward. "We don't care what the Novices think. Half of them will be gone in a month. A few more will hold on longer than that. Only a handful will make it all the way."

When I arrived here this morning, I was determined not to accept anyone's assistance. Somehow in the space of mere hours, I've had multiple offers of help. Having a safe place to eat is one I'm prepared to accept.

Before the meal is over, Thomas tells us that he and the other new Superiors are heading out on a mission tonight, so they won't see us again until dinner tomorrow.

When we finish eating, Slade stands with me, remaining at my side for the walk back to the dorm. As the cool outside air washes away some of the security I felt inside the food hall, I allow my senses to spark again, paying attention to my surroundings, especially to the other Novices following behind us.

We're just out of earshot of the others, so I lower my voice and say to Slade, "Don't eat breakfast before Superior Ridley's combat class tomorrow morning. You'll only throw it up again."

"Thanks." He's quiet for another moment. "There's a washroom at the front of the dorm. It's tucked around the corner past the service elevator. I wasn't sure if you saw it earlier."

"I didn't. Thank you." I guess he came to the same conclusion I did: There will be no showers for me.

Unlike me, Mom stayed in the Master Assassin's quarters, which is why she never had the same privacy issues that I do. The fact that she lived with him also made it very clear who my father was. I used to wish I could have met him, but he died soon after Master Gareth took over.

When we reach the dorm, I study the contents of the locker that stands beside the empty space where my bed used to be. The cupboard contains a few simple toiletries: deodorant, hairbrush, soap, and a washcloth. Also a towel.

The space where I will hang my clothes is empty pending Ridley's quest for clothing that will fit me. But in the bottom of the cupboard I'm surprised to find the bag I handed in when I arrived.

I almost laugh out loud when I find it's been emptied of the few things I brought with me except for one pair of jeans, a T-shirt, and the mountain of female necessities that will last me a year. I guess they decided they didn't want to have to buy sanitary items for me.

Tucking the bag away, I grab the soap and washcloth, and close the locker, leaning back on it. I fold my arms and cross one booted foot over the other. I will wait until all the men have gone to shower before I head to the washroom. Then I'll make sure I'm out of it before they get back. For my own safety, I will maintain visibility of them at all times.

I look up to find Slade sitting at the end of his—*our*—bed opposite me, arms folded loosely across his chest, fresh clothing resting on his lap.

He's watching over me.

I wonder if I should be offended. *I'm* the only one who watches out for me. That's who I am and how I've lived my life since Mom died. But despite my best efforts to dig deep and find any feeling of outrage at the fact that he's trying to be my friend… I can't.

Maybe it's the way he does it without invading my space or making a big deal about it, but I don't mind that he's remaining vigilant about my safety.

His apparently casual gaze shifts from me to the door. All of the other Novices are forced to walk between us to get to their beds and lockers, and it seems to be making them nervous.

All except Lutz, who arrives last, swaggering along the walkway, singing out to me, "I missed you at dinner, sweetheart."

My fingers twitch around the bar of soap I'm gripping. A good assassin can turn any object into a deadly weapon. I'm pretty sure I could ram it down his throat and choke him to death with it.

But there's always that pesky rule… Assassins don't kill each other.

It's the biggest lie I've ever heard.

If it were true, my mother would still be alive.

CHAPTER FIVE

Slade is the last to leave for the showers. He gives me a quick nod and I wait another few moments to make sure the others are all gone before I race to the washroom.

Locking the door, I strip off and quickly use the washcloth and cold water from the tap to clean myself. I dry off fast and dress in tomorrow's jeans and T-shirt, ready in case I need to move fast in the morning.

I let my hair down for the first time, brushing out the waves that fall down my back. When I check myself in the mirror, I don't like the effect my loose hair has on my appearance. I look far too feminine. Far too vulnerable. I should put it back up, but I hate sleeping with my hair tied up…

I growl at the mirror and pull my hair over one shoulder, twisting it around so it doesn't look so carefree.

Finishing up in the bathroom, I cut my return to the dorm a little too close. I can already hear the men coming up the stairs. I shove my toiletries inside my locker and hang the washcloth and towel over an empty clothes hanger to dry.

Then I eye the bed. I'm not getting into it until Slade does.

I'm not sitting on it, either—that paints the wrong picture too. So I cross the room and lean up against his locker instead.

Lutz is the first to arrive. I return his hard stare as he prowls past me. Satisfied that he's keeping to his end of the dorm, I focus on the returning men, watching for Slade. I'm half-dreading what will happen when he gets here.

Am I really going to cram myself into that bed with him? Maybe I should just curl up on the floor, after all…

Ten guys file into the room one after the other, stride to their beds, and flick on their lamps. There isn't a curfew, but the main lights will go out soon.

The beds fill up.

All of the Novices have returned. But not Slade.

I stare at the empty doorway. It's been two minutes since the last guy came back and still, Slade hasn't appeared. I wait another minute, carefully studying the other men. If I was friends with any of them, I could ask them what was going on.

Maybe one of the teachers asked Slade to do something?

While I'm trying to decide whether or not to risk approaching one of them, I find Lutz watching me. He's sitting on the side of his bed and he seems far too happy about the fact that I'm alone.

My stomach plummets. Only bad things could make Lutz happy. Maybe Slade was right when he said he needed someone to watch his back.

I grit my teeth and wade through the testosterone filling the back of the room, stopping at the end of Lutz's bed.

Everything becomes quiet around me. The other men watch me, the tension around their eyes and mouths telling me they're on edge and wary about what I might do.

I make my demand clear and concise. "Where is he?"

Lutz's lips curl up at the corners. "Do you want a piece of me, sweetheart?"

I grind my teeth together and turn my hands into fists, taking an offensive stance. "Where is Slade?"

He shrugs, his forehead crinkling in an innocent expression. "I guess lover boy likes long showers."

I assess his facial expressions and the movement of his eyes, ignoring the sounds coming out of his mouth.

It takes a liar to know a liar and I'm an expert. One day, I'll meet a man I won't be able to lie to—that man will be my equal and my match, the one I'll give my heart to. Luckily, I haven't met him yet and until I do, I'll keep perfecting the deceptions that keep me alive.

My skills at deceit tell me that, despite Lutz gloating about Slade's absence, Lutz doesn't know where Slade is. He's just making the most of the fact that he has my attention.

That means… something is definitely wrong. I need to look for Slade. And quickly. Because if he's injured, every second will count.

I spin to leave, but Lutz is faster than I expected. I've only made it two steps when his thick arms encircle me from behind, yanking me hard up against him, trying to pin my arms and pull me backward.

He croons into my ear, "Come back, sweetheart. Slade can't have all the fun…"

My reflexes kick in without a second's hesitation.

I drop my weight and at the same time, my elbow slams back into his stomach. The air whooshes out of his lungs and he releases me like I'm a hot iron, leaning forward at the same time, gasping for breath.

I spin back to him with a quick uppercut that snaps his head back.

The resulting *crack* makes everyone wince.

Lutz backs up fast, hitting the side of his bed, clutching his jaw. "Damn, woman! You hit like a man."

He's right. I am stronger than most women. It's a gift from my mom. Because of her, I am… not entirely human.

"Believe it, asshole." I glare in the direction of his groin. "I warned you what would happen if you touch me. You're lucky I'm leaving you intact."

Sometimes I forget how strong I am. Sometimes I forget that there is a power hidden deep inside of me that I can never show to anyone. Keeping the true nature of the Clave hidden is important, but protecting my own secret is even more so. It's my biggest lie—my most important deception.

If these men knew what I was…

Part of me—the furious part—wants to fly back at Lutz, knock him on his back, and pulverize his face.

But I won't.

Not only because the more I fight, the more likely I am to reveal my inner power, but also because I'm wasting time. If Slade is hurt, then I need to find him.

I turn and stride from the dorm. I don't waste time putting on my boots. They'll make my footsteps noisy and I don't want to draw attention from any nearby Superiors by clattering down the stairs.

Racing from the dorm, I glance once at the dark middle level where Slade's cousin and his friends sleep. If they were here, I could ask them for help, but they said they'd be out on a mission tonight.

Running to the showers first, I find the building lit by a single lamp outside. Inside, it's quiet, the air filled with steam as I head down the hallway. The building is divided into two sections: one for the Novices and one for the new Superiors. The more senior assassins have private bathing facilities on the other side of the Realm.

I head to the shower room on the right—the one that Superior Ridley said was for the Novices. I check the dressing area before looking inside the shower room itself. The white-tiled area is empty and my panic increases.

Slade, where are you?

CHAPTER SIX

My instincts are screaming at me that something isn't right about the aura in this room.

I close my eyes and open my senses.

A faint wash of old magic lingers in the air. It has an aggressive tinge to it... It was definitely used in an attack...

Mom taught me every combat move she knew, but she barely taught me anything about assassin's magic—not how to use it or what it can do, or even where it comes from. She flat-out refused to tell me. She said it was because assassin's magic has a particular feel to it and another assassin would detect it on me and know that I had been trained. It seemed to be her way of protecting me from this life. A life I've dived right into.

The only thing she taught me about magic was how to detect it—how to use my own power to see the glow that magic creates in the air.

I follow the magic's trail, my eyes half-open to give my other senses better control so I can trace the thread. It takes me through the Novice's dressing room, into the hall, and across to the new Superiors' dressing room.

I finally locate Slade two steps inside.

He's lying up against the far-right wall, positioned on his right side facing me. The lighting in here isn't great, but the cut above his eye tells me everything.

"Slade!" I run and drop to my knees next to him.

He doesn't move, lying perfectly still. He's breathing, but the aura of assassin's magic around him is so thick, it tells me someone hit him hard.

He's out cold and the intensity of the magic will most certainly keep him that way. For how long, I'm not sure, but someone really didn't want him to be awake tonight. Maybe they even intended to make him miss training tomorrow morning. Superior Ridley said we'd be eliminated if we didn't turn up on time…

I can't leave him here. I have the strength to carry him back, but showing it would be a bad idea, and even then he'd still be unconscious.

I run my hands through my hair and rub my eyes as indecision grips me.

He and I aren't friends—are we?—but he was right when he said we could both use someone watching our backs. I'm not sleeping in that dorm tonight without Slade. I tell myself I'm only helping him because it's in my best interests to do so. Definitely nothing to do with friendship.

I may not know how to use assassin's magic, but I do know how to use my own.

Carefully resting my forefinger against his temple, I seek my inner calm, the quiet place deep inside my mind.

My shoulder blades burn at the same time, but I fight back against *that* sensation. I don't need to have a full-on power explosion right now. I want to access enough of my power to draw Slade's consciousness back—but no more than that.

Warmth builds beneath my fingertips. I sense his sleeping mind but try not to see his thoughts. As the nature of his breathing changes, I withdraw my hand, but not before I'm overwhelmed with the image of a bakery... sunlight... apple muffins... family... a happy place...

Cinnamon. Just like the scent that surrounds Slade.

I'm leaning so close to him that the warmth of his scent envelops me. It's surprisingly comforting and more than a little disarming, given that he's one of the strongest Novices.

His eyelids flicker, a faint groan passing his lips. He tries to move, but I press my palms flat against his chest and shoulder to stop him. "Stay still. Let me check you over."

His stunning eyes open, squinting at me. "Hunter?"

I snort. "Do you know any other women around here?"

Now that he's awake, I examine the cut above his eye. It's shallow; his skin is split, but not deeply. From the looks of it, the wound was more likely caused by a fist than a weapon. I gently check the rest of his face for concealed wounds, especially to the back of his head.

He allows me to check him over, his eyes half-closed, relaxing under my touch. When I run my hands through his hair, he sighs. "None crazy enough to come to the men's bathroom."

Well, at least he has a sense of humor about it. That has to be a good sign that he wasn't hit too hard.

Satisfied that he doesn't have any other wounds to his head, I quickly check his neck and shoulders, running my hands across his skin while I visually check for signs of bleeding.

He's half-dressed in pants but no shirt, so it's easy enough to check his torso. His eyes are open fully now, his gaze following my movements with the faintest hint of surprise.

I guess I'm touching him an awful lot for someone who threatened to harm him if he didn't keep his hands to himself.

Judging that he's more alert now, I ask, "What happened?"

What I really want to ask is: Who did this?

His forehead creases. "I got to the showers after the others but made sure to finish first so I could get back to you. Then I got dressed, heard a sound… turned around…" He shakes his head. "I've got nothing after that."

"They were aiming for the back of your head, but you must have turned into the blow." I rest one palm lightly across his chest as I check the wound above his eye again. "If you were alone in the dressing room, it made you an easy target. You've been hit with a fist strengthened by assassin's magic."

"What?" He jolts upright, but I was prepared for that, my hands positioned to restrain him.

"Take it easy." I wrap one arm behind his back, helping him to sit up while I stay close and watch carefully to make sure he isn't concussed.

"I thought it must have been Lutz," he says, "but none of the Novices would know how to use magic."

It's more alarming that it could have been someone other than Lutz. He's a bully, but at least that makes him predictable. An unseen and unknown assailant is worse.

"It probably wasn't Lutz," I say. "But you can't rule him out. We don't know much about the other Novices. Any of them could have been trained by family members."

Actually, anything is possible. I'm playing a ruse pretending not to have any assassin's skills already. Pretending to be *normal*. Although I revealed a few combat skills when I hit Lutz earlier.

Slade leans back against the wall, allowing me to stay where I am, one of my arms still partially supporting him. "I hate to say it, Hunter, but this might not be about me."

I can't stop the sigh escaping my lips. "You mean it's about me."

He maintains eye contact, his gaze steady, but with the slightest hint of worry. "I helped you. It doesn't take a genius to know that Master Gareth doesn't want you here. Somebody could want me out of the picture so that you're alone and… I hate to use this word to describe you, but… *vulnerable*."

I attempt a shrug, pretending that I don't care. "Then you'll be safer if you stay away from me."

His gaze travels from my hair to my lips and up to my eyes. As his focus shifts, his expression changes in a way that makes the hard lines of his face seem softer.

I suddenly remember that my right hand is pressed against his bare waist while my left arm hugs his back. I'm much closer to him than I ever intended to be.

His lips part. "That could be difficult."

I never really understood what people meant when they said that a look could be like a caress, but the way his gaze passes from my eyes to my cheeks to my lips feels almost… tangible. Like he reached out and grazed his thumb across my skin. It's so unexpected that despite my best intentions, my breathing increases and I find myself leaning closer to him.

I've never been able to let go of my inhibitions easily. My heart is locked away in a cage and my body is locked in there with it. When my last boyfriend, Oliver, broke up with me soon after Mom died, he pretty much broke the key off in the lock of the cage I built around my heart.

My emotions were so damaged from losing Mom that I didn't realize how much he hurt me when he abandoned me at my most vulnerable time. For the last four years since then, I've plastered over the wound, adding layer after layer until I buried the part of me that feels like… a woman.

Suddenly, it all rushes at me in an enormous wave as if Slade ripped through all the careful layers I constructed around myself.

His left arm is wrapped around me because he reached for me when he was trying to get up and now his palm rests lightly against the small of my back, strong fingers conforming to the curve of my spine. I sense his hand flex against me for a moment as if he wants to draw me closer but changes his mind.

Instead, he lifts his free hand and carefully runs his fingers through my hair, unfolding the twist I'd determinedly placed it in. "You let your hair down."

My breath hitches as his knuckles brush my neck, making me tingle all over. It's the first time he's deliberately touched me and it has such an unexpected effect on my heart rate.

My hand shifts against his waist, an instinctive response, and I can't stop my eyes from closing as I soak up the feeling of the hard planes of his muscles beneath my palms.

But... I can't afford to get involved with him. Not least because we're rivals. We might be allies now, but Master Gareth will pick Slade over me in a heartbeat. I have to beat all of the other Novices if I'm going to become a Superior—including Slade.

I force my eyes open to find him contemplating me. Like me, he has hidden himself behind a mask all day. It's what we have to do in this place. But right at this moment, there's honesty in his expression.

"I just got hit on the head," he says, "so I'm about to say more than I should. But I want you to know that I won't step across any boundary unless you invite me to cross it."

I swallow against the fiery sensations his touch set alight, my mouth suddenly dry. I can't stop the question that passes my lips or the surprise that goes with it. "You want to cross a boundary?"

His gaze settles on my eyes, holding steady. "Hell, yes."

CHAPTER SEVEN

ontrary to his declaration, Slade withdraws his hand from my back, a gentle slide away from my waist that makes me shiver.

He flattens his palm resolutely against the floor as if he's emphasizing that he won't cross boundaries with me.

I bite my lower lip, trying to process the surprising fact that the more he withdraws, the more I don't want him to. It would be so easy to lean into him, narrow the gap between us, press my lips against his...

Get it together, Hunter. That path will only lead to pain and regret. It's the nature of my kind that when we fall, we fall hard. And I can't commit—or risk committing. Not least because I'll run the risk that he could be my match and then I won't be able to lie to him.

I clear my throat. "Well, like you said... you just took a hit to the head."

I try to refocus the conversation, forcing myself to take on a business-like tone. "The cut above your eye doesn't look too bad. It doesn't need stitches. But assassin's magic is designed to stun, so you should be careful when you stand up. Here... let me help you."

I really need to put some physical distance between us right now, which requires him to stand up on his own so I can stop supporting him—preferably without my conscience pricking me because I'm worried he'll fall over when I let go.

He gives me a small smile. "It's okay, Hunter. I can stand on my own."

"Okay." Biting my lip, I drag my hands back to myself and give him space.

He takes it slow, rising in increments, testing his balance, finally lifting up to his full height.

I study him with concern, worried in case he topples over. Holding up a timber plank is one thing. Holding up Slade would be another. It's not that I don't have the strength to carry him—I actually do—but it would lead to a lot of questions I'd rather avoid, including what happened to him. We can't tell anyone about it. Violence is to be expected here. I'm concerned about who might have done this and why.

Unfortunately, I think Slade's theory is correct: Someone was trying to make me vulnerable. It doesn't take many guesses to suspect it was Master Gareth or, more likely, one of the Superiors acting on his command. I expect them to target me, but I don't want to be responsible for Slade getting hurt.

He rests back against the wall for a moment, a satisfied smile appearing on his lips. "You're worried about me."

I lift my chin, not sounding very convincing when I say, "I'm worried about carrying you back to the dorm if you fall over."

"Right."

I take a full step back. "We should get back before someone finds us here and things get awkward."

More awkward than they already are.

He follows me from the shower room, collecting his things from the dressing room along the way, but his brow is furrowed by the time he draws level with me outside the building. "How do you know what assassin's magic feels like?"

I miss a step. I told him that whoever hit him had strengthened their fist with magic. A Novice wouldn't know how to sense that. Once again, I employ the technique of answering a question with a question.

"You don't?" I deliberately inject surprise into my response, making it sound as if I thought everyone knew how to do that.

The furrow in his brow deepens. "My grandmother was the assassin. My parents own a bakery. They work hard and live normal lives. They didn't want me to have anything to do with this life. Unlike Thomas's parents, mine made sure our grandmother didn't teach me anything."

Now I'm genuinely surprised. If what he said is true, then he's here on true grit and determination alone. "Then why choose this path?"

He's quiet for a moment. "It's the only path for me."

He could be repeating my own mantra back at me. *Death is in my blood. There is no other way.* "I can respect that."

"What about you, Hunter?"

Damn. I should have seen that question coming. I pick up my pace. We'll reach the dorm soon and I need this conversation to be over. Not that I'm totally calm about our sleeping arrangements.

I give him the most honest reply that I can. "I don't have any other choice."

I'm a step ahead of him and I can't see his expression. I don't wait for his reply as I hurry up the stairs, my bare feet slapping the wooden rungs. I pause at the top, suddenly regretting racing away from him. He just took a blow to the head. I should have watched him ascend. I don't want him to take a tumble because he's off-balance…

I turn and bump right into him. My chest collides with his and his arms sweep up around me, steadying me for a moment.

His chin is at my eye level. I tilt my head back to meet his eyes, sensing the cascade of my hair down my back across his arms.

My quick inhale only serves to press my chest closer to his.

I guess he wasn't so slow to climb the stairs after all.

Steadying both of us, he speaks in a throaty growl. "Watch it, Hunter. I don't want to add a fall to the injuries I've already sustained today."

Seeming satisfied that neither one of us is going to take a tumble, he steps back to give me space, but his hands linger around my shoulders in a way that tells me he wants to check my balance before he lets me go.

Despite my vague response to him about why I'm here, he seems more relaxed than he was before. Maybe he detected the honesty in my response and understood it. Maybe our reasons for being here are not that different—neither one of us has another path.

I decide not to run from the feeling of his hands around my upper arms and instead relax into it for a moment. If I tell myself he's my friend, then I can take as much as I want from this feeling and not read anything into it.

Matching his smile with a wry one of my own, I say, "Don't worry. After training tomorrow, we'll all look worse than you do now."

His forehead crinkles with disbelief. "Something tells me you won't." He doesn't let me go yet. "You have walls, Hunter."

Whatever relaxed emotion I felt flees in an instant, but what he says next surprises me most.

"That's a good thing. You need walls in this place."

He finally releases me, but his grin is back. "So tell me before we go in… Do you want to sleep facing the door or the wolves?"

By 'wolves,' he must mean the other Novices. The warrior inside me wants to face the Novices, but it would be better for me to be hidden behind Slade's big frame. Visibility is not my friend in this place.

"The door," I say.

He nods once before he walks ahead of me.

The dorm is quiet when we enter. Most of the lamps have been switched off. Somehow, I don't think anyone is asleep. Certainly not Lutz. I sense his sharp gaze following every move I make.

I track Slade to his bed and wait for him to put away his things before he slides under the single blanket. True to his word, he turns to face the side of the room where everyone else sleeps, but he reaches back to flip the blanket open for me to get in.

I slip beneath the blanket and press my back to his, tensing for a moment before I relax.

Normally, I would strip down to a sports bra to sleep, but I want to remain as fully dressed as possible so I'm ready right away in the morning. Not to mention... my bare back pressed against Slade's might be a little too pleasant and I really need to reconstruct my emotional shields right now.

My bent knees extend beyond the edge of the bed, but I can't complain. I'm sure it's worse for Slade. At least this way, we'll keep each other alive.

I feel a little bad that my bare feet are filthy from walking around outside, but I'm guessing the staff will change the sheets daily, given how wounded I'm expecting us all to be on a daily basis.

This will be the last night we sleep without pain.

CHAPTER EIGHT

I awake to the sound of a food trolley being wheeled into the room from the service elevator.

I sense Slade's deep breathing, the rise and fall of his chest, but it changes with the rattling noise, becoming wakeful.

He remained exactly where he was all night long. I'm actually shocked to discover that the night passed without incident. I'm even more surprised that I slept so deeply. I try to shake off the feeling that being with Slade might have made me feel… safe.

I remind myself: There's no such thing as safe here.

I stretch my cramped legs and check the clock on the wall. It reads 4:30 A.M., which is half an hour before combat training starts. Sliding my legs over the side of the bed and stretching out my body, I turn to check on Slade, gently placing a hand on his shoulder.

He covers my hand with his. Warmth spreads through my fingers from his touch as he murmurs to me, keeping his voice quiet, "I'm awake."

"Bathroom," I whisper, indicating that's where I'm going. I

reluctantly pull my hand free. "Remember what I said about breakfast before class."

The trolley is full of plates containing freshly cooked bacon and eggs, the aroma of which follows me to the washroom like a cruel taunt. The staff member who brought the food watches me but doesn't say anything.

When I return, I find Slade sitting on the edge of our bed. He's pulled on a shirt and boots, but he hasn't joined the other Novices, who crowd around the food cart, stuffing their faces. I guess they figure they should eat while they can. I would have thought so too if it weren't for Ridley's warning.

I take a moment to check the wound above Slade's eye, happy to see that it's healing. He watches me closely as I check him over. He wears a small smile on his lips. It's impossible to read what he's thinking unless I consider that he might be enjoying the fact that I'm running my fingers across his cheek and forehead.

I narrow my eyes at him, but it's hard to feel indignant, especially when he raises an expectant eyebrow at me, waiting for me to tell him about the state of the wound.

I grumble, "It looks fine."

He gives me a nod, the seriousness returning to his expression. "I'm going to the bathroom. Will you be okay while I'm gone?"

I nod. "Thanks for asking. I can hold my own."

He's gone and back within five minutes. In the meantime, I swipe two bottles of sports drink from the food cart, handing one to Slade on his return. From the other side of the room, Lutz belches loudly before eyeing the drinks we're consuming.

He seems to only notice now that we haven't eaten anything. The slightest hint of worry enters his narrowed gaze. Not an expression I expected to see, but he's smart enough to realize that his two biggest rivals have teamed up against him.

I meet Slade's eyes as I finish my drink. Neither of us has to say anything. Together, we head to the door and out to the courtyard, where we're supposed to meet Ridley.

He's already waiting for us, dressed in long pants and a sleeveless shirt, showing off his enormous biceps. As Slade draws level with him, I find it interesting to see that Slade is actually taller, broader in the shoulders, and more muscular in his arms and thighs than Ridley. But there's this thing that Slade does with his body to make himself look smaller and less challenging: a sort of hunch to his shoulders, a slight lowering of his head.

It's a subtle mask that he wears very well.

It reminds me that Slade is far more dangerous than he looks.

A shiver runs through my spine at the reminder and I'm not sure if it's fear or anticipation. A very big part of me wants to see how Slade does in combat class this morning. Someone might have gotten the better of him last night, but that was a coward's move—a hit from behind. I'm certain Slade won't let that happen again.

Ridley acknowledges our arrival with a curt nod, but he doesn't say anything until the other Novices catch up. Then he orders us to form a line while he paces in front of us.

"Good morning and welcome to a world of pain. You're mine this morning, but this afternoon, you will have your first magic lesson with Superior Fallon. You might think this morning is bad. You have no idea how much worse your day is going to get."

We haven't had much to do with Fallon so far. In fact, he hasn't said a word to us. A shiver runs down my spine and this time, it's anxiety. I'm not looking forward to his class. I may be able to recognize assassin's magic but controlling it is the one skill I don't already possess.

Ridley continues. "We'll start the day easy. With a run. Follow me."

He takes off at a quick pace. Slade settles in beside me and we keep close to Ridley's heels. I understand now why Mom always got me up at the crack of dawn to run a mile before breakfast. She might not have wanted me to come anywhere near this place, but she prepared me well.

Ridley takes us to the edge of the Realm, where we run around the walled perimeter. The weirdest part about the Realm is that I can hear the cars and voices coming from outside—from the normal world. I even smell the coffee, a beverage I haven't seen since I arrived. I don't think they have any within the Legion, so it's a good thing I weaned myself off caffeine months ago.

Ridley points out the buildings inside the Realm as we pass them, telling us what they are, projecting his voice at a bellow so even the stragglers can hear him. He finally indicates a wooden building with a wide porch along the front. "That is the combat room where I will train you. But we won't stop there yet."

The perimeter is over one and a half miles and we run it three times before Ridley shows any signs of changing his speed.

It's a shame he speeds up instead of slowing down.

"Anyone who doesn't beat me to the combat room has to do fifty push-ups when they get there."

We're a quarter mile away from the building, a distance he seems to expect us to run at full pelt.

Off he goes, feet pounding.

I take one look at Slade and we launch into a sprint. Our breathing is still even, though increasing, but some of the other Novices must be beginning to regret breakfast and I'm certain this last race will be their undoing.

I push my legs faster, keeping pace with Slade, arms pumping, pushing him faster too.

Together, we catch up with Ridley. For a second, I think he's going to speed up just to beat us, but he ends up maintaining the same pace.

Slade and I reach the combat room with ten seconds to spare, racing up the steps and skidding to a halt, pacing the porch to walk off the sprint.

Lutz reaches us moments later. He pulls up short of the balcony and hurls his breakfast into the bushes at the side of the building—*all* of his breakfast by the sounds of things. He then stumbles across to the water tap at the corner of the building and sticks his face under it, gulping water and spitting it out.

Two other Novices make it to us before Ridley does— Brandon and Rowan—but the others are ordered to do push-ups on the pebbled pathway outside the building—after they also empty the contents of their stomachs into the bushes.

I eye the stones lining the pathway with caution. They're jagged and sharp, and I have a feeling they've been deliberately placed there to teach Novices a hard lesson. Their winces as they start their push-ups tell me the rocks are breaking skin. They'll find it hard to train with bleeding palms.

Ridley orders the first five of us inside the room.

I've only taken three steps inside when he turns and swings a giant fist at my face.

don't have time to be shocked.

My reflexes kick in. I duck, swerve, and land a retaliatory punch to his exposed ribs before I leap away from him. The novice behind me isn't so lucky. It's Brandon Baker.

Thud.

Brandon hits the porch after the fist I ducked smacks into his face. He shouts, gripping his jaw. Beside him, Lutz leaps out of the way, dancing out of Ridley's reach.

Ridley ignores both me and Lutz as he looms over Brandon. "Always expect violence! Fifty push-ups on the stones, Novice!"

He doesn't wait for Brandon to obey, turning on his heel and striding past us. I'm still catching my breath from the suddenness of Ridley's attack, but I'm satisfied to see him rub his ribs where I made contact. I definitely hurt him.

"Nice hit, Hunter," Slade whispers to me, suddenly appearing beside me again.

I narrow my eyes at him. In the entire short episode, he somehow managed to stay clear of it all. My forehead creases as I replay it in my mind. Slade was right behind me, I'm sure of it, which means Ridley's fist should have landed on him instead of Brandon, but I see it again in my mind...

Slade side-stepped when I did, shadowing my moves. Smart. But also unsettling. He must have been very confident that he could anticipate what I would do. If he misjudged my steps, I could have knocked him over.

I'm not sure I like the fact that he read my mind so clearly and moved with me so seamlessly.

There are now only four of us inside the building with Ridley.

Steering clear of the teacher, I take a quick survey of our surroundings. At the head of the room, a wooden table displays about a hundred different knives. Every wall is covered in weapons of all descriptions and dummies are positioned a few paces from the back wall.

Ridley heads to the table, his footsteps appearing casual, but from the corner of my eye, I witness him give Lutz a sharp nod.

Always expect violence, Ridley said.

Luckily, I always do.

I spin to meet Lutz's attack, ready for his fists. But it seems he learned from his altercation with me last night.

He charges at me with his chin tucked in, head down, barreling into me. His arms close around my torso as he scoops me right off my feet and throws us both down toward the ground.

I land on my back but manage to get a knee up between us as we fall. I use his own momentum against him, shoving him off me so he can't pin me to the ground. Quickly rolling to my feet, I launch myself right back at him.

As I speed toward him, my back tingles, a sharp sensation shooting all the way from my head to my toes.

No! Not now! Fear rakes through me, but I clamp down on it. The hidden power inside me responds to threats, but I can't use it here.

You can control this, Hunter. Focus.

My distraction is enough to give Lutz time to get back to his feet. This time, he comes at me with a swinging fist, but I grab his arm, block the blow, and land two quick jabs to his face, followed by a boot to his chest that shoves him backward. He tumbles, hitting the floor but rolling to his feet, growling at me before he barrels back at me again with brute strength.

I jump aside, but not fast enough. He catches me and we both go down. I manage to land closest to the top, swinging my legs over him to straddle him before he can pin me down. I use my position and the full force of my fists while he tries to defend his face and neck against the blows.

I know I'm hitting him hard. Hard enough to draw blood. But I want him to think twice before he comes at me again.

He doesn't give up easily. I'll give him that.

He risks exposing his face to grab my waist and swing us onto our sides, pinning one of my legs under him. He lands a quick hit to my cheek at the same time. It's not as hard as it could have been if he'd had more leverage, but it hurts. He shoves my shoulders, trying to force himself on top of me, where he has the advantage of weight to pin me down completely.

In that position, he'll end up between my legs.

That is *not* happening.

A quick assessment of my surroundings tells me Slade is pacing at the edge of the fight, but Ridley holds a firm, almost angry, hand up to him, forbidding him to get involved. The force of Ridley's expression makes me think Slade has already given significant signs of intervening before this moment.

I punch a fist into Lutz's upper arm—the one he's trying to use to press me onto my back. As his arm swings wide, I use the movement to shove him in the opposite direction, freeing my leg so I can roll away from him.

I leap to my feet, only to be grabbed from behind. Not by Lutz.

Now I know why Slade looks so unhappy. Ridley must be sending the others after me too.

I grab the arm that holds me, bend, pull, and use my smaller frame combined with my strength to flip my assailant onto his back with a thud that knocks the wind out of him. It's Rowan Robertson. I land a hard kick to his ribs before he can get up. It's vicious and makes him shout, his arms reflexively shooting up to protect his head in case I kick there too.

I'm beyond caring about causing pain at this point.

More Novices rush at me. I catch a glimpse of bleeding palms, but I have no mercy. One meets my boot, the other meets my fist, and a third takes the full impact of my backhand as I swing in his direction.

As they fall backward, I give a growl of my own and launch myself back at Lutz, who has regained his feet. I duck his fist, land a hard blow to his ribs, spin, leap upward, and slam a boot into his temple from the side.

He stumbles backward and this time, he throws both hands up, backing away, indicating that he's had enough.

He shoots a glare at our teacher. "I'm done fighting her."

Ridley's brow furrows but he doesn't disagree.

Lutz strides away from me, checking the cuts I opened on his face, wincing as he heads to the side of the room.

I turn to find the remaining Novices watching from the other side, where they stand just inside the door. I guess they finished their push-ups in time to see part of the fight.

I take one step in their direction and cause them to flinch backward, making it clear they don't want to take me on. Especially not right now when they're nursing their wounded palms and I've got a head full of battle rage.

One thing is certain: They won't be late to the combat room tomorrow.

Without a word to me, Lutz, or even Slade, whose expression has turned very dark, Ridley gestures everyone further inside the room. "Sit down. On the floor."

I find a place on the far left, satisfied to discover that nobody but Slade wants to sit anywhere near me. I take a quick moment to check my wounds—nothing serious—before I eye the others, knowing that Ridley can order another attack at any moment. They seem to know it too, all of them crouched as if they believe they'll have to move at any second.

I wait, on edge, as Ridley folds his arms and speaks as if nothing happened. "The second rule in the assassin's code is this: Every assassination must be sanctioned by the Guardian before it is carried out."

The Guardian is the arbiter of the assassin's world—the only neutral party between Factions. She alone gets to decide if a planned assassination is legal. Not legal in the ordinary sense because everything we do is illegal. But *permitted*. She basically gives the nod to death.

The Guardian is always a woman. In the male-dominated assassin's world, she gives an appearance of gender balance.

I watch Ridley warily as he paces around us. With each passing second, I regain my own equilibrium, calm my breathing, and return to a state of readiness.

Ridley says, "Breaking this rule doesn't lead to death. But it means being stripped of your qualifications. You will no longer be an assassin. That means... rule number one no longer protects you. *From anyone.*"

He stops in front of me, towering over me while I remain sitting. I watch his legs. He could just as easily kick me as speak with me.

He spreads his arms, half-turning back to the table. "Tell me, Hunter, if you want to cut a man's throat, which weapon would you choose?"

It sounds like a casual question. Which means I need to treat it with suspicion. I eye the weapons from where I sit.

"You may get up to look at them."

I rise to my feet, giving him a wide berth, and don't take my eyes off him for a second. Reaching the table, I attempt to keep my distance as Ridley prowls around me.

I quickly run my hands over the knives on the table, past the thick ones, the heavy ones, the ones with serrated edges. I pause, surprised to see a dinner knife also set up in the array. It looks exactly like the one I picked up the night before and nearly pitched at Lutz. I brush over it, though.

Instead, I look for the smallest, sharpest dagger and then I point to it. "That one."

"Hmm. What if you needed to hit a target from a distance?"

I shrug. "Any knife will do."

"Really?"

"Yes," I say. "Even a dinner knife."

I dart left as Ridley lurches at me. He tries to grab me, but I snatch up the steak knife and run the length of the table, adjusting my grip as I go. Still running, I take aim and pitch it neatly into the opposite wall.

Right above Lutz Logan's head.

Then I skip out of Ridley's grasping hands. He growls at me but lets me go, allowing me to stop near the door so I can take in the sight of Lutz hunched over after he shouted and ducked.

Lutz takes rapid glances from me to the knife quivering in the wall. The look in his eyes tells me he's teetering between a healthy respect for my skills and a desire to murder me slowly.

A clapping sound draws my attention back to Ridley, who has edged up closer than I wanted him to. "Well done, Hunter. Top of the class already, but I'm not surprised."

He turns to the Novices, cajoling them. "Are any of you surprised by what Hunter has done today?" He waits a beat before he continues. "Come on. She's a woman and she already knows how to fight off an attack and pitch a blade. Who's surprised? Be honest."

Everyone except Slade lifts their hands. It's like watching kids in kindergarten, but I don't blame them for obeying Ridley. He will likely flatten them with a fist if they disobey. Nobody will want to do more push-ups on the stones.

Ridley laughs. "You don't know who she is, do you?"

I've remained standing near the end of the table and now I back up, taking glances from him to the others.

I suddenly regret my display. Massively. I should have fallen in the attack. Certainly not picked up a knife and thrown it like a pro.

I don't need Ridley telling them who my mother was. Silently, I beg him not to say anything. If there is ever a time I want to cash in on that favor he owed Mom, it's now.

But he's not looking at me to see the pleading in my eyes.

"She's the daughter of the Glass Fox," he announces.

CHAPTER TEN

Every Novice jolts. Eyes snap to me. But there's only one person whose reaction I care about.

Slade's gaze is unwavering, but his eyes are suddenly wide. Then his shocked expression slowly changes, his forehead creasing. And then... he gives me a grin. But it's a dangerous grin and I don't know how to read it.

Maybe he's pleased he teamed up with me. Maybe he's smiling like a caged wolf because he realizes that he has invited a whole load of trouble into his life and literally into his bed.

I can't tell if Superior Ridley just did me a favor or put an even bigger target on my back. After all, everyone knows my mother was killed.

The Glass Fox was mortal. As it turned out, glass could be shattered.

I raise my head and square my shoulders as I announce to the class, "She taught me everything she knew. Remember that when you come at me."

Because I know they will. On top of the fight today, this knowledge about my mom will make them smarter about any attack now. Thanks to Ridley, they'll come at me in the shadows, not in the light.

I glare at him.

He gives me a shrug and leans over to me while he rubs his side where I punched him. "Expect to be tested, Hunter."

He takes up a stance at the head of the room, facing the men. "Get up. Pair up."

He shakes his head when Slade strides toward me. "Slade, you're with Brandon Baker. Hunter, you're with Rowan Robertson."

Rowan looks even unhappier than Slade. It's not surprising, considering that I kicked him so hard.

Once we pair up, Ridley says, "There's one more rule you need to know before we begin. This is *my* rule."

He pauses to make sure we're all listening. "You can sweat on my floor. You can bleed on my floor. But you do *not* puke on my floor. If you need to throw up, do it in the bushes. Now, let's begin."

~

Three hours later, when we leave the combat room and head to the food hall, we're bruised and bleeding.

I have a split lip from the fight with Lutz and multiple sore ribs from learning new maneuvers with Rowan, who took advantage of every opportunity to seek revenge for his own bruised ribs.

I have nothing broken, though. Superior Ridley demanded nothing less than brutality but drew the line at broken bones. Still, there were no pulled punches or going easy on each other. I'm glad now that he didn't allow me to pair with Slade.

I didn't have an opportunity to speak with Slade after Ridley's revelation about my mother and I'm worried about what he's thinking. It's not a conversation I will avoid, though. I always tackle everything head on.

His cousin's table is empty. They said they wouldn't see us until this evening and no doubt they're sleeping off their mission.

As soon as Slade takes a seat, I say, "So now you know."

He's quiet for a moment while a staff member places food in front of us—which neither of us touches. After Ridley's warning about Fallon's class, I'm not taking any chances with the contents of my stomach. Hydration is more important so I grab two sports drinks before the staff member can wheel the food cart away.

Slade accepts one of the drinks from me, his expression closed off. "I imagine there could be many reasons why you didn't tell me. I'm trying to figure out which one makes the most sense."

I uncap the drink and take a sip, keeping my posture casual. "What are you tossing around?"

He shrugs. "That you don't want to live in your mom's shadow. That would be understandable."

I nod, keeping my emotional distance. "Sure. That would make sense."

"Another reason is that you'd be an even bigger target if everyone knew who your mom was. You'd have to watch your back around not only the Novices, but the Superiors as well. I'm sure your mom humiliated a few of them in her day."

"That, too."

The look he gives me is suddenly chilling. "Or maybe you're hiding something. Nobody knows how your mom died. Or why."

My grip closes around the bottle, pressing into the plastic. He's hit a sore spot and I'm sure he knows it. Slade is way too clever. "We're all hiding something. Aren't we?"

He blows out a resigned sigh before he takes a final gulp. "Maybe."

It doesn't look like any of the other Novices are eating before Superior Fallon's class, either. Ridley warned us that combat class would be a walk in the park compared to Fallon's. A lot of sports drinks disappear very quickly as we continue to huddle at our tables until Fallon rises from the head table and calls, "Novices to the Magic Room."

We hustle after him before he tests us like Ridley did. Nobody wants to be late.

The Magic Room is very similar in appearance to the combat room, although its name makes it sound like some kind of kids' playroom. I half-expect to sit on big, plastic toadstools surrounded by stuffed unicorns.

Not so. The room is mostly bare, with nothing more than a row of flat cushions laid out on the wooden floor.

Once we file inside, Fallon orders us to find a cushion to sit on. I take the far left while Slade sits between me and the others. As we were for Superior Ridley's class, we are all watchful and wary of what might happen next.

Fallon crosses his legs as he settles onto the cushion at the front of the class. He is a slight man, tall and lanky with elegant hands and dark eyelashes that would make any woman jealous. His eyes are earthy brown like the color of an old oak tree. He rests his hands on his knees. A slight smile remains on his lips the entire time he talks, as if he has a secret that only he knows.

"I encourage questions in my class," he says. "Ask anything, and I will answer."

He pauses as if he expects us to ask something right then, but nobody does.

"Okay, then… Lesson number one: There are magical beings all around us. They come in all shapes and sizes, but most of them appear human. I will teach you how to identify their auras to see through their disguises. On your missions, you will encounter witches, warlocks, shifters, and mages, as well as goblins and centaurs, just to name a few."

He peers at us as he continues. "You may even encounter the odd dark elf, although they are rare. So are the fae. Fifty percent of your targets will be magical beings who have harmed a human. The other half will be humans who must answer for a heinous crime. Most of the time, your targets will live in the shadows. Rarely, you will target a well-known figurehead."

He pauses again but still, nobody asks anything. "You do not need to fear any magical being, no matter how powerful they appear. All of them have weaknesses that can be exploited and dealt with using assassin's magic. That is what you will learn in my class. Any questions?"

To my surprise, Lutz speaks up. "Which magical species is the most dangerous?"

The corner of Fallon's mouth twitches upward. "Are you planning on targeting them first?"

Lutz shifts uncomfortably. "I'd like to avoid them until I'm more skilled."

I never expected to hear anything so sensible or honest come out of Lutz's mouth. I take another look at him. He seems quiet. Much less confident. Not like himself at all. It's… odd.

What's gotten into him?

My forehead creases. Maybe there's something about being beaten up for hours, having a knife thrown at your head, and finding out that the woman you thought you could bully is actually the most dangerous enemy you could have.

Still, it's out of character for Lutz to admit any weakness.

Fallon purses his lips as if he's chewing on his answer. "There are only two species you need to fear. They are the Valkyrie and the Keres. They have no magical aura and are therefore completely undetectable."

The group was quiet before, but now it becomes perfectly still. The Valkyrie and Keres are magical beings with the power to choose who lives and who dies in battle. The Valkyrie are known for their mercy, ferrying dead souls to heaven, while the Keres are renowned for their brutality, killing wounded soldiers on the battlefield in their greed for death. At least... those are the stories.

I smother a smile about the fact that the Valkyrie and Keres are all female. According to the stories, they don't have male children, so they have to mate with humans. I love that the only species these men have to fear are two races of women.

Lutz asks, "How do we kill them?"

Fallon's eyebrows rise. "You can't. That's why they're so deadly. But you have nothing to fear because they're extinct."

Lutz's brow furrows. "But you said they can't be killed..."

Unlike Ridley, Fallon is a picture of patience. "I said *you* can't kill them. Oh, you might be able to make them hurt, but there are only two ways to kill a Valkyrie or a Keres. The first is to make them kill each other—they are vulnerable to each other's magic. The second is to force them to sacrifice themselves. Believe it or not, they can choose to die."

As Fallon speaks, I cast my gaze around the room again. The lack of weapons and furniture doesn't seem quite right.

I narrow my eyes at the patch of sky through the open door. We've only been in here for a few minutes and it was early afternoon when we entered, but it looks like the sun is going down already.

I blink at the fading light, finding it increasingly confusing.

Fallon continues speaking, the sound of his voice like a lulling melody describing the war between the Valkyrie and Keres, how it lasted for centuries before they wiped each other out, how the final two women—one Valkyrie and one Keres—faced each other across a battlefield littered with the bodies of their dead brethren and struck each other down at the exact same moment in time.

A half-smile remains on his face the whole time.

He is far too serene. In fact, the atmosphere in this room is far too peaceful.

The cushion I'm sitting on is thin, but my backside hasn't gone numb and my legs don't hurt. The air smells sweet. Birds chirp outside—despite the descending dark.

Superior Ridley said we should be afraid of Fallon's class, but so far, I feel safer than I have all day.

Cold panic begins to push at me because there's something very wrong here.

CHAPTER ELEVEN

Slade's gaze follows mine and the way his forehead creases at Fallon and then the beautiful sunset hues visible through the door tells me he's also searching for answers.

Something cold suddenly slides across my legs, but I can't see it. I brush at my ankles, trying to ease the sensation.

There's nothing there.

But... just because I can't see it, that doesn't mean it isn't real.

The hairs on the back of my neck shoot upward.

We're being deceived.

Everything we see right now—this entire room—must be an illusion.

It's the oldest and most dangerous form of assassin's magic to create an illusion around a target and lull them into a false sense of security. It's magic that can only be used by the most skilled assassin.

Fallon must have cast a spell on us to dull our senses and our reflexes, taking over our sight and our feelings, controlling our emotions. That alone would be bad enough—losing control of my body and my feelings is something I avoid at all costs—but the reason he will have done it is so that we can't see what's really happening to us.

It's like being blinded.

It's what assassins do right before they kill their target.

A scream rips out of me as I shoot to a standing position. "Slade! Get up!"

He leaps to his feet immediately, not questioning me. The edges of his body blur as he moves, telling me that he's pushing through the magic around us. It's like he's moving through water. He meets my eyes and his expression tells me he's ready to act.

Fallon watches us closely, also rising to his feet. He loses his smile, scowling at me while the other Novices stare in shock at my sudden outburst.

Fallon glowers. "You can't escape my magic, Hunter."

I glare right back at him. "Watch us."

If I could use my inner power, I would, but I need to keep it hidden. I wish Mom had taught me how to use assassin's magic, and not just how to recognize it, because there's bound to be a simple counter-spell. I just don't know it yet.

I murmur to Slade, "We need to attack the source." Which basically means: We need to attack Fallon.

Slade squares his shoulders and rises up to his full height, losing the obedient posture he wears as a disguise. "With pleasure."

I allow him to stride ahead of me toward our teacher. The air burns white around every movement Slade makes, creating a slipstream as if he's coursing through air. I don't need protecting, but I can't risk revealing my power. Or rather—I can't risk my power revealing itself. If I'm truly threatened, it will pour out of me in full force.

Fallon takes a step back, the air crackling around him as he reveals his magical defenses, a layer of icy flame covering his entire body.

To my surprise, Slade doesn't hesitate. He punches right through the magic, his fist connecting with Fallon's jaw. The force Slade puts behind it makes me gasp and jolt. Even in combat class, he didn't reveal this much strength.

It makes me wonder if, even now, he's holding his true strength back.

The *crack* echoes through the room.

The sound is more indicative of the snap of magic, which absorbs the full force of the blow, allowing Fallon to remain standing with a twisted smile on his face.

Slade isn't deterred, throwing another punch, and it only takes me a beat to decide to stand clear of the two men. Every time I consider getting involved, my power tingles inside me, rearing up, wanting to be released. The sensation only disappears when I step away from the fight.

Damn. I want to get in there! I hate that Fallon is someone I won't be able to combat without putting myself in serious danger.

Still… it doesn't look like Slade needs much help.

While Fallon moves fast, avoiding the next blow, Slade is ready for the evasion, anticipating exactly where Fallon will step—right into Slade's fist. Just as he anticipated my moves earlier today, he predicts Fallon's with exact precision.

Their fight is like a deadly dance. Every time Fallon evades a move, Slade anticipates it. Each time Fallon attempts to land a blow of his own, Slade has already moved out of the line of fire —even when Fallon employs magic.

Icy flames sizzle around them in dazzling strikes, hitting the floor or the ceiling instead of Slade, who tackles the magic fists first, taking advantage of every pause when Fallon's magic has to build again.

Fallon's frustration increases and the more annoyed he appears, the more the illusion around us frays and thins.

Behind the classroom veneer is a very different room: dark walls like the fake night outside and dank air as if we're deep underground, where fresh oxygen can't reach us.

Even though our bodies are moving in the illusion, it's possible that we're perfectly still in real life. We could be tied up and immobilized, or we could be floating in air, or even swimming in water. Anything is possible.

The other Novices jump to their feet as patches of reality show through, confusion and alarm spreading across their features.

Lutz is the first to storm toward the fight.

"I've had enough of this." He ducks a fireball, darts in close to Fallon, and follows Slade's fist with a hit of his own.

Suddenly, the nature of the fight changes. Fallon's eyes widen as Slade changes his approach, landing a blow to Fallon's temple that forces Fallon right into the line of Lutz's fist.

Lutz follows up with a perfect blow that clips Fallon's chin.

The two punches in sequence are enough to knock Fallon off his feet.

The Superior hits the floor, momentarily unconscious.

For a second, Slade and Lutz are still in my line of sight. Slade spins, seeking my position, a crease in his forehead while Lutz grabs my attention as he strides past me, growling, "Don't read anything into that, sweetheart. I'm helping myself, not you."

A second later, a high-pitched shrieking sound breaks the air and the spell seems to shatter. The illusion of the classroom peels away like wallpaper being ripped off.

Slade reaches out a hand toward me, but he's ripped away too, spinning backward, slamming up against the nearest wall.

On my other side, Lutz grunts as he slides backward, pulled to the place where his body really is: chained against the wall. The other Novices slide backward too, clawing at the air.

The illusion of nighttime becomes reality as I find myself standing in the middle of a dark room. Actually, 'room' is a nice description. This place is more like a dungeon made of what looks like iron, as if we're inside a very large, metallic box.

Chains of icy flames encircle the other Novices' ankles and wrists, keeping them pinned high on the walls.

I'm the only one who isn't restrained.

That alone is strange enough, but the weirdest part is that Fallon is nowhere to be seen. I spin, expecting him to leap out from behind me, but I can't see him anywhere. Although... I sense the same magic that was used to hurt Slade last night wafting through the air around me.

I suppress a shudder. Fallon is even more dangerous than I feared.

I jump as he materializes out of nowhere.

His eyes are cold and hard, more angry than Master Gareth's. "How are you defying my magic?"

I calculate the distance between us and decide not to let it narrow. I dare to scoff in the face of his anger, keeping my cool. "It wasn't hard to know something was up. You were being too nice. Next time, don't be so chatty."

He circles me. I pace in the opposite direction, maintaining the gap between us.

"I'm not talking about breaking the illusion," he says. "I'm talking about the fact that I can't chain you."

I take a quick glance at the other Novices since it's true that I'm the only one standing free. I assumed I had somehow broken free, not that he couldn't chain me to begin with.

But, *dammit*, I have no answer for that. None that I can voice anyway.

A line of flame suddenly shoots out from Fallon's hand,

forming a rope that darts toward my ankles, but just as it is about to encircle my legs, it recoils with a hissing sound.

I feel the same tickle that I sensed while I was in the illusion, but the chain of fire fizzles and dies instead of imprisoning me.

I meet his eyes. There's only one explanation and I'm not about to give it to him. "I guess I'm stubborn."

"Or," he says, "you are something else."

CHAPTER TWELVE

I suppress the shudder that races down my spine, hiding it with another laugh. "I'm a *woman*. Are you sure your spell isn't formulated for men? We have different hormones, different responses, different fear receptors…"

He scowls, but some of the suspicion fades from his eyes. "You may be right. I've never used it on a woman." He huffs. "I will perfect it next time."

I'm determined that there won't be a next time. I glance at Slade, who hasn't stopped wrenching at his restraints since the illusion faded. He's fighting against them so hard that marks are starting to form across his wrists and ankles. He will want to be free like I am.

I take a deep breath to maintain my calm as I ask Fallon, "Where are we?"

He raises his voice, addressing everyone. "This room is made of iron. Magic can't get out." He gives a short laugh. "It's made that way so you can practice magic without burning down the Realm."

"How did you appear so suddenly just now?" I ask, trying to

ignore how much Fallon makes my skin crawl. His presence is a thousand times worse in reality than it was in the illusion.

He chuckles. "It's called 'blurring.' It's the ability to disappear into your surroundings, an essential skill for all assassins. It will be the subject of your first lesson."

He snaps his fingers and the flames disappear from around the other Novices' arms and legs.

Slade drops to the ground, rubbing his wrists. For the barest moment, Fallon narrows his eyes in Slade's direction. Clearly, he's unhappy about the way Slade fought him.

Slade, on the other hand, is now deadpan, expressionless, not challenging at all. I can't help but admire the way he knows how to play this game.

Sensing no threat, Fallon seems prepared to let the fight go, turning his attention to teaching us how to blur. "First things first. To harness assassin's magic, you will each need a ring."

He snaps his fingers again and a table appears. Twelve silver bands rest on top of it. "These are training rings. They're all made of simple silver. If you succeed in becoming a Superior Assassin, the Guardian herself will bestow on you a ring that matches your skill and personality. Like mine."

He holds up his hand so we can see the ring encircling the first finger of his left hand. It's a thick, gold band inlaid with multiple diamonds that shine in the dim light.

He beckons us to take a ring, saying, "As humans, we have no natural magical power to draw on, so assassin's magic was created by powerful warlocks. Over time, they imbued their power into five hundred rings, which the Guardian protects. When an assassin dies, their ring goes back to her to be passed on at a later time."

I allow the other Novices to step forward first, watching carefully to see what Fallon will do.

"Each ring is unique," he says. "Some are made of gold, some silver, iron, even steel, and some are decorated with precious stones."

When I finally step forward to collect my training ring, Fallon darts right up to my side and grabs my forearm, stopping my outstretched hand.

The hairs on the back of my neck stand on end as he leans in toward me and whispers, "That's how your mother got her name. She was the first assassin allowed to wear the legendary glass ring. It was indestructible; tempered by the ancient warlock himself."

He sighs and his breath washes across my ear like a rushing wave. His grip tightens when I try to pull away. "Unlike your mother."

Pain and anger rush through me. I want to smash his face in. I want to let loose my power and destroy his smug expression. I picture myself thumping my free hand down on his arm—the one he's using to restrain me—and breaking his bones to make him feel the pain I feel right now.

But he's baiting me. If I react, I'll let him win.

I close the fingers of my free hand into a fist and press it hard against my other side, where he can't see it. I focus all of my rage into my fingernails, knowing that my choice is to break my own skin or to break his, and the second option is not open to me. I fight everything inside myself as I tell myself to be like Slade, to play the game.

Just play the game, Hunter. You will end this smug bastard. One day.

I swallow a sigh. Maybe I will. Maybe I won't. But telling myself that helps me get through the rage.

Fallon slides the last silver ring over my forefinger. It's far too big, but the magic in the ring causes it to shrink to fit me snugly so it won't fall off. I'm ready for him to let me go, but it seems he isn't done with me when he maneuvers me around to face the class.

I flinch as he places his free hand across my forehead, his grip on my arm tightening even further. "Harnessing the ability to blur requires you to forget your own body. To stop believing in boundaries. To understand that you are nothing more than what surrounds you: the iron walls, the table, the floor. You are part of everything and nothing at the same time."

I squash the rising power inside me and try to focus on the ring instead, but all I feel is a faint pushing sensation, as if the ring wants to slip off my finger. As if it doesn't want to be there. There's no rush of power or sudden influx of energy.

Did he somehow conspire to give me a dud?

The other trainees appear to focus in concentration, their foreheads slightly creased and lips pressed together. I sense the power from their rings, but not my own. I'm surprised when Rowan's form is the first to flicker at the edges, his body becoming transparent to the eye. It's only for a moment, but it's more than anyone else manages.

I close my eyes and try to sense something—*anything*—from the ring, but still, there's nothing.

Fallon leans to the side, narrowing his eyes at me, but when nothing happens, he finally lets me go. I take a deep breath. The other candidates have avoided me ever since the fight this morning, but now they look at me again, bolder now that Fallon has mishandled me without any retaliation from me.

They must now believe they can use magic against me. That I'm not experienced in it like I am with combat.

I want to scream with frustration. When Mom refused to teach me magic, she said it was because an assassin would detect it on me, but now I find out that assassin's magic is contained in rings that assassins wear. She never told me that.

I wonder if it's because assassin's magic somehow doesn't mix with ours. Maybe it's dangerous to me... But then, why wouldn't she warn me about it? I try to calm myself with the knowledge that I'm wearing one of the rings, so if it was going to hurt me, surely it would have already.

But then... I never saw her wear the fabled glass ring that Fallon talked about. Ever. Not even when she was on the job.

I also never saw her blur.

I don't understand any of it.

All I can focus on right now is the fact that she never wanted me to come here and be exposed to any of this. Maybe this whole room is some sort of death trap...

I'm close to panic when I sense eyes on me and look up to meet Slade's steady gaze across the room. His chest expands as he takes a visibly deep breath and it's like he's telling me to do the same.

Breathe, Hunter.

I maintain eye contact with him as I allow air to slip into my lungs, filling my chest, calming me. Slade gives me an imperceptible nod and after that, I focus on remaining calm no matter what.

When we leave the class, I feel like I've been pulled out of my own skin. We spent three hours trying to blur and by the end of it, most of the Novices succeeded to some degree, with Rowan and Slade being the only ones to disappear entirely. Leaving me as the only one who didn't even get close.

Fallon's final instruction is that blurring inside the Realm is strictly forbidden except within the walls of the magic room. At the end of the class, we are required to give back our rings. I've never been so happy to take off a piece of jewelry.

After we drag ourselves up the staircase into fresh air, I turn back to see that the opening to the dungeon is right outside what we thought was the magic room—the opening consisting of an iron door in the ground like the entrance to a cellar.

I have to find a way for my own magic to coexist with assassin's magic. Or rather, to use my magic in a way that looks like assassin's magic so that Fallon won't know the difference. It's the only way I'll get through his class.

As I head to the food hall with Slade walking silently beside me, I chew my lip in thought before I realize I'm making the cut on it worse. I've managed to ignore the pain all day, but it's returning to me now that my adrenaline is dropping. *Ouch.*

When we reach the table, Thomas takes one look at us and grabs a handful of ice from the bucket on the trolley. He wraps the ice in a table napkin to form a makeshift ice pack and hands it to me before making a pack for Slade.

I press the ice against my lip while Slade tucks his pack under his shirt next to his ribs. I won't ask him to show me his wound out here in the open, but I'm worried that he didn't completely escape Fallon's magic today.

Thomas slides back into his seat. "We heard they were rough on you today."

Slade grumbles as he sits down, taking the seat between Thomas and me. "We didn't expect anything less."

I throw Slade a glance. I appreciated his silence on the walk over, but now I'm not sure if he's okay. I'm not about to ask him in front of the other Superiors, though.

I add a defensive: "We're fine."

Thomas and Matthew chortle into their food. Thomas spins in his seat and grabs two plates of food for us, eyeing the bruise on Slade's jaw. "Here, eat up. If you can."

Slade is clearly not impressed by the humor. He makes a two-syllable noise that sounds like "Thank you" but could just as easily be "Get lost."

Thomas isn't deterred and neither is Matthew. The green-eyed Superior leans across the table from his habitual spot opposite us. Once again, I have the impression that Matthew could move much faster than he allows himself to.

I find myself checking for the ring on his finger, even though I know I won't see it. In class, Fallon told us very firmly that only the Master is allowed to wear his assassin's ring all of the time in the Realm. The others are required to remove theirs unless they're teaching or on a mission.

With assassin's rings, people could blur, which is forbidden except during training, but I also imagine that the rules are about power and control. Only the Master may have constant power here.

"We heard you kicked butt in combat training today, Hunter," Matthew says.

I shrug, willing to eat now that my lip is somewhat numb. I take a bite instead of answering him. I'm starving, so the shrug will have to do.

Thomas nudges Slade. "It's a good thing Ridley didn't order you to fight her, Slade."

Matthew grins, watching us both. "That's a fight I'd like to see."

Slade becomes very still. Darkness settles around his eyes. He focusses on his food. "He did."

Thomas lifts an eyebrow. "What's that?"

"He ordered me to fight Hunter. I refused."

My eyes shoot wide. I study Slade, who glares at his plate. Ridley signaled a lot of Novices to attack me today, including Lutz. I didn't know he'd tried to make Slade fight me too. Instead, Slade made moves to fight my opponent, going against Ridley's orders. At which point, Ridley ordered Slade to stand down.

Thomas leans back in his chair, his expression becoming serious for the first time. "Well, you've got some balls, cousin."

Slade drops his fork onto his plate, his lips pressed into an angry line. He looks like he wants to throw something.

He's mad and I'm not entirely sure why. I hold my breath...

At the last moment, Slade exhales, easing back in his chair. He taps a finger against the edge of the table and relaxes. "I'm not a fool. Hunter would have kicked the stuffing out of me. Only an idiot takes her on."

His eyes meet mine for a moment.

He's lying about his reasons. I saw him fight Fallon today. I heard the crack of his fist against Fallon's magic and saw the glimmer of alarm on Fallon's face.

Slade has no fear. He's certainly not afraid of me. Every move he makes is strategized before he makes it.

A shiver races through my spine as I realize that Slade is more like me than I thought.

He's hiding his strength. Just like I am. And now he's using me to do it.

CHAPTER THIRTEEN

The other Novices take longer than us to eat dinner, and the new Superiors give us space, so Slade and I end up walking back to the dorm alone.

He's very quiet, but it's not a calm kind of silent. Tension bubbles in the air between us and I don't like it because I can't pinpoint why it's there. If it was because we were enemies, it wouldn't surprise me, but it doesn't feel like distrust so much as… frustration.

Trying to break the tension, I gesture to his ribs and ask, "How bad is your wound?"

His response is short. "It's a bruise. Nothing more."

I narrow my eyes at him. *Okay, he doesn't want to talk to me, but that's not good enough for me...*

I stop walking, forcing him to stop, too. "I'm confused. Something's gone wrong in the last few hours and you're not telling me what it is."

He shakes his head and walks past me, but I won't let him go.

"Are we allies or not?" I demand to know. "Because I can't afford to misjudge where I stand with you."

He stops, his back to me, shoulders tense. He half-turns, his expression hooded in the moonlight, but he doesn't say anything, not even when the furrow in his brow deepens as his gaze travels from my eyes to the straight line I'm making with my lips.

I shift, planting my feet. "There's something you want to say to me, so... say it."

He turns fully, crossing his arms. "What happened in magic class? You almost had a panic attack and everyone saw it. Including Fallon. He grabbed you and you just stood there. What was that about, Hunter?"

"I... can't..."

"You were the only one who was free, the only one who *somehow* resisted his magic, yet you didn't fight him. At all. Why not?"

I can't begin to answer that question without opening up a very large can of worms: that I'm terrified my power will reveal itself, that they'll find out I'm not quite human, that Fallon's presence ignites my defense mechanisms in a bad way, that my only choice today was to shut down and not fight back because the consequences of fighting back would be catastrophic.

Slade must interpret my silence as an unwillingness to explain because all of the unforgiving lines have returned to his face. In fact, his whole posture is like granite.

"It wasn't until I heard myself talking about you at dinner tonight that I realized just how far you've gotten under my skin," he says. "I've known you for a day and I'm already compromising everything I've worked for."

I search his expression, but I can't read it at all. "What do you mean?"

"I refused an order today, Hunter. Because of you."

My shoulders lift and my hands splay, trying to shrug it off. "Well... good. I hit one of the teachers. They aren't going to kick us out because of it—"

He shakes his head at me, closing the gap between us, making me swallow whatever I was about to say next.

His presence this close to me has the unwanted effect of making my heart beat faster. The way his eyes change as he speaks reminds me of a deep ocean and I can't see what's beneath the surface, so many layers hidden from me.

"I thought I could make this work," he says. "I thought that teaming up with you would work out in my favor, but right now, you are a major distraction to me. A distraction that I want, but I can't afford."

I take a step back. It's a reflex. Like being kicked in the stomach.

Yes, I froze in magic class today and I hate that I can't explain why, but now he's saying that he sees me as a liability. He's about to tell me he wants to go it alone.

He's about to ditch me.

I tell myself I don't care.

I don't care if I sleep on the floor. I was prepared for that. I don't care if I have to eat dinner alone. I was ready for that, too. I don't care if he follows Ridley's orders and fights me in class. I understand fists and fighting better than I understand anything else.

I definitely don't care if I have to treat Slade the same way as I treat Lutz—with extreme distrust.

But I do care that for a few moments today... I actually thought he...

What, Hunter? Was a friend? Someone who has your back? Could even be more than that? Only Mom ever had my back. Right up until she died.

It's time for me to remember that I'm on my own. That I have a mission. Slade is right. This alliance... or whatever it is... is a distraction.

He says something else, but I don't hear it. My ears are buzzing and I need to get away from him so I can kill off these emotions rising like a wave inside me.

I am not an emotional person. I am not that woman. I don't feel things. I just… don't.

I haven't felt anything since Mom died. I've covered myself in ice since that day and I'm not about to thaw out now.

I pull away from him, stepping aside, deliberately moving off the path to avoid walking anywhere near him. "It's okay, Slade. I'll sleep on the floor."

He looks confused. "That's not what I…"

Passing clear of him along the grass, I veer back onto the path, my boots click-clacking on the pavement. I focus on what I have to do next, each small step. I plan out the mundane things to clear my mind: bathroom first, then figure out a pillow.

Don't feel…

Maybe I can wad up yesterday's jeans to rest on. They're not that dirty.

Don't feel…

Swift footfalls sound behind me. Slade moves fast, stepping right into my path, blocking me, but he doesn't touch me. His gaze flashes across me, insistent.

"I'm not pushing you away," he says. "I want answers so I know what to do if it happens again."

I can't give him answers. I shake my head at him. "If you think I'm a liability, then stay away from me."

"That's what I'm trying to tell you, Hunter. I *can't*." He runs a hand through his hair. "Did you listen to what I said?"

"I'm a distraction you don't need."

He waits as if he expects more. Was there more? Did he say something else?

He tips his head, his forehead creased.

"Get out of my way, Slade."

He doesn't budge.

I lower my voice, dangerous now. "Get out of my way."

A muscle ticks at the edge of his jaw. "Make me."

"What?"

"Fight me. Right here." He takes a deep breath and remains right where he is, as if he's daring me to move.

I glance around at the nearby buildings and along the path to check that we're still alone.

He growls. "If I win, you tell me why you froze today."

I stare at him in disbelief. "No."

"Why not?"

I try to step around him, but he gets in my way.

"Why not, Hunter? C'mon, you can't be afraid of me. In fact, I know you're not. You must be certain you can beat me. So, let's go. Fight me!"

"No!"

He grinds out each word. "Why. Not."

I burst out, "Because that's not the way I want to touch you."

Wait... Did I just tell him the truth?

That's not possible.

He appears as stunned as I am, his eyes widening and his lips parting. His gaze searches mine, taking in my posture, the set of my lips, and what I'm sure is my horrified expression. I can't believe I said something I never intended to say.

The air between us is suddenly electrified.

My heart is pounding in a way that makes me feel like I'm going to pass out. Slade and I have barely touched. Aside from sleeping back to back... I barely know him. It's like he said: We only met a day ago.

Mom warned me that when I give my heart, I'll give it completely. That is the nature of our kind. Once we commit, we commit for life. It was the reason I always kept something back when I was with Oliver, to make sure I didn't commit to my first like Mom did. But now...

The fact that I just told Slade the truth is the first sign that he could be my match and it terrifies me.

I take a step back. He takes a step forward, not threatening, but not allowing the distance between us to widen. With great caution, he holds out his hand to me. I stare at his calloused palm while he waits.

He wants me to take his hand. When I lift my eyes to his, his gaze won't let me go.

His voice is a compelling rumble when he says, "Come with me."

Despite myself, I step toward him, not away. I slide my hand into his and shiver at the contact, a reaction he doesn't miss. His palm closes over mine. With a quick check of our surroundings, he gently tugs me in the direction of the dorm.

I glance behind us as we walk, my sense of self-preservation saving me from ignoring the fact that anyone could be watching us right now. Luckily, I don't see anyone and better yet, I don't sense anyone's magic. Blurring in the Realm is forbidden, but it's possible that someone could break the rules and blur so they can spy on us.

I don't allow the sensation of Slade's hand over mine to swamp me until we reach the steps to the dorm, but I'm surprised when he leads me around the side instead.

We step onto the neatly cut grass, veering behind the building. The dorm is located on the edge of the Realm, so there are no other buildings behind it and no windows on this side of it. A wide patch of grass greets me and that's all.

Without releasing my hand, Slade draws me toward the side of the dorm building, where he quickly taps a series of bricks.

I raise an eyebrow at him. *What is he doing?*

He smiles like he has a secret he's about to share with me.

I gasp when the night air swirls in a large patch on my left, shifting and forming shapes I couldn't see before. A lush garden appears before my eyes, weeping willows around its edges forming a canopy that sways in a breeze I can't feel.

Slade tugs my hand. "Quick. Before the door closes."

He holds aside the weeping willow fronds for me to step

through into a clearing containing a pond, a mossy rock bed, and a bench seat at the side. Once inside, the weeping willows provide a complete curtain around us, their fronds descending all the way from their tall branches to the ground, some right into the pond.

"What is this place?"

Sound dies in my throat as Slade draws me close, one arm sliding around my waist, the other gliding up my back. He searches my eyes again, an intensity in his own that I haven't seen before.

In fact, from the moment we stepped into this place, he became completely unguarded. The harsh lines of his face fade away and the heat in his eyes makes my heart skip a beat.

His voice is a throaty growl. "I need to know what you meant just now, when you said that's not the way you want to touch me."

I struggle to concentrate as his hands stroke my back in slow, circular movements. I glance around us, worried about someone seeing us, but he says, "Nobody can hear or see us here."

I need to know where we are, what this place is, but I can't concentrate on anything except his question. "I don't want to hurt you."

He demands more. "How do you want to touch me?"

My eyes widen. I want to lie, pull away, escape, but ever since he reached out to me last night when I found him in the bathroom, that single light touch when his hand grazed my neck...

I have no answer except the truth.

My lips part as I lift up on the points of my toes, leaning into him to keep my balance.

I press my lips to his. Just the briefest touch.

His mouth is warm, his lips soft against mine, much softer

than I expected. I break the contact before I'm incapable of pulling away.

He looks stunned, even confused. The way he's holding me suggests he wanted me to kiss him, but the disbelief in his eyes tells me he didn't think I would. After all, I threatened to do him serious damage if he ever so much as looked at me the wrong way.

Now I'm the one making moves on him.

I'm confused too. What is going on with me? I refuse to believe that Slade is my match. He can't be the one.

Most of all, because it would be very dangerous.

Mom warned me: *When you bond, you won't be able to lie to him. You can lie to everyone else, but not to him. It's our one weakness. Your heart will force you to tell him the truth. Always.*

I *need* to be able to lie in this place. Telling the truth will only get me killed.

He doesn't try to kiss me back. Instead, he speaks slowly and deliberately, as if he's choosing his words with care. "We have seven months of training to get through. The challenges are only going to get tougher. Neither one of us needs things to be more complicated than they already are."

I nod, agreeing, but it's mechanical and at odds with what I feel every time his hands graze my back, soft and slow, sending tingles to my toes.

He continues. "Despite all of that…" He draws me closer, our hips pressed together, his gaze burning mine. "If you ask me to cross a line right now, I will."

I've never wanted anything more. I want to explore the curve of his lips, the shape of his shoulders, and the muscles in his torso and stomach.

I open my mouth to tell him that I'm leaving now, that this is too complicated and we need to keep things simple.

That I'm sorry I kissed him and it won't happen again.

Instead, I say, "I want you to cross a line."

CHAPTER FOURTEEN

His gaze softens, dropping to my lips and drawing back to my eyes.

Very slowly, he tilts his head, the barest brush of his lips across mine making me gasp.

His mouth whispers over to one corner of my lips, kissing the sensitive curve before traveling with the lightest touch over to the other side, nuzzling the other corner.

At all times, he avoids the cut on my lower lip that would hurt me, focusing on my upper lip instead, tingling touches that make me forget I'm injured at all.

My toes curl and his arms tighten. He coaxes my lips apart and his mouth fits to mine, making me sigh and run my hands up his broad back, across all the perfect muscles and hard contours until I reach his neck, tangling my fingers in his hair.

He backs me up against the nearest tree, but slowly, still kissing me.

Every move he makes feels considered, as if he's drawing out the moments as long as he can. His arms cushion me against the rough bark, his mouth moving against mine, until his hands move to my sides, my waist, resting against the curve of my ribs, sliding upward… but stopping…

I moan and kiss him back, fierce now, wanting more. I want all of him. And I'm very frightened about what this means.

I fill with agony as he pulls away, breathing hard, cupping one of my cheeks with his palm as he regains his breath. His callouses are rough against my soft skin.

He's searching my eyes again and I don't know what he's looking for. I've let all of my guard down. He's cracked through all the layers of ice that I wrapped around myself.

His voice is thick and it surprises me how much emotion he reveals as he says, "You're terrified of what you just said to me. And I *never* want to make you afraid."

His thumb brushes my cheek, his hand trailing away from my face and neck. "So I'm going to stop us from doing something that could hurt us both."

I try to find my voice, swallowing hard but unable to speak.

He exhales. Slowly. Drops his forehead to mine. "Even if it kills me."

He pulls me into a hug and it's much too soothing and comforting, considering that he could have asked for more and I would have said *yes*. But it's just what I need to calm my frayed senses, to come back to Earth from the place he so quickly sent me.

He waits for my breathing to settle back to normal, his arms firm and unmoving around me. Then he begins to speak as if he knows that will help. "You wanted to know what this place is. It's a sub-realm."

I'm astounded at how vulnerable I feel right now. Vulnerable but safe. Two opposing emotions. *Is this what trust feels like?*

I finally find my voice to ask, "How did you know it was here?"

He strokes my cheek, coaxing me to look at him. A smile lights up his eyes when I do.

"The new Superiors created it as a place to retreat when they need some head space. Thomas let me in on the secret. I guess he figured I'd need to escape sometimes. I didn't think I'd need it so soon…"

My eyebrows rise. "That sounds a little too deep for Thomas."

Slade shrugs, the movement causing his arms to shift around me. "He's deeper than he looks."

"I guess we all need wells of determination to survive in this place."

Slade nods. "The Legion is designed to beat us. This is one way of fighting back."

He eases away from me but draws a hand down my arm. He turns his palm up, open, cupping my hand and allowing it to rest freely in his. I could break the contact at any time, slide away from him whenever I want.

When I don't, his thumb and forefinger graze across my palm, making my skin tingle. "I understand why you don't want to talk about the things that scare you. So I'm going to go first."

He takes a deep breath. "I'm a built assassin. When I was ten, I beat up a bully twice my size. When I was thirteen, I got in the way of a mugger's gun and left him in the hospital. My parents tried to channel my aggression into sports, but as soon as I stepped onto the football field, I happily ripped guys up. Violence is part of me. It could turn into something really bad. I want to make it something positive."

I allow myself to smile. "By killing people?"

"By killing *killers*. The Guardian will never sanction the death of an innocent person." He holds my gaze, switching the conversation on me. "I know enough about you to know that it takes a lot to scare you. But you were afraid of Fallon today. Why?"

I take a deep breath. It's time to test my theory that Slade has gotten under my skin as much as he says I'm getting under his.

I open my mouth and prepare to lie. I'm going to tell him that I'm scared of failing magic class. It's that simple.

I tremble when the truth comes out. "I was afraid I'd kill him."

Slade visibly startles. "What?"

It's too late to take it back. I shake my head, trying to swallow my emotions. "He said... that my mother... was weak."

Slade's eyebrows draw down. "I'm sorry."

"I watched her die, Slade, and she was anything but weak. So, yeah... I wanted to kill him. The feeling was so strong that I had to freeze. It was the only thing I could do. That rage... It clouds everything. I had to stop myself from lashing out. Killing him would be a very bad idea because of the first rule of the Assassin's Code."

Slade draws me across to the bench seat. "I know about rage," he says, but he leaves it at that.

I'm glad that he hasn't let go of my hand. It's like a lifeline holding me together. I stare at our entwined palms. "I didn't see Mom's final fight. I only got there after. By then, there was nothing I could do. She didn't have much time. Just enough to tell me what mattered."

He is quiet for a moment. "Which was?"

Tears burn behind my eyes. "She told me: *Just because you're born into darkness, that doesn't mean you can't overcome it.*"

He listens quietly while I meet his eyes.

"I was born into darkness," I say. "My father was the Master Assassin Soren—the one before Gareth. And my mother was a ruthless killer of mobsters and criminals. Death is in my blood. Maybe you and I have that in common."

"Maybe," he says, but he's suddenly far away, and it reminds me of how he responded to my assertion earlier that we all have secrets.

I sigh into the silence around us, closing my eyes in the soothing breeze. "You don't have to worry about me freezing up again. I'll find a way to deal with it. I'm good at putting aside my emotions. I promise I won't put you in danger."

"Actually, I think I'm in a lot of danger right now."

His declaration startles me into opening my eyes. His focus is on my parted lips before his gaze moves up across my cheekbones to my eyes. A shiver runs down my spine, chasing away any sadness I felt, replacing it with a very different kind of ache.

How does he do that?

I want the distance between our bodies to close, but if that happens, I won't stop. I've told him the truth several times now. I can't deny there's a very real possibility that he will claim my heart. The only way I'll know for sure is if we have sex. If I've bonded to him, then my back will burn and my power will reveal itself—*during* sex.

For better or worse.

It can only be for worse.

Mom was lucky. Master Soren saw her worth and didn't betray her. But me? I'm only just starting to trust Slade and I have no idea how he would react if he knew the truth.

I'm suddenly incredibly grateful that he stopped us before we went further. No matter what happens, I can't take that risk.

Slade has tensed beside me. He searches my face again. "That's the second time you've looked at me as if I could destroy you. I won't hurt you, Hunter."

I don't know what to say. Before I can reply, he stands in a smooth, fluid movement. "We should go, but I'll show you how to access this sub-realm. It won't open if someone else is already in here, so you can be assured you'll always have privacy."

I nod, swallowing down my emotions, preparing myself for going outside again. Quickly, I shut down everything I'm afraid of—Slade's kisses, telling the truth, being exposed. Feeling something for him that I'm not prepared to feel.

When I raise my head again, my guard is up.

So is his. We are both ready to leave this place of safety.

He gives me a last smile as we exit the sub-realm onto the empty patch of grass outside.

CHAPTER FIFTEEN

The next morning, I wake to find I'm not the first to rise. Most of the other candidates are already up, including Slade, who gives my shoulder a gentle nudge.

I take in the sight of his naked chest, sculpted to perfection, as he leans over me. I didn't think I'd go to sleep at all, resting my back against his, but somehow, sleep claimed me.

I slide my feet out of bed and stretch my shoulders and neck. I'm sore from training yesterday, but it sounds like everyone else is too. Groans and murmurs greet me as the men wince and stretch their sore bodies.

Lutz is in a particularly bad mood. When the elevator doors open and staff members wheel in the trolley laden with greasy food, Lutz barrels straight toward them, grabbing a sports drink but shaking his fist at the plates.

He gets right up into the nearest staff member's face. "If you bring us food tomorrow, I'll wring your neck."

I narrow my gaze at Lutz, closer to him than anyone else, including Slade. "He's just doing his job, Lutz."

Lutz lurches at the guy and grabs him by the collar of his shirt. "Well, he's doing a crap job of it."

"Hey!" I dart between them and ram my fist against Lutz's forearm, making him drop the staff member, who jolts backward and hurries to get away.

"He brings us whatever the Superiors tell him to," I say. "It's their sick joke, not his. If you want to hate on someone, hate on them."

Lutz's fist flies at me, but I dodge it.

My defensive gesture makes him laugh. "Are you going to panic again, sweetheart?"

I narrow my eyes, zeroing in on his face. "Do you want another bruise on your jaw, Lutz? You're looking a little lopsided today. I can hit the other side if you want."

He rubs his face, which clearly hurts. He gives a grimace and appears to lose steam. "Whatever," he says, retreating to the back of the room.

I watch him go. I catch Slade's eye. He grins at me. I can't help but return it.

Yeah, I'm back.

The blip I experienced yesterday in Fallon's class is over.

After we make it through another brutal training session with Ridley, Slade and I march into the dungeon for our second magic session with Fallon.

This morning, Ridley told us that every third afternoon will be spent with the poisons teacher, Superior Lincoln, since combat and magic require more training. So I'll get a break from Fallon tomorrow.

Today, I'm determined to find a way to use my own power without exposing myself. The rings wait for us on the table, already pre-shrunk to the size of our fingers, so I'll get the same one as yesterday.

I dart forward and snatch it before Fallon can manhandle me. He seems surprised when I throw him a challenging look, an answering sneer settling around the cruel curve of his lips.

I guess he expects me to fail like I did yesterday.

I take myself off to the far side of the room as he orders us to attempt blurring again.

Slade is a comforting presence on my right. It amazes me to realize that talking to him about my fears yesterday helped to lift them off my shoulders. I'm not weighed down by them anymore. It's incredible how talking to someone you trust can really help.

The silver band on my finger is cold and dull. Today, it almost... pushes back at me.

For all I know, Fallon could have been messing with me by telling me that Mom wore a glass ring. I only have his word for it.

From now on, I'm going to treat every word out of his mouth as a lie.

I close my eyes and seek my inner power—the power I hide from the world. I let it unfurl inside me, but only the tiniest bit, only the smallest amount trickling through my senses like a pencil drawn across a page.

I've never tapped into the full depth of my abilities. My number one lesson was to keep it under control. Always. But the few times I've explored it, I discovered that it's like a deep well of possibility.

What I want to do now feels like a mere drop.

Forget my edges. Merge into my surroundings. Become one with the dank air...

When I open my eyes, the room has become hazy, like looking through water. Nearby, Slade is suddenly standing very still, but his gaze shoots around the room, traveling from where I was ten seconds ago to sweep across the other occupants.

I clap my hand over my mouth before I let out a sound of exhilaration.

I've done it! I must have. I've blurred. I guess I shouldn't be so surprised that assassin's magic is a lot like mine. My power is anchored in death too.

I feel a little bad that Slade exhibits a moment of worry, but he soon relaxes. I'm not sure to what extent he can sense me or to what extent he can hear me.

I test how far the blur can take me, carefully taking a few steps, keeping my footfalls as quiet as possible.

The other trainees are still busy trying to make their own blurs happen, so I decide to push myself even further by maneuvering around them, refraining from making faces at Lutz Logan. Sure, that would be childish, but right now, I'm not above wrinkling my nose at him. The deodorant they give us is not up to task.

Fallon lifts his attention from one of the others to glance at the place where I used to be.

He jolts and looks around, appearing perplexed at first and then increasingly agitated. A deep furrow forms in his brow, darkening his features. "Where is Hunter?"

I pause. His question makes it sound like he can't even *sense* me, let alone see me. Yesterday when Slade and Rowan blurred, he walked right up to them to congratulate them while they were still invisible.

Judging from the considerable alarm spreading across his face right now, he can't find me at all.

I prowl toward him, testing how far I can go.

Fallon glares at Slade, who gives him a shrug of his shoulders, which only seems to make Fallon more agitated.

He roars, "Everyone, be quiet!"

The men hush while Fallon closes his eyes, visibly concentrating.

I stop moving. He must be able to hear me… mustn't he?

I take a step, willing my foot to land gently. Fallon doesn't so much as shift in my direction. I tread a little more heavily, testing the situation.

Still, he gives no indication that he heard me.

I make it within two paces of him, close enough to hear him muttering to himself, "Where is she?"

I study the way his dark lashes fall across his pale cheekbones while his eyes are closed. Darkness oozes from every part of him, not to the same degree as Gareth, but close.

My senses are heightened in the blur, mostly because I'm accessing my own magic, allowing it to flow through me, and I can hear his heartbeat, his breathing. His facial expression doesn't betray it, but his pounding heart tells me it's his turn to panic.

He can't find me and it's scaring him.

I consider the assassin's ring he's wearing, as well as the dagger at his waist, which is an ornate one with a jeweled handle.

Then I make a decision.

Calming my breathing, I prepare myself to materialize, but before I do, I very gently wrap my hand around the dagger's hilt, testing whether I can blur it, too.

I know when I've succeeded because its edges become clear to me, as if I pulled it from my watery surroundings into the clarity of the blur with me. It's just like the way my clothing and everything else touching my body is blurred from the view of others but clear to me.

I check to see if anyone noticed Fallon's dagger suddenly disappearing, but it doesn't look like they did.

Fallon's heartbeat is loud in my ears, whereas my own heartbeat is the calmest it has ever been.

He snarls beneath his breath, "Where is she?"

I was built for killing. It's what my kind does. Slade called himself a built assassin. Well, I'm a bred assassin.

So I press the blade against Fallon's throat. I expect him to retaliate and I'm shocked when he doesn't. It must mean he can't feel the blade yet and won't feel it until I stop the blur.

No wonder blurring is an assassin's most deadly skill.

I materialize behind him and whisper, "I'm right here."

Fallon freezes. The nearest Novices quickly step away from us.

Slade also appears alarmed, but that would likely be because of what I admitted last night about wanting to kill Fallon.

Before Fallon can react, I very carefully remove the dagger from its position against his throat, raising both of my hands to show I'm not going to attack.

As I do, I whisper, "Don't ever talk about my mother the way you did yesterday."

His glaring eyes swivel to me.

I've made my point. I lower the knife to the table and step away from him. But I maintain eye contact the whole way, ensuring my message is loud and clear: *Don't mess with me.*

Fallon returns his dagger to its place on his hip and snarls at the staring men, "Get back to work."

Slade gives me a smile of approval as I return to a position near him. He disappears in the next heartbeat, but now I sense what Fallon does: a shift in the air, a presence. I have to concentrate, but now that I know what blurring feels like, I can identify it in others. This must be what Fallon expected to sense when I blurred. But instead, I disappeared entirely.

Slade stays near me, still blurred, and when Fallon's attention is turned to the other side of the room, Slade wraps his arms around me from behind and drops a kiss against the back of my neck that sends delicious shivers to my toes.

I close my eyes and absorb the sensation. How does he still manage to smell so good?

I bite my lip before I make a sound. By the time Fallon swivels in our direction, Slade has shifted to a nearby stance again, materializing so that Fallon sees him.

Fallon scowls but lets it go.

I consider returning the favor to Slade, but if my experience with Fallon is any indication, I could kiss Slade fully on the lips and he wouldn't feel it. As the other Novices gain in expertise, he won't be able to hug me again. They'll sense it, but for now, the gesture tells me…

He likes me. Actually, the grin he gives me as his gaze runs the length of my body, a visual caress, tells me it's something more than *like*.

I hide my smile before anyone sees it.

CHAPTER SIXTEEN

Superior Lincoln, the poisons teacher, stops in front of my desk.

To my surprise, poisons class is set up like an ordinary science lab and, what's more surprising is they actually seem to take our safety seriously in this class. We've been given gloves and protective eye wear and we're all sitting at separate locations at desks around the room.

Lincoln folds his arms across his chest. "The third rule of the Assassin's Code is this: Collateral damage is unacceptable. If you kill or hurt anyone other than your target, you are nothing better than a common criminal and you will be punished."

He strides around the desk, eyeing each of us in turn. His long legs take him quickly around the class. "If you cause collateral damage during a mission, you will bring shame on your Faction. The form of your punishment will be up to your Master. Anything short of death is permissible."

I bet Master Gareth would love it if I broke that rule.

I tally up in my mind the rules we've learned so far:

1. Assassins don't kill each other.

2. Assassinations must be sanctioned by the Guardian.

3. Collateral damage is unacceptable.

Lincoln continues. "Every magical species is susceptible to a particular substance. What is harmless to one species may cause death to another. Some substances are so lethal, they kill merely upon absorption into the skin. For that reason, all poisons must be treated with extreme care."

He stops in front of me again. "Each of you will discover your primary method of killing. For some of you, it will be combat; for others, it will be magic; and for a smaller number of you… poisons will be your forte." He smiles at me and I'm not sure how to read his expression when he says, "Poisons are particularly favored by female assassins."

I brace for some sort of derogatory comment—at least from Lutz, who is bound to associate poisons with weakness—but I guess the dressing down Lincoln gave him on the first day keeps him quiet.

Lincoln steps away from me. "There is one substance that is deadly to all creatures: the sap from the verdan plant." He pronounces it 'veh-*dan*' with emphasis on the second syllable.

"However, it grows only in the darkest crevices of the highest mountains," he says. "It has only ever been found once. So we make do with the various substances we already have. Today, we will focus on poisons for goblins."

The remainder of poisons class is positively peaceful. I might even describe it as *restful*. I have the chance to employ my brain, rather than my body, observing the way Lincoln dissects snakeroot and extracts the pulp and juice.

Then I have the chance to attempt it myself. I'm not sure if Superior Lincoln meant the comment about women in a condescending way, but I enjoy working with the plant and learning about its poisonous attributes.

When I emerge from poisons class, I'm calmer than I've been since I first came to the Legion, but the peace I found quickly disappears when Lutz shoves past me.

We won't have another poisons lesson for two more days and in the meantime, I expect more vicious combat and brutal magic.

My momentary rest time is over.

~

By the end of the first two months, seven of the candidates have dropped out, leaving only five: me, Slade, Lutz, Brandon, and Rowan.

Each night we fall into bed, exhausted and bruised. Poisons class becomes more demanding as we learn about different methods to administer poisons, but it's always a welcome break from combat and magic.

Lutz is too tired these days to bother hassling me.

When the guy in the bed next to ours drops out, Slade and I take one look at the empty cot and push it next to Slade's, forming one larger bed. We still sleep back to back, but our knees don't stick out over the edges anymore.

Every time I leave the dorm in the morning, I expect to come back and find that the staff have taken away the second bed, but they haven't. I don't think it's because Master Gareth has decided to go easy on me. I'm certain he's simply biding his time.

I only visit the sub-realm that Slade showed me a few times to clear my head and always by myself. I'm too afraid of what will happen if I take Slade with me. The only times he touches me now are to check over my wounds and even then, those small touches... I want so much more.

It shocks me how quickly my body responds and how hard it is to clamp down on those feelings.

He seems to sense my struggle and keeps our contact to a minimum, allowing us to settle into a quiet routine.

I watch his back and he watches mine. We never fight each

other in any class—we just flat-out refuse.

Now that there are fewer Novices, I'm not sure how much longer the teachers will tolerate our alliance. Not to mention, Lutz is getting tired of me kicking his butt. His combat skills have improved, but so have mine. Every time he thinks he's got the upper hand, I turn the tables on him.

I'm excelling at all of my classes, particularly magic, although Slade dominates combat now. Even though we don't fight each other, he consistently beats all of the other trainees, including Lutz, at every kind of hand-to-hand combat and with every kind of weapon.

At the end of the fourth month, the teachers start sending the remaining Novices out on reconnaissance missions to support Superiors, who are working outside the Realm. The purpose of the reconnaissance is to track a target, observe their routine, study their home and place of work, and report back to the Superior who will carry out the mission.

At this stage, the Superiors don't trust the Novices to get everything right, so they rely on their own intelligence to carry out their mission, but it's intended to teach us what to look for and what we missed.

At least it would, if I were allowed to do any of it.

To my frustration, Master Gareth refuses to send me out of the Realm. He rotates the other trainees through pairs so they have to work with each other to get the work done, but I'm never sent out.

Slade tries everything he can, but the teachers don't budge.

It gets to the point that I consider asking Superior Ridley for that favor he owed Mom. If I'm not sent out, I won't become a Superior. If I don't become a Superior, then I can't get into the Cathedral. And if I can't do that... I'll never get the Clave.

It's the only reason I'm here.

I suspect that Gareth is running out of ways to get rid of me and wants me to become so frustrated that I'll choose to drop out.

I won't.

I can't.

At the end of the fifth month, Master Gareth breaks his dinner routine by standing and delivering an announcement.

"We are expecting a visit from the Master of the Horde tomorrow."

My eyes widen. It's rare for Masters to visit each other.

At our table, Thomas and Matthew straighten in their seats, surprise etched across their features. It won't be long before they're allowed to leave the Realm to resume their lives in the outside world.

Across the table, Slade's eyebrows rise like mine.

Gareth continues. "A new Horde Master has been chosen and introductions will be made." His lips twist. "The Guardian will accompany the Master and the Heir Apparent to ensure that peace is maintained between Factions during the visit."

Strong rivalry exists between the Factions. Some might call it a healthy rivalry. Most would admit it's savage. The Assassin's Code may stop assassins from killing each other, but that doesn't mean they can't beat the hell out of each other if a slight is perceived. Most 'misunderstandings' occur along the borders between the east, west, and south. Closer to the center of a Faction's territory, skirmishes are rare.

"No assassinations will be carried out during the visit; however, training will continue as normal."

Slade and I exchange glances. No reprieve for us, then.

Master Gareth smiles, his gaze landing on me across the distance. "In fact, I intend to show the Horde what we're made of."

Now I'm worried.

Then he says, "They will stay one night. To commemorate

the occasion, a dinner will be held in the Cathedral. You will all be expected to attend, including the Novices."

The Cathedral! I can't stop the widening of my eyes. The only reason I'm here is to get inside that place.

Now Gareth is *ordering* us inside it.

I can't help the thrum of excitement that shoots through me, but I shut it down quickly. Gareth is still watching me and I hope my response will be interpreted as surprise that he's giving us access to his private quarters.

I can't smother all of my excitement, though. Getting inside the Cathedral means I could be out of here by tomorrow night.

CHAPTER SEVENTEEN

$\mathcal{I}$ wake before dawn. My back isn't quite pressed to Slade's, but his arm reaches back, his big hand resting on my thigh.

My eyes shoot wide as I realize this could be the last time I wake up beside him. If I succeed in stealing the Clave tonight, then I'll have to run as far and as fast as I can away from the Realm and everyone in it.

I already have a safehouse set up outside of Boston. From there, I'll have to keep moving.

I'll never see Slade again.

My heart squeezes. I take a chance to turn from my usual position to face him instead. His big, bare torso rises and falls in the rhythm of his breathing, telling me he's fast asleep.

I dare to reach out and press my flat palm against the muscles below his shoulder blades, closing my eyes and soaking up the feel of his skin.

Maybe for the last time.

I carefully pull my hand away. I didn't expect to meet someone like Slade here, and I'll have to go back to relying on myself again.

As I rise from the bed and stretch out my shoulders and neck, I turn to find Lutz sitting on the edge of his bed at the back of the room.

He tips his chin at me, the most cordial 'good morning' he's ever given me.

My brow furrows at him before I turn away and gather my hair up into my usual ponytail. I definitely won't miss Lutz.

When we reach the courtyard, I'm surprised to find Superior Ridley more surly than normal. He orders us into a run and then quickly to the combat room. True to Gareth's warning that he expects us to show the Horde what we're made of, Ridley pushes us relentlessly. So hard, in fact, that I expect to turn around and find the Horde Master already standing in the combat room's doorway.

Partway through the training session, Ridley calls us to a halt. We're all breathing hard and sweating harder since he's just put us through wrestling drills. The other men like to wrestle me because I'm lighter, but I don't go easy on them.

We draw to our feet and stand in a row, waiting silently for his next instructions.

Ridley watches the door and a thrill of anticipation washes through me when I sense a tremendous power approaching the room.

Assassin's magic ripples through the air moments before three men appear in the wide doors: Superior Fallon and two men I don't recognize.

The older man is tall and lean, graying slightly at the temples, an air of calm control surrounding him. His age indicates that he's the Master of the Horde.

The younger man standing beside him is as massive as Slade, all muscle, with striking, almost-black hair that's long on top and short at the sides. His eyes are green with stunning blue rims.

There's no doubt in my mind who he is.

Fallon's polite tone is underlain with a dangerous edge. He clearly doesn't like having to show the Horde Master and Heir Apparent around.

Fallon drips with politeness as he says, "Excuse me, Superior Ridley, may I introduce Horde Master Abraham Kolko, and Heir Apparent Cain Carter?"

Both Horde men appear to assess Ridley, the room, and everything in it—including us—within seconds.

"Well met, Horde Master," Ridley says, giving the Master and Cain a quick bow. It's a warrior's bow—short and sharp, performed by bending at the waist without taking his eyes off them.

To my surprise, Cain speaks first. "Well met, Superior Ridley," he replies, his voice reminding me of a storm that's about to break.

Ridley opens his hands wide to introduce us. "These are the Legion Novices of the twentieth year."

The years are counted according to the length of time a Master has held power. Each time a new Master is chosen, the years reset. It's a reminder that the Master's reign is not endless.

Both Cain and Abraham nod in our direction and we return the gesture with quick bows, none of us taking our eyes off them.

"This is the group from which the Heir Apparent will be chosen," Cain says, his gaze pausing on me for long enough that Slade stiffens beside me, his shoulders squaring.

"Y-es." Ridley's reply is uncharacteristically faltering and I guess it could be because Cain made a statement instead of asking a question.

I'm filled with unease as I consider the fact that nobody in our group has ever spoken aloud the reality: one of us will become Master.

Inwardly, I shake my head. I don't really care who becomes

Master so long as I get the Clave and leave. Although... admittedly... I'd prefer not to see Lutz take up that position...

Cain says to Ridley, "With your permission, Superior Ridley, I'd like to join your class tomorrow before I leave."

Ridley nods, but he appears unsettled. "Of course."

The men move on, but Slade gives me a worried look. He won't have missed the way Fallon glared at me the whole time.

After that, magic class is more unpleasant than usual. Fallon seems to be taking out his frustration about being a tour guide by making us practice hitting each other with fists strengthened with magic.

Each time we knock each other out, he revives us to start over again. I'm relieved when he cuts the class short so we can prepare for dinner. But with each passing minute, I'm also more nervous. I don't know what will happen tonight and what my chances are of finding the Clave.

When we return to the dorm, new suits and crisp, white shirts have been laid out on the four men's beds, but there's nothing new for me so it looks like I'll be wearing my standard trainee's navy clothing to dinner.

I sigh, but I shouldn't be surprised. Gareth never passes up an opportunity to humiliate me.

I open my locker to retrieve my towel and head to the washroom, but I've only taken two steps when I inhale the scent of death and swing to find Master Gareth himself standing behind me.

"Hunter Cassidy, you will come with me."

I glance at Slade, who looks wary and worried on my behalf, but his expression wipes clean before Gareth passes his cold gaze in Slade's direction.

I paste a pleasant expression on my face before returning my towel to my locker and following Gareth to the door. "Yes, Master Gareth."

What could he want with me?

We walk in silence, heading into a part of the Realm where I've never been allowed to go before. This is the section reserved for the experienced Superiors who have remained in the Realm, including the teaching staff. I've run past it around the perimeter, but I've never been allowed close to any of these buildings.

We approach a multi-level building with grand pillars outside. It's lavishly decorated inside with gorgeous ornate furniture and old-world paintings. The lower levels are busy and I catch sight of men and staff I don't recognize—maybe only fifteen of them, but I'm certain they aren't Legion Superiors and there are enough of them to make me feel unsettled about what I'm doing here.

I maintain a polite tone as I take a guess and ask, "Excuse me, Master Gareth. Is this the guest house?"

"It is."

I exhale slowly. This is where the men from the Horde will be staying, which explains why I don't recognize them.

Master Gareth doesn't stop on that level, though. Instead, we climb a flight of stairs all the way to the top of the building, leaving the busy levels behind.

By the time we travel down a hall and stop outside a large room that appears just as opulent as the ones downstairs, we're completely alone.

"I'm sorry your accommodations have been less than pleasant so far," Master Gareth says, his lips pinched.

I raise my eyebrows at him. He's clearly anything but sorry.

My forehead creases as I wonder what I'm doing here and what he's really trying to say.

A quick glance tells me the room contains a large bed, a table, and chairs, and it looks like there's a door to a private bathroom off to the side.

"You will find everything you need to prepare for tonight's festivities inside this room," he continues. "Including your choice of clothing. But don't get too comfortable. You will return to the dorm to sleep. You will not stay here. This is simply to allow you to dress properly for tonight."

So it's intended to be temporary then. Another glance tells me that the wide-open closet is filled with dresses, which is nice, but oh, a private bathroom means my first shower in months.

I want to run to it, but then I determine with a glance that there's no lock on this bedroom door. I'm not close enough to the bathroom door to know for certain, but it's possible it won't lock either.

My anticipation fades. There's definitely no such thing as 'safe' in this place.

Gareth's cold expression is piercing. "Don't worry. Nobody is allowed to enter while you're here."

The corridor behind Gareth may be empty right now, but I don't trust him one bit.

His actions can't be intended to be thoughtful because I know he doesn't care about my wellbeing. I haven't taken much notice of my appearance lately, but maybe he's realized that it won't look good if the Master of the Horde—the Faction with the most respect for female candidates—thinks I'm being mistreated.

Despite my distrust, I really do need to wash my hair. I've been pulling it back into a tight ponytail for weeks now to hide the dirt. There's only so much I can achieve with soap and angling my head under the tap in the washroom basin. At the very least, I can put my head under the shower to clean my hair properly.

"Thank you, Master Gareth," I say. "You are very generous."

His lips crack apart into a wolfish smile before he swings away from me. "You have one hour."

I hurry to close the door and get my bearings. I don't have time to study everything. The closet contains too many different dresses to count while a section of drawers at the side contain underwear, some of it incredibly lacy. All of it appears to be in my size.

I guess Ridley did take all my measurements that first day.

The bathroom is a compact room that somehow manages to contain both a shower and a bath, as well as a toilet and washstand. The cupboard above the washstand is stocked with shampoo, perfume, and even makeup.

To my very great surprise, the bathroom door has a lock.

Quickly choosing some clean underwear to get me started, I head to the shower first, letting the hot water steam up the small space.

Oh my... How have I survived without a shower for the last five months?

I don't want to get out. But as much as I enjoy being thoroughly clean for the first time in a long time, I have to focus on my goal: getting the Clave.

My biggest problem is that I don't know the inner layout of the Cathedral. I have no idea where Gareth keeps the Clave. It could be anywhere inside that large building.

My plan had always been to become a Superior and then find a way to visit the Cathedral a few times, map it out, and make a plan once I knew what I was up against.

Every move I make tonight will be spontaneous and I rate my chances of finding the Clave at, oh, about ten percent. Not great odds, and I don't intend to take any risks since I still have my first plan to fall back on.

I towel-dry my hair, slip on some underpants, and consider my bruises in the mirror. Most of them are across my torso and back. I'm better off choosing a dress that will conceal them, but I'm not sure how I'll hide the new bruise across my shoulder where Brandon hit me in magic class today.

I shrug at myself. Maybe that's what the makeup is for.

I clip on a bra and head out of the bathroom.

It's only when I'm a single step through the door that I replay the last three seconds in my mind. The *click* as I unlocked the bathroom door, the swish as it opened, the change in the light outside…

And the furtive shadow cast across the opening that shouldn't be there.

CHAPTER EIGHTEEN

My reflexes kick in.

I whirl to my left, sweeping my arm upward to block the downward thrust of a knife from a masked attacker. If there's anything I know how to do, it's steal an attacker's knife.

A quick kick to his groin causes him to reflex downward. Lightning fast, I grab his forearm as I run past him, bending his hand at the wrist in the direction I'm moving and sliding the knife neatly out of his grip.

I spin and slash at his suit, but it doesn't cut through.

Oh, great. He's in full assassin gear.

He's also wearing an assassin's ring.

But I'm shocked to realize it's a plain silver one.

Only the Novices wear those.

Rage courses through me that one of the trainees would attack me like this. Pitching the knife into the bathroom door to keep him from grabbing it again, I launch myself at him. His eyes widen through the slits in his mask. He can't have missed the way I focused on his ring.

He tries to blur before I reach him, the edges of his form

fading out of view, which tells me he either intends to run or to attack me unseen.

I grab him before he can disappear, bite his hand as hard as I can, and rip the ring off his finger, hurling it into the bathroom through the gap of the swinging door. It clangs against the tiles, far out of his reach.

Then I harness my power to give me greater strength and prevent his escape, taking hold of his shoulders and driving him bodily forward to thump his head against the side of the doorframe.

He tries to fight me, tries to use his fists to punch his way out of my hold.

I snarl at him. "Tell me who you are! Which one of those assholes are you?"

I bang his head with every name. "Lutz? Brandon? Rowan?"

He stops fighting me on the last, throws out his hands, and drops his weight, but that seems to be because his legs have given out.

I let him go as he drags himself across the floor, unsteady and shaking, bumping up against the bed, one hand held out to ward me off.

I don't want to let him go. I want to kill him.

The bathroom door swings shut behind me and the knife he used to attack me sways into view, right at my eye level.

It's engraved with the crisp emblem of a thick, stylistic 'X.'

No, wait… that's two 'Cs' back to back that look like an 'X.'

Two 'Cs' is… *Cain Carter*.

I whisper, "The Horde." This dagger is engraved with the initials of the Horde's Heir Apparent. But the Horde isn't responsible for this attack.

Gareth must be trying to get rid of me while making it look like the Horde was responsible. I guess he wants to kill two birds with one stone.

My attacker is breathing hard. I've winded and dazed him,

probably hurt him, but I'm certain he'll recover. I drop across him, straddling his legs, not caring that I'm nearly naked.

Squeezing one fist around his thick throat with my unnatural strength, I rip off his facemask to expose his identity.

Rowan winces at me. Blood trickles down the side of his face from his head wound, matting his blond hair.

"Give me one good reason why I shouldn't use that knife on you right now," I say.

He presses his lips together, refusing to answer.

"That knife was meant to be your get-out-of-jail-free card," I continue. "Well, I can use it too. I can kill you and make it look like Cain Carter did it so I'm not guilty of breaking the Code."

"You wouldn't do that," he says.

"Really? You don't think so?"

He shakes his head. "You always fight with honor."

I lift my hand, ready to break his nose and show him just how honorable I am when his head drops, chin to chest.

He murmurs, "Sorry, Hunter."

My fist freezes. "What?"

He doesn't lift his head. "I didn't want to do it."

I struggle to speak. I just… can't right now. "You came here to kill me, Rowan. Why?"

"I was about to be kicked out. Master Gareth said I could stay, but only if I ended you."

My forehead creases, but he won't see my confusion with his head down. "But you're not failing any classes," I say. "You were one of the first to blur."

He shrugs. "I thought I was doing okay, but Gareth told me I was out."

My eyes narrow. "Were Ridley or the other teachers present in the room when he spoke to you?"

"Fallon was there, but none of the others." Rowan finally looks up at me, taking in my scowl. His expression clears and his jaw drops. "Do you think he was lying?"

"Hell, yes. He was playing you. Fallon is in Gareth's pocket, so he would be in on it too. You're not failing. They just want you to think you are."

"They weren't really going to kick me out." He groans, rubbing his forehead. "My head is mush."

I exhale a sigh. I've long ago lowered my fist. "Gareth is a master manipulator. He knows how to find your weak spot."

Rowan scrubs at his eyes. "So… what now?"

"Now we both get dressed and go to dinner like nothing happened."

His eyes widen with disbelief. "You're not going to report me?"

"What would I report, Rowan? That you tried to kill me with Cain Carter's knife? And to whom would I make this report?" I scoff. "Master Gareth?"

I slide off Rowan and glide to my feet, towering above him in all my very intimidating underwear. *Great.* All the adrenaline made me forget how little I'm wearing.

He also seems to suddenly notice that I'm mostly naked. I guess he was completely focused on my fists up until this point.

He stares. Shakes himself. Has the grace to look away. "You're like my best dream and my worst nightmare rolled into one."

"Get out of here, Rowan."

"Yes, Hunter."

He rolls to his feet, moving slowly as if he's testing his legs before he makes his way to the door. He doesn't look back and within seconds, the door closes behind him.

Well, now I know why Gareth put me in a room without a lock.

I sag against the bed, staring at the knife jutting from the bathroom door. I'm going to have to give Cain Carter's dagger back to him somehow. If I knew for sure that I was getting out of here tonight, I could wipe it down, leave it where it is, and let everyone figure out how it got here, but I have no guarantees I'm going anywhere, so I have to think ahead on this.

I dig around in the drawers at the side of the closet and come up with a pair of leather gloves. I wrap a glove around the blade so I won't impale myself and secure it with multiple hair ties.

When I'm done, I finally pick out a dress to wear, changing my bra first to accommodate its plunging neckline. The dress is a royal blue color and it's beaded all over the bodice in delicate white pearls that catch the light. It's A-line, so there's plenty of movement in the legs, and the top is a V-neck that extends right down to my waist. It's cinched in with a wide, separate band that wraps tightly around my waist and conceals a small pocket.

The pocket is too small to be of use to me, so I slip the dagger, still gloved, beneath the waistband of the dress on the outside, where the blade rests down the front of my stomach while the hilt rests horizontally beneath my breasts.

It's completely visible, which is what I want so nobody can accuse me of trying to smuggle it into the Cathedral. But I also want people to be reluctant to snatch it off me.

I jiggle around a bit to make sure it won't slide down to the floor—because *that* would be awkward—but it sits snugly.

Cain Carter's dagger now rests neatly across my stomach beneath my breasts. Let *that* raise some eyebrows.

As for the silver ring that Rowen left behind, I slip it into the little pocket. I'll have to find a safe place to leave it. Worst case, I'll put it somewhere in the Cathedral once I have the Clave.

I let out a laugh that's half panic and half determination. Maybe this evening will be more fun than I thought.

CHAPTER NINETEEN

I stride down the stairs, full of purpose, only to discover Fallon pacing at the bottom of the staircase wearing a black suit and looking both angry and uncomfortable in it.

I'd expected to find Master Gareth waiting for me, but Fallon's presence gives me a solution for the silver ring.

I stop briefly on the stairs and crouch demurely, giving him a full view of my cleavage to distract him while I pretend to scoop up something from the floor.

Reaching the bottom step, I hold out Rowen's silver assassin's ring to him with an innocent smile. "I think someone dropped this by mistake."

He has no choice but to take it, his cold gaze flashing to the dagger nestled at the front of my dress.

"People seem to be dropping things today," I say.

His response is stiff as he holds out his hand for the dagger. "I will return the knife to its owner."

I don't pause, gliding past him. "That's okay. I can do it."

His magic boils around him, his jeweled ring lighting up, but I hurry out into the open.

To my relief, a sporadic line of men walk along the path, heading in the direction of the Cathedral. Not all of them are Legion. A handful of men I don't recognize exit the guest house behind me wearing suits with pins on the lapels matching the symbol on the dagger.

They pause to allow me to proceed ahead of them. Either they're being polite or they want a good look at my backside. I sigh inwardly as I accept their gesture. I've forgotten what it's like to receive common courtesy without treating it with suspicion.

The closer I get to the Cathedral, the more anxious I become. How am I going to flee in this dress? Why did I choose heels instead of boots? And… why does my heart lurch painfully when I catch sight of Slade pacing the paved entrance outside the Cathedral?

It's hard to miss him because he's a full head taller than everyone else. He stops dead when he sees me. His gaze rakes me from head to foot, his angular features taking on an intensity I haven't seen before, not even when he kissed me in the sub-realm.

I put it down to the fact that he's never seen me in a dress, let alone anything this figure-hugging.

Just as it appears that he's about to relax, his focus shifts to the dagger resting against my stomach and he stiffens again.

I take his arm as I reach his side, keeping my voice low. "I'll explain later."

Slade doesn't move, his eyes narrowed at a point past my shoulder, a warning passing across his face.

A new voice speaks at my ear. "You could try explaining right now why you have my dagger?"

Wait…

I spin to face the speaker, my hand still resting on Slade's arm.

Cain Carter stands directly behind me, a towering mass of muscle and threat. He's flanked by several other men, all Horde.

To reach me this fast, Cain must have been walking behind me the whole time.

Was he blurring so I couldn't see him? He's wearing a thick, gold band on his finger, so it's possible, but I quickly dismiss that idea. He's allowed to carry a weapon here, but he isn't allowed to blur.

Assuming he follows the rules, it means he must have been among the men who gave way to me on the path.

I shiver at this realization. It's a true skill for an assassin to blend into his surroundings, to appear much less deadly than he is. Especially since I already know exactly what Cain looks like, so I should have recognized him.

It's the skill I've seen Slade show multiple times in class, keeping his true nature hidden until he needs it.

I guess Cain Carter is Heir Apparent for a reason.

I meet his striking emerald eyes and it's like looking into a mirror in that he reflects only what he sees. He doesn't give anything away.

I lick my suddenly dry lips and the gesture doesn't appear lost on him. The dangerous lines of his mouth soften and a smile plays around one corner of his lips.

He holds out his hand, palm up. His eyebrows rise, questioning. "I could take it back myself, but in its current location, that might appear impolite."

Slade bristles beside me, his muscles flexing beneath my fingers, causing Cain's attention to snap to him.

Just like Cain, Slade knows how to blend in. Now he squares his shoulders and steps in close beside me, an ominous protective force as he stares Cain down, as if he's daring him to touch me.

The dark clouds filling Slade's demeanor say loud and clear that Cain had better not force this situation.

Seeing them now, standing opposite each other, it's clear that the two men are equals but also opposites. They're eye-height and similar builds, but while Cain's aggression appears casually controlled, Slade's is tightly held, a coil waiting to spring.

Surprise flickers across Cain's expression, turning quickly to respect. He glances from Slade to me, his focus lingering for a brief moment on my hand where it rests on Slade's arm.

I can't tear my eyes from Slade. The way he stepped up to protect me is heart-wrenching. It makes me wonder how many times he's pushed away that instinct when the teachers or the other students have targeted me.

He can't fight back against them, but he can against Cain.

My end goal has always been to get out of this place—to escape with the Clave—and now…

The dull ache in my chest becomes unbearable because escaping means leaving Slade behind too.

Cain withdraws his hand and continues smoothly. "Of course, if you'd rather hold on to the dagger, you can consider it a gift."

I wonder what Master Gareth would think about that. I have to admit the dagger could come in handy, but it could also be misused.

I clear my throat, knowing that I have to defuse the tension between the two men. "Not at all. I was hoping I'd have the chance to give it back to you."

Without releasing Slade's arm, I slide the dagger free, blade pointed downward, unthreatening, and hand it to Cain, hair ties and all.

He gives the hair accessories a quizzical glance before he accepts it, passing it quickly back to one of the other men with a quiet order, "See that this is put in a safe place."

The man nods and disappears back the way he came.

Cain's lips part as he returns his attention to me, as if he's about to say something more, but he takes one look at Slade and gives me a polite nod instead, striding onward.

Slade is a picture of growing worry. "Hunter?"

I casually check for passersby, waiting another moment before I whisper, "Someone tried to kill me with it. They wanted it to look like the Horde."

Ahead of us, Cain misses a step and my stomach plummets.

Slade and I are only now learning how to hone our hearing and sight by using magic, but Cain would have mastered those skills already and he's allowed to wear his ring.

I wish I could swallow back what I said—I don't know what Cain will do with this information—but it's too late. Luckily, there's a wide space around us, a break in the stream of men, so only Cain could have overheard me.

I unfreeze when Cain keeps moving.

Slade draws my attention back to him. If he was worried before, now he's transforming into full combat mode. It's scary and also... makes my heart burn.

I told him that someone tried to kill me and it looks like his protective instincts are about to spiral out of control.

"I'm okay, really," I say.

He growls. "Who?"

I shake my head. "I've already said too much."

"Are you hurt?"

"No, I'm okay."

He looks me over with an expression that tells me he doesn't believe me. What is it about this dress that's turned his protective switch up a million percent?

Obviously not satisfied with a visual inspection, he draws me aside into the shadowed walkway beside the Cathedral, quickly checking me over.

"Really Slade, I'm okay. *Really*." My declaration ends on a sigh as his hands brush the side of my neck. Somehow, he always finds that sensitive spot beneath my earlobe. I relax a little too much against the wall and it seems to be the only permission he needs to drop a kiss against the spot he just touched.

"Don't get hurt." He growls against my neck, as if I have any choice about pain in this place.

I raise my eyebrows at him as he withdraws enough to meet my eyes. He rapidly shifts from angry and worried to... *Damn, why aren't we in the sub-realm right now?*

As his palms brush my shoulders, his lips follow the curve of my cheek to my jawline.

"In another place and another time..." He sighs, not finishing his sentence, drawing me away from the wall before I'm ready to leave.

"Wait," I whisper, pulling him back to me. If this is the last chance I have to kiss him, then I want it to count.

I press my mouth to his, feeling his lips soften, our kiss deepening as our mouths move against each other. With a sigh, I draw up onto my tiptoes to reach him better. Drowning in the taste of his mouth, I lose myself to his touch, to his fingers tangling in my hair and the shivers racing down my spine.

I don't know how we've lain side by side at night for months without doing this.

When he draws away from me, he seems surprised, grazing my cheek with his thumb, gently untangling his other hand from my hair, smoothing it back into place.

Did I really mean that kiss as goodbye? I lean toward him again, struggling with the thought that it could be the last. But he places distance between us, determinedly drawing me away from the wall and leading me out of the shadows.

I calm my breathing, compose my features, and prepare myself for the task ahead as we pass effortlessly through the doors of the Cathedral, a feat I thought I'd have to wait another two months to achieve.

Beyond the entrance, we find a grand dining room

containing multiple tables laid out with fine cutlery and wine glasses at each table setting. I don't plan on drinking tonight since I'll need all my wits about me.

The walls are covered in tapestries, and an elevated platform is located at the front of the room, but it's the gruesome images on the tapestries that stop me dead in my tracks.

Some depict titans rampaging across the Earth, while others show winged women dressed in armor fighting each other. The women are Valkyrie and Keres and they rage over battlefields strewn with dying and injured humans, battling each other to decide who gets to take each human's soul. I recognize the Keres' wings because they're a brilliant copper color while Valkyrie wings are sleek silver.

Slade makes it two steps in front of me before he realizes I've stopped. He turns back to me but freezes again, focused on someone behind me.

It's definitely a day for people to creep up on me, but the scent of death tells me exactly who it is this time. "Master Gareth."

"Hunter, you will sit with us tonight."

It's the most pleasant tone he's ever used to address me and I soon see why as I take in the beautiful woman standing beside him. With glossy, caramel hair falling straight to her waist and luminescent brown eyes, the Guardian is a picture of grace and power. A hush descends over the room as her presence becomes known, all eyes staring in our direction.

Master Gareth is the first to move, striding ahead of us to the table nearest to the dais. The Guardian catches my eye and scoops up my arm at the elbow to propel me along with her.

I throw Slade a helpless look. His protective face is back as he watches me disappear.

The Guardian murmurs to me, "There must be fifty men in this room and it takes one woman to shut them up."

I swallow my disquiet and allow myself to smile. "You have to admit, your presence is a little daunting."

She laughs. "Oh, you thought I meant me. No, Hunter, look around. I assure you the silence was not for me."

I carefully consider the room as we pass through it, wondering if everyone had quieted before the Guardian arrived. I was too shocked by the tapestries to take notice when it happened.

When I don't respond, she says, "I take it you don't often wear a dress, dear."

"Or have clean hair. Or wear a push-up bra."

She says, simply, "Ah."

We're only ten paces from our destination table now, which I identify because Master Gareth has stopped at it.

The Guardian glances at my exposed shoulder and a quick check tells me that Slade must have rubbed off some of the makeup I had applied earlier to conceal the bruise.

"I take it your training has been challenging so far," she says.

"That's one way to put it."

She sighs. "It's a far cry from the treatment your mother received. The Legion was a different Faction then. Its inhabitants worked together, not against each other. I'm afraid Gareth has encouraged distrust and disunity during his reign as Master."

I consider the Guardian carefully. She would be around my mother's age if Mom were still alive. They must have met at some point. Possibly more than once. I want to ask her whether or not they knew each other, but we've reached the table.

Cain waits there, along with the Horde Master and two Horde Superiors, as well as Master Gareth and Superior Ridley. There's clearly no love lost between Master Gareth and the current Horde Master. They give each other stiff nods before taking their seats.

The Guardian gestures for me sit at her right, between her

and Cain. After my encounter with him outside the Cathedral, I'm not sure how I feel about this arrangement, but of all the men at the table, he seems like the lesser of the evils.

It's only when I take my seat that I realize I'm facing the dais. There's a single pedestal on it, on top of which is a glass case. And inside the case…

My breath catches and my eyes widen before I can stop them.

It's right there. Ten paces away from me, displayed in plain sight, closer than I ever thought possible is the Clave.

CHAPTER TWENTY

I can't tear my eyes away from the single, beautiful feather resting inside the glass case.

Mom and I called it "the Clave"—the key—but that word doesn't do it justice.

It's more lovely, more delicate, than I remember, and the sight of it brings all my memories to the surface, all the pain I've pushed down. Mom hid that feather for years, kept it safe for almost two decades before it was stolen from her.

I wrench my focus away from the feather before I draw attention to the fact that I'm staring at it.

The Guardian leans toward Gareth, grimacing at the tapestries. "I don't understand why you keep such violent images in this room."

Gareth waves her comment away. "These pictures depict the struggle between life and death, the battle for our souls. It's a reminder of why we're here."

I stare from the tapestries to the feather. *Why we're here, huh?* That feather is the only reason I'm here.

As the entree arrives, the Guardian gestures to the feather. "And what is this relic you've wheeled out tonight?"

Wheeled out...? My forehead creases because that makes it sound like the Clave doesn't always remain in this location. But of course... he would keep it under lock and key. Not out here in the open. That means that after tonight, it will be hidden away again.

Gareth's eyes light up in a way that tells me he was hoping someone would ask about it. He swivels to beam at it. "Ah, that is something truly priceless."

He swings back, his gaze piercing mine. "I think Hunter knows what that is."

I jolt at his comment. For all appearances, the feather could be from a swan or an eagle, but I know it's something much more priceless. I fill my face with a blank expression, sensing that Cain has turned slightly in my direction. So far, he hasn't spoken to me apart from a polite "Good evening" when I sat down. It's as if we never spoke outside the building at all.

Oh, what a game we're all playing.

I say to Gareth, "I apologize, Master, but it looks like a swan's feather to me."

His lips thin. "It is the birth feather of the last Keres."

Silence falls around the table. A sort of tension fills the air. It's almost comical to see the other men trying not to stare at the feather when it's clear they all want to get up and study it now. That is... except Cain, who remains angled in my direction.

I keep my expression blank, reminding myself that I can't give anything away.

I remember Fallon's warning that the only creatures an assassin needs to fear are the Valkyrie and the Keres. That every other species has a weak point, but not them. It's odd the way we're drawn to things we fear.

The Guardian pauses, soup spoon half to her mouth. Her comment sounds deliberately light. "How intriguing."

Gareth continues. "There's a very interesting story that goes with that feather. You see, it was found long ago by a man who dedicated his life to studying the Keres and everything related to their war with the Valkyrie. He wanted to discover the source of their power to kill. To harness it for assassins to use."

I shiver. The man Gareth is talking about is himself. This story didn't happen "long ago," like he said. He's describing his own search for the source of the Keres' power. Their power is the weapon he has been seeking his whole life. It's the weapon the Clave can lead him to. *I'm just grateful he doesn't know that.*

Gareth leans forward. "The story is that he found the feather in the possession of a beautiful Romani woman. Apparently, she was so determined to keep the feather that she encased it in her dying blood so that nobody could ever touch it."

Pain grows in my heart, but I push against it, trying not to feel anything. There was no "Romani woman." The woman he's talking about was my mother and the blood around the feather is hers. It was her last desperate attempt to stop Gareth from taking it.

He points. "If you look carefully, you can see the substance surrounding the feather. It looks like clear resin, but I assure you it's blood. It dried transparent and is completely indestructible. The feather is untouchable inside it."

The Horde Master folds his thick arms across his chest. "Well, that is an interesting story. But how did this feather come to be in your possession, Gareth?"

"It was handed down through the generations and eventually put on the black market. I was lucky enough to acquire it."

I can't help asking, "How much did you pay for it?"

His eyes narrow at me. "Too much."

For once, he's telling the truth. My mother's life was far too high a price.

He clears his throat. "I haven't given up trying to get the feather out of the resin. I'm determined that it will reveal its secrets to me."

The Guardian gives him a dubious look. "A feather as old as that will surely perish as soon as it is exposed to air. The Keres have been extinct for hundreds of years."

Gareth shrugs, apparently undeterred. "Perhaps, but I can only try."

As the meal progresses, my thoughts whirl. The feather is displayed in front of everyone and is now a topic of discussion and focus. Stealing it is going to be very difficult. My best option may be to use my power to blur and take the glass case with me. I can make it disappear too, just like I did with Fallon's dagger.

But... I'm not sure if I can do that in front of so many people. Now that everyone's looking at it, someone is bound to see it disappear. Even if I run with it while I'm invisible, Gareth can place protective spells around the Realm before I get out. Then I'll be trapped here.

I tell myself that my reluctance to snatch the Clave tonight has nothing to do with Slade. Absolutely nothing at all.

I make a decision. If the crowd thins and I have a chance to snatch the feather, then I will. Otherwise, I'll make do with the knowledge that I know what the case looks like. At least I know the protective layer around the feather is still intact.

Halfway through the meal, Cain finally speaks up. He has been a quiet but powerful presence beside me. It's difficult to see his expression because of his location, but I don't miss the unspoken communication he has with his Master across the table. It's clear they trust each other—a sentiment I doubt Gareth will share with his replacement.

Cain says, "Master Gareth, I have recently learned that I have family here in Boston."

Gareth appears uninterested. "Really?"

"I am not required to take up my post for another six months. In the meantime, I would like your permission to stay in Boston."

Gareth chokes on his drink. "Not in your current role."

Cain's countenance turns icy. "Of course not. I would live here like any other civilian until I take up my position as Master of the Horde, at which time I will leave Boston permanently."

A shiver of apprehension speeds down my spine. I'm not sure what this means.

Gareth doesn't seem to know, either. For the first time since I met him, he seems thrown.

The Horde Master turns in his seat. "The Horde would consider this a gesture of goodwill. For the future peace between Factions."

Gareth swallows a mouthful of wine. "Does the Guardian sanction this?"

The Guardian remains serene beside me. "I do. As future Master of the Horde, Cain Carter will not jeopardize his Faction's reputation nor the harmony that exists between Factions."

Which is basically her way of saying she trusts Cain. When it's clear she doesn't trust Gareth at all.

I contemplate Cain. He didn't say what sort of family he has here, but they're obviously important enough for him to take a very big risk staying in Boston.

The most surprising emotion I feel right now isn't worry but envy. I don't have family anymore. It was always Mom and me. I would do anything to spend one more day with her so I can understand why Cain would want the chance to get to know the family he apparently didn't know he had.

"Very well." Master Gareth looks like he's spitting inside. "As a gesture of goodwill between Factions, I will agree to this."

The tension around the table eases and the rest of the meal passes without incident.

At the end of the meal, I hover near the glass case while my table clears, waiting to see where everyone is headed. The Horde Master, the Horde Superiors, and Ridley bid the

Guardian goodnight and head for the door. Cain gives me a quick acknowledging nod and meanders off to the side of the room, blending in once more. It's scary how well he does that.

A drinks table has been set up at that side of the room, and most of the men flock to it.

I resolve to stay right where I am. These men are unpredictable at the best of times, let alone drunk. Although… it could work in my favor if they're too inebriated to notice the feather go missing.

I consider my timing as most of the occupants of my table depart, but unfortunately, the Guardian has drawn Gareth to the side of the platform, too close for me to make a move.

On top of that, I discover that I'm not free from scrutiny. Off to my left, Slade hasn't taken his eyes off me, although he's doing a good job of disguising it.

To my surprise, Cain is watching me too, where he's now located farther toward the center of the room, casually finding ways to check my location every few seconds.

What's more, Rowan has positioned himself directly in my line of sight, his posture relaxed as he leans against one of the tables.

It's impossible to make a move right now and the longer I stand here, the more conspicuous I get.

Off to the side, the Guardian leans toward Gareth, her voice traveling to me, and I'm suddenly distracted by what she has to say. "Whom have you chosen as your successor?"

Gareth stiffens. "It's too soon to tell."

"Too soon? The current Novices have only two months left in their training. If none of them is suitable, you are allowed to choose from the intake in the year before this one. As you know, Cain was chosen from the year before. But for generational purposes, you must choose a candidate from one of those two years."

He snaps, "I know the rules."

"Indeed, you do. See to it that you follow them."

She turns from him, but he seems to want to stick a barb in her side. "You look old, Catherine. Remember that your own retirement is not so far away."

She smiles, graciously. "But under the Code, my retirement will occur one year after we have three new leaders of the Factions. You are the last to select your replacement, Gareth. The longer you take to choose, the longer I remain where I am."

She glides away from him with a final remark. "Remember, you have two months or the other Faction leaders can choose for you. You might not like the outcome of that."

She heads in my direction, not taking my arm this time but speaking plainly. "My advice to you at this point, Hunter, is to leave the room as quickly as you can. Manners quickly fly out the window where assassins and honey mead are concerned."

Honey mead is a particularly potent form of alcohol and its effects are fast and strong. It hasn't escaped my notice that the teachers have now left the room. It looks like the older Superiors are prepared to allow the younger men to have a little fun.

Fun… drinking and… this is the part in the outside world where there would probably be whoring. Given that I'm the only woman here, sticking around is suddenly a bad idea for me. Even with Slade and Cain in the room, things could get nasty.

Slade is already on edge, no longer blending in with the crowd, switching back into full-on protective mode as he pushes through the crowd toward me.

What's worse, while the Guardian was speaking with me, Gareth gave the order to have the glass case wheeled away. The feather is disappearing from my reach with every passing second.

This is not how the evening was supposed to go.

I want to curse. Wildly.

I catch Slade's eye—he's still twenty paces away—and indicate that I'm going to follow on the Guardian's heels. Just as I head in her direction, someone tugs on my arm and a couple of guys get in my way. I recognize them as older Superiors, ones who have remained in the Realm at Gareth's invitation and who, judging by their breath, have already had too much to drink.

When one of them grabs me, I prepare to slug him in the face, but before I can, he suddenly drops, clutching his stomach. Rowan rears up beside him, gives me a quick nod, and shoves the guy into a nearby empty seat before knocking him out cold with another punch.

I'm shocked. I knew Rowan was watching me, but I didn't think it was with the intention of helping me.

I hurry for the door, sensing that Slade is not far behind, and find the Guardian waiting for me outside. She throws a disgusted glance back at the Cathedral and blows out an exhale like she's blowing off the evening.

"Well, at least you made it to the door unscathed. Can I walk you back to your dorm, Hunter?"

I'm about to give her an affirmative when she stiffens.

Master Gareth steps out of the shadows at the corner of the building. "I'm sure I can see Hunter safely to her bed. She is, after all, a member of my Legion." He gives me a slimy smile. "I will take good care of her."

The Guardian has no choice but to let me go. "Very well. Good night, Hunter."

"Good night, Guardian."

Gareth waits for her to leave and then he waves his hands, causing the air around us to shimmer.

I take a step back, wary of what he's doing. "Are you blurring us?"

"Of course not; blurring is forbidden in the Realm except during class, even for me. I don't break my own rules. I've created a mobile sub-realm with modifications. We're visible but can't be heard."

He keeps his distance from me while firmly gesturing for me to walk with him. I glance back to try to locate Slade, but I don't see him anywhere. He must have been held up inside.

I'm on my own.

Gareth says, "You're an exceptional liar, Hunter, but I won't judge. Your life depends on it. For example, if anyone were to find out what you are—"

My back burns as my power threatens to ignite. "What do you want?"

"I want to know what you thought of my story. About how I acquired the Keres feather."

I snap, "Now who's talking about lying? You made it sound like it happened hundreds of years ago. Not four years ago when you stole the feather from my mother."

He shrugs. "Assassins believe that the Valkyrie and Keres are extinct. Only you and I know the truth."

I remain tight-lipped, knowing that my anger will cause me to say things I'll regret.

"It always disturbed me that your mother was so determined to keep the Keres feather out of my possession that she gave her life's blood to stop me touching it," he says.

So that's what he wants from me. He wants to know why she would go to such great lengths to protect something that most people would see as a mere relic of times long past.

When I remain quiet, he rounds on me. "Why would she do that?"

I can't stay silent anymore. "Isn't it enough that you killed her?"

His response is swift and fast. "I didn't break the Assassin's Code. She killed herself."

Pain rips through me, because he isn't lying. He attacked my mother and stole the feather, but she chose to die. I arrived on the scene too late to stop her.

I still don't know why she would choose death when she could have fought back.

Gareth's hand snakes out, grabbing my arm, his grip filled with assassin's magic, using it to pin me to the spot so I can't get away from him.

He snarls. "She killed herself the way that Valkyrie do."

I shudder so hard that I rattle in his hold.

"You're Valkyrie," he says. "Just like your mother."

CHAPTER TWENTY-ONE

"Let me go."

He laughs. "Or what, Hunter? You won't use your power to kill me. If you were here to kill me, you would have done it already. For some reason, you're determined to become an assassin. Why? Is it simply because of your nature? Even though you're the last of your kind, death draws you like a magnet, doesn't it?"

Magic trickles from his body into mine, stronger than I've ever encountered. I push back, harnessing my own power, but every time I force his grip to loosen, he increases his hold.

With a sudden pull, he yanks my arm across his chest, maneuvering me so that he's behind me. He runs his hands across my back, pressing on my shoulder blades. "Where are your wings, Hunter?"

I grit my teeth. My wings have wanted to spring out so many times to protect me, but I always push them away as soon as I feel the warning burn in my shoulder blades.

I'm pushing them away right now.

Gareth made it clear that we're fully visible to anyone who

could be watching us, so revealing my wings would be incredibly dangerous. Assassins are all humans who hunt supernatural creatures like me.

I fight to constrain my wings.

There are only two times when I can't control their appearance. One is when I take a life using my power, but there are so many other ways to kill that using my power is a last resort.

The second is the moment when I bond. When I sleep with the man who is my match, my wings will reveal themselves, whether I want them to or not.

I gasp. "You will never see them."

"I saw your mother's."

I am suddenly, intensely cold. "She killed someone while you were watching."

He whispers, "No. I saw them the other way."

The foundation falls out of my world. My entire soul just plummeted far, far below me. "You're lying."

He spins me to face him. "I'm not."

But that means… he and Mom… Which also means…

I stare at him in horror. "You can't be my…"

He laughs again. "Your father? I'm not. I was her match but not her choice. That's how I came to hate her. She took my heart and crushed it."

I struggle to believe him. I don't want to think that Mom could ever… with this man… *No.*

But something clicks into place. "She knew you were obsessed with the Keres' power."

"Ever since I got here."

I always thought that Mom left the Realm because of me—because she was pregnant. But now I wonder if she left because she knew the Keres' secrets, the key to their power, and if Gareth was her match, she would have to tell him the truth.

He was the only one who could force the truth out of her.

She had to stay away from him at all costs.

The same way my relationship with Slade is becoming dangerous.

"My focus was always on the Keres—on their thirst for death," Gareth says. "I should have spent more time studying the Valkyrie. I only found out after she died that I could have asked your mother anything and she would have been compelled to tell me the truth."

He strokes my hair. "Now I'm determined to know everything about your kind. So I won't make that mistake again."

Tears drip from my eyes. I could kill him in a heartbeat. It's what Valkyrie do. Clearly, Gareth bought into the whole idea that Valkyrie only kill as acts of mercy and that Keres are the real killing machines. Otherwise, he would have come after our power sooner.

I force myself to remain calm. I'm done speaking with him. I'm done listening to him. "Stay away from me, Gareth. Or I will kill you and burn the Code to the ground."

I allow my power to burst through me so suddenly that it knocks him backward. Steam rises from his skin and a flash of fear streaks across his gray eyes.

I always wondered why Mom didn't kill him.

Now I know it was because she couldn't.

The only person we can't kill is our bonded mate.

I don't have that limitation when it comes to Gareth. If push comes to shove, I will end him and everyone who stands in my way. I'll take back the feather and disappear.

I'm almost ready to try it now, but the protective spells around the Cathedral would have reverted back into place the moment I stepped out of the building. Even my power can't get through them. But Gareth will have to let me back into the Cathedral once I become a Superior. It's just a matter of time.

Of course, he'll do everything he can to get rid of me before then, but for now, we're stuck in this place together.

I hurry away from him, picking up my pace along the pathway, but I don't go to the dorm. I need space. I need a place to calm my thoughts and re-focus.

Most of all, I need a safe place to cry.

Even more than that, I need a safe place to unfurl my wings and to remember what it's like to feel their strength.

I hold it all in, slipping off my heels to hurry around the side of the building, hitching up my dress so I can run faster.

I tap the required sequence of bricks to enter the sub-realm, but just as I step through the canopy of weeping willows, running footfalls sound behind me.

I whirl toward the sound, fear raking through me. I can't see past the fronds to know who is coming after me and the opening won't close for another three seconds, which means they'll be able to get through.

I harness my power, one hand flung out, ready to use it if I need to.

Slade slides through the opening a moment before the sub-realm closes. "Hunter!"

Energy crackles around me, but I shut it down fast. I'm not wearing an assassin's ring, so I shouldn't be able to wield any power right now. If I don't hide it, he'll question me. And then… Oh, help me if I have to tell him the truth.

He strides right up to me. "Are you okay?"

My hand is still flung out, making him pull to a sharp stop when I don't drop it.

"What happened?" he asks. "What's wrong?"

My emotions are going haywire. I was ready to release my wings within the privacy of this place. My cheeks are still wet from angry tears, and I'm a mess.

My voice is a hoarse whisper. "You shouldn't be here."

He can't be here when I'm feeling more vulnerable than I've

felt since I came to the Legion, when all my shields are down and his presence alone is enough to send all logical thought into oblivion.

It's too late. My body takes over. I drop my hand and cross the distance between us, crashing into his chest and kissing him the way I've wanted to ever since I found him injured in the shower room. Maybe even before that when we stood shivering in the rain during the first endurance test.

"Hunter... What...?"

I smother his surprise with my mouth and he responds instantly, meeting my demanding kisses with his own, pulling me closer with a groan, his lips moving against mine. I push him backward against the nearest tree, still kissing him, pulling at his shirt, needing his skin against mine. He allows me to remove the garment before he seems to register what I've done, his eyes widening.

I run my hands across his broad back, loving the feel of his skin, the contours of his muscles, the way he shivers when I slide my fingers across his chest and stomach.

I sigh against his mouth. "This is how I want to touch you."

He takes a mere beat before his arms sweep up around me again and his mouth claims mine, taking control of our kisses. His lips caress the corner of my mouth, tracing down my neck. One big hand slides the dress strap from my shoulder, exposing the upper curve of my breast. I arch against him as his mouth finds all the soft curves across my shoulders and collarbone.

I glimpse the strength he keeps hidden from the world when he easily picks me up and swaps our positions so that I'm the one with my back pressed against the tree. He lifts me up so I can wrap my legs around his hips, bracing against the solid wood behind me.

But... damn. We're still clothed. I can't change that while we're in this position. And he seems to know it.

He's breathing fast, but he's all power and control when he

draws back to search my eyes. He holds me tightly, doesn't let me slide, but his gaze follows a line down the left side of my face and it's only then that I realize he's tracking the tears still falling down my cheeks.

"Tell me what happened," he says.

CHAPTER TWENTY-TWO

I can't speak about it.

I pull Slade back to me, curving my spine to press against him, wanting to taste his lips again, wanting the clothing between us gone. He has lifted me into a completely compromising position and my body responds with a need of its own.

A slow smile spreads across his face, but he doesn't give in to my attempts to kiss him before his expression becomes serious again. "Talk to me, Hunter."

I'm ready to let go, to take the chance that my wings will reveal themselves, to take the chance that he could be the one for me—my match. I'm ready to take the biggest risk I've ever taken in my life.

As the weeping willow fronds sway beside us, I decide that I can use them. I can sweep them over myself. Maybe… Maybe… for the few seconds that my wings appear, I can hide them in the thick curtain of nature spreading out on either side of me.

As the fronds glide through my fingers, Slade suddenly freezes. "Wait…"

He stares at the greenery resting across my shoulder. Still

holding on to me, he very slowly lifts a leaf to examine it. His sudden tension and focus on the tree tells me that whatever stopped him has nothing to do with me.

I whisper, "What is it?"

He elevates one of the fronds for me to see. "The leaves shouldn't be this color."

"What do you mean?"

"They shouldn't have gray streaks in them. I'm sorry, Hunter. The sub-realm is compromised. It's breaking down."

I look around us, shuddering as Slade allows me to descend to the ground, holding me close while I find my feet.

"How long has it got?" I ask.

"It could be minutes or it could be days. But it means Gareth knows about it."

I don't intend my response to be so high-pitched. "What?"

"Sub-realms aren't against the rules, so we won't be punished, but we can't stay here now."

I want to scream with frustration, both physical and mental. Instead, I manage a quiet, "Oh."

He wraps his arms around me and I can't believe how much I'm trembling. Defeat burns inside me. I've never let myself feel so much before. I've always been able to pull back and shut off my feelings whenever I need to. I haven't been with anyone since Oliver and even when I was with him it was mechanical… sometimes downright awkward. But with Slade…

It's so hard to shut off this burning need.

Defeat rips through me and I want to growl my anger, but all that comes out is a sob.

"I'm sorry, Hunter. This was our only safe place."

I refuse to accept that this moment with Slade is over. "When do they teach us how to make sub-realms? We have to make a new one."

He shrugs. "Not until the final month, I think."

"I can't wait that long."

Laughter rumbles against my ear. Slade draws back and smiles at me in a way that makes my heart skip a beat.

"You are incredible," he says.

"I'm serious, Slade. How am I going to lie in the same bed with you after this?"

"We'll find a way. We have so far."

"It sucks so far."

He laughs even harder. When I glare at him and all his glorious bare-chested-ness, he grins at me.

"Like I said, you're incredible, Hunter." He runs his hands through my hair, kissing my lips in a way that reminds me of what I can't have right now.

He draws away from me and I let him go, leaning back against the tree while he pulls his shirt back on. He takes a step toward me, reaching for me, but he stops to take me in, his gaze traveling from the top of my head, down the curve of my neck, the cascade of my hair over my shoulder, to my waist, and all the way down to my bare feet.

My lips part as he closes the gap. I want one more kiss, but I say, "If you kiss me again, I won't let you stop."

A wicked smile grows on his face. He shifts so he's within touching distance and then he leans down and picks up my discarded heels, handing them to me.

"I'll remember that the next time I kiss you."

I slip the heels back on my feet while a shiver chases the contours of my spine, making me tingle.

He asks, "Are you ready to go back out there?"

I sigh. Close my eyes. Shut everything off.

I am Hunter Cassidy. I am an assassin-in-training.

"Yes." I follow Slade out of the sub-realm, seeing now how it's thinning at the edges, becoming more transparent with every passing moment. Slade was right to stop us.

Up the stairs and inside the dorm, we pull up short when we find Ridley pacing back and forth, his boots clomping impatiently on the floor beside our pushed-together beds. Everyone else must still be at the Cathedral, getting drunk probably.

If Ridley's here, it means something's about to happen. I brace myself for whatever that might be.

His tone is clipped and concise. I take note of the fact that he keeps his eyes on mine, although his gaze darts briefly to my crumpled dress. "Hunter, you will no longer sleep in the dorm."

I blink in surprise. "Why not? Where will I sleep?"

He doesn't answer my question. "Get your things. Come with me."

Fear shoots through me. I don't obey him. Don't budge.

Ridley scowls. "Now, Hunter."

"Not until you tell me where I'm going."

He presses his lips together, glowering at me. He doesn't answer, grabbing my arm instead, wrenching me toward the door, seeming prepared to make me move regardless of whether I have my things or not.

I quickly smack him in the face with a full fist.

He jolts away from me but manages to keep hold of me, pulling me off-balance so I stumble against him.

He growls. "This is not the time to fight me, Hunter."

I tip my head back, balancing by leaning against his chest. "Then tell me where—"

The sight of me losing my balance seems to trigger something in Slade.

He steps up, steadies me, spins to Ridley, and slams a palm against Ridley's chest, propelling him backward, shoving him easily with one hand away from me.

Ridley's eyes fly wide, but his surprise turns into a dangerous grin. He reacts by flinging his arms wide, not retaliating.

"I was wondering when you would show your true strength, Slade," he says.

Slade's response is low and menacing. "Tell me where you're taking Hunter."

Ridley grins back at him. "If you want to survive the next two months, you need to let your anger out, boy."

Slade's wrath remains a dark cloud between them. "If you hurt Hunter, you won't even see my anger coming before I bring you a world of pain."

Ridley's eyes narrow, but he seems to remain determined. "Hunter is getting her own room."

Slade's eyes widen in apparent surprise before he retreats a little. "Where?"

"In the guest house."

That's where I was this afternoon, and I don't exactly want to go back there. "But I'm not a guest."

If they'd put me there to begin with, I wouldn't have questioned it, but to make this change now… I have to treat it with suspicion.

Master Gareth doesn't do anything to be kind or thoughtful. My mind is already whirling with all the evil possibilities: like separating me from Slade and giving me different treatment so the other trainees will hate me more than they already do.

"True, but the decision has been made," Ridley says. "Get your things, Hunter. That's an order."

I meet Slade's eyes. I don't know how I feel about having my own room or what this means, but I don't have a solid reason to rebel against this new arrangement.

Reluctantly, I gather my meager belongings into the bag I've kept at the bottom of my locker. I try to stretch out the moments. A few minutes ago, the idea of sleeping back-to-back with Slade felt like agony. Now I won't be sleeping near him at all and it's worse. So much worse.

Seeming satisfied that I'm going to obey him, Ridley strides for the door, waiting there impatiently.

I pause beside Slade, but I can't say anything meaningful to him in front of Ridley.

I can't tell Slade that I don't want to go, or that I'll miss him at night, or that I'm actually… a little bit scared right now.

Despite my hostile roommates, I felt safer with people around me. Now, I'll be alone. Gareth just shifted the rug under me and I don't know whether or not I'm going to land on my feet.

I keep moving.

Slade watches me go, his expression unreadable.

Outside the dorm, farther along the lamp-lit and deserted path, Ridley says, "Your alliance with Slade has to end."

"No."

"You have to fight him in class."

"No!"

He growls with frustration. "Listen to me very carefully. If you don't fight Slade, then I can't rank either of you. Without rankings, Master Gareth can delay choosing his successor. Do you understand?"

My forehead creases. The Guardian spoke to Gareth about choosing his replacement. She seemed worried about it, while Gareth appeared to enjoy his control over the process.

Ridley continues. "You think you're rebelling against Gareth, but you're giving him exactly what he wants."

The air is suddenly cold on my bare arms. Slade and I have been refusing to fight each other since the beginning—and we've been getting away with it. That fact, combined with being allowed to push our beds together, makes me wonder if Gareth has been playing me all along.

I sigh into the night. I didn't want to believe it was so easy.

I surprise myself by saying, "I don't want to fight Slade. I hate hurting people I respect."

Ridley rubs his eyes. He looks tired for the first time, his footsteps slowing. I've retaliated against him often enough for him to read an insult into what I just said.

"I know my classes are brutal, but I'm not here to be your friend. I'm here to make sure you survive." He runs his hand through his hair. "Maybe if your mother hadn't been so adored, she would still be alive."

"Adored?"

He gives me a frank stare. "Her training was a stroll in the park compared to yours."

His comment gets my back up. "Mom was the toughest person I know. What do you even know about her?"

He sighs, suddenly defeated. "Hunter… you could just as easily be my daughter as you could be Gareth's."

CHAPTER TWENTY-THREE

I miss a step. Stumble badly.

Ridley reaches out to steady me, but I jump away from him like a frightened cat. I refuse to believe I heard him correctly. "What did you say?"

He stops walking, shoulders tense, folding his arms across his big chest in a defensive gesture. That makes two of us. My defenses have gone way up, like a thousand percent higher than they were a minute ago.

He speaks carefully. "Everyone thought that your mother and the old master were sleeping together." He lifts his shoulders in a slow shrug, up and then down. "Maybe they were. I don't know… All I know is that she meant everything to me."

I wobble in my high heels before I rip them off my feet, needing to be grounded in something right now, even if it's the patch of dirt beside the path. My stomach has plummeted so far, I don't know where it is anymore.

Gareth denied being my father. He said he was Mom's match but not her choice. I always assumed that old Master Soren was my father and what Gareth said supported that assumption.

But now…

I'm in so much shock, I feel like I'm rising out of my body. I've been hit by a number of revelations already tonight— Rowan trying to kill me, the location of the Clave, Mom's relationship with Master Gareth, and the fact that he saw her wings, then the sub-realm was destroyed, and now I find out that Ridley might be my—

I can't even consider it, but I immediately find myself studying the contours of his face, his eye color, hair color, seeking any similarities, any resemblance to me. Or rather, me to him.

It would mean that I have a living parent.

I might actually have a family.

I hear myself say, "There are tests we could do."

He shakes his head. "If you're mine, then I'll have to protect you."

Oomph. His words are a knife to my heart.

My voice sounds empty. "You don't want that burden."

It's like an ice bucket dumped over me and I shut down whatever thoughts I had about family, my shields shooting up.

He winces and I don't know why. Maybe I looked vulnerable for a moment. Maybe I reminded him of her. Maybe he realizes that he struck hard enough to hurt. I'd rather he'd slammed a fist in my face than make me feel like this.

I return to the path, but before I stride ahead of him, I say, "I know where I'm going. You don't have to take me."

He doesn't let me out of his sight or his reach, catching up with me within seconds, his strides forceful. "End your alliance with Slade, Hunter. And whatever else you're doing with him."

For someone who doesn't want to be my father, he seems determined to make my other activities his business.

I want to retort that I won't make the same mistakes my mother did. Before I came to the Legion, I went to the doctor for a less temporary form of contraception. I'm good for another five years. But it's none of his business. Neither is the fact that Slade and I... haven't really done much more than kiss.

My heart aches by the time I climb the stairs to what will be my new bedroom.

Ridley doesn't make the mistake of touching me, but he places his hand on the door before I can open it. "Stop giving Gareth the power to stall. The Legion needs a new Master."

I don't make any promises to fight Slade. I won't. Even though I know Ridley's right even if I don't want him to be. Gareth is using me, using my determination and my loyalty.

In fact, he might even encourage Slade and me to be together. If I bond with Slade, Gareth could manipulate Slade into making me say things about the Clave, about why Mom tried so hard to protect it.

I shudder so hard that I have to brace against something, my hand landing right next to Ridley's. The shape of his fingernails, the way they fan out a little, matches mine. His might be man size and mine might be delicate, but we have the same fingers.

I can't take any more of this. I have to forget what he told me.

I have no family.

"I want locks on this door," I say. "Enough locks to slow an assailant down."

He steps away from me, releasing the door, eyeing me like I'm a wounded animal. "I'll get them put on."

I hate the look of sympathy in his eyes. "Don't expect me to get any sleep until you do."

I open and close the door, shutting him out.

Inside the room, a lamp has been switched on. The cleaners have been through here. The bed is no longer rumpled. The blood has been cleaned off the bathroom door.

I throw my bag into the bottom of the closet, but it's the last thing I can manage.

I drop my heels right where I stand and slide to the floor, curling up into a ball on the carpet.

I haven't broken down since Mom died.

I can't... start... now...

A sob tears out of me. I try to smother it with my hand, swallow it, push it away, but another one follows, too strong to stop. I clutch my stomach, curling my knees to my chest to bury the pain in my heart. I press my back against the door. This is the only safe location anyway. This way, I'll keep the door closed with my body so that anyone who tries to sneak in will wake me up.

I give up trying not to cry.

Who was she? Who was my mother?

I feel like I didn't know her at all.

CHAPTER TWENTY-FOUR

Just because you're born into darkness...

I wake to a knock on my door, my mother's voice fading from my dreams.

I startle at the sharp thud so close to my current location, my eyes snapping open. I'm still in my dress, lying right next to the door.

My limbs ache, my chest feels empty, and my eyes are... I rub them... so puffy.

The knock sounds again, firmer and more insistent this time. The magical energy seeping under the gap beneath the door curls around me. It's not cold, or threatening, but it is seeking...

I snatch up one of the discarded heels, hold it in a firm grip, and then leverage myself away from the door. I'm a mess, but I won't be surprised by an attacker again.

I take hold of the doorknob, my shoe raised in my hand, its stiletto heel ready to be used as a weapon if I need it.

I wrench the door open.

Cain Carter jolts backward, his defenses leaping up so fast that it's like a physical energy-force slamming up between us.

I glare at him. "What do you want?"

As I speak, I note the new sunlight shining around him, the breaking dawn visible through the wide windows opposite my room. It must be almost five A.M. already.

I slap the back of my hand to my forehead, still clutching the stiletto while I peer around him. "Damn. I'm going to be late for combat class. Ridley is going to kill me. Not that I care what he thinks anymore." I freeze. "I said that out loud. And that too."

I need to curse and scream and maybe hit a punching bag.

His brow furrows. "Have you been drinking?"

I scoff. "Pfft. Drinking."

I've been *crying*. It has the same effect on me. I turn into a wobbly, uncoordinated, illogical mess after I cry. I swore I'd never do it again. Now that I'm standing up, it's like the filter between my brain and my mouth has descended to my feet, far away from where it needs to be. "I wish. I could really use a strong drink right now."

He raises an eyebrow at me, a carefully blank expression pasted over his features. I finally notice his short-sleeved T-shirt and sweatpants. Unlike Slade, he does not hide his strength. He's all power and muscle, head held high, keen eyes taking everything in, including the fact that my bra has slipped a little and I'm showing way too much curve.

"I thought we could walk together," he says. "But it looks like you need a moment."

I need coffee. I need something for my headache. I need a cold shower to shock me awake. "Well, if they'd put a lock on my door, I wouldn't have to sleep right next to it. But now that you're here, you can stand guard while I change."

I stagger into the bedroom, my knees buckling badly. I clutch the dressing table at the side of the room and slide along it, using it to stay upright as I waggle my finger at him. "That's if *you're* not here to accost me. Despite present appearances, I promise you, I will kill you if you come any closer."

He stays at a respectful distance, his only response a slight tip of his chin.

I strip off before I've even made it to the bathroom, throwing the dress and underwear out behind me before I lock the door.

Give me cold water. That's all I need to get my brain working and my coordination back. Hopefully, Cain was too distracted by my cleavage to notice my tear-stained face. I prop myself against the bathroom sink, peering into the mirror.

I sigh with defeat.

There's no way he missed those tear tracks. Damn mascara.

At least he isn't Slade. Slade would demand to know what was wrong and then I would have to tell him. My worried expression changes in the mirror, a wan smile on my lips as I remember Slade growling at Ridley last night, but my humor quickly fades.

Slade won't do that again after today.

Today I stop giving Gareth what he wants.

Today I will fight Slade. I just have to find a way to communicate my reasons to Slade first so he understands why we need to do this.

I turn the shower on full cold and stand beneath it until I'm shivering. The adrenaline finally kicks in. My inner power gets his backside into gear, mending back together like droplets in a pond.

I inhale a long, sharp breath and allow my back to burn, sensing my wings, their strength, not letting them out, but allowing the deadly power to flow through me.

When I open my eyes again, I'm back.

After I dry off, I wrap the towel around myself and emerge to find Cain leaning against the bedroom door. It's closed behind him, leaving us alone in my bedroom. Not what I expected.

My gaze flicks to my other stiletto heel resting a few paces away on the floor. My hand flexes as I prepare to dive for it if I need to and ignore the fact that the towel will come loose in the process.

It seems to take him two seconds to realize that I'm back to normal and he suddenly looks uncertain, shuffling a little on the spot. Great, towering beast that he is. I think I've startled him with my sudden focus. But his uncertainty quickly fades and his confidence returns.

He asks, "What was that all about?"

I'm not about to tell him. Instead, I shoot back at him, "What are you doing in my room?"

"Do you like it?"

I narrow my eyes at him, not understanding the meaning behind his question. "What?"

He takes a step away from the door. "Your new room. It seemed like the least I could do after you thwarted an attempt to frame me."

"You're responsible for my staying in this room?" My eyes are dangerous slits. "How did you make this happen?"

"The same way I'm staying in Boston for the next six months."

When I raise a questioning eyebrow, he says simply, "I asked."

"Yes, but why did Master Gareth agree?"

A smile plays across Cain's lips, but he remains where he is. Despite the fact that he's stepped into my room and the fact that I'm naked under this towel, I don't sense any interest from him that suggests he's going to make a move on me.

In contrast, his attention seems... not *cold*, but... professional.

It dawns on me that he's expecting Gareth to pick a new Master from my group. I guess from Cain's perspective, that could be me. Of course, I know how laughable that is. Gareth would never in a million years pick me, so Cain is wasting his time if he's trying to create alliances.

"I honestly didn't think he would," he says. "I just figured it couldn't hurt to ask."

I snap. "Well, you didn't do me any favors. I was safe in the dorm with Slade."

And now I need to worry about why Gareth agreed to give me my own room. Unless... My gaze flicks to the bed and my shoulders sag a little.

A private room can be used for private purposes. Once the Horde leaves, the whole building will be deserted. It's like an open invitation to do whatever I want here.

Sick, old bastard.

Cain's smile fades. "Don't fool yourself, Hunter. You aren't safe with anyone. There's no such thing as a friend in the assassin's world."

"Then what are you doing in my bedroom?"

A worried crease quickly forms in his forehead. "Gareth will pick Slade."

"What?"

"As the next Master," Cain says. "As soon as he does, Slade will have enemies everywhere. You're safer if you're far away from him. I want you to know that you can call on the Horde if you need help."

I'm shocked. "Why are you saying that? What happened to no such thing as friends?"

He presses his lips together. "You could have kept my dagger and used it against me, but you didn't. It would have taken someone highly skilled to steal that dagger from me—an act that I'm still investigating. You could have kept the dagger and used it as leverage against me, but you gave it right back. I don't like owing favors, but I think the situation requires one. Whatever happens, remember that you can call on me."

I'm confused by his offer. If I suspected he wanted to get

inside my pants, it would explain it, but as it is... What is his motive?

I refuse to believe it's because he might actually be a decent person underneath the whole deadly assassin persona. Of course, he did see my tears.

Now I'm angry because he probably thinks I'm vulnerable. Then I try not to be angry because he didn't have to offer friendship at all.

I say, quietly, "If Slade becomes Master, then I'll have nothing to worry about."

"You trust him?"

"I do."

"I hope you're right about that."

I try to diffuse the sudden tension. "I need to get dressed, so you'd better get out."

The bedroom door clicks and he's gone, but a shadow remains under the door, telling me he's waiting for me outside. I have to hurry or we'll be late. I don't want today to be the first day I do push-ups on the stones.

I dig through the bag I brought with me and retrieve my regular sports bra and training clothes, pulling on the T-shirt and pants, then my gym shoes.

Meeting Cain outside, I check the angle of the sun. "We need to run or we won't make it."

I can't help my sudden smile. I'd love to see Ridley try to order Cain to do pushups on the stones.

Cain gives me a nod and we take off down the path, jogging to the courtyard. It's farther from the guest house than from the dorm, but by running there, we arrive with five minutes to spare. I check to see who's already present, noting that Ridley hasn't arrived yet.

The other trainees mill around the courtyard, straightening when we appear. Rowan watches me intently, undertaking a quick assessment of me from my head to my toes. Lutz keeps to himself off to the side, but he undertakes a similar evaluation. Brandon is the closest, maintaining a firm focus on my face. None of them seems worse for wear, making me wonder if they avoided the after-dinner party after all.

Slade is the farthest away. He folds his arms across his chest, seeming unsettled that I arrived with Cain. I read a thousand questions in his gaze, none of which I can answer right now.

Brandon surprises me when he unfolds his arms and speaks first. Of all the trainees, he's the quietest, the one I've interacted with the least.

His tone is guarded. "Where were you last night, Hunter? We missed you in the dorm."

I don't detect any hint of sarcasm. A quick check of the others indicates they're waiting for my explanation. Even Lutz is quiet. I keep expecting some lewd comment from him, but he doesn't make one.

"I don't sleep there anymore," I say.

Brandon immediately looks at Cain and back to me. My stomach sinks. Oh, he thinks I slept with Cain.

"I have my own room," I say, a little too forcefully. "Where I sleep. On my own. By myself. In my own room."

Ugh. I take a deep breath, flustered, the color rushing to my cheeks.

"Easy, Hunter," Brandon says, suddenly smirking at Cain. "You're too good for him anyway."

I suck in a sharp breath. That is the Heir Apparent of the Horde he's talking about right now.

Cain wears a grin. Is he the reason the others are being so polite? Has he sucked the aggression out of the air or something? Or maybe they think they have to be nice to me because he's standing right next to me.

Or maybe... I remember Cain heading into the throng last night before Slade and I left. Cain was recently a Novice, so he knows what we're going through. He also seems to have a disarming way of getting to know people. He could have buddied up with the other trainees after I left.

Slade hasn't taken his eyes off me. He knows what I look like in the morning. The cold water did wonders, but he knows my eyes aren't normally this puffy. He will guess I've been crying.

I can't quite look at him because I don't want him to see me like this.

I use Ridley's arrival to turn away. But Ridley isn't looking at me, either.

Great. Now nobody is looking at anybody.

All Ridley says is, "You know the drill."

So we run. We follow Ridley around the perimeter two times before he orders us into the combat room. As soon as we get there, he tells us to do stretches. Slade maneuvers his way to my side, a quiet presence close beside me. Cain positions himself on the other side of the room, away from both of us.

My embarrassment about my puffy eyes fades. Normality returns. For the next ten minutes, I can immerse myself in the usual routine.

But the calm doesn't last long.

Too soon, Ridley says, "For the benefit of the Heir Apparent, I believe we should have a demonstration of the Legion's strength this morning."

Ridley meets my eyes for the first time this morning. "Hunter and Slade. Fighting positions."

The other trainees cast surprised glances at Ridley. They know that Slade and I don't fight each other. I guess they're wondering why he'd invite us to disobey him in front of Cain.

I know that Ridley's testing me. His intense gaze tells me that. He wants to find out if I listened to him last night.

I did listen, but I need more time to let Slade know. I don't want Slade to think that I've changed my mind about how I feel about him.

Lutz doesn't hide his surprise. "Are you sure about that, sir? You know she's going to mess him up."

"I don't know that," Ridley replies, challenge oozing from every inch of his body. "Is she?"

My heart is pounding. This is where I would ordinarily flip Ridley the bird and stand my ground.

Slade, on the other hand, has no hesitation about staying where he is. He doesn't budge. Doesn't take up position. He remains relaxed at my side.

But as I shift on the spot, he gives me a sideways glance, his stunning eyes suddenly narrowing, his shoulders suddenly tensing. He's too smart not to sense that something's going on.

I turn fully, taking a deep breath. "Slade Baines, will you meet me in combat?"

CHAPTER TWENTY-FIVE

Slade turns to me, disbelief clouding every inch of his posture. "Hunter?"

I swallow, trying to find the words that will make him understand, keeping my voice low and calm, clear but not challenging. "I believe Superior Ridley needs to rank us. At some point, we have to show him… which one of us can beat the other."

What I don't say is that right now is the best time for us to do it. With Cain Carter watching, there can be no denials about who won, no underhanded behavior to change or influence the outcome. Cain Carter's presence guarantees a fair fight and a known outcome.

One glance at Cain tells me he sees everything, including my emotions. He's probably using his assassin's power to assess my heart rate and know that I'm torn into pieces right now. He saw the protective way Slade reacted last night in front of the Cathedral, not to mention the hand I placed on Slade's arm.

Slade searches my eyes. It's the same search as always, as if he's looking for something lost, something he really needs to find.

I will him to say *yes* to fighting me. I need him to go with me on this. We don't have to hurt each other. We just need to go through the paces and in the end... there has to be a clear winner.

Slade takes a step into position.

I don't know what he's thinking when he says, "I accept the challenge."

Ridley visibly relaxes, and he and the other trainees take up places around the room, standing back against the walls so that Slade and I have the whole floor to ourselves.

We bow without taking our eyes off each other.

As soon as I return to an upright position, Slade steps in with a halfhearted punch. It's easy to miss and I dance to the side with a smirk. *Really?*

His forehead creases, but it's a questioning look that tells me he isn't sure how seriously he needs to take me right now.

Smiling, I step up and quickly sweep his feet out from under him, but I fall with him, deliberately getting tangled up in his legs. He tenses, still seeming uncertain, but his eyes widen when I whisper, "Go with me on this."

His surprised expression becomes a grin. His gaze quickly rakes my body in a way that tells me fighting me is a good way to touch me.

I leap to my feet and he rolls to his.

We've gone through practice drills enough to know each other's movements. Fighting is just like dancing: a fist avoided, followed by a kick, also avoided. The moments stretch out, calm, almost relaxed as we beat out our own rhythm, not hurting each other until... too soon... I sense a dark energy enter the room.

Master Gareth stands in the doorway, creating a tension in the space around us that wasn't there before.

I wasn't counting on him watching us.

His pinched expression tells me he isn't happy that Slade and

I are fighting. I guess Ridley was right. Gareth doesn't want us to be ranked.

His presence changes everything. If there isn't a clear winner, Gareth will find a way to say the fight doesn't count. If Gareth weren't here, we could have gotten away with a mock fight and Ridley could have claimed a clear ranking. Cain would have backed him up.

But Gareth's presence means I no longer have a choice.

I always believed that I had to outrank Slade to be a Superior. But Slade needs to be the clear winner. If I can't control anything else, I can control who the next Master will be. The outcome of this fight will be a big factor in that.

Everyone is here to witness it. Even Fallon and Lincoln appear in the background.

I guess news travels fast.

They've come to see the fight they've been waiting for.

The next time I duck Slade's fist, I slide in close to him, grab hold of his shirt, and speak fast. "I'm sorry, Slade, but we have to fight for real now."

He shakes his head at me—*no*—but I hit him. Hard enough to make him wince.

It takes every shred of determination inside me to shut down my feelings and fight him as if he were somebody else. Not someone I care about.

I hit high—he blocks. I hit low—he blocks again.

I use my knee, connect with his stomach, and he retaliates on instinct with a solid defensive hit to my chest that pushes me backward. He looks shocked at what he did, but I follow up with a kick to his side before he can keep thinking about it, striking in fast succession, twice to his chest and then high at his chin, knocking him backward.

They're hard hits, intended to provoke the anger he keeps under tight control as I try to force him to react on instinct.

C'mon, Slade, where's that rage you talked about?

I just need one solid hit from him. One to end the fight.

I don't let him regain his balance before I strike again, relentlessly, fists and boots so fast that he's flat-out defending against the blows. Four rapid blows to his chest followed by an uppercut to his jaw and I know the exact moment that his instincts take over. I recognize the second his reflexes kick in.

The look in his eyes tells me he's stopped thinking.

A whole mountain of muscle is about to thud down on me.

Slade places the full force of his strength behind his fist. It's a blow that would knock out a bull, let alone a woman.

I see it coming, and I know the impact it's going to have.

I should dodge it.

He *wants* me to dodge it. I see it in his eyes as he comes back to himself in that split second before the punch will land.

I pretend to mistime my step, pretend to stumble. But I stumble in the opposite direction to the one Slade wants.

I step right into his fist.

Crack.

The impact is so powerful that my body flips midair. I spin, air rushing around me, the room shifting as I hit the floor with a bone-jarring thwack that rattles every part of me.

Pain explodes in multiple places—my head, my back, and my right arm.

The room continues to spin and blur as I tumble and finally come to a stop, lying on the floor several paces away.

I can't move, can only lie still to the sound of running footfalls and Slade's shout. "Hunter!"

I welcome the darkness to overcome the pain.

The room goes black.

CHAPTER TWENTY-SIX

"Lie still, Hunter."

Ridley leans over me, his hands pressed gently on either side of my face. Beyond him, I make out the combat room, the other trainees, Master Gareth a dark force in the background...

Cain Carter pacing on my right-hand side...

Slade pacing on my left.

Warm liquid trickles down the side of my cheek. The bone above my left temple feels like it was hit with an iron club. I replay the image of Slade's fist in my mind, the impact, the full force of his strength.

If I weren't Valkyrie, he would have shattered my skull. The strength behind his punch was immense. Far stronger than I ever expected from a human, even one as skilled at combat as Slade.

I find my voice. "Uh...?"

Slade stops pacing as soon as he hears me speak. His face is paler than I've ever seen it and his chest is heaving. He's breathing hard and not in a good way.

He runs his hand across his forehead. He looks like he wants to close the gap between us, kneel next to me, but he also looks like he's beating himself up in a savage way.

Self-loathing is written all over his face.

To my shock, the others give him death stares. Rowan looks like he wants to punch Slade in the face. Even Lutz is glaring.

Slade's voice is a hoarse whisper. "Is she okay?"

Ridley captures my attention, using his body to create a visual block between me and Slade. He keeps his tone even as he says to me, "You were out for a full two minutes, Hunter. That's long enough to cause concern. I need to check if you have bleeding on your brain."

Assassins don't go to a hospital. Ever. There are too many questions and too much official paperwork. My eyes snap to Ridley's and then to the glittering assassin's ring on his finger so close to the side of my face. "How are you going to do that?"

"Shh. It's okay. Assassin's magic allows us to sense when someone is near death. I'll use it to check you over."

I don't like it. I don't want him to take a deep look into my body, but it seems like I don't have a choice. The impact was bad. They are genuinely worried about me. I can try to tell him that I'm okay, that I *know* I'm okay, but it would be hard to convince him. I can't exactly tell him not to worry because nothing can kill me other than a Keres.

That or a situation that forces me to choose my own death.

I've been trying so hard to focus on getting the feather back that I haven't allowed myself to think about what could happen if I don't.

The feather leads to the source of the Keres power, a terrible weapon.

The Keres power can kill me.

I can't let Gareth get his hands on it for so many reasons, but my own death is one of them.

Finishing his examination, Ridley's hands drop to my

shoulders and he lets out a tightly held breath. "She's okay." Then to me: "You'll be okay."

That seems to be the only news the others were waiting for.

Rowan rams into Slade. "You could have killed her!"

He punches Slade full-on the jaw and Slade takes the blow, turning back, appearing to wait for more. When it looks like Rowan will be happy to oblige, Brandon grabs him and pulls him away, driving him to the side of the room.

Rowan grapples with Brandon, still shouting, "He almost killed her!"

Gareth strides up to Slade and places a big hand on his shoulder. "Well done, Slade. Your ranking is clear."

I guess if Gareth has to accept there's a ranking now, he's going to make the most out of the triumph over me.

Slade's shoulders sag. His lips twist in an expression of self-disgust. I want him to look at me, silently beg him to look at me, but he doesn't. I want him to know—*surely, he knows*—that I stepped into the punch.

Cain's voice interrupts my thoughts as he kneels on my other side. "Can I help carry her back to her room?"

Ridley shakes his head. "I'll take her." He lowers his voice. "It might be wise for you to remain here when we leave. Your presence will help diffuse this situation."

Ridley glances meaningfully at Gareth and Slade before he scoops me up into his arms, supporting my head against his shoulder. He's right. Slade looks like he wants to punch Gareth for what he said.

Up close, Ridley smells warm, like aftershave and freshly cut grass. Too many nice Dad smells that I should resist, but I relax into him anyway.

Gareth's cold gaze glitters over me as we pass. He alone knows that I will be okay.

Ridley says, "Hunter's training is over for today. She needs an ice bath. She will not attend magic class. There will be no penalty for her absence."

He glares at Fallon as if daring him to challenge the decision.

Fallon scowls, glances at Cain, who is watching closely, and says, "Of course."

Ridley carries me across the Realm to the Guest House and up the stairs without losing breath. All assassins train like elite athletes, so it doesn't surprise me. He manages to get the door open before placing me carefully on the bed.

He looks down at me. "Don't ever do that again, Hunter."

"Do what, Ridley?" I ask.

"Step into a punch like that."

I exhale. So he noticed. Of course he would—he knows how I fight. He knows I don't make mistakes.

"It worked, didn't it?" I can't avoid the challenge that enters my voice as I lie still, looking up at him. "Slade and I are ranked now."

"You are, although I'm at a loss to understand why you chose to allow Slade to rank above you."

He seems genuinely disappointed. I'm surprised to realize that when he said he needed to rank us, he may have wanted to rank me highest.

Even if I'd won, Gareth would have found a way to de-rank me. This way, the outcome is certain.

Besides, I can't stay here. If I were to become Master, I would have to keep the Clave here too. I can't do that. I have to run with it. Run for my life. And eventually, I have to find a way to destroy it.

Mom couldn't bring herself to do it. She told me it was precious. But she should have burned it when she had the chance.

I have to do what she couldn't.

CHAPTER TWENTY-SEVEN

When I don't answer him, Ridley says, "I'm getting the ice bags."

"I'm fine, Ridley."

"I'll be the judge of that."

He disappears, returning a few minutes later carrying two massive bags of ice that he deposits into the bath. The frozen cubes clatter against the enamel and the sound pounds around my head. So does the rushing water as he leaves it to fill, returning to check on me.

I exhale any annoyance I felt about being babied. I do need that bath and my legs aren't steady enough to get me there on my own.

"You'll have to go in fully clothed because I can't leave you alone," he says. "In fact, you can't be left alone for the next twenty-four hours in case something happens."

I sigh. "You don't have to stay with me."

"Actually, I might not be able to…" He taps his thigh. "But somebody should."

I raise an eyebrow at him. "The only person I trust is Slade."

Ridley presses his lips together in an unforgiving line.

Without a word, he lifts me into his arms again, pulling me against his chest, his big hand cradling my head. He squeezes me tightly for a moment. "You scared me, Hunter."

He clears his throat in a way that tells me he's already regretting the admission of his feelings before he carries me into the bathroom and lowers me into the freezing water.

I gasp at the sudden cold and then close my eyes with relief at the numbing sensation that calms all the bruises I've sustained, including the ones from yesterday.

Before I relax too much, Ridley fills the cup at the sink with water and tells me to drink it. When I give it back, he fills it again.

"You need to stay in there until you're numb, but no longer than that."

I manage a "Got it" before I allow my eyes to close.

I'm not sure how much later it is when there's a polite knock on the far bedroom door. Ridley rises from the chair he dragged into the bathroom so he could watch over me.

I recognize Cain's voice but can't hear what he says. A few moments later, he appears in the doorway.

Both men are too large to fit side by side in the opening—it only accommodates one of them—so Ridley has to make way for Cain.

It's like watching bears trying to be polite to each other.

The younger man gives me a nod. "I wanted to say goodbye. I'm leaving the Realm now, but as you know, I'm staying in Boston for a while."

I attempt a smile. "I'm sure our paths will cross again, Cain Carter. Don't go losing any more daggers."

He gives me a grin. "I'm going to find a good witch to spell them for me. Anybody who tries to touch them will get a nasty surprise."

"Good plan."

He pauses. "Remember what I said, Hunter."

"Yeah… I will."

Then he's gone and Ridley takes a seat on the chair again.

A little while later, I shake myself, realizing I almost fell asleep. Ridley isn't in his chair. I rise up in the bath, looking for him until I hear his voice outside in the bedroom.

Ridley says, "You shouldn't be here."

"I need to talk to her." It's Slade. His voice is quiet. Subdued. "I won't stay."

"You'll stay if she wants you to," Ridley suddenly commands Slade.

There's a pause. "But you said…"

"Forget what I said. Now that you're here, you'll do whatever she wants. She handed you the keys to the kingdom. You owe her." Ridley exhales loudly enough for me to hear it. "I'll wait outside. Don't take your eyes off her. We need to watch for concussion."

Slade's voice remains quiet. "I won't."

I sense his presence outside the bathroom before he appears in the doorway, his expression shadowed and unreadable. Like Cain and Ridley, he fills the entire space but even more so because his presence is so much stronger to me.

He takes in my wet hair, my lips, the chunks of ice floating around me, but he doesn't come any closer.

He asks, "Why did you do it?"

I relax a little, relieved that he knows I stepped into the punch. "There needed to be a clear winner."

"Why me?" he asks.

"Because it can't be me."

He shakes his head and I sense his suppressed anger trying to surface. "I could have killed you, Hunter. I could have crushed your skull."

"But you showed everyone what they needed to see."

He meets my eyes. "Which is what, exactly?"

"That you can be the next Master."

He flinches like I struck him. "I don't want to be the next—"

"It's worth it to me if you are."

Anger bursts out of him. "Nothing is worth hurting you! You are the last person I ever want to hurt. I... Look at you! I did that. Me. I'm responsible."

His chest is heaving. He won't release my gaze. It feels like the floodgates have opened and he can't seem to close them. "I've never laid a hand on a woman in my life. That's not the way a man treats his woman. Ever. A man protects his woman, gives her freedom, supports her. He never hurts her. But *I* did this to you."

His regret and hurt are so strong, it breaks my heart, but there's only one thing that sticks in my mind.

His woman.

"Tell Ridley he can go," I say.

Slade stares at me. He's so full of emotion, I don't think he heard me.

I repeat what I said, even more softly, forcing him to focus on my voice. "Tell Ridley he can go. You will stay with me."

He swallows, taking deep breaths, his forehead crinkling. I read sadness and frustration in his expression and so many other emotions that I can't absorb them. Then he disappears through the door, and I listen for his muted conversation with Ridley outside.

Ridley finally says, "Okay. I'll send staff with food in an hour."

The far bedroom door clicks closed and Slade's footsteps sound as he returns to me.

I reach my arms up to him. "Help me get out, please. I've had enough of the cold."

He grabs a towel from the rack and quietly reaches for me, taking a firm grip of my shoulders and sliding his arm behind my back to support me, leveraging me out of the water so we don't slip. As soon as I'm on my feet again, he wraps the towel around me, rubbing my arms and back.

"I need to get out of these wet clothes," I say.

Indecision is written all over his face. "I'll give you privacy."

"No, please don't." I slip my arms free from beneath the warm towel and raise them above my head. "I need your help."

His hands pause on my waist, but only for a moment before he slides the wet material up over my head. I'm still in my underwear. He dries off my exposed shoulders and torso, resolutely avoiding my lady parts before he wraps the towel firmly around my shoulders.

Then he peels off my long pants, leaving my underpants where they are. The material sticks to my legs and I'm sure I would have fallen over trying to get the pants off myself. Shimmying out of drenched clothing is not as easy as it appears, and as much as I don't like to admit it, I haven't quite recovered my balance.

It scares the wits out of me that even though I'm Valkyrie, one hit from Slade did this to me.

While my upper half remains wrapped in a towel and mostly warm, he reaches for the second towel to dry off my legs. His touch is efficient but gentle. He doesn't make a move on me at all, wrapping and tying the second towel around my lower half. "Let's find you some dry clothes."

I think he's going to offer me his arm, but instead, he picks me up, leverages me expertly through the door, and returns me to my feet in front of the closet. The close contact is over so quickly that I don't have time to process it, other than a sense of missing him the moment he sets me down.

I try to focus on the task at hand. I have a second set of workout clothes in my bag, which I haven't had a chance to unpack yet, but I don't want to get back into training gear.

I ignore the slinky dresses and pull open the drawers I didn't have time to open yesterday, happy to find jeans, T-shirts, and multiple pairs of sweatpants. I'm surprised to also see what looks like a full body protective suit that I'll probably only be allowed to wear on a mission.

Slade prepares to turn around to give me privacy while I change, but I challenge him with a smile, saying, "You're not supposed to take your eyes off me."

CHAPTER TWENTY-EIGHT

Slade answers me with a serious look. "The closer we get to the end of our training, the more danger we're in. Gareth was more than happy to see you wounded this morning. I don't want you to get hurt. I sure as hell will *not* be the one who hurts you." He exhales. "You just took a hit to your head and I'm not going to take advantage. I'm turning around."

He presents me with his back.

I wait another moment, but it looks like he's determined to be a perfect gentleman.

I push away my own reaction to this. I'm... disappointed, actually. Sad that he thinks he can't touch me right now, and maybe a little anxious that something might have shifted in our relationship and I'm not sure what the fallout will be.

He's right that I'm in no fit state to do more than get dressed. My hands shake when I reach for clean underwear in the top drawer. I wrap my fingers in the material to hide the unwilling movement, pulling on the underwear along with sweatpants and a top. I focus on the small movements to help me get through them, counting the seconds it takes to become fully clothed again.

"I'm done." I turn back to him and collide with his chest, finding him suddenly right beside me.

His voice turns to a growl. "Hunter. I'm sorry that we have to wait."

The sound of his voice rumbles through me, striking a chord deep inside. One look in his eyes tells me he's still hurting about what happened this morning. In fact, he's probably more hurt than me now. My body is still getting its act together, but it won't be long before I'm fully functional again. My power will make sure of that.

But Slade's pain can't be seen. It's emotional and that makes it harder to heal.

I drop my head to his chest, needing to speak the truth. "Trust goes both ways, Slade. You trusted me this morning, that I wouldn't put myself in danger. You trusted me to keep myself safe. I broke your trust." My voice becomes very small. "I'm sorry."

When I look up, he cups my cheek in his hand. "Promise me you won't do anything like that again."

"I promise." I cautiously reach for his hand and lead him to the bed. After I curl up on one side of it, I pat the other.

When he lies down, quiet on the other side, I shuffle over and curl up next to him, wrapping his arm around my waist. Unasked, he strokes my hair from the top of my head down my back.

I close my eyes, soaking up how comfortable I feel lying like this. We've always lain back to back. This is much better.

He murmurs, "I don't think you're supposed to fall asleep."

"Then you're going to have to stop stroking my hair."

He kisses my forehead, whispering, "This is how I want to touch you."

I lift my eyes to his. "Only this?"

He smiles. "Other ways too, but this will have to do for now."

We stay like that for a long time until food arrives—a hearty stew with crusty bread—and then we eat at the table at the side of the room.

In the middle of the meal, he says, "I've been thinking about assassin's magic."

"What about it?"

"That story about how the rings were created… It sounds like a fairy tale when you think about it: Ancient warlocks created five hundred rings and gave them to a Guardian to then give to assassins? Why five hundred? That's a lot of work. Why create the rings at all? How did it all come about?"

"I don't know," I say, speaking honestly. "Mom didn't tell me much about assassin's magic. She never mentioned the rings or the warlocks. I never even saw her wear her ring."

I swallow, quickly focusing on my food. That last piece of information was more than I should have shared.

A light crease forms across Slade's forehead while he pokes at his plate with his fork. "She never used assassin's magic?"

"Not that I saw."

"Well, that makes her even more remarkable," he says. "My parents might have kept me out of that world, but I heard she had a hundred kills under her belt. She was singlehandedly responsible for cleaning up the Boston mob, wasn't she?"

"That's what they say." Now we're getting into dangerous territory. Mom made alliances where she needed to. What Slade calls "cleaning up" the mob actually amounted to killing off all of the opponents of one particular mobster: Patrick Ryan.

Mom never told me why, but she gave him full control of Boston's underground. And then she let him reign to his heart's content for many years. He had a son whom he was grooming to take over in his place. I don't even want to think about what they did that she allowed. That was one alliance that I never understood.

"She even managed to kill Patrick Ryan," Slade says. "In the end."

Ah, yes. The story was that he was so hard to kill, so untouchable, that it took years to do it.

The Superiors haven't taught us this rule yet, but there's a rule in the code that an assassin only gets one try. If they try and fail to kill their target, it's considered a mark against them and their entire Faction is prevented from targeting that person again.

I bite my lip, trying not to speak. Mom *is* credited with killing Patrick Ryan, but she didn't do it. I know that for a fact because Mom died on exactly the same day Patrick did—a few hours *before* him.

I don't know who killed him, or whether or not the timing of his death was in any way coincidental, but she wasn't responsible.

In fact, I often wondered if he died because she wasn't alive to protect him. His son disappeared too.

After that, control of the underground was up for grabs. Now the Boston underground is chaos and as much as I hate to admit it, maybe Mom had a method to keep the uncontrollable controlled.

Slade changes the subject so abruptly that I have to catch up.

"I think we can do more with assassin's magic," he says.

I blink at him. "How so?"

"So far, we've learned how to blur, how to immobilize and deceive our targets, and how to strengthen our bodies with magic, make ourselves faster and stronger. But whenever I put that ring on... I don't know... it feels like there's more."

I suggest, "Ridley used it to check me today."

"More than that. We only use it in an assassin's sense, as a method of attack or related to death, but what if it's bigger than that? What if it's not as limited? What if it's more like sorcery? What if we can create things with it?"

He stops, shakes his head, and laughs at himself. "Sorry. I guess I wondered if you ever sensed that."

I can't lie to him. "I'm sorry. I don't feel much at all when I put on that ring. In the beginning, I wondered if Fallon deliberately gave me a fake one."

His forehead creases. "But you can blur with it."

I force myself to nod. "I can now, yes."

It's not untrue. I blur while wearing the ring. I just don't blur *because* of it.

He shrugs, but it's more at himself than at me. "Once we get through training, I plan to find out more about the magic within the ring and how to use it. I don't think Fallon's telling us everything."

On that, I definitely agree.

After lunch, Slade asks if I need to rest. As much as I want to spend the next few hours in his arms, I finally have the chance to really study my new room for the first time. Not to mention, I'm feeling much better.

He seems content to stand aside as I consider the closet's contents more closely than I could before. I shake my head at all the dresses. They look expensive. Some of them are designer brands. There's a row of heels in the bottom in multiple colors to match the dresses. The bag I threw in there last night has knocked some of the shoes over. There are designer handbags, too. Not to mention the lacy lingerie in the top drawer at the side of the closet.

Ridley had said: *What you wear can save your life.*

I'm guessing that's what the stilettos are for. I'm not sure what he thinks I'll do with the lingerie.

Turning away from the closet, I then set about investigating the chest of drawers that sits beside the bed.

"What the…?" I let out the exclamation before I slam the drawer shut.

I really don't know what anyone thinks I'm going to do with a thousand condoms. I mean, of course, I know what I'd do with them—I even know what I *want* to do with them, like possibly right now. But the fact that someone bought them and put them in my room sends shudders down my spine.

My suspicion that Gareth is trying to manipulate Slade and me might be truer than I thought. He's certainly making it easy. What are the odds that he'll insist that Slade has to stay with me tonight?

Slade jumps to his feet on the other side of the bed. "What's wrong?"

My face flames. *Please don't tell him the truth...*

I point at the drawer. "That was surprising, that's all."

His blue eyes narrow as he gives me a quizzical smile. "What was?"

"Uh." I shake my head, dying inside. I pull open the drawer and step aside, chewing my lip ferociously.

He makes his way to my side and peers at the contents of the drawer. His reaction isn't what I expected. I thought he'd laugh, brush it off, but instead, his expression turns serious. Becomes clouded with darkness.

"They expect you to use your body."

He glances at the dresses, the lacy underwear I didn't quite push back into the drawers, and now the million foil packets resting in my bedside table.

My stomach sinks very slowly toward the floor.

I was so caught up in Gareth's scheming that seducing targets was one scenario I hadn't considered. The new Superiors, Matthew and Thomas, had said very plainly that women can make the best assassins because of our bodies. I took it as a joke at the time, not a reality.

Slade's voice becomes wooden. "Even when we become Superiors, we have to stay here for a year like Matthew and Thomas have. We take the missions Gareth gives us. We don't have freedom to choose our targets. Or how we get close to them."

I sink to the side of the bed, speaking without thought. "I

guess that's why Mom left so soon. She was no use to them with a pregnant belly."

And despite the usual rule about staying, the old Master would have let her go.

Slade closes the drawer. "Don't do anything you don't want to do, Hunter. They can't make you."

I fold my hands in my lap. "I wish we'd met in a different place, Slade. In a different time. Maybe a different life."

Always expect violence, Ridley said. It turns out I also need to expect to be used.

Slade suddenly leans toward me, scooping up my hands, practically kneeling to get my attention. "Hey. Did you hear what I said?"

"Yeah." I focus on his eyes. My voice becomes stronger. "I'll kill my targets before they touch me."

Now he smiles. Grins. "Yeah. You will."

I break into a smile. His lips are so close to mine.

Hesitantly, I say, "You could stay in my room. You don't have to go back to the dorm. Ever."

He sucks in a sharp breath. "Don't tempt me, Hunter."

I whisper, "Why not, Slade?"

"Because I'll take you up on it."

I'm stepping into dangerous territory. But I'm ready to face the danger. I lean forward to kiss his surprised lips. "How about now?"

Before he can answer, the aura of death invades the space behind us. My skin crawls and I know without a doubt who is about to knock on my door.

I pull back from Slade and mouth: *Gareth.*

Slade growls. "You need a lock on that door."

He straightens and I quickly relocate to the table and chairs while Slade opens the door just as Gareth is about to knock.

The Master drops his upraised hand. "How is Hunter?"

"Doing well," Slade replies smoothly.

"Good," Gareth says, his mouth smiling while his eyes are like dead weeds. "Because she's being sent out on reconnaissance tonight."

Slade's brow furrows. "She needs to rest."

Gareth raises an eyebrow. "I'll be the judge of that. For as long as I am Master, I will say what my Novices do."

His speech carries a veiled threat. Slade may be the first-ranking Novice, but Slade is not Master yet.

I rise to my feet as Gareth peers at me. He gives Slade another mirthless smile. "She looks fine to me. Hunter, report to central headquarters in half an hour."

He spins and leaves without another word.

Slade shakes his head at me. "I don't like this. Ridley won't, either."

I sigh. "I'm fine. Really. I've rested enough. I need to go out on reconnaissance at some point. This is actually a good thing."

Gareth has left the door wide open and it's like a wall has sprung up between Slade and me.

For a few hours, we could be ourselves. Now it's time to put our masks back on.

"Okay," Slade says. "But be safe."

CHAPTER TWENTY-NINE

When I arrive at the administration building in central headquarters, I'm unsettled to find Lutz waiting outside the room too.

He seems surprised to see me, but he hides it quickly behind his own mask. For all intents and purposes, he couldn't care less whether or not I'm okay.

He leans against the doorframe as we wait to be called in. "Looks like you're going to be my friend this evening, sweetheart."

Within moments, Superior Fallon opens the door for us, revealing Gareth sitting at a desk on the far side of the room.

Hmm. After what Rowan said about Fallon and Gareth telling him he was going to be kicked out, seeing the two of them together doesn't inspire me with confidence.

Master Gareth remains seated, giving a brief gesture with his hand to indicate that we should enter. Once we're seated opposite him, he lowers his hand to rest on a thick book sitting on the desk in front of him.

"This is my ledger."

I glance at Lutz, but he looks bored. I guess he's heard this speech before.

I know what a ledger is. Gareth knows I know, but it looks like we're going to go through this speech anyway.

"All assassins have one," Gareth continues. "If you succeed in becoming a Superior, the Guardian will assign a ledger to you. When a client wishes to engage your skills, they must write their name and the name of the target in your ledger. Every time a ledger is written in, the ink appears in the Guardian's ledger too. She will either sanction the assassination or refuse it."

He opens the book, but I don't lean in to read it. I know what will happen if I try: The writing on the page will turn to squiggles, wriggling across the page as if it's alive.

It will be completely unreadable to me.

Gareth smirks. "Only I can read my ledger. Only you will be able to read yours."

He slams the book shut. "Written in my book is the name of a particularly violent goblin who has disguised himself as a human. He currently poses as the owner of a bookshop on a street called Saber Lane not far from here. He is responsible for the disappearance of a number of children, but the police can't prove anything. That's where we come in."

Gareth folds his arms over his chest. "His death has been sanctioned; however, it is not your job to end him. You will go tonight to map the layout of the street, identify vantage points, and study his movements. You will be permitted to use magic, including blurring, for this task."

Superior Fallon hands us our rings and I slip mine on.

"You will meet each other at the door to the Realm at sunset and proceed from there. You must spend the rest of the afternoon preparing."

"Thank you, Master Gareth." Lutz stands and I follow.

As we reach the door, Gareth calls out to us. "One last

thing… This goblin can't be allowed to remain on this Earth. While your job is to observe, obviously, every day he lives, more people are endangered. Should you have the opportunity to take him out… well… let's just say it would go well toward your chances of becoming a Superior here."

I stiffen, because our job is supposed to be to surveil and observe, not kill, but Lutz is suddenly alert.

Gareth continues. "That is, for whichever one of you has the courage to do it."

As soon as we leave the room, Lutz rounds on me. "Don't get in my way tonight, Hunter. We all know that Slade is the golden boy. I want a place in the Legion too, and I'm going to get it by whatever means necessary."

I keep my response monotone. "You're forgetting who I am, Lutz. You won't even notice I'm there."

Mom never took me on a mission, but every morning when we went running, she would point out vantage points from which to survey targets; all the places to hide and disappear into. I know this city well. Although I've never been to Saber Lane, I've heard of it—it's some sort of tourist destination off Shawmut Avenue. The perfect place to set up a bookshop with which to lure potential prey.

I spend the afternoon studying our destination on different maps, as well as determining different routes to get there. Then I choose my clothing: jeans and a long-sleeved T-shirt, the kind of attire that won't draw attention on the streets of Boston in the middle of fall.

I meet Lutz at the entrance to the Realm at the required time. He's also dressed casually.

"We'll walk to Saber Lane and then we'll blur," he says.

It looks like he wants to take charge of the situation, but I sense a sort of anxiety in him. I've never been out on reconnaissance and Gareth made it clear this mission is a make-or-break deal.

Still, I raise an eyebrow at his command.

He shuffles. "That's what I think we should do."

"I agree."

He grunts before he turns to the wide mahogany door that's set in the wall surrounding the Realm, quickly pulling it open.

Exiting the Realm is like surfacing from deep water. As I step through the door, I take a deep breath of clear, Boston air.

The outside sounds flood in. The Boston Opera House is located opposite our current location. I remember why I loved growing up in Boston despite the bitterly cold winters. There's so much history here.

I push away my own painful history. I won't let it cloud my thoughts tonight.

When I glance back, the Boston Common stretches out behind us, the lush green park turning to burnished orange and gold with the change of season. A tall memorial plaque sits at the side. When we place our palms on it, the magic will recognize us and give us access to the Realm again.

When I first came here for the endurance test, I had to prick my finger and mingle my fingerprint with my blood. Even then, Master Gareth could have denied me access. Although I could have taken it up with the Guardian. All Masters are required to allow potential Novices through no matter what.

I don't feel the need to make conversation with Lutz as we stroll down Tremont Street in the direction of Shawmut Avenue. To a casual observer, we could be a couple heading out for dinner at one of the cafés.

Half an hour later, we pause at the entrance to our target street.

A dark gray lamppost sits at each corner of the entrance. Attached to one is a forest green street sign with white lettering: *Saber Lane*. The street itself is paved, but in the form of a very wide walkway rather than a passageway for vehicles. There are no cars outside the various buildings.

Before I can say anything, Lutz says, "Time to split up and blur."

He doesn't wait for me to agree, checking for passersby before he merges with the shadows at the side of the street.

I don't like the idea of letting him out of my sight, but it's preferable to him breathing down my neck.

Stepping into the shadows, I pause there for a moment, and then allow my power to trickle through me. I've long ago stopped trying to harness any magic from the ring.

The streetlights flicker on around me as I take a deep breath and enter the lane.

CHAPTER THIRTY

It's the strangest street I've ever seen.

The entrance is made up of old-world traditional brownstones that give the vibe of a place that time forgot, but farther in it's more like the street where time got jumbled up.

Buildings iconic of every era line the pavement on both sides. The three brownstones on my left are jammed up against a bakery with a 1950s shop front complete with bright pink, yellow, and green iced cookies in the window, which in turn is rammed up against a grocery store that heralds from the 1980s with an orange-and-cream checkered linoleum floor visible through the still-open door while fluorescent green graffiti sprawls across the outside window.

Farther along is a diner with a jukebox that I can see through the swing door, followed by an apothecary's shop that looks like it hails from the late 1800s. I peer closer, surprised to see an old wooden telephone on the wall outside that shop.

No wonder tourists come here.

Several of the shops are still closing up, although the diner remains open. Two figures sit inside it at a table closest to the window, easily visible in the bright store light.

The guy's sleeves are rolled up around his large biceps while his black hair is slicked up and back in typical 1960s style. The young woman's dark blonde hair sweeps down her back as she leans toward him over the counter, laughing at something he said, playfully swatting his arm.

They create the picture of a flirting couple. Except that there's an aura around both of them that tells me neither is completely human. Lutz will be able to see it too, if he bothers looking. As a human, he wouldn't normally be able to see that sort of thing, but with an assassin's ring he can.

The guy in the diner looks up. I'm disconcerted when he looks directly at me.

I jolt, but his chocolate-brown eyes move past my location. I remain perfectly still as he slides out of his seat and heads to the door, where he surveys the street.

The woman follows him, concern written all over her face. "What is it, Dean?"

A crease forms in his forehead. "I thought I felt someone's pain..." He rubs his forehead. "I feel... secrecy... death... I haven't felt this much pain for a long time."

I take another step back. *Is he an empath?*

I've never encountered an empath before to recognize his aura from my own personal experience and Fallon didn't describe their aura in magic class.

The woman's clear green eyes flash across the space. "Well, it must be coming from somewhere." She rubs her fingers together in a soundless motion, whispering, "Illuminate."

The streetlights flare brightly, and I quickly step into the nearest shadow. They shouldn't be able to see me, but I can't take any risks. The woman is definitely a witch, but I can't tell if she's a good witch or a bad one.

She shakes her head at the empty street. "Maybe it was someone passing by at the end of the street. Remember how you felt when there was that car accident a while ago?"

"Yeah, I guess." He rubs his head some more, groaning and wincing. "Damn. This isn't good..."

She draws him away from the door. "Come inside. Let me get you an ice pack."

If she's a bad witch, she's certainly a caring one.

If it's me he's sensing, then he's an accurate empath. Pain, secrecy, and death pretty much sum me up. But still, I'm surprised. When I blur, I disappear from detection completely, even to other assassins. I didn't expect to encounter an empath here, let alone one powerful enough to sense my emotions through my blur.

I feel momentarily guilty that I'm causing him that much pain. Have I really bottled that much up?

I hurry along the street to the bookshop. Gold lettering on the sign reads: "The Tomb Bookshop."

Lovely name for a bookshop.

I sense Lutz at the side of the store, sneaking along one of the narrow alleyways between it and the next shop. He's checking the windows.

Through the wide storefront window, I can see bookcases lining the right hand side of the shop. There's a simple counter on the left with ornaments on shelves behind it. Set out in a neat row toward the front of the space are glass cases containing books that are open to pages with vibrant illustrations.

I stop still and study the older man sitting behind the counter as he leans over an open book with a magnifying glass. Goblins have notoriously bad eyesight, so I'm not surprised, but what does unsettle me is that he has no aura around him.

I give my power a little more freedom, trying to use it to see beneath the glamour that Gareth said the goblin is wearing. I should be able to detect it and see his true identity—the same way I detected the magic surrounding the empath and the witch.

This man…

I shake my head. I don't see anything.

Maybe he's not our target. He could be a shop assistant.

I spin to the sound of running footsteps.

The witch approaches at a run, her blonde hair flying behind her, and at first, I think she's headed straight for me until I realize she's aiming for the front door.

I quickly sidestep but not quite fast enough.

Her shoulder grazes mine and she jolts to the side, thudding into the doorframe, her wild eyes searching for what she touched.

The force of the impact causes the older man's head to snap up.

He lurches up from his seat and hurries to the front of the store to open the door. "Tansy? What's wrong?"

She shakes herself, spinning to him, her hair flying again and her speech flying faster. "It's Dean. He needs help. I don't know what to do. It's never been this bad before. I can't find the right spell! He's in pain, William. I don't know what's wrong—"

He swings the door wide, props it open with his foot, and places both hands on her shoulders. "Slow down, Tansy."

She's standing right beside me, facing into the shop. Tears streak her cheeks. "He's hurting and I don't know which spell to use."

His voice is low and calm, gentle. "Look at me."

She meets his eyes, takes a deep breath, and lets out a sob on the next one.

"You've got this," he says. "Believe in yourself. You can find the spell."

"I'm scared."

He nods. "Fear is normal. Especially when someone you care about is in pain. Put your fear into action. You can do this."

"Will you come with me?"

"Of course."

He steps out from the shop. The door creaks closed very slowly behind him. I take the chance to slide through the opening before the door shuts, easing back against it so its closure isn't noticeably *too* slow.

I make it inside the shop without detection, watching them hurry away up the street.

The older man is definitely our target: William Sloane.

Gareth said he was a goblin in a human disguise, but for someone who is supposed to be an evil monster, he was really... *normal*.

I shake my head, my brow furrowing as I take a step inside the shop.

The scent of paper and ink stops me in my tracks. I'm suddenly transported back to when I was a girl, sitting in the library with my head stuck in a book. It was my one escape, my one indulgence. The library held the wonders of worlds that lived only in my imagination, a place where I could become anyone and anything inside my mind. It was limitless.

Inhaling the amazing scent, I prowl around the shop. The books inside the glass cabinets appear ancient. A quick walk around the bookshelves tells me that most of the inventory is made up of first editions, all beautifully-bound, many gold-trimmed. Definitely rare. They're all carefully shelved and lovingly labeled in curly, handwritten script.

I peer inside the nearest glass case—one that looks a lot like the case that houses the Clave—studying the ancient-looking manuscript inside it. It's open to a page in the middle depicting a battle scene. Human warriors fight each other on a bloody battlefield, swords clashing, but above them in the air, winged creatures also fight each other: Valkyrie and Keres. It's similar to Gareth's tapestries.

When I make my way to the counter and examine what William was studying, I find another illustrated book, but this one looks much older. It's open in the middle, but the binding has a lock at the side. I don't have to touch it to know the book is infused with magic. The aura around it is a strong glow.

There's no visible text on the page, but the image depicts a woman holding two babies, one in the crook of each arm, while a feather floats on either side of her.

The ink is extraordinary. It looks like it's made out of real silver and gold. Every detail is visible, including...

I lean across the page, trying to distinguish the individual strokes making up the feathers, surprised to discover that it looks like there's writing hidden within the image.

That's when something glints from the corner of my eye.

I stare at the glittering ring that sits on the counter beside the book. It looks like it's made purely from diamonds.

Without thinking, I reach for it, and that's when the magic within it reaches out to me.

It's an assassin's ring!

That's why I didn't sense any magic around William.

He isn't a goblin. He's a man.

He's an assassin.

CHAPTER THIRTY-ONE

Gareth tricked us.

My head snaps up as I detect movement on the street and see that William is walking back.

I need to get out of here fast.

Reaching the door and sliding through it, I inch it closed behind me and head around the farthest corner of the shop to watch him approach. As soon as he's inside the store, I'm going to find Lutz and get out of here.

This man is not who we thought he was.

Just as William reaches the door, I catch sight of Lutz creeping up behind him, his dagger poised to sever William's spine at the base of his skull.

Without a sound, I run for Lutz, my arms outstretched. I barrel into him before he can reach William, pushing as hard as I can.

Lutz grunts, but as soon my hands connect with his chest, I draw him into my blur with me and I can speak without anyone hearing us. "Lutz! No!"

He snarls back. "Get out of my way!" A dark cloud descends over his features. "I want my place in the Legion."

He tries to shove past me, but I keep hold of him, using all of my strength to pull him back to me. "You can't kill him!"

He grits his teeth and shoves at me, his own strength increased because of his ring. "Move, Hunter!"

"No." I manage to keep hold of his shirt, to keep him in my blur, following up my shout with a fist strengthened with my magic. He jolts and stumbles, clutching his jaw, but still, I keep hold of him.

"Listen to me, Lutz. He's not a goblin."

Lutz snarls. "You want the kill for yourself."

"He's an assassin, Lutz. It isn't sanctioned!"

Lutz stares at me, actually focusing on me now. "What are you talking about?"

"Gareth told us it was sanctioned, but it can't be. That man is an assassin. I saw his assassin's ring. The Guardian would never sanction his death. It's rule number one."

The blood leaves Lutz's face. "Killing an assassin means death. Why would Master Gareth send us here to do that?"

"Because for whatever reason, he must want that man dead. And he wants someone expendable to make it happen. That's you or me."

Lutz peers through the shopfront window to where the man has gone back to reading his book. "If he's an assassin, he'll sense us."

"He's not wearing his ring. It's on the counter."

Just as I point, William reaches for the ring, pulling it upward.

"We need to get out of here before he puts it on," I say. "Otherwise, we're—"

"In deep trouble," Lutz finishes for me.

I grip his shirt even more firmly. "Stay in contact with me so you remain in my blur. Let's move."

One of his fists lands on my shoulder, allowing me to let go of his shirt, and he runs beside me, racing past the diner, the grocery store, and the bakery.

I don't release the blur until we're halfway up Shawmut Avenue. Then I pull us into a shadow at the side of the street from which we can emerge, visible again.

Lutz staggers away from me, running his hand through his hair. We've stopped in a clear patch of street, but there are people walking farther along.

His eyes are wild, his face tense with shock.

"We don't talk about this," he says. "We go back and tell them what we saw on the street. I tell them about the exterior of the building. You tell them what you saw in the shop. We carried out surveillance. That's all."

"For once, we are in agreement, Lutz."

He lifts his hand, palm out, as if he's warding me off. "Don't follow me back, Hunter. I was ready to kill that man. If I had, I would have broken the code and then I would be dead. I have to think. Just stay away from me right now."

"Wait. I think we should go back together."

But he's already striding away from me, blending in with the other passersby like we've been taught to do.

Part of me isn't sorry. I need time to think too. It can't be a coincidence that the bookshop owner is in possession of what looked like a detailed description of Keres feathers. It's exactly the sort of book Gareth would kill to get his hands on.

I stroll up the street, maintaining a casual appearance, even though my thoughts are churning. I'm not against blurring if I have to, but I don't sense any danger around me and Saber Lane is far behind me now.

It hits me then that I'm alone outside of the Realm.

There's nothing forcing me to go back other than my own determination. The resin is still in place around the Clave. Gareth hasn't figured out what the feather can do. I can tell myself it's safe. I can tell myself that I don't have to worry about it.

I could leave right now, leave Boston, go to my safehouse, get my things, and disappear.

Nobody would come after me.

Except maybe Slade…

I'm kidding myself. I can't leave. I have to go back.

I calm my breathing on the way, block my emotions, and by the time I reach the Boston Common, I've tucked all my feelings away again.

I touch my palm to the memorial plaque. When the door appears, I stride through it like nothing is wrong and head to the administration building to write my report—a report I know nobody is going to read.

When I'm done, I return to my room, shut the door, and breathe again. My room is empty, and the only person I want to be here isn't. I've missed the usual dinner time, so there's no point going to the food hall to see Slade. I can't exactly go back to the dorm, either. I pace my room until a staff member brings me food and then I fall into bed, sleeping fitfully.

I wake at dawn. Nature calls, so I slide out of bed and head to the washroom. Finishing up, I quietly push open the door.

A body pushes me backward, a large hand covering my mouth, arms snaking around my back as he pushes me against the bathroom wall. The arm at my back cushions me and softens the thud as I hit the wall, but one of his legs hooks around mine, prepared to pull outward, keeping me off-balance and pinned against the wall.

I struggle, but I'm completely immobilized.

"Shh. Please." Lutz draws back far enough that I can identify him.

It's only because of the "please" that I don't launch into a full-scale attack and punch the living daylights out of him. It's so unlike Lutz to have any sort of manners that it gives me pause. Still, I grind my teeth, preparing to bite the hand he holds over my mouth if I have to.

"Relax, Hunter. I just want to talk."

He slowly draws his hand away from my mouth but remains pressed against me, using his full weight to pin me to the spot and that one wretched leg hooked behind mine to keep me in place.

"Then let me go, asshole."

He exhales a sigh. "*Asshole* pretty much sums me up, doesn't it?"

I narrow my eyes at him. It's an interesting insight from him.

He returns my glare. "How did you know it was a trap last night?"

I exhale slowly. "Master Gareth doesn't want to choose a new Master. He wants all of us gone, including Slade. We're not the first Novices whom he's tried to trick."

Lutz's eyes narrow. "Rowan?"

I nod, although I'm surprised he guessed.

He grimaces. "I thought there was something going on with him. He suddenly got all protective of you. I'm guessing you saved his neck."

"That's one way of putting it."

"Well, don't expect me to owe you one."

I snort. "I would never expect you to think about anyone except yourself, Lutz."

I expect him to react with anger, but to my surprise, my declaration appears to have a different effect on him. A slow smile spreads across his face. He's still all pressed up against me and it doesn't take a genius to know what's going on with his body. "Actually, I think about you all the time, sweetheart."

I roll my eyes and growl at him. "It's time for you to let me go, Lutz."

To my even greater surprise, he does.

Easing away from me, he backs up against the washbasin.

What with the bath and the shower taking up most of the space, there isn't a lot of floorspace left. It makes me even more surprised that Ridley and Cain managed to maneuver so agilely around in here yesterday.

Lutz is suddenly serious. "You and I are opposites. I'm an asshole who doesn't give a damn about anyone and you care about people even though you pretend not to. I like killing things and you like saving them." He folds his big arms across his chest. "You're gorgeous, and I'm ugly. We could be good together."

My eyes widen as his meaning registers, and I can only stare at him. "Are you... propositioning me?"

He shrugs. "At first, I thought you and Slade... but it's obvious you're not pounding him, so why not me? What do you say?"

I can't help it. A laugh bursts out of me, but I cover my mouth before I'm too loud. "Seriously, Lutz? *Pounding*? You need to wash your mouth out."

"Damn, you're beautiful when you smile."

My laughter dies. I assess him more carefully. His reactions are all over the place. He's angry, worried, determined, and now... vulnerable?

That is *not* an emotion I thought I'd ever see on Lutz Logan's face. What happened last night must have really shaken him up.

He takes a step toward me. "Do you know what your power is, Hunter?"

I shake my head, speechless. Of course I know what my real power is, but I don't think Lutz has figured out that I'm Valkyrie.

"You change people. I don't know why, but I'd do anything to see that smile again. Even be a better person."

My shoulders sag a little as I contemplate him. "I guess you'd better get out of here before that happens, then."

"Yeah. I guess." He pauses at the door. "There's a world of

danger around you, Hunter. Sometimes I want to be part of it and other times I want to get as far away from you as possible." He eases open the door and disappears outside of it.

I dare to call him back. "Lutz?"

He pokes his head around the door. He looks almost hopeful. "Yeah?"

"You're only ugly when you act it."

"Thanks, Hunter." His forehead creases. "I think." His usual cocky smile returns. "Let me know if you change your mind, sweetheart. I promise to make it worth your while."

I wait to hear his footfalls disappearing and the click of the door closing.

Then I drop back against the wall. *What just happened?*

I replay recent events within my mind: Brandon telling me they missed me in the dorm, Rowan wanting to kill Slade for hurting me, and now Lutz coming after me in a weird sort of grateful way. Maybe. I'm not really sure what that was with Lutz.

It feels like everything has been tipped on its head.

CHAPTER THIRTY-TWO

*T*he sun has barely risen but there's no point in going back to sleep.

I dress and head out to run laps around the perimeter before class.

When I step outside my room, there's a table beside the door that wasn't there before, with a single bottle of sports drink on it. Maybe this is how they're going to leave me food from now on.

Running clears my head, and by the time I show up to the courtyard for training, I'm focused. I've decided what I need to do. As soon as I have another chance to leave the Realm, I will go back to Saber Lane and figure out what that book says. And why Gareth wants William Sloane dead.

Superior Ridley is already waiting. So are the other Novices, but I'm certain I'm not late…

He strides right up to me in front of the others. "Why were you on reconnaissance yesterday?"

"Master Gareth sent us out."

"Us?"

"Lutz and me."

Ridley glances at Lutz, who gives a confirmatory nod.

Ridley's forehead creases and he seems perplexed. "I wasn't told about it."

I press my lips together for a moment before saying, "I can't speak for Master Gareth's reasons."

Lutz and I can't tell Ridley what happened. The fact that an assassin was nearly killed implicates us in a near breach of the code. Gareth holds all of the power in this situation.

Ridley takes a step back, but he looks unsettled. "No, of course not." He addresses everyone. "Today is your last combat class. Your progress has been accelerated. From today on, you will start going out on missions."

Startled murmurs rise up around me. Brandon speaks up first. "That's a month earlier than normal, isn't it?"

"Correct," Ridley replies. "Master Gareth is fast-tracking your progress and decreasing your overall training time from seven months to six. You have one more month to prove you should be Superiors."

"Will we carry out missions in pairs?" Slade asks, his eyes meeting mine.

"No. You must carry out missions on your own. Take your time planning each one. Seek help if you need it. Even though the kill is up to you, a successful mission is never a completely solo task."

As much as I'm nervous about this change—Gareth's intention to spook us into making mistakes?—inwardly, I smile.

Saber Lane is close enough that I can slip out to it during reconnaissance on other missions.

It's the perfect cover and I plan to use it.

Three days later, I'm called up to the administration building again. My stomach churns because this can mean only one thing: my first mission.

When I reach the room, all of my teachers are there, which gives me reassurance that this time, nothing underhanded is about to play out.

Gareth sits behind the desk as usual, while Superiors Ridley and Lincoln stand to his left and Fallon stands to his right.

But, surprisingly, they aren't alone.

An older woman stands off to the right-hand side. She has long, knotted-looking hair not quite hidden under an old beanie. Her skin is weathered and she wears a tattered brown coat. She's thin and doesn't look like she's eaten a lot lately, but her eyes are bright. It's only a guess, but at first glance, it's possible she's homeless. She's visibly quivering and the way she grips the edges of her coat tells me she's afraid.

Gareth's sharp voice makes her jump when he barks at me, "We've had a very perplexing request."

I study him, remaining aloof. I'm a little concerned about the lady's safety, but I remind myself that Superior Ridley is in the room. He and I might not be best friends, but he's not a complete asshole. "Oh?"

"Normally, the Superiors choose to allow a trainee to carry out a mission on their behalf," Gareth says. "This is because the trainee situation is the only exception to the requirement that a target must be written into a specific assassin's ledger. This then requires a lot of trust on the part of the Superior that the mission will be carried out correctly. After all, the target is written in their ledger, not the trainee's."

He rises from his seat, places his hands on the table, and glares at the woman. "However, we have had a request for an assassination to be carried out by you. And you alone."

"Me?"

Gareth's glare would cut steel and I'm not sure how the lady hasn't transformed into jelly yet.

She straightens her old coat, draws herself up a little, and turns to meet my gaze.

"Milady," she says, bowing deeply in my direction, a gesture that makes Gareth scowl. "I wish to acquire the skills of the Glass Arrow."

Gareth's mouth pinches. "Apparently, that's you, Hunter."

The old lady points to my tattoo. "That is the name your mother gave you."

My eyes widen. The tattoo on my arm forms the vague shape of a letter 'A,' very stylistic and not obvious. Not even to me until this woman pointed it out. "You knew my mother?"

The lady inclines her head and some of her fear disappears. Beneath her outer façade, I now detect a will of steel.

Could it be that her fear is all for show?

She's definitely smarter than she looks. I really want to know why she's here and what mission she wants me to carry out. There's one problem, though…

"I'm not a Superior yet," I say. "I don't have a ledger."

Gareth looks like he's dying inside. "The Guardian has granted you one."

I'm in shock. I stare at the leather-bound book he pushes toward me across the table. *That's mine?*

It's gorgeously bound in leather the color of an amethyst. It's wide, with thick, cream pages visible at the edges that remind me of the books in William's bookshop.

I try not to hold my breath with the incredible realization that I now have a ledger.

Mom's ledger is safely tucked away in storage, not that I could ever read it, but I can't bring myself to destroy it. It contains history, even if it's not accessible to me. Somewhat symbolic of my relationship with my mom, actually, considering the things she kept from me.

I reach for the book, sensing the magic oozing from its brand-new pages. All books are magical, but this one is *mine*.

One look at Gareth tells me he's sucking rotten eggs right now. His fingers twitch against the cover as if he wants to open it, but he can't. It will only open for me.

He finally removes his hand and, without hesitation, I flip open the pages. Each page contains seven columns for all of the important details to be filled in.

"Pen?" I ask.

The pen is also assigned by the Guardian. It stays filled with ink that never runs out.

Those rotten eggs must get so much worse when Gareth hands it to me.

I place the pen carefully in the center fold of the ledger and step aside, saying to the lady, "Please fill out your details and the details of the target, as well as what date you would like services to be rendered. Also, the offered payment and the reason why services are required."

She will be able to read what she writes, but if there were already entries in the ledger, she wouldn't be able to read those.

Gareth raises his eyebrow at my smooth rendition of the standard instructions, but I ignore his condescending eyebrow twitch. I heard Mom say those words a thousand times. I know the drill.

The lady fills out the details with a steady hand but leaves the target's name until last. Having quietly observed Mom's clients in the past, this is not surprising to me. Most clients take a final moment to decide if they want to go through with it. Writing the name of the target seals their side of the bargain.

She speaks as she writes. "My name is Briar, milady."

"It's nice to meet you, Briar."

I'm puzzled that she keeps calling me "milady," but what surprises me most is what she writes in the offered payment section. I stare at the two words:

My loyalty.

I consider her offer. She knew my mother—knew what the

tattoo meant even when I didn't. She looks like she has no money to her name, but the ones who live on the streets see things that the rest of us miss. She could be an incredibly valuable ally. Her offer could be worth more to me than the highest monetary figure.

She finally writes the name of the target:

Anthony Gallo.

It's not a name I recognize until I think harder about it. If I reach back into my memory of the days before Mom died, his was a name she mentioned in connection with the underground.

In the *Why?* column, Briar wrote:

Otherwise, more women will die.

It makes me pause for different reasons. You can never take a client's reasons at face value, but it's not very often they cite reasons that don't result in some gain to themselves personally. If Briar's reason is genuine, then this guy needs to be stopped.

Briar swiftly signs her name and hands over the pen.

It's my turn to decide if I will accept the mission and then we will wait for the Guardian to sanction the kill.

I follow my instincts and sign without hesitation, then I place the pen in the middle of the book.

We have to be patient; it could be an hour until the Guardian makes a decision. I might even have to come back later to find out what she has decreed. It depends how much information she already has on the target, if more research is needed, and how long it takes her to decide on the target's guilt or innocence.

Only I will be able to read what she writes, but her writing will glow golden if the kill is sanctioned and sapphire if it is not. Everyone around us will see which color glows and know whether the mission can go ahead.

I try not to hold my breath as I wait.

CHAPTER THIRTY-THREE

Within seconds, curvy script appears across my ledger and golden writing lights up the page.

Sanctioned.

A sanction this fast tells me that this guy has been on her radar for a while. Assassins can never act on their own accord, so it looks like the Guardian has been waiting for this request.

I take a moment to consider how hard that must be for her. The Guardian may be aware of a violent crime, but she can't do anything about it until someone requests our services. Of course, the usual channels of justice should take care of things first, but sometimes justice needs a little help.

"The mission is sanctioned," I say.

Even though I signed my name so she knows I accepted her terms, I say to Briar, "The offered payment is gratefully accepted."

She gives me a toothy grin. "Yes, milady."

Gareth says to Briar, "A staff member will see you out." He can't seem to get rid of her fast enough. She's shown a lot of grit to seek entrance to this place and make her request.

When she's gone, Ridley steps up. "There are two things you

need to know before you start preparing. The first is the fourth rule in the Assassin's Code."

It's the one I already knew about. "I can't fail."

He gives me a stern nod. "A failed assassination can't be attempted again. You have one shot, Hunter. If you fail, your target is protected from the Legion forever."

"I understand. And the other thing you wanted me to know?"

His stern expression softens. "This is perhaps the harshest rule in the Code: a bystander who prevents an assassination forfeits their own life."

I'm startled. Mom never mentioned that one. "So if someone is walking past, sees me trying to kill someone, and tries to stop me… they… what? Become my target as well?"

"Correct."

"I don't like it," I say.

"It's important, Hunter."

My voice rises. "Explain to me how killing a bystander could possibly be justified."

Ridley remains quiet but firm. "For starters, you should be so quick and fast that nobody sees you. If they do see you, you've either been sloppy or the bystander has perceptive skills that are a real danger to assassins."

He gives me a hard stare as he continues. "Further to that, anyone strong enough to stop you is a direct threat to us. We train you to be the strongest and fastest. Someone like that can't be allowed to get in our way. We can't afford to become ineffective."

I close my mouth before I argue, thinking it through. I still don't like it, but I'm unhappy to discover that he has a point. Someone with the skills to get in my way and to stop me would have to be very dangerous indeed.

I wonder for a moment how this rule works with the third rule that collateral damage is unacceptable, but I guess it's the difference between accidentally shooting the wrong person or having a person try to take the gun out of your hand.

"It's also important to remember that the rules have a hierarchy," Ridley says. "The first rule trumps the second, and so forth."

I think it through. "So if an *assassin* gets in my way, I can't kill them, after all."

"Yes, which is why there is a sixth rule: An assassin must not intervene in an assassination. That assassin's Master will decide on the punishment if they do. However, the worst case scenario is if a Legion assassin gets in the way of another Faction's assassination. In that case, the other Faction's Master is entitled to draw blood from the Legion Master."

"In other words," Gareth snarls from his seat, "if you ever dishonor me by getting in the way of a Horde or Dominion assassination, their Master is entitled to draw blood from *me* as compensation. Believe me when I say, you will regret causing me that dishonor."

Superior Ridley jumps back in, speaking quickly. "Luckily, the geographical limits of each Faction make that a very rare possibility, which is to say that it hasn't happened yet."

I count the new rules in my head:

4. A failed assassination can't be attempted again.

5. A bystander who prevents an assassination forfeits their own life.

6. An assassin must not interfere in an assassination (with a large helping of shame heaped on their Master if they do).

It's enough to make me want to get in the way of a Horde assassination and watch Master Gareth submit to a beating from Cain Carter. I'd like to see that.

I swallow my wicked grin before it shows on my face. Master Gareth would make my life hellish afterward.

"I understand," I say.

Ridley concludes with, "The Guardian has sanctioned the

kill and therefore, she will have more information to get you started. That information will be couriered here by tomorrow morning. You should start planning as soon as you can."

I'm keen to leave now. I don't need to wait until the Guardian sends her information to get started. There's this neat little thing called the Internet that I can use to get a head start. I need to know who Anthony Gallo is, what his skills are, and most importantly, his weaknesses.

I turn to leave, but Superior Lincoln calls me back, speaking up for the first time. "Hunter?"

"Yes, Superior Lincoln?"

"You need to tell us who your target is so we can judge the success of your mission."

He's right. They only know that I have a target and that the target has been sanctioned. I'm the only one who knows the name or the reasons. Or the price Briar promised me.

"His name is Anthony Gallo."

On the other side of the room, Fallon twitches, but when I glance at him, he appears completely relaxed.

I leave the room, unsettled for the first time. Fallon's surprise tells me he knows my target.

That can't be a good thing.

CHAPTER THIRTY-FOUR

My target is human. I always thought that would make it harder, but in this guy's case... not so much.

The package the Guardian sends me is thick with photographic evidence, voice files, crime scene photos, along with bank and telephone records. As well as a long list of all the technical legalities that stop him from being charged with anything.

I spread the entire file out on top of my bed, studying his movements and associations, memorizing faces.

He's a suspected associate of the Tirelli Family, one of the groups that rose up after Patrick Ryan died.

I want to close my eyes when I get to the photos of the women, but I force myself to look at them. They're the reason I'm doing this.

He's sickeningly clever. He also likes to stay in the public eye. Four nights from now, he will attend a charity ball—a children's hospital fundraiser that's being thrown by one of Boston's millionaires, which means I have days instead of weeks to plan, so I'll have to work fast.

I ask to see all three Superiors at the same time to request what I need for the mission. That way, I can keep Fallon in my sights and ensure he can't fail to provide me with the resources to carry out my mission.

Meeting Fallon, Ridley, and Lincoln in the administration building, I don't mince words. "As you may know, my target is a known associate of the Tirelli Family, so taking him out will stir up a hornet's nest. To succeed, I need three things."

Ridley contemplates me without any obvious reaction. Lincoln waits politely. Only Fallon leans forward a little. I'm sure he really wants to know how I'm going to do this.

"Name them," Ridley says. "We'll do our best to help."

"First, I need thumbtacks."

Ridley gives me a bewildered smile. "Thumbtacks?"

"Yes."

"Okay… What's the second thing?"

"I want permission to come and go from the Realm freely over the next four days so I can carry out reconnaissance."

"Of course," Ridley says. "Granted. And the third thing?"

I take a deep breath. "I want my mother's katana."

Now he sucks in a sharp breath.

I maintain my even expression, giving nothing away of the anger I've buried inside.

It's the one thing they haven't taught us here—sword skills. But Mom took me to learn Japanese swordsmanship as soon as I was old enough to hold a blade. It's my weapon of choice and I can't afford my own sword yet.

"I know you can find it," I say.

Silence settles around the room, but Superior Lincoln is the only one who looks confused. "What is Hunter talking about?"

I level my gaze with Ridley's. "I believe my mother's katana was taken into safekeeping by another assassin during a mission. You will find out who has it and return it to me."

I don't actually know the details. A week before she died,

Mom came home without it. All she would tell me is that another assassin was holding it for her.

Superior Ridley clears his throat, his face now as expressionless as wood. "I don't have to find it. I'm the one who has it. I'll bring it to your room this evening."

Him? I can't read his expression since he seems to have retreated completely into himself.

"Thank you," I say.

Superior Lincoln now seems puzzled for a different reason, his brow crinkling at me. "That's all you need?"

I nod, but say, "I assume from your question that the other Novices have asked for more, but I assure you, that's all I need."

He shrugs, accepting my answer. Of these three Superiors, he's always been the least confrontational. "Okay, then. Good luck, Hunter."

I return to my room and continue studying the file on my target until a knock on the door tells me Ridley has arrived. A thrill runs through me. To hold my mother's sword in my hands means the world to me.

I open the door to find him holding the weapon wrapped in velvet cloth.

He bows, head down, and holds it out to me in the traditional gesture, palms upward and spaced apart, the wrapped sword resting across both of them.

I take hold of it with my left hand, loving its sturdy weight, balancing it and allowing the velvet covering to fall to the floor.

I fold my right hand around the cord-wrapped handle and sweep the blade halfway out of its scabbard, turning it so the blade ridge and edge catch the light. It makes a beautiful humming sound at the moment.

I slide the katana back in with a snap. "Thank you."

I'm grateful he gave it to me respectfully. It makes me more confident that he looked after it for the last four years.

He lifts his head for the first time. Watching me carefully, he pulls a packet of thumbtacks from his pocket and hands them to me.

I give him a quick nod of thanks. "And for these."

Turning back to the room, I prepare to close the door, but he stops me. "Don't you want to know why I had it?"

"If I ask you, will you tell me?"

I expect him to admit that he won't, but he surprises me by saying, "Yes."

Do I want to know? I'm not sure that I do. But I sense that I have one opportunity to ask him and I shouldn't pass it up just because I'm afraid of what he might say. "Then tell me."

"May I come in?"

I sweep my arm wide and gesture to the table inside the room. He eyes the scattered files as he steps through the door: the documents on the bed, the pictures of women that I've placed carefully side-by-side across my pillow, all four of them.

I rest the sword across my lap when I sit down, trying to hide how much I love its weight across my thighs. How comfortable I am with it.

"Do you know how to use that?" he asks.

"Of course."

He starts speaking, never quite focusing on me. "A week before your mother died, my path crossed with hers. I hadn't seen Anna for ten years. She was… just as fierce as the last time I saw her."

He stops and clears his throat. "Our targets were in the same location. Except that I didn't know that. She was tracking a dark elf and I was tracking a wolf shifter. Dark elves are nearly impossible to sense. I didn't even know it was creeping up on me."

"She saved you," I say.

"In the worst possible way."

My forehead creases. "What do you mean?"

"She killed them both."

The crease in my forehead deepens. "I'm confused. How is that bad?"

"Hunter, your mother was what we call a Rogue Master. When she left the Legion, she severed all ties with this Faction. She didn't belong to *any* Faction."

"But I thought…"

He considers me carefully. "That she was still Legion?"

"Yes."

He shakes his head. "She wasn't. So the sixth rule applied."

I whisper, "An assassin must not interfere with an assassination. You said that never happened before."

"I didn't tell anyone about it. I could have demanded that she fight Master Gareth, but I knew that would end very badly. So she offered me her sword as compensation for taking my kill. I think you understand how hard that was for her. When I returned to the Realm with her sword, I didn't tell anyone why I had it."

My hands shake. For more reasons than one. If she had fought Master Gareth, maybe she would be alive today. Or maybe she would have died even sooner than she did. But what it means for me now cuts a piece out of my heart.

"Then this katana didn't belong to her anymore. Which means… it doesn't belong to me."

I push my chair back, honor demanding that I give it back to him. Dropping my head, I prepare to lift it in my arms and give it back to him.

"Stop," he says, inhaling deeply when I meet his eyes. "I am entitled to give it to whomever I choose. I always intended to give it back to her, but she was gone so soon afterward that I never got the chance."

He leans forward and for the first time, I see the pain he keeps hidden. "I'm glad you asked for it. It's yours now."

I don't know what to say. He has made it clear he doesn't want to know if I'm his daughter, but with every interaction I have with him, he seems to struggle even more with what could be the truth: I could be his child.

At some point, we might both have to face that reality.

He stands, inclines his head toward the pictures, and says, "I hope you cleave his head from his shoulders."

I give him a close-lipped smile before he shuts the door behind him.

The truth is, I don't intend to use the sword at all. I just needed a reason to get it back.

And… I needed a decoy, a deception.

The Superiors will now believe that I intend to kill my target by attacking him with one of the deadliest katanas ever created.

But, no. When I end him, I don't intend to kick the hornet's nest at all.

CHAPTER THIRTY-FIVE

When I leave my room the next morning, one wall is covered in documents and images from the file, all neatly tacked using the thumbtacks I asked for.

I head out for a run, hoping that I might bump into Slade.

Since the night of my bogus reconnaissance mission, I've been completely isolated from the other Novices. Food is brought to me. I shower in my own bathroom. Nobody comes to visit. Sometimes it feels like I'm the only person in the whole Realm.

I've come out for a run every morning, hoping to see Slade, but I haven't. In fact, I haven't seen him since I invited him to stay in my room. I should probably feel insecure, but the longer I stay in this place, the more I realize that nothing is what it seems.

I pass by the combat room and pause when I see a light on inside. It's still dark outside, so the light spills from the room and across the porch.

As I glide up the stairs, I'm happy that my breathing is still regulated so I can approach quietly, but I pull up short in the entrance.

The room is empty and dark.

Huh. I was sure I saw a light…

I remain where I am for a moment. My senses are never wrong and I definitely saw something. As I need to do sometimes, I replay what I saw in my mind, asking myself if I was accessing my power when I saw the light. If I was, then I didn't see it with my eyes but sensed it with my power instead.

I retreat into the shadows at the side of the entrance, waiting quietly, allowing my power to surface, sensing its warmth filling my veins.

There.

I sense again the presence inside the room.

A glow begins in the far corner, revealing a luminescent male outline. Powerful arms, broad shoulders, narrow waist, making deliberate and calculated movements.

I would know Slade anywhere.

He's completely concealed in assassin's magic. A bright spark fills my vision every time my power-filled gaze passes over the hand on which he wears his assassin's ring. But because he's hidden from the eye, he's not hiding his true self.

With my power, I can see him as he is, truly unhidden for the first time.

The breath catches in my throat. I've caught glimpses of the power he hides, but I've never seen it fully revealed.

He's completely absorbed in the warrior's routine that he's practicing, but it's not only his movements that make my heart skip a beat. His skin glistens, his body taking on a starlit sheen, magic shimmering across every part of his naked chest.

He said he thought assassin's magic could do much more than we've been taught and now his power fills every part of the room, energy streaming around him as he moves. He has completely assimilated to the assassin's magic, using it to strengthen every move he makes.

With two swift movements, he removes the daggers he's

wearing at his waist and spins them into his routine. The blades light up with golden flames, two blazing edges following his movements.

His body is a translucent glow, blades whirling, the most skilled display of swordsmanship I've ever seen. In fact, his skills rival mine. I can't stop a smile spreading across my face.

Damn, I'd love to see him wield a katana.

I want to step into the room so badly. Every part of me is called to him, my legs moving before I remember that I'm not wearing an assassin's ring, which means I shouldn't have the power to see him right now.

I try to stop myself, but it's too late.

He pulls up short, but unlike every other time, he doesn't hide himself behind a mask, his chest rising and falling as he contemplates me, his head slightly tilted.

He emerges from the magic but keeps it close around his body, a soft glow. "Hunter."

I try to find an excuse, a reason why I'm here. "I felt…"

Your power.

I felt your power.

He pitches the blades into the far wall, one after the other, and strides toward me, his arms sweeping around me, pulling me upward, one hand gliding into my hair.

His lips crash against mine and my world spins. I inhale the scent of cinnamon and taste his lips, responding to the intensity in his kiss, returning it, our lips crashing against each other, our bodies pressing closer. Never close enough.

He draws back just enough to whisper against my lips, "I don't care how you sensed me just now. Just say you'll stay."

His eyes search mine and maybe it's the power around him or my own power responding to his, but I'm not afraid of the possibility that I'll show him my wings.

"I'll stay."

Without moving away from me, he untangles one of his

arms to extend his hand, palm out, toward the doors. In the next moment, the doors slide shut, slowly and quietly, glowing at the edges as they seal tight, giving us complete privacy.

My eyes widen. "Did you just...?"

He kisses me again, stopping whatever I was about to say, drawing me closer to him, his hands finding the edge of my shirt and stroking up my back under the material. Every second of contact sends intense sensations shivering through me from my head to my toes.

His lips soften against my mouth before he kisses the corner of my lips, making his way along my jaw, nuzzling my neck and planting kisses beneath my earlobe. At the same time, my shirt rises as his hands find my shoulder blades, his fingers spreading out across my back, supporting me as he plants kisses across my collarbone and the tops of my breasts through my shirt.

My breathing is rapid and my head is spinning, my hands finding the contours of his back, his sides, his arms. I can't touch enough of him at once. The more I want, the more he slows us down, until I want to scream when he stops completely.

He groans against my mouth, but it sounds like frustration. "Hunter, I want this more than anything, but I'm not prepared."

My forehead creases because I don't understand. "Prepared...?"

"I almost lost my head right now. But I don't have protection on me. We can't do this."

Oh. All those foil packets. Too far away to be any good to us.

My whisper breaks the silence. "Damn. They're all in my room."

He gives me a rueful smile. "I should have swiped one the other day, but I never thought you'd come to me like this."

I press my face against his neck in the nook between his jaw and shoulder, holding him tightly with my arms as he strokes my back, seeming intent on trying to slow my breathing.

I murmur, "Or maybe ten."

"Or maybe a lifetime's worth." He draws back, urging me to look up at him. "Is it possible that you're my match, Hunter?"

A shiver races down my spine.

"I've never cared this much about anyone before," he says. "But it's more than that. Your strength matches mine in ways I never dreamed I'd find."

I allow myself to smile. "Because I could beat you in combat?"

"Because you challenge me in ways that I never expected."

I want him. My whole body wants him. But there's no point telling him that human diseases don't survive in my body—that my power obliterates them. I can't tell him that I won't pass on any illnesses to him, either. That we don't actually need protection.

I can't tell him because it isn't normal. It isn't human. And I don't want to encourage him to go against his sense of responsibility.

But maybe there's a way around it.

With a question in my voice, I say, "You know… my blur is undetectable. We could make it all the way back to my room and nobody would know."

He grins, but his expression quickly becomes confused when his gaze falls to my bare finger. "Hunter, you're not wearing—"

Realizing my mistake, I speak quickly. "Can I use yours? The training rings aren't specific to a person like our final rings will be."

He seems to forget his confusion. "If it means you can pull me into your blur. Who knows what we could do while we're completely invisible?"

I smother a laugh. We have two hours before anyone else is awake and we have to take hold of this moment or lose it forever.

I hold out my hand with a command. "Hand it over."

Without hesitation, he slides his assassin's ring off his forefinger and drops it into my palm.

It takes me a split second to know I made a mistake.

Sharp pain shoots through my palm, burning through my arm and spine like electricity.

A scream bursts out of me before I can stop it, agony ripping through me.

CHAPTER THIRTY-SIX

iery pain burns through my body.

I need to drop the ring, and do it fast, but for some reason I can't let go of it.

I fall to my knees as Slade shouts, "Let it go, Hunter!"

But I can't. I can't even turn my palm. I'm stuck with the ring resting on my upturned hand, my arm frozen in an upward position, agonizing pain rocketing through me.

He darts forward, plucking the ring from my frozen fingers.

The pain stops immediately and I collapse to the floor, doubling up over my knees, moaning as the aftershocks rip through me.

I can't form coherent words as he flings the ring as far away from me as he can and drops to my side, pulling me into his arms, gathering me up into his lap. "Hunter! What happened? What was that?"

I shake my head, shivering uncontrollably, trying to form sound. "I don't know. It felt like my heart was being ripped apart."

"Please tell me you're okay."

I take a shuddering breath. The pain finally eases, but my

palm still burns. I turn it so that only I can see it, quickly hiding it again. A circle the size and shape of the ring has burned into my palm. I tell myself it will heal. "I am… okay."

His arms are tight around me. His voice rumbles against my ear, a regretful growl. "All I do is end up hurting you."

"No!" I draw back, determination in every part of my body. "You didn't cause that. I shouldn't have tried to take it. It's probably assimilated to you now that you've been using it for a while."

The tightness around his lips and eyes tells me he's not so sure. "Maybe."

I cup his cheek with my good hand. There's more rage in his eyes this morning, something different. I sense a darkness that wasn't there before, and I consider him more carefully. "Slade, what is it? What happened?"

He inhales and exhales so deeply that his giant chest presses against me. "My first kill."

I'm startled. "When?"

"Last night."

I won't withdraw or run away from this, holding his gaze instead. He needs to talk about it. "Tell me."

"Ridley gave me one of his missions. I think he thought it would help me get ahead. But it was this guy who abused his wife. Her sister wrote in Ridley's ledger a week ago. I was supposed to do reconnaissance last night."

His gaze becomes far away as he speaks. "I got to their house. She was unconscious on the floor, blood dripping down her face. And he was kicking her. Yelling at her to get up. I gained access and…"

"What did you do?"

His expression is blank, somewhere else. "I wrapped a rope around his neck and strung him up in the basement. Made it look like a suicide."

I consider the physical strength it would have taken to do that. Then I consider the impact it had on Slade.

"The first kill is the worst," I say. "It's okay to feel whatever you feel."

"Rage, Hunter. That's all I felt. We're not supposed to get emotional during a kill, but I needed to watch the life drain out of that bastard. To end his time on this Earth. If I could have broken every bone in his body and made it look like he did it to himself, I would have."

"But you didn't."

He shakes his head. "I called Ridley and told him to call an ambulance for the lady. She was barely regaining consciousness by then. Did you know the Legion has burner phones and voice distorters to call the authorities when someone's hurt?"

"I didn't." I place a kiss on his cheek and press my head into the crook of his neck, wrapping my arms around him. "It's okay, Slade. It will be okay."

"I wanted to become an assassin so I could do something good with my rage, but what's going to happen when I see something I can't do anything about?" he asks. "What about when it isn't sanctioned?"

"You'll follow the rules," I say.

"Or break them."

"No," I whisper. "You'll be the Master Assassin one day. You'll follow the rules to the letter."

"Do you really think I'm going to be the Master?"

I kiss him full on the lips, sensing his breathing changing as soon as our mouths connect. "Without a doubt."

He gathers me up and pulls us into a standing position. "What if I don't want that?"

"Why wouldn't you?"

"The Master Assassin is tied to this place. To the Realm," he says. "Where will you be, Hunter? Will you be here too?"

My face falls. I won't be here. I'll be long gone. I don't want to tell him this truth, but the compulsion is so very strong. "I can't stay here."

"I want you in my life," he says, his blue eyes burning into me. "I don't want to live here without you and turn into a sad, old man."

He's breaking my heart. I can't stop the sob-laugh that wrenches out of me. "You will never be a sad, old man, Slade."

"You're right." He nods. "The next Master will kill me before I get old. Somehow, the Legion's Masters never seem to live long after retirement."

My smile fades. "That doesn't have to be the way of things. The Horde Master and Cain Carter aren't enemies. Both of the former Masters of the Dominion are still alive. You can change the Legion. You can change so many things if you become Master."

I don't dare hope that Master Gareth will leave the Clave in the Realm when he goes, or that Slade might simply give the feather to me if he inherits the Realm.

Gareth will surely take the Clave with him, and then I'll have no chance of finding it. I'll have a small window between the time I become a Superior and when Gareth hands over the title to the new Master.

"I hope you're right, Hunter."

"Slade, no matter what happens over the next month," I say, "don't accept any missions unless Ridley is also in the room."

He tilts his head. "Why? What's wrong?"

"The reconnaissance mission that Gareth and Fallon sent me and Lutz on… It was messed up… pretty badly. I can't give you details because I don't want to implicate you or make things more difficult for you than they already are. You have to be able to trust the person giving you the mission and so far, the only Superior I trust is Ridley. Promise me you'll keep that in mind."

So far, Gareth has targeted me, Rowan, and Lutz. He hasn't gone after Brandon or Slade yet, but he's bound to have a plan.

Slade brushes the hair out of my eyes and kisses me again. "Okay. I promise."

We separate, and it's as if part of me remains behind with him when I leave the room. I may not have bonded with Slade yet, but my body acts as if I have.

Now, my choice is whether or not to give in to it.

wo hours later, I head out on reconnaissance, checking out the hotel where the charity ball will be held before I wander down the street and stop in at a café and pretend to sip coffee.

I indulge in a moment to nurse my injured hand before I tuck the pain away again. I have too much else to worry about right now.

As much as I love to inhale the scent of coffee—especially now that the days are getting colder—my seat at the window gives me the ability to casually survey the street, including the tail I've acquired. I recognize him as one of the older Superiors. He's pretending to window shop on the other side of the street.

As if I wouldn't notice him.

I can only assume that Fallon has ordered him to follow me and report back about my movements.

I head into the bathroom at the back of the café, step into a stall, and initiate a full blur, becoming completely invisible. Slipping out of the bathroom, I wait for someone to leave the store and follow them out through the open door.

Three streets over, I know I've given my tail the slip. And that's when I go where I'm really headed this morning.

Back to Saber Lane.

I lose my blur in a shadow at the corner of the street before I pass the bakery and then the grocery store. I've almost made it past the diner when a figure pulls away from the doorway.

I startle and swing in his direction since I didn't see him there.

The man the witch called "Dean" rises from a lean against the doorframe next to a large, white icebox. Despite the cold, his sleeves are rolled up around his biceps, jeans taut across his thighs. His eyes sparkle even though he isn't laughing, somehow drawing me in. Combine those eyes with a killer smile and… whoa… Now *this* guy could be an assassin.

He leaves his position at the front of the shop and saunters across the pavement, his smile fading the closer he gets, replaced with growing concern. He stops three paces away from me, far enough that I don't feel threatened.

"You're hurt," he says.

I raise an eyebrow at him, but I'm struggling to find anything unlikeable about him. "I'm fine, thank you."

He crosses the gap between us in three quick strides, reaching for my hand, turning it upward to reveal the circular burn mark across my palm. "That's not fine. You need ice on that."

He swivels and tugs me in the direction of the icebox, lifting a soft cloth from the top of it and reaching inside to shovel a handful of ice into the material. Then he presses it against my palm, closing my fingertips around it.

I suppress a sigh at the cooling sensation that seeps through my skin.

He asks, "Where are you headed?"

"I'm going to the bookshop." I decide to play dumb. "Which way is that?"

"The Tomb is that way." Dean's voice is like honey. I swear he could be living in a beehive, he's oozing with charm. For a second, I forget what I'm supposed to be doing, swimming in the sweet nectar of his voice instead.

I shake my head, clearing it of the cobwebs that have gathered. I remind myself that empaths not only detect pain, but also try to soothe it in any way they can. I don't think it's deliberate on his part. What I've read about empaths indicates that they can't control their own compulsions. Pain hurts them and they want to make it stop. His voice is designed to lull me to sleep so I can rest while my hand heals.

I tug out of his hold. "Thanks for your help."

He smiles at me. "Keep the ice pack. Come back and see me when you're healed."

I laugh. His smile is so open, so obviously flirty, but he hasn't taken a step after me, making a point of letting me leave. I can't be offended and I'm definitely not threatened.

I head in the direction of the bookshop. As much as I want to, I can't carry the ice bag inside. It will draw too much attention. With regret, I deposit it beside the stairs, where I won't skid on it if I have to make a speedy exit.

As soon as I step inside, the familiar scent of paper overwhelms me. I've thought my next moves through carefully. I already considered blurring and gaining access that way, but I need answers, so I've decided to try a more direct approach.

I pause, thrown when I see the witch—Tansy—behind the counter instead of William.

She looks up and gives me a smile. "Welcome to the Tomb."

I head for the nearest bookshelf, pretending to be a customer while I consider my next move. It could be very dangerous, but I want to speak with William. I have to figure out what he has that Gareth wants, and why Gareth wants him dead.

If I had weeks, I could watch his movements and figure it out for myself, but I don't have that long. I've only got a few days of freedom. Speaking with him directly is the fastest way to get answers.

I turn to find the woman studying me from behind the counter. She has shiny blonde hair that falls in waves around her shoulders and gentle, olive-green eyes. She's chewing her bottom lip. Oddly enough, her focus is on my tattoo. Valkyrie run warm, so I'm not wearing sleeves. My tattoo is easily visible across the room and she's paying a little more attention to it than most people do.

She must realize that I've caught her staring because she stammers, "Are you here about the position?"

I raise my eyebrows at her. "I'm sorry, what?"

She points at the flyer printed on blueberry-colored paper inside a plastic case propped on the counter.

It reads:

Feeling lost? Find yourself in books. The Tomb Bookshop is hiring now.

I shake my head. "No, sorry. I have a job."

"Oh." She babbles nervously. "I guess I'll keep helping out for a while longer, then. Not that I mind working here. Don't get me wrong. I love it in the store. It's just that William... uh, the owner... he's getting older and I won't be able to help out forever. If you know anybody...?"

"Sure. I'll tell them you're hiring."

Her gaze darts to my tattoo again before she asks, "Can I help you find something?"

I quietly assess the tension around her mouth and the way her hands grip the counter a little too tightly. She's nervous, but she's trying to hide it.

"Actually... I was wondering if the owner—William—is around?" I ask.

Her fingers tighten even further. "He's upstairs, but I can get him if you like?"

"Thank you, I'd appreciate that."

She sweeps past me in the widest arc possible. She can't possibly know what I am. I have no aura for her to detect. That's what makes me so deadly. But I'm certain my tattoo has unsettled her.

I prepare myself for William to appear wearing his assassin's ring and ready to defend himself. I'm going to have to convince him fast that I'm not here to harm him.

To my surprise, Tansy pauses beside me on her way past. She's slightly shorter than me, but she's graceful and lithe in her jeans and heels. She takes a deep breath before her eyes meet mine—a brave move, considering how nervous she appears.

Her tone sounds forced as she says, "Nice tattoo. What does it mean?"

I shrug. "It's just an abstract design. My mother created it for me."

"Your mother. Okay. I'll be right back."

I watch her head to the back of the shop and disappear up the stairs. I'm guessing this means William lives above the store.

I consider my surroundings while I wait, calculating everything I need to make a hasty getaway, including positioning myself with a clear path to the door and bracing for what could be coming my way: raging assassin being my best guess.

Contrary to my expectations, William descends the stairs slowly and with measured steps. He pauses at the base while Tansy hovers behind him in the shadows.

I check his fingers, and my forehead creases when I realize he's not wearing his ring.

He meets my gaze as he emerges into the light.

"Welcome, Hunter Cassidy," he says.

CHAPTER THIRTY-EIGHT

Shock ripples through me. He knows exactly who I am. That is *not* a good sign.

I back away from him. "I think I made a mistake."

"Wait, please." He doesn't come near me, doesn't take a step closer, but he reaches out toward me as if he can make me stay. "Don't you remember me?"

I edge toward the door. "Am I supposed to?"

He remains where he is, his hand still partially raised. "I shouldn't expect you to. You were very young when you lived here."

"When I lived…?" I choke on the words. My world spins, and I can't quite breathe.

I lived here?

I don't remember this place. Not at all. But the scent of paper and ink is too familiar, too overwhelming. I associated it with the library, but maybe it wasn't that at all.

I take another step back, shaking my head. I don't know William. I really don't, but he claims to know me. As much as I want to detect a lie in his expression, there is none.

His forehead creases a little. "If you don't remember me, then why are you here?"

There's no way I can answer that question. I can't exactly tell him I was sent here to kill him. The back of my foot hits the door. My hand finds the handle, preparing to open it, run, and never come back.

The widening of his eyes tells me he knows he's about to lose me.

"Please. Don't go," he says. "You must be here for a reason and there's a lot I need to tell you. I always hoped you'd come back. I hoped Anna would come back, but she never did." He's speaking very fast since he must recognize that he only has seconds before I rip open the door and disappear.

I shudder against the wood paneling. I have no reason to believe anything he says, but the fact that he knows who I am has shocked me to my core.

"Please," he says again. "Stay."

My demand for answers is swift. "When did I live here?"

He slows his response down. "Anna came here when she left the Realm. She stayed with me until you were four years old. She left once she could afford her own place."

He places his hand on the corner of the counter. "Her assassin's ledger used to rest right here."

I test him. "What color was it?"

"Emerald with silver edging on the pages, just like the silver rings around your eyes." He takes a step toward me, speaking very carefully. "Please, if you allow me to show you, I think I can prove that you were here. Will you come upstairs with me?"

Go upstairs with a complete stranger? Sure, why not?

I smother an almost hysterical laugh and then shout at myself: *Get it together, Hunter*. He took me by surprise, but I have to focus.

I take a deep breath, reaching for my power, feeling its calm wash through me. I quickly assess him and Tansy, who hasn't stopped staring at me with wide eyes. I tell myself I have nothing to fear from either of them.

The irony is that *they* should be afraid of *me*.

I give William a quick nod. My power will protect me from both of them, no matter what they try.

Without taking his eyes off me, he says, "Tansy, can you please turn the sign to *Closed*? I think we need to take the rest of the day off."

Tansy glances between us. For the first time, I notice that she's breathing very quickly. Panic is spreading across her face and I realize that I was wrong: Her wide eyes don't indicate surprise, but rather, fear.

She gasps. "Her mother was the Glass Fox. She's the Glass Arrow. That tattoo has been circulated as a warning through the ranks of witches for years. She kills people like me, William."

I try to back up but I can't go further without stepping through the door. I've never killed a witch, and her accusation grates on me, even if I recognize that it comes from a place of deep fear.

William quickly reaches her side, holding firm to her shoulders. "Take a deep breath, Tansy. Everything is going to be okay."

She snaps back at him. "How do you know? Darkness grows where she walks. Death is in her blood."

It's true, but it's so much more confronting to hear someone else say it.

Tansy's eyes begin to glow, the olive-green color becoming more intense, deeper, her face glowing.

William cups her cheek with his hand, forcing her to look at him and away from me. "Tansy, remember: Just because you're born into darkness, that doesn't mean you can't overcome it."

I recoil against the door in surprise. Those were my

mother's last words, and now I wonder if she got them from William. Or if he got them from her.

Tansy demands to know, "Can she? Overcome it?"

"She already has," he says.

Some of the fear fades from Tansy's eyes. "Do you really believe that?"

"I know it." He rubs her arms the way a father would calm his child, dropping a kiss on her forehead. "Now, come upstairs with us. There are things you need to see, too."

He turns to me. "Please, both of you. Tansy, you go first because you know the way. Hunter can follow both of us. That way, if she changes her mind, she knows she can leave."

I eye the staircase at the back of the shop. It's narrow and only accommodates single file. I'm glad he told me to go up last or I would have felt trapped. I don't need my fight-or-flight instinct triggering right now. I'm already on edge as it is.

I follow them up, watching carefully. Ahead of us, Tansy pushes open the door at the top of the stairs when she reaches it. When I follow behind William, I find a simply furnished apartment at the top consisting of a kitchen and a bathroom, which we pass by, followed by a short hallway with a door on either side.

William takes a key from his pocket and opens one of them. He swings the door wide. "I kept it pretty much the same as when you were here, Hunter."

Then to Tansy, he says, "I know you always wondered what was in this room." He shrugs and gives a soft smile. "Not a secret lair, after all. Just happy memories."

She peers in after me but draws back sharply when she seems to realize how close she's standing to me. She doesn't trust me, no matter what William says.

I enter the room and it's like stepping back in time. A bed rests in the far left corner with a child's cradle beside it. There's a rug on the floor, a closet at the side, and a set of drawers. I gravitate toward the drawers and the photographs sitting on top of them, framed in silver.

Pictures of Mom and me.

One of them shows her snuggling me while I'm sleeping beside her on the bed. I guess that was when I grew too big for the cradle. In another, she's holding my hand—little girl me—while we stand on the doorstep to the bookshop. My hair is much shorter. Hers is piled up on her head in a loose bun. We're both pointing at the camera. She's laughing and she looks... truly happy.

I rub my forehead to ease the tension and my sudden sadness to see her face again. I brace against the chest of drawers for a moment before I run my finger across the top of the picture frame. "You said we were here for four years."

William nods. "She needed a safe place when she left the Realm."

I chew my lip. The pictures tell me that we were both safe here.

William remains standing just inside the door, giving me space. "I did everything I could to make sure she felt at home."

"You're an assassin too," I say.

He jolts and glances at Tansy. Her eyes widen in alarm.

"No, I'm not," he says.

I swivel to him, on my guard again. "But you have an assassin's ring."

He arches an eyebrow at me. I guess he's wondering how I know about the ring, but he doesn't press me for answers.

"Of course I do," he says. "But it's not mine. Look in the top drawer."

Wary now, I pull open the drawer. A glass case rests inside it, its contents easily visible. The ring I saw the other night glitters at me. I pull the case out, my forehead creasing.

William says, "It was your mother's glass ring."

Glass, not diamond.

I suck in a sharp breath, freeze, and then unfreeze so fast that I'm already opening the case and pulling the ring out before I even think about it.

I hold it in my hand, gripping it like it's part of her and I can bring her back by holding it.

"It belongs to you now," William says.

CHAPTER THIRTY-NINE

It's the first assassin's ring I've touched that doesn't repel me or make me feel a confusing nothingness.

"Why is it here?" I ask in a whisper, trying to process the sadness and happiness it brings me because it was hers and now it's mine.

"Your mother left it with me for safekeeping." William's response becomes hesitant. "I think you already know you don't need it. Your assassin's power comes from within you."

I take a big chance that I've interpreted his meaning correctly. "You know I'm Valkyrie."

He nods. "Your mother chose to reveal that to me."

I sigh, a sense of relief filling me. "I know I can use my own power, but I don't understand why assassin's rings have no effect on me. Or worse, they burn me." I hold up my blistered palm to show him.

William's eyes widen. "An assassin's ring did that to you?"

When I nod, he glances at Tansy and she quickly leaves the room. I'm not sure where she's going and I don't have time to ask before William reaches for the glass ring, redirecting the conversation. "If I may?"

I'm reluctant to hand over the ring, but I manage to give it to him.

He holds it up to the light. "This ring is made of glass because it has no power."

I'm aghast, because I'm certain I sensed its power the other night. "What?"

"It's the only one of its kind," he says. "It's made to look like an assassin's ring, tempered, and indestructible, but it's spelled to give off an aura of magic to deceive other assassins."

Damn. That must be how it tricked me into sensing magic around it.

William's smile is gentle, but there's a twinkle in his eyes. "Anna told me that she had it made in secret and she tricked the old Guardian into assigning it to her. She said the real assassin's rings repelled her. She couldn't stand wearing them during her training."

"I feel a similar way," I say. "But I don't understand why."

"I've been trying to find the answer to that for the past twenty years. As a Valkyrie, you are the embodiment of assassin's power. Killing is what you do. Anna didn't understand why she couldn't assimilate with the rings like others could. In contrast, they made her feel physically ill. She said she even had different reactions to different training rings."

"The first time I put my training ring on, I had a panic attack," I say. "Most of the time, I feel nothing from it. Other times, I feel like it's pushing back at me."

Tansy returns in time to hear me talk about panicking. Her expression softens. Judging by her panic the other night, she knows what it's like to have moments of crippling anxiety.

She hands me an ice pack. "For your hand."

"Thank you." I can't stop myself from closing my eyes with relief at the cooling sensation. My power is taking an unexpectedly long time to heal this wound.

William hands the ring back to me and all I want is to put it on. So badly. But then I would have to take it off again when I leave and that would be far too painful. I close the fingers of my uninjured hand around it, gripping it tightly.

I ask William, "Why did Mom come to you for help in the first place?"

Tansy sucks in a sharp breath and William places a comforting hand on her arm. He asks her, "Do you want to tell Hunter or will I?"

"You should tell her," Tansy says. "I was only three years old at the time."

"Well, then… I think we should make a cup of tea first. Both of you, come with me."

He takes us to the little kitchen and puts the kettle on, offering us both herbal tea before pouring it out. Then he pushes all three cups toward Tansy. "Will you place a calming spell on them, please, dear? We're already emotionally stretched today. We need resilience for this conversation."

She takes the slip of paper he hands her, reading the words while she holds her hand over the top of the cups.

I'm confused by this. Witches don't usually need to read their spells, but I accept the cup from her, sensing nothing harmful about it.

When I take my first sip, a warming sensation fills my body and I'm grateful. I'm not sure what William is about to reveal about my mother, but I've already learned there's a lot I don't know about her.

William speaks quietly and calmly. "Your mother's first mission was to track and kill an old witch who was stealing other witches' powers. This woman had become very powerful, so it was a dangerous mission to give to a Novice, but Anna insisted on taking it.

"She tracked the old witch here to Saber Lane just in time to see her kill Tansy's mother and snatch baby Tansy. The old woman tried to use Tansy as a shield against your mother, sucking Tansy's power from her at the same time."

I whisper, "Collateral damage is unacceptable…"

"Anna asked for the mission because she knew that no other assassin could kill a woman who had stolen the power of ten witches. Not even the Master himself. Anna made a choice. She revealed her wings and pulled the life from the old witch."

I nod. "If we use our Valkyrie power to kill, our wings reveal themselves." Just like the gruesome images on Gareth's walls. It's a double-edged sword, though. Sure, we can kill, but it means exposing ourselves. I'm sure there was a time in the dark ages when that might have been totally fine. Not so much in the modern world.

William sighs sadly. "It was already too late for Tansy."

"I can't remember spells," Tansy says, her chin held high, her posture defensive as she folds up the scrap of paper with the calming spell on it. "I can perform spells if I read them, but I can't keep them in my head like other witches can."

"I'm sorry," I say. "That never should have happened to you."

She presses her lips together. I'm not sure why she hates me so much if Mom saved her life. I'm also not sure why she could think I'm the Glass Arrow who kills witches. Sure, Mom killed a witch, but it was to save another witch's life.

William says, "I heard the fight and saw Anna reveal her wings. She let me live, even though I knew her secret. I proved to her that she could trust me."

"She came here when she needed a place to stay," I say.

"She visited often while she was training at the Realm, regularly checking on Tansy," William says. "Then she came to live here while she was pregnant with you."

"My grandmother raised me until she died," Tansy explains. "Now the house at the corner of the Lane is mine."

"The brownstone?" I ask. "It's beautiful."

Tansy's response is stiff. "Thank you."

I turn to William. "So you're human?"

He smiles. "Plain old human. A historian, actually. Knowing rare and antique books requires understanding history—and believing that there's truth in fairy tales. After I met Anna, I dedicated my time to finding out more about the Valkyrie."

I challenge, "And the Keres?"

He meets my eyes. "Why are you really here, Hunter?"

It's time to tell him the truth, but I decide to keep Lutz out of my explanation. "You're being targeted. I was sent here several nights ago to study you and map your home. I was told it would look good for me if I killed you."

He turns pale. "But you didn't kill me."

"They said you were a goblin, which you clearly aren't," I say. "As soon as I discovered that I was misinformed, I left."

"That was the night Dean got sick," Tansy whispers. She glares at me. "It was your pain that he felt."

I return her stare with an apologetic shrug. "I didn't know my presence would have that effect on anyone."

William's brow is furrowed. "What does Gareth want?"

"He wants to know what the Keres feather does."

William sucks in a sharp breath. "He wants the *Keres Coda*."

"What is that?" I ask.

"A book that contains code hidden in the illustrations. I searched for the book for years until I finally acquired it a few months ago, but I'm still decoding it. I'm close to cracking it. Very close, in fact." William leans forward with a hopeful expression in his eyes. "I will understand if you don't want to tell me, but what do you know about the feather?"

I hesitate. "I know that it leads to a weapon, but I don't know what the weapon is or what it does."

His shoulders slump. "That is the extent of my knowledge also. I was hoping you might know more. The *Keres Coda* can tell us what the weapon is and how to locate it. We have to keep the Coda out of Gareth's hands."

"How did Mom get it? The feather, I mean?"

He shakes his head. "I'm sorry, I don't actually know. When you were one year old, she was out on a mission and she didn't come home for three whole days. I was beside myself with worry. When she finally returned, she was bloodied, bruised, and carried the feather. She placed it in that glass case I've kept her ring in. She wouldn't tell me how she got it or where she'd been. She wouldn't stop hugging you and she cried herself to sleep that night. After that…" His expression hardens. "That was when things with Patrick Ryan started."

He peers at me with a question in his eyes.

"I know who Patrick Ryan is," I say. "But what does he have to do with the feather?"

"I don't know, Hunter. Your mother had a lot of secrets," he says. "All I know is that after that night, she was relentless in eliminating his competition. A constant stream of clients arrived at my store for three years. That was when she truly became the Glass Fox. And her reputation spread like wildfire."

He leans back in his chair. "I wish I knew more, but one thing I do know for certain is that we can't let Gareth get his hands on the *Keres Coda*—or the weapon the feather hides."

"Agreed," I say.

With a glance at Tansy, he asks me, "Will you come back here, Hunter? I think we can help each other. If you trust me?"

I find myself saying, "Yes."

CHAPTER FORTY

ansy follows me out.

She's stony-faced and tense, showing me the door and then walking alongside me with a short explanation that she needs to head home, which is in the same direction I'm going.

I can't help but think it's because she wants to make sure that I leave.

As we pass the diner again, I find Dean waiting, a slight crease forming in his forehead as he considers Tansy and me. The unhappy tension between us would be noticeable to anybody, let alone an empath.

He focuses on the new ice pack I'm carrying. "How's your hand now?"

Tansy wears a cynical expression. Before I can reply, she says, "I take it you've met each other, then. Dean, this is Hunter."

He continues to scowl at my palm, turning his unhappy expression on Tansy. "Why haven't you healed her already, Tansy?"

She can heal me? I probably should have guessed that. But it's her reason for not healing me that I can't guess at all.

Her response is unyielding. "I don't have my spell book."

"I can get it for you," he says.

"No."

He blinks at her sharp retort.

I round on her. "Okay, you need to tell me why you hate me so much, and why you think I'm out to kill witches. Because, otherwise, we're going to have a problem."

She glares at me. "I might not be able to remember spells, but I remember everything about the night my mom died. Every detail. Crystal clear."

She advances on me, but I stand my ground. "That old woman who stole all of the other witches' powers… she was my aunt. The bad witch in my family. And yes, that means that my own aunt tried to kill me. But it was your mother's fault that my mother died."

I'm defensive, standing my ground. "How so?"

"She hesitated!" Tansy sucks in a sharp breath. "She hesitated for long enough that my aunt struck my mother dead."

"You were being held as a shield," I say, cautious. "Mom couldn't risk harming you—"

She bursts out, "She didn't want to reveal her power! It was about not exposing herself. It wasn't about saving me."

It's my turn to suck in a sharp breath, indignant that she's placing judgment on my mother. "You don't know that! And she's not alive for us to ask her."

I advance on Tansy until we're inches apart and the air crackles between us.

Her eyes begin to glow the same way they did in the shop. No matter what she says about not remembering spells, there are some magical powers that can be used on instinct alone. Right now, my own power is rising to meet hers, the space between us rapidly glowing in a myriad of swirling colors.

I whisper, "We've both lost our mothers."

Tansy pales, but she doesn't back down. "Valkyrie don't fear death. They cause it. They welcome it. I think everyone has the Keres and the Valkyrie mixed up. *Your* kind are the cruel ones."

I flinch.

Just because you're born into darkness...

I used to believe that Mom told me that because she was trying to help me overcome whatever obstacles I encountered in my life. But now, I wonder if she was trying to warn me.

There is darkness in my soul. I do crave death. Just like Slade said, it could turn into something really bad unless I use it for good.

Tansy snarls. "*Where she walks, darkness grows, paving the way for death with every step.* Those words are in the *Keres Coda*, but they aren't about the Keres. They were writing about the destruction caused by their sworn enemy: the Valkyrie. They're about you: *the hunter.*"

"I'm not that person, Tansy."

She snaps, "I'll believe it when I see it."

I sigh and back off, deliberately tucking my power away. She blames me for a moment in time that I have no control over, a moment's hesitation that cost her mother her life.

But when I think about it, I at least got to grow up with Mom around, even if I lost her too soon. Tansy didn't get that chance at all. Seeing me must bring all of that back to her. I can't expect her to push that kind of pain aside and forget about it.

"I guess I'll just have to make sure you see it, then," I say, turning and heading back up the Lane.

On the morning of the charity ball, I stroll around the streets of Boston, stopping in at a café and then a homewares store, and finally, I pop into the hotel where the ball will be held.

I make a single phone call from the hotel lobby. Then I wander back to the Realm.

Everything is in place for my first mission. I'm as ready as I can be.

~

My target is the guy in the expensive blue jacket. Anthony Gallo's overloud laughter is raucous enough to carry across the immaculate ballroom and reach me at the bar.

I don't need to look to know he's headed in my direction. I let my power trickle through me, ensuring that my senses are razor-sharp. I can isolate my target's heavy tread from among the other hundred guests at this charity ball, especially since he walks with the arrogance of someone who thinks he's untouchable.

The woman on his arm has no idea that he's her worst nightmare.

Laugh while you can, buddy. I pretend to take a sip of wine, but it doesn't pass my lips.

I'm wearing a black dress with a full skirt and a silver strapless bodice, my mahogany hair a glistening, sculpted wave across one shoulder. I chose the only black dress that was hanging in my closet. It's the color all of his victims were wearing.

Anthony bumps against the bar, leaning on it as if he's the only customer the bartender should pay attention to.

"Hey, you!" he calls while his date squeezes herself into the space on his other side. "Two martinis."

When his gaze swings in my direction I casually cross my right leg over my left, allowing the thigh-high slit in my dress to open all the way from my lower hip to my stilettos. I appreciate that most of the dresses in my closet have a full skirt because they're easier to run and fight in. High heels, on the other hand, are awful for running, but a good stiletto is like carrying a weapon in plain sight, so I'm okay with them for now.

Anthony's gaze travels up my leg, beyond my narrow waist, but stops at the level of my chest, traveling no higher. Thanks to a push-up bra, I've put my figure to its best use in this low-cut dress.

I lean forward to give him a better view. "Oh, babe, you don't want to be drinking *that*."

It takes him a moment to catch on. I'm not talking about the glass the bartender just slid in front of him.

I have to incline my head directly at his date to make my meaning clear.

I've done my research on this guy. Subtlety is not his strong point. He tips his chin up as if he's looking at my eyes, but he's not. His gaze remains solidly on my cleavage. "You got something better I should drink?"

I scoff as if it's obvious. I slide off my chair into a standing position, my legs pressing up against his in the tight space.

He grins at me, licking his lips. It doesn't seem to occur to him to wonder why a complete stranger would suddenly throw herself at him. He also doesn't appear to care that his date looks lost and uncertain now. He's forgotten her. He's *that* arrogant.

I slide one hand across his shoulder and lean in, my lips close to the corner of his mouth before diverting to his ear.

"Take me somewhere private and I'll show you how much better."

A smile spreads across his face as I lean back, slowly biting my lip, waiting to see how he'll respond. The black dress has definitely caught his eye. So has the fact that I'm a brunette. My eye color isn't consistent with his other victims, but he seems willing to ignore that, seeing as I pretty much dropped myself in his lap. I'm closer to his type than the girl he arrived with.

He flicks his hand, causing two large guys to appear from the crowd. Bodyguards. Thugs. I pay no attention to them.

It's Anthony's turn to lean into me. "You ready for some fun?"

I smile and nod. He slides an arm around my waist, pulling me from the bar stool, leaving his date to watch us go. She's glaring daggers at me right now, but she has no idea of the favor I'm doing her.

By the time we reach the elevator, Anthony has already groped my backside and attempted a full-frontal grope of my pelvis. I force a giggle and push him off, tugging on his hands so I can guide his arms around my waist instead.

We enter the elevator that way while his thugs take up position in front of us to stop anybody else getting in.

Longest elevator ride of my life.

By the time we reach his room, I'm grateful for the fact that I'm wearing a dress with a structured bodice. There's no way this asshole can get inside it without undressing me completely and he seems to draw the line at getting naked in the hallway.

The thugs remain outside the door as we enter the room. It's a typical hotel layout: large bed, closet, bathroom at the side. It's not as opulent as I expected, so I guess he's small fry.

I avoid his grasping hands and head straight for the champagne bucket beside the bed. A bottle of wine rests inside it. I drip ice water across the cups as I quickly pour out two full glasses while his hands continue to roam everywhere on my body that I'd rather they didn't go.

I'm going to have to step this up if I want to maintain any shred of dignity.

I spin and shove the glass between us as his arms snake around me again.

In a husky whisper, I say, "For every sip you take, I'll take something off."

For a second, I think he's going to pitch the drink off to the side, which would be annoying, but I have a backup plan if that happens.

He grins at me and takes a large gulp, stepping back to get a full view. "You're not wearing that much."

"Oh, you'd be surprised." I sashay my way toward the bed. I'd prefer a little more distance between us, but I'll take what I can get. I twist a little so he can watch me pull the zipper down my back, allowing the bodice to separate. I slowly step out of the dress, letting it to fall to the floor, leaving me in my underwear.

He takes a step toward me, but I waggle my finger at him, pointing at the glass.

He takes another large gulp.

I slowly unclasp my bra, but I take my time.

Any moment now and my plan will come to fruition...

CHAPTER FORTY-ONE

*A*nthony inhales, shudders a little, and stares at the glass in confusion.

He licks his lips and tries to inhale again, but his throat will already be closing over.

Severely allergic to crustaceans.

It was such a tiny notation in his file.

His eyes bulge, darting to the satchel on the bedside table. After tailing him for a day, I've already confirmed that's where he keeps his epinephrine: lifesaving medicine I don't intend to let him have.

I leap toward the bag and snatch it into my arms before he can get to it. It's heavier than I expected it to be. Much heavier.

I don't have time for more than a quick glance inside: wallet, keys, multiple burner phones, and a thick book with a Latin title... *Mecum* something. It must be the book that's weighing the satchel down.

Anthony stumbles, gasps for breath, and clutches his throat, the anaphylaxis overpowering him fast.

He launches himself at me, knocking the lamp over instead. It crashes to the floor, the *thud* muted somewhat by the carpet, but it's certainly loud enough to be heard from outside in the corridor.

I hold my breath as I dart out of his way, wondering if his thugs will rush in to see what happened.

Nope. I guess they're used to things getting rough inside this asshole's bedroom.

He rages after me, but I evade him, dancing aside, lithe as a wraith. I want nothing more than to slam a fist into his face, but I can't leave any bruises. Nothing to suggest this was anything more than a tragic accident.

He tries to shout, but he can't breathe. He's desperate for his medicine now. He flails, falls to the floor, gripping his throat, his face becoming blotchy and red. He crawls toward me, hands and knees desperately trying to push himself closer, stalking me around the room at a snail's pace as I take step after step away from him.

Soon enough, he sags to the floor and I wait for him to stop moving. Then I nudge him over onto his back while he wheezes. Dropping his bag onto the floor where he can't reach it, I retrieve the champagne bucket, and upturn it over him.

Ice cubes spill across his chest and legs, along with about a dozen prawns.

My phone call that morning had been to order the champagne bucket to be delivered to his room half an hour ago when I was sure he would be downstairs.

Of course, the hotel had stern instructions he was in no circumstances to be delivered any food with fish in it, so I had to plant the crustaceans in the bucket myself. There's nothing like a full blur to allow me to slip around unseen.

I'd crept in behind the hotel staff when they delivered the champagne to the room, and I walked out when I was done. Then I dripped seafood-infused water into his glass before he drank from it just now.

I angle my stiletto over his wrist as he stretches out his arm one last time toward his bag. I pin his wrist neatly between my heel and the ball of my foot before leaning down to him, whispering names into his ear.

His eyes are so puffy that they're nearly closed, but I see the final moment when he recognizes the names of the women he butchered.

"This death is too quick for you," I say, tears dripping down my cheeks as he rattles a final breath and finally lies still.

Then I tip my head back and scream.

I wait a moment.

Still no thugs. I guess they're used to women screaming, too.

I pull on my dress but don't zip it up. Ruffling my hair, I rub the tears across my cheeks, smearing my mascara with it before I clutch my bodice to my chest and take quick breaths to heighten my breathing.

Then I run screaming to the door.

I rip it open, colliding with the nearest thug, and crying as loudly as I can, "You have to help him! He's having an allergic reaction! I don't know what to do…"

The guy shoves me out of the way so hard that I rocket to the other side of the hallway. He runs inside, the other bodyguard close behind.

I rub my shoulder where I banged the wall and back away quietly, quickly harnessing my power. As soon as my blur is complete, I zip up my dress and stride down the corridor. I straighten my hair and wipe my eyes, heading for the nearest bathroom so I can fix my makeup.

Once there, I go straight to the mirror and wipe away the eyeliner smudges with balled-up paper. I didn't bring extra makeup with me because I didn't want to carry a purse, so I'll have to be satisfied with—

My thoughts stop for a moment.

I inhale. Exhale.

I killed him. Anthony Gallo is dead.

I told Slade that the first kill is the worst. But I'm calm. So calm. *Too* calm. My hands aren't shaking. I didn't feel any fear. I felt anger on behalf of the women who died, but not an uncontrollable rage like Slade talked about. I was the calmest I've ever been.

Killing is what I was born to do. It was like breathing.

That should scare me.

But it doesn't.

All I want is another target. Give me another target and I will end them too.

I take another deep breath, smooth my hair over my shoulder, and head right back out into the ballroom. I'll leave the same way I came in: through the front door.

As I make my way past the dancing couples, I take note of my observer—a blurred presence at the edge of the room. He's been following my moves all evening, right up to the corridor outside Anthony Gallo's door.

I haven't figured out who he is yet. Not Slade, I know that for certain. It could be the Superior who was following me the other day, or Fallon himself, or even Ridley if he's worried about me.

For now, I've decided that my best option is to pretend I don't know he's there and wait for him to reveal himself.

While my attention is momentarily diverted to my observer's position, I take another step and—

I trip over someone's foot.

My brain tries to catch up with my falling body. *How did I misjudge that step?* I know the location of every single person in this room. I calculate every step, every move.

Where did this guy come from?

"Whoa there," he says, drawling out his speech like he's calming a frightened foal. So much so that I'm surprised he doesn't add *darlin'* at the end.

My head snaps up.

Cain Carter might be allowing his Southern accent to show, but I'd know his voice anywhere.

CHAPTER FORTY-TWO

Cain Carter is the only man, other than Slade, who is powerful enough to blend in to his surroundings and trick my mind into not seeing him.

He's more casually dressed than anyone else here, wearing a white-collared shirt that's open at the top, leaving an exposed triangle of bare chest situated right at my eye level.

I tilt my head back to meet his eyes, choosing to remain where I am, pressed tightly against his chest. "Cain Carter."

He clears his throat, his dark eyebrows arched at me. "Hunter Cassidy."

I wait another moment, but he doesn't say anything.

Okay, so it looks like neither of us is going to explain why we're here.

He frees one hand, keeping his other arm wrapped around me. His thumb tracks down my cheek. He's seen me cry before. He's too observant to miss it. A hint of concern enters his eyes.

His lips part, and I think he's going to ask me what happened.

Instead, he says, "I'm glad to see you looking well."

The last time he saw me, I'd just taken a serious hit to the head. I'm about to thank him for his concern when someone shifts beside him and a beautiful redhead clears her throat pointedly.

I glance at her, quickly taking in her figure-hugging dress and the very expensive diamond earrings she's wearing, along with a matching necklace. I don't like the way she's looking down her nose at me.

Oh my gosh. I guess I'm not wearing enough diamonds or something. How trashy of me.

I allow a smile to grow on my face as I turn my attention back to Cain. I'm still all tangled up in him and it's making his date tap her fingers impatiently against her thigh.

"Hmm," I say loudly, pretending to think about it. "The last time you saw me, I was enjoying a nice bath."

Of course, I mean "an ice bath," but I deliberately run the words together so that's not what she hears. It's impossible to miss her reaction, the instant possessive scowl and pouting lips.

I lift myself up onto my tiptoes, lean right into his broad chest, and whisper into his ear so she can't hear me. "You can do better, Cain."

I slide away from him and he lets me go.

Before he can respond, a guy in a tailored suit hurries up to him and murmurs, "It's time for your speech, Mr. Carter."

My brow furrows. *Speech?*

Cain shrugs at my confusion. "It's my party."

But... the guy throwing this thing is some anonymous millionaire. I kick myself for not digging deeper into this event. I only saw it as a means to an end. My surprise turns to a smile. Cain Carter is certainly a mystery.

He closes the gap between us again. Even without his assassin's ring, his presence is powerful. There's a moment of true honesty in his eyes as he murmurs, "The moment a woman looks at me the way you look at Slade Baines, that's when I'll do better."

I mean it when I whisper, "I hope that happens, Cain."

He turns back to his date and takes her arm, giving her his full attention like a perfect gentleman. It hurts me to realize that what he said is true: I have strong feelings for Slade. It hurts because I'm still fighting them.

I make my way out of the ballroom, collect my coat, and wander down the street. I'm not sure what my observer will have made of the interaction with Cain, although it should have been obvious that I didn't bump into him deliberately.

Halfway down the street, making sure he can see it, I initiate a partial blur, the kind that a human would simply blink away thinking it was a trick of the light. I quickly duck into an alleyway, once again making sure my observer saw my detour.

I pause just inside the entrance, ready for him.

As soon as I sense him step around the corner, I grab him and push him up against the far wall, wrapping my hand in his shirt and keeping a strong hold on him. I consider drawing him into a full blur with me, but I want to force him to expose his identity. "Show yourself!"

His blur disappears.

Brandon winces and throws his hands up on either side. "I'm not here to fight you!"

"Who sent you?" I demand to know.

"Ridley. He wanted to make sure you'd be okay. He was worried when you didn't take any weapons."

I exhale, but I don't let Brandon go. I click my tongue in annoyance. "Ridley."

"And maybe the other Novices as well."

I narrow my eyes at him. "What?"

He quickly adds, "Not Slade. He said you didn't need help. But he didn't try to stop me, either." Brandon shrugs. "I have to tell you, Hunter, when I heard you scream, I was ready to run in there and pull you out."

By the time I screamed, my target was already dead, but if

Brandon had interfered, my ruse would have been discovered. Not to mention, it would have looked like I'd failed and needed help.

I snap, "I had it under control."

"Good thing I'm not such a nice guy, after all." He gives me a hopeful look, as if he's asking for forgiveness. "It was a good kill."

I finally let him go, stepping back a little, but not so far that I can't kick the stuffing out of him if I decide he's up to no good. "What about your first?"

"A few days ago," he says, his eyes turning dark, but he doesn't elaborate with the details. "Lutz has two kills under his belt already. Rowan has one. Slade has another tomorrow. The Superiors are keeping count."

"Count of our kills?"

"We all know Slade is in front," he says. "But your kill was requested by your own client, so that counts for extra. You're not far behind."

My forehead creases. "Behind what?"

"To be the next Master."

I laugh. "Gareth won't choose me."

"Why not?"

I stare at him. "Are you serious?"

He returns my stare with a firm one of his own. "Hunter, you're as physically strong as any man, more magically powerful, and we all know you stepped into that punch that day."

He gives me a dark look, daring me to deny it. "Nobody can beat you. Not even Slade. Rowan was really pissed at Slade about that fight, but he calmed down. He respects your right to choose your destiny. I'll follow Slade if he's chosen to be Master, but you… I'd follow you into hell if you asked me."

I press my mouth into a fierce line. "Why?"

He leans down to me. He's smaller than the other guys, but

he's still taller than average, lean in a way that makes his movements efficient. His gray eyes flash with the illusion of steel. "Because you're a stone-cold assassin."

The corner of his mouth rises into a half-smile before he slips away from me, quickly checking his surroundings. He pauses in the entrance to the corridor. "I have to say, Hunter, you let that guy touch you in places the rest of us can only dream about. I kept waiting for you to break his fingers. I hope he died happy."

With that, he strolls away down the street.

I'm left with a sense of surprise and unease. I wait a few minutes before following him out, stepping into the shadows beside the nearest building and staying out of the golden streetlight as I walk lightly, traveling the distance on foot.

Close to the Realm, I pause, assessing the shadows beneath the trees within the park. Because I know that the Realm rests right on top of the Common, I find it hard to walk into the park itself, as if there's a mental barrier stopping me.

A thin figure detaches from the nearest tree and I recognize Briar's green beanie and disheveled hair. She shivers in the cold as I cross the distance.

She asks, "Is it done?"

"Yes, Briar, it's done."

"Thank you, milady."

I pull off my coat, handing it to her. "Here, have this."

The cold air rushes in, but I'm so close to the Realm that I won't freeze before I make it back to my room. She hesitates and then draws the new coat around her shoulders, giving me a grateful smile.

She asks, "What do you need to know, milady?"

Her question tells me I was right about her loyalty: She will be my eyes and ears in this city. I open my senses and check our surroundings before I speak, confirming that there's nobody else around. "I need to know what Superior Fallon does when he leaves the Realm. Specifically, I need to know if he has ties with the Tirelli Family."

"Consider it done."

"And from now on, we meet on Saber Lane. There's a bookshop there—"

"The Tomb," she says, nodding. "I know it. William Sloane is a good person. The witch who lives on that street is also my friend."

I'm glad she's fully aware of the non-human inhabitants in the city. Most humans are oblivious to them. I wasn't sure if I would have to break that news to her. "Excellent. Thank you, Briar."

"Goodnight, milady." She disappears into the trees, a fleeting shadow that merges with the dark. I should have given her some food or money. I make a mental note to do that the next time I see her. She's far too thin.

I hurry back to the edge of the Common, gain entry to the Realm, and take off my stilettos to jog back to my room. Once there, I take down the pictures from the wall and place them neatly back into the file. Then I retrieve my ledger from the closet, lift the pen, and mark the mission as complete.

I wait a moment for the Guardian to respond.

I'm not exactly sure when she sleeps—maybe never. Within seconds, her golden writing appears on the ledger, but it's not what I expect.

She's supposed to write "Acknowledged" beneath the row.

Instead, her curly script forms different words...

Be careful, Hunter.

I close the book quietly, a cold shiver shooting down my spine.

I'm still a month away from becoming a Superior, and a lot can happen in a month.

CHAPTER FORTY-THREE

The next day, I'm called to the administration building and told to bring my ledger.

For some reason, Gareth seems very happy. I was expecting him to be upset that my first mission went so smoothly. It surprises me that he's not angry I succeeded without bringing the wrath of the Tirelli Family down on myself.

Instead, he gives me a wolfish grin as he gestures to not one, but two new clients waiting for me. As soon as they write their requests in my ledger, the Guardian sanctions the missions.

For my own part, it feels like some sort of floodgate has opened. Almost like the last four years of my mother's absence have been accumulating, waiting for me to take her place. Both clients are women. Both targets are men. But I'm sure that is bound to change eventually.

Five days later, I have a total of three kills under my belt. I've barely seen Slade in that time. My missions have been all-consuming. But snippets I hear around the Realm tell me he has succeeded at each of his missions so far.

On my way back to my room the day after my third mission, I catch sight of Slade making his way across the Realm, disappearing toward the entrance. He's wearing full combat gear, with a full-body protective suit, a weapons belt around his waist and another one crisscrossing his back.

In fact, every part of his powerful figure is being used to carry a weapon, a blade, or a gun. It looks like he's going after an army of assholes.

A shiver of apprehension shoots through me. What kind of mission have they sent him on?

I stalk after him, determined to catch him before he leaves, picking up my pace to match his quick stride. But as soon as I do, he blurs ahead of me, breaking into a run, becoming a streak of light in my vision.

Within seconds, he's completely gone.

I stare in shock at the empty space he leaves behind. Nobody but me can blur so completely. Or at least, that's what I thought. But Slade has been perfecting his skills and now... he's clearly more powerful than I imagined.

By the time I gather my thoughts, it's too late to follow him. I don't know which way he's gone. And I won't be able to detect him. Not with that kind of power.

I tell myself not to be worried. Slade is strong, smart, and skilled. He's the guy whom others should fear. But I suddenly understand why Slade didn't stop Brandon from tailing me on the night of my first mission. Even though he knew I could pull it off, it's hard knowing that someone you love is about to willingly put themselves in danger. You want to be there for them, even if you know they don't need your help.

I pull myself up. Not *love*.

No. Nope.

Uh...

I place my focus on working out in the combat room. Now that we don't have scheduled classes, we're free to use the facilities as we see fit.

As the afternoon wears on, I grow more uneasy, and not

about whether I'll get more missions. A quick walk around the Realm confirms that Slade hasn't returned.

I decide to head down to the food hall for dinner for the first time in a while, heading toward my old table in case Thomas or Matthew knows what's going on.

They grow quiet when I approach.

"Slade?" I ask.

The tension around Thomas's eyes is stark. Even Matthew is on edge. He's usually the more relaxed of the two.

When Thomas sets his drink down, his fist is clamped tightly around it. His gaze shoots toward Gareth with barely concealed fury. "They sent him on a suicide mission."

I eye them both with growing fear. Now I wish I'd raced after Slade. I should have gone with him. "Where did they send him?"

Matthew shakes his head. Thomas doesn't answer, either, glaring at his food without touching it.

I grab Thomas's arm and grind out, "*Where*, Thomas?"

"You can't help him. He has to live or die on his own."

I growl. "If you don't tell me where he is, I'm going to start killing things, beginning with you."

His shoulders slump. "If he was going to die, he's dead already."

My knife thuds into the table with a wallop that echoes through the suddenly silent food hall.

I leap out of my chair, step onto the table, and jump down the other side, taking the most direct route to the Superiors' table on the far side of the room.

If Gareth gets rid of Slade, then the most viable candidate for Master disappears.

Ridley drops his cutlery, as does Lincoln, both watching my oncoming wrath with open concern. Gareth, on the other hand, continues to chew his steak as if nothing is wrong.

I stop in front of him, my focus zeroed in on him, my heart rate deadly calm. "Where did you send Slade?"

Gareth glances up, his expression shuttered, giving nothing away. "That's none of your concern, Hunter."

The entire food hall is quiet behind me. I lean down to him. I'm pretty much ready to pull out all of the stops right now.

My back is burning. My wings want to burst out so I can end this monster. I allow my power to flow through my fingertips as I reach out, very slowly, to stop his hand before it rises to his mouth.

He inhales sharply. His eyes widen. A tiny wisp of smoke rises from his hand where I ran my finger across his skin. The air above his arm becomes hazy, like summer air above a burning street.

I just took a tiny piece of his life away.

To take his whole life, I will have to reveal my wings, but I'm angry enough to risk exposing myself. And I'm certain he knows it.

He freezes before he leans back in painfully slow increments, trying to put distance between us without making it obvious that he's attempting to retreat.

My gaze drills into his as I speak very softly. "Tell me where you sent Slade."

Gareth's gaze flicks to his left. "Ridley? Escort Hunter from the food hall and tell her what she wants to know."

CHAPTER FORTY-FOUR

Ridley rises from his seat. "Let's take a walk, Hunter."

He's one of the few Superiors whose life I won't threaten. I don't think Gareth knows that, but it's the only reason I don't let my rage loose right now.

Beneath my anger is an intense fear. Thomas said that if Slade was going to die, he would be dead already. I spent all afternoon ignoring my instincts.

If Slade is hurt because I failed to act…

I stride after Ridley as he exits the hall at a quick pace. As soon as we're outside, he says, "Slade is in a very rough part of Boston. You can't help him, Hunter."

I growl at him. "Don't tell me what I can't do!"

He doesn't know it, but if I want to, I could fly to Slade's location in minutes.

Ridley says, "He was sent after a violent gang."

"A gang. As in multiple targets?"

He quickens his pace and I imagine it's because he wants to put more distance between us and the food hall, where Gareth remains. The farther we get away from it, the more information Ridley gives me.

"Seven of them. Heavily armed. Holed up in a fortified warehouse in South Boston. They have an arsenal of black market weapons—and know how to use them. It's practically an army base."

"Give me directions. I'm going."

He grabs my arm. "No."

I glare back at him, yanking my arm out of his grip. "Try to stop me."

His expression softens. "You can't get involved. All of the Faction Masters are watching this mission and waiting for its outcome. If Slade pulls this off on his own, he will be unbeatable. He will have their respect. Gareth will have no choice but to make him Master. You can't assist Slade. It's important, Hunter."

I hate that my vision blurs. Tears burn behind my eyes and I try so hard to shake them off, but I can't seem to halt them. "But I can't… stay here and wait. What if he dies? What if he doesn't make it out of there?"

Ridley places one big hand on each of my shoulders, gripping me firmly, anchoring me to the spot. "You have to trust him. He wasn't ordered to take this mission. He was given the choice. He said *yes*."

"Why? What did these guys do?"

"Some pretty bad things to a lot of people, Hunter."

I drop my head into my hands. "I feel sick."

"I felt that way when your mom went out on her first missions. Then I saw her in action and she was mind-blowing."

I lift my eyes. "But she died, Ridley. Not that day maybe, but far too soon. She wasn't immortal."

He whispers, "Yeah."

He's never asked me how she died. Maybe he doesn't want to know. To find out that the Master of the Legion—the man he has followed for the last twenty years—caused her death would be devastating. Just like finding out whether or not I'm his daughter. It seems to me that there are some things Ridley simply doesn't want to know.

I back away from him. "I have to go for a run. Don't worry. I won't leave the Realm, but I can't stand still right now. I'll do laps."

"I understand."

I fight the impulse to take to the sky and look for Slade. Instead, I race around the perimeter, trying to outrun my fear.

I picture Slade practicing his moves in the combat room, how agile and strong he is, picture him blurring as quickly as light, imagine him deftly evading an oncoming blade in a fight, literally dodging bullets.

I can imagine his safety all I like. It doesn't make it reality.

All I want to do is scream out my fear.

Eventually, I have no choice but to go back to my room. I stand beneath the shower, turning it to full cold to trigger the strength of my inner power, but even that is not enough. My stomach won't stop churning.

When I'm done, I throw on my underwear and pace my bedroom, wearing a track in the carpet, stretching my nerves thin. I slip on my pajamas but rip them off again. Anything against my skin is too much sensory input right now.

Maybe… if I just take a small flight for a few minutes, spread my wings, I'll feel better.

I race to the door and fling it open, ready to run out of there, but I immediately halt.

Slade stands on the other side, a quiet presence, his power so muted that I didn't sense him until he was right in front of me. His assassin's ring glints as he rests a hand against the doorframe.

His dark brown hair falls across his eyes, obscuring his face. His protective suit is torn in places: a slash across his chest, rips along his arms, another crossing one knee. But most alarming to me are what look like bullet holes across one shoulder.

He's covered in blood. It's gruesome and awful, but he's alive. He's standing straight as if nothing has touched him. He looks... okay.

I've never felt such relief in my life. "Slade. You're back."

He draws up tall, his hair matted with blood across his face. "I reported to Gareth and the Superiors already. They know that the mission was a success. The targets are dead."

He takes a step forward but stumbles, his fist clenching around the doorframe before he rights himself.

Fear shoots through me. It was such a small misstep, corrected so quickly, but very unlike him. "Slade?"

He steps into the room as I back away. Then he closes the door behind himself with slow, deliberate movements. It clicks shut and nobody can see us now.

His voice cracks. "I couldn't tell them. I couldn't let them see. I need them to think that everything's fine. But, Hunter..."

He finally meets my eyes through the curtain of his hair. "I think I'm hurt."

I catch him as he drops to his knees.

CHAPTER FORTY-FIVE

My heart pounds as I use my inner strength to support his weight, keeping him from hitting the floor.

He leans against me, his arms hanging limply at his sides, his torso a mountain of heavy muscle. His weight would crush anyone else, but not me.

I draw on the burn in my back, accessing my inhuman strength to keep us both upright for a moment, trying to decide if he's better off lying down anyway. "Tell me where you're hurt."

His voice slurs. "Left shoulder. Bullets. Machine gun. I got four of the guys before they realized I was there, but after that… all hell broke… I couldn't… I wasn't fast enough."

"What were you thinking, Slade? Nobody can dodge bullets."

He shrugs, a smile tugging at his mouth while he rests his head in the crook of my neck. "I did. For a while."

I support his torso against my shoulder while I brush the hair out of his eyes, checking over his face and head for wounds.

As I run my hands through his hair, he sighs against my neck, wrapping his arms around my bare waist, planting a soft kiss against my neck. "You know what, Hunter? If I'm going to die, can you please keep doing that until I'm gone? It's not a bad way to go."

My brow furrows as I check his eyes. Glazed. Unfocused. I'm not sure if he knows what he's saying right now. I carefully leverage him back onto the floor, supporting his head and torso all the way down. His arms slide away from me with the movement, barely enough grip in them to hold on to me.

As his hand brushes my side on its way to the floor, his assassin's ring burns my hip in a long streak. I wince and suck in a sharp breath. I need to get the ring and the suit off him and figure out where he's wounded. I won't be able to cut the damn suit off. It's designed to resist a blade. I shudder at what must have made the rips in it. A chainsaw, maybe?

Grabbing a pillow from the bed, along with a leather belt from my closet, I use the pillow to support Slade's head while I turn him onto his side, undoing the hidden closures at the side of the suit, peeling it off his chest and arms. Then I wrap the belt around his finger and slide the assassin's ring off his hand, dropping it as far away as possible so I don't accidentally touch it again.

He doesn't resist or even acknowledge my movements, his body becoming increasingly heavy. I run my hands across every square inch of his chest, checking every wound. Some of the cuts are deep enough to require stitches, but he's right about the bullet wounds.

There are three entry wounds across his shoulder, but only two exit wounds in his back. One of the bullets is still lodged in his chest. I don't have the tools to get it out or to stitch him up and my power can't help with this.

He needs a hospital, but he can't go to one. That's the choice we made when we became assassins in training. No professional medical help. The Superiors have a medical room—they know how to deal with wounds like this—but Slade made it clear he can't let them know he's hurt. If I take him to them now, the entire mission will be for nothing.

I run my hand through my hair in frustration, resting my palm against his heart. "Dammit, Slade, is your life worth this?"

He doesn't respond. He's out cold.

There's only one way I can help him. I don't know if it will work, but I have to try. At least if he's unconscious, it will make what I have to do much easier. He'll ask far less questions this way.

I slip on a pair of jeans but leave my top bare except for my bra. I need my back as clear as possible. I open the door in preparation for what I need to do. There's nobody in the corridor and I have to hope I won't be seen before I can implement a full blur. A woman with my physique shouldn't be able to do what I'm about to do next.

Taking a deep breath, I bend my knees, slide my arms under Slade's torso, and access my strength before I pick him up.

Big, bulky… beautiful man.

Don't die on me, Slade.

It's not his weight that's going to defeat me, but his sheer size. I can't exactly throw him over my shoulder. Instead, I hook one arm under his knees and the other behind his shoulders, tilting him toward me. Yep, I'm carrying him like a bride over the threshold.

I harness my blur as fast as I can, drawing him into it with me, making us both completely invisible. Then I carry him from the room, along the corridor, and down the stairs, leveraging him out through the big doors at the side of the building.

It's a good thing they're left open all the time. I used to hate that—it made me feel vulnerable. Now it's a good thing because I don't have enough hands to open or close doors right now. Leaving my own bedroom door wide open is risk enough. Not to mention the bloody pillow I've left lying on the floor.

His back is slippery, which tells me he's still losing blood and it scares me.

As soon as I exit the building, I find a clear patch of ground, close my eyes, and tell myself, "I can do this."

I allow the burn to spread across my back, sensing the shift in my body, the blossom of my power like a butterfly breaking out of a cocoon.

I sigh out the sensation as the composition of my back changes, my muscles shifting, allowing my wings to grow and unfurl. They spread and spread, silvery feathers not soft, but sculpted as if from metal, light as air, but tough as iron. I stretch them out, a full five feet at either side of me, power shimmering through them.

I'm not afraid of touching Slade like this. When I take a life using my power, it is a very deliberate act. Merely touching Slade won't hurt him.

I wish I could savor this moment, the first time I've opened my wings in nearly a year, but I can't delay. Taking two quick steps, I beat my wings and soar up from the ground, holding tightly to Slade.

Once I'm airborne, I fly across the Common and head south, speeding over the city, locking my arms and legs around him as best I can.

The protective barrier around the Realm gives way as I exit the boundary. It's similar to leaving the Realm via the door. It's getting back in that requires more effort.

Five minutes later, I descend onto Saber Lane and quickly tuck my wings away before I exit the blur. It's late and all the lights are turned off along the street. Even the diner is dark. But I'm certain that Dean will sense my arrival—and the pain that Slade is in.

I don't waste time, quickly heading for Tansy's door, gripping Slade with one hand and propping him against my shoulder with the other so I can thud my fist against her door.

When Tansy doesn't answer, I stare at her dark windows, then I beat against her door again, cold fingers of panic growing in my chest. If she's not here…

Dean's honeyed voice makes me jump. "Hunter?"

"Dean, where's Tansy?"

He stares, wide-eyed, at Slade. I can't tell for sure in the dim light, but I suspect that Dean is as pale as Slade.

"She's at the Tomb. William was worried about something. She went over there an hour ago and hasn't come home yet."

His gaze darts between Slade and me. "The two of you together…" He rubs his forehead with the back of his hand as a deep crease appears between his eyes. "There's a hell of a lot of pain between you. You need to get him to Tansy right away. Here, let me help you."

I'm about to say that I'm fine, but I'm not sure if Dean knows I'm a Valkyrie. Carrying Slade along the street in front of him might raise too many questions.

He holds out his arms with a stern look. "You think you're fine, but you're not. You're tired, Hunter. Accept my help, please."

As soon as I nod, Dean puts his big biceps to good use, bending and leveraging Slade over his broad shoulder. His muscles strain and I honestly don't know how Slade doesn't slip off. I'm also not sure how I held on to him for so long. Dean is right. My power is stretched thin now.

I hurry after him as he rushes down the street toward the bookshop. "Why isn't my pain hurting you this time?"

"The first time I sense someone's pain is the worst. Usually, after the first time, I can handle any further interactions. In some cases, Tansy can create a spell that's tailored to protect me from that individual."

"I'm guessing you needed that for me."

He gives me a wry smile. "In a big way. But you shouldn't feel bad about it."

"I don't feel…" *Okay, Hunter, don't argue with an empath. I do feel bad about it.* "What about Slade's pain?"

"He's unconscious, so his pain is muted, but if he has any sort of history like you do, I suspect I'll need Tansy's help before he wakes up."

We're approaching the Tomb now, so I run ahead, grateful to see the light switched on inside the shop. Racing up the front steps, I knock on the door, conscious now that the noise is disturbing the other occupants of the Lane. A number of lights flicker on in the upper and lower levels of buildings farther along.

I don't know who else lives here. But since the street is a home for a witch and an empath, I can only assume that the other inhabitants may have powers, too.

Tansy wrenches the door open with a deep furrow in her brow. "Hunter? What…?"

Her gaze takes in Dean holding Slade and I'm pretty sure it's only because she doesn't want Dean to strain himself that she says. "Come inside. Put him on the floor."

Dean complies with her curt order while I help him lower Slade to the floor, resting his head on my lap.

I peer up at Tansy as she scowls down at me. I try to keep the begging tone from my voice as I say, "I need you to heal him."

Her chin juts out. "What's wrong with him?"

"A bullet is lodged in his shoulder. I can't get it out or stitch up his wounds. He's been unconscious for ten minutes now. He's already lost a lot of blood."

She folds her arms across her chest, unmoving. "You should have taken him to a hospital."

Dean gives her a disapproving look while he hovers at the other side of me. "Tansy—"

I snap. "I can't take him to a hospital. He just killed seven thugs. I can't get the police involved."

"Why should I help him?"

I stare at her in disbelief. "Because he's dying!"

"Why should that bother me?"

My eyes widen. "Are you freaking serious?"

Across the way, Dean glowers at her, disappointment carved into his features. "Tansy!"

"No, Dean! She doesn't get to dump a load of trouble on my lap and expect me to fix it."

I try to keep the anger out of my voice. "Slade is not a load of trouble. He's my..."

"What, Hunter? He's your what?"

"Look, I know that you hate assassins because of my mom, but please... *please*, Tansy. He means a lot to me and I can't..." My voice breaks. "I can't lose another person."

She glares down at me. I'm in a position of weakness sitting where I am, but I'm not going to move Slade's head onto the cold floor so I can stand up.

As I consider her unyielding features, I realize that nothing is going to change her mind. She hates me that much.

I thought I could ask her to help him. I thought she'd be willing to put aside her dislike of me if it meant saving a life. I shouldn't have brought him here thinking that I could ask for help.

I can't rely on anyone but myself.

CHAPTER FORTY-SIX

Grinding my teeth, I say, "There isn't time to take Slade anywhere else now. He'll die on the way. If you're not going to help, then back away. I'll do it myself."

I place my hand over his wound. I was hoping I'd have another choice, but now I have to take the worst chance.

I didn't want to reveal my wings in front of Dean, but he'll find out soon enough what I am and I no longer have a choice.

Slowly focusing on my power, I allow the burn to spread across my back, enabling my skin to begin the shift and my wings to unfurl. As my giant, silver wings expand behind me, Tansy scrambles out of the way, her eyes wide, the color draining from her face.

She's shaking so hard, it looks like she's terrified of me.

And suddenly I realize… that's why she won't help Slade. It's not because she's angry with me. She's afraid to go near him, doesn't want to touch him. He just returned from carrying out a mission, so I guess he smells like death, the same way I do.

I block out her emotions, focusing on what I need to do.

I choose a feather from the base of my wings and take a deep breath, shut my eyes, and brace as I rip it out.

My scream echoes around the room. Pain rakes through my back and arms and into my stomach. I double over, focusing on Slade's closed eyes. I'll never grow that feather back. Our feathers are finite. We don't shed them. They can only be removed by our own hand.

But he's worth it.

I'm grateful that he's unconscious for the next bit. I focus on the bullet stuck in his shoulder, using the feather to dig around in the wound and locate the bullet, leveraging it out with a lot of difficulty. Luckily, the tip of the feather is as hard as steel and acts like a narrow scoop. Still, it scrapes the inside of his wound, cutting him on the inside.

He jolts in my lap.

I'm hurting him, but I have to get the bullet out. I'll deal with the damage in a minute.

A sob tears out of me. I didn't even know I'd started to cry.

The bullet slowly, painstakingly, appears and finally emerges. My hands shake hard as I drop it onto the floor.

Now to heal him.

This is the truly dangerous part. I'm built for killing, not saving things. My feathers are weapons, not instruments of healing.

I hold the feather between my palms and focus my power into it, heating it until it's pliant between my fingertips, transforming it into putty. Reaching over him, I'm preparing to press a lump of it into the empty bullet wound when a shout stops me.

"Hunter! No!"

My head snaps up to find William standing at the base of the stairs, staring at me, aghast. "You can't do that."

He races to my side in an instant, dropping to a kneeling position, moving much faster than expected for an older man. His gaze flies wildly from my melted feather to Slade. "You're about to give this man a part of yourself. If you do that, you will never be able to kill him. Ever."

I say, with complete honesty, "I will never want to."

I proceed to lean over Slade again, but William grabs my hand in an iron grip. "Don't take that risk."

I grind my teeth. "I have no choice, William. He's dying. And I can't let that happen."

"Why not?" His eyes widen. "Hunter... do you...?"

Love him? Maybe. Even if I didn't, I can't let him die. "He is very important to me."

"Your mother did everything she could to make sure you would never be weak like she was," William says. "If you give him part of yourself, you'll never have a choice."

I consider William carefully. There's something about the way he talked about my mother. She raised me to be strong, to trust only myself, to never make myself vulnerable to anyone—let alone a man. But the way he spoke, it sounds like something more.

I don't have time to think about it. Slade is even paler now, his breathing shallow, his wounds weeping. Every moment that I delay is costing him.

"Let me go." I shake William off.

My forceful glare is enough to make him retreat and I turn my attention back to Slade, quickly pressing the putty I made from my feather into the worst bullet wound. Then I place two more lumps into the other wounds, sealing them.

Slade's body reacts quickly to the magic, rapidly healing over the top of the wounds. I use the remainder of the putty to smear sparingly over the other cuts, trying to make the most of the quantity I have, waiting for the wounds to heal as he absorbs the power of my feather into his body.

I literally gave him a little part of my immortality. A tiny part of my life is now part of him. It's so dangerous that Mom told me never to do it. When I tried to do it for her as she lay dying, she pinned my hands, imprisoning me with her last strength, so I couldn't reach my wings to pluck out a feather.

But I won't watch Slade die.

His breathing evens out. As I run my fingers across his cheeks, the first signs of color return to his bloodless features. I slump over him, waiting for a long time as his body relaxes and finally I sense… he's asleep now.

Beside me, William is resigned, but Dean glares daggers at Tansy while she presses up against the cupboard behind the counter, as far away from me as she can get.

I retract my wings, grateful I didn't smash anything with them. They came awfully close to one of the glass cabinets.

William is the first to speak. "Hunter, that was very dangerous."

"I know." I acknowledge his concern, but it's done now.

CHAPTER FORTY-SEVEN

William asks, "Who is he?"

"An assassin-in-training," I say. "His name is Slade. William, can we stay here tonight? I don't have the strength to fly back."

Maybe it's my exhaustion, but William seems to put away his disapproval of my actions. He gives me a sad smile as he says, "Of course. Let me help you get him upstairs."

I consider William's offer warily. He's sturdy, but he's not young. Dean immediately moves beside me, reaching out to help, but I shake my head at both of them. "I'll do it."

I brace and lift Slade into my arms, grappling again with his size while William stares after me in shock. I guess I must look a bit ridiculous, a woman of my stature carrying such a large man.

I pause long enough to ask, "Can we stay in my old room?"

His expression softens at the way I call it *mine*. "Of course."

As I ascend the stairs, climbing them sideways so I can carry Slade up them, I have a full view of the room below and Dean shaking his head at Tansy before he strides toward the door.

She cries, "Dean!"

He whirls back to her. "Stop letting fear rule your life, Tansy."

"But I can't—"

"No! Fear is a choice. Stop choosing it." He spins on his heel and stalks through the door, leaving her to slump against the cupboard, her shoulders sagging.

I continue up the stairs to the room on the right, surprised to find the bed freshly made. I place Slade onto it, realizing then how tired I am.

Unfortunately, I still need to undress him and make sure there aren't any other wounds I don't know about. I'm prepared to rip out another feather if I have to. I maneuver the blanket out from under him, pull off his boots, and peel off the protective suit, exposing his hips, thighs, and calves.

Checking him over, I'm grateful to discover that I didn't miss anything. If he has any internal injuries I can't see, the magic within my feather will heal him as it absorbs into his body. I can already see the more minor wounds healing even though they aren't in direct contact with parts of my feather.

I pull the blanket up over him and drop to the rug on the floor to watch over him, studying the curve of his cheekbones, the features I used to think were harsh, that appear all smoothed out while he sleeps.

Tansy may have let her fear overwhelm her, but I'm not without my own fears. I succeeded in pushing my worries aside before so I could make a choice. I was certain it was the right one, but now… well… I'm in trouble if I chose wrong.

Don't betray me, Slade.

A soft knock sounds at the door before William opens it a little. "Hunter? Do you have the energy to talk? I'm afraid it's important."

As I open the door, he runs his hand through his hair and I notice for the first time how disheveled he looks. Tansy hovers in the background, her expression blank. She looks like she'd rather be anywhere else but here right now.

"Do you have a shirt I can borrow?" I ask, since I'm still wearing nothing but my bra and jeans.

"Of course." He strides into his room and out again in two seconds flat holding a man-sized T-shirt with a cartoon picture of a dragon on it. He shrugs when I raise my eyebrow at the picture.

Then I follow him into the kitchen, where Tansy turns away from me to put the kettle on, her movements stiff.

William doesn't mince words as he sits down. "I've decoded part of the *Keres Coda*. But I don't like what I've found."

I pull up a chair. "You're worried."

"Very." He sighs, dropping his head into his hands. His eyes are dark-ringed, the creases along his forehead deeper than before. "The knowledge in the book was coded for a reason. The more I decipher, the more concerned I am that we shouldn't be digging so hard."

I glance at Tansy, but she's a blank page right now, giving nothing away about what William might have found.

"Everything in that book affects my life and my future." I exhale slowly, trying to decide if that's a good enough reason to ask him to reveal what he knows. Maybe it isn't. Maybe Mom hid things from me for good reasons. But not knowing what she died for has slowly eaten me up for four long years.

"I won't force you to tell me what you've found," I say. "All I can do is promise to do everything in my power to protect that information."

His shoulders tense, concern oozing from every part of him. "I know how to trigger the feather to locate the weapon. And I'm afraid… it's connected to you."

What could it have to do with me—a Valkyrie?

Maybe I shouldn't be surprised. Tansy told me that the Coda described the Valkyrie. In less than flattering ways, actually. It practically described us as death on legs. In fact, it makes me a little worried about what else might be in that book about my people.

Are there things I don't know about my own race?

I'm the last living Valkyrie. I only had Mom to teach me the things I needed to know. There could be a thousand pieces of knowledge that didn't get passed down to her and therefore haven't been passed down to me.

William rubs his eyes, wiping at his tired face. "We know that the feather can be used to locate a hidden object. I've long imagined what it could be: something with killing power, maybe the power of flight, or worse, the power to steal a soul, not just a life." He shrugs, his old arms lifting in an almost helpless gesture. "It could be anything."

Unlike the Valkyrie, the Keres are extinct, so I've never seen the Keres power in action to understand its nature or its limits. I know that a Ker—the name for a single Keres—can kill someone the same way the Valkyrie can—by sucking the life out of them. But I'm not clear about the differences between our powers. Quite frankly, I'm grateful they're extinct. They're the only creatures who can kill me.

William continues. "Unfortunately, I've discovered that your mother did a very dangerous thing when she coated the feather with her blood."

"How so?"

His eyes meet mine. "The feather is triggered by Valkyrie blood. One drop will reveal the weapon it hides."

My eyes widen. "One drop of my blood can trigger the feather?" My forehead quickly creases with confusion. "But Mom *covered* it in her blood. Why didn't it reveal the weapon?"

William is hesitant, cautious. "Obviously, I wasn't there, so I can't say for sure, but in order to coat it, I believe she had to sever a major artery. I would guess that she bled out so fast that it covered the feather before it could reveal the weapon."

I wince, closing my eyes against the memory. William wasn't there, but I was. Afterward, at least.

I remember Mom's pale face. All the blood she'd lost. The way she lay there. I don't want to picture what must have happened moments before I arrived on the scene... The feather lying in a puddle of her blood. The way Gareth must have carefully stepped over her to pick up the feather and walk away from her, ignoring the fact that she was bleeding out before his eyes.

But as soon as he touched it, it would have sealed over. Human touch turns Valkyrie blood to the consistency of smooth stone. As soon as Gareth picked up the feather, he sealed it.

That must have been very frustrating for him.

But it poses a big problem for us now.

I shudder. "As soon as the resin is removed..."

"The feather will burst into life and reveal the weapon it hides."

CHAPTER FORTY-EIGHT

I rub my eyes. "Gareth will have all the answers he wants."

William contemplates me from the other side of the table. Tansy is still quiet. Everything we're talking about is dangerous. Dangerous because we don't know what we're dealing with.

"You're right," I say. "That book shouldn't be decoded."

William nods in agreement. "Which is why I asked Tansy to destroy it."

"What?" I'm surprised. Dean said that William had called Tansy to his place and that he was troubled. Still, I never expected him to take such drastic action.

Tansy's expression is wry. "Don't worry. It's not possible. I've tried every method—magical and non-magical. I tried burning it, disintegrating it, gluing it closed, trying to cut the pages, you name it." She slumps against the cupboard, her normally bright eyes dull. "The book is untouchable."

I grimace in frustration and then a worrying thought occurs to me. "Is this the only copy?"

William is pale. "There is only one copy of the *Keres Coda*, but unfortunately..."

My heart sinks. "There's one for the Valkyrie too, isn't there?"

He nods, a single downward beat, and it's like a knife falling over me. "It's called the *Valkyrie Vade Mecum.*"

Wait... I know that title...

I go into shock. "It's called... what?"

He repeats the name, even though I don't need him to.

That was the book in Anthony Gallo's satchel. I had it in my hands and I didn't know how valuable it was. I rub my forehead with a groan. "Gareth has it already."

"How?"

"I saw it on my first mission, but I didn't know what it was. My target had it. Superior Fallon knew him. He must have been bringing the book to Gareth."

No wonder Gareth looked so happy the morning after I completed my first mission.

William looks shell-shocked. "It's only a matter of time before Gareth decodes it."

Tansy has forgotten the kettle. It sings on the stove before she yanks it off. "William, you need to tell her what else you know."

I raise my eyebrows at them, preparing myself for more bad news.

William says, "The resin can only be dissolved by the sap from the verdan plant."

I relax a little. "That's a poison. Deadly to all creatures. Superior Lincoln told us about it, but it's incredibly rare. Nobody has found it in a very long time."

"Good." William lets out a breath, appearing to relax a little, too. "Let's hope it stays that way."

As I stand, I rub my forehead, my energy nearly depleted. "Now I have two things to steal from Gareth: the feather and the *Valkyrie Vade.*" Even as I speak, I'm losing focus. I need to put my head on a pillow and sleep. "Forgive me, I need to rest."

"I understand," William says. "We could all do with some sleep."

I push my chair back and stumble away from the table. It's not the flying or even carrying Slade that has drained me. It's losing one of my feathers, a tiny part of my life. I head to the bathroom, wash up slowly, and try not to notice how pale I look in the mirror.

I'll be fine after I sleep. I hope. I've never given up a feather before.

I make it back to my old room, where Slade is sleeping soundly. The medicinal properties of the feather will keep him asleep until he's totally healed.

Instead of making a bed on the floor, I slide in beside him, squeezing into the remaining space, burying my head against his chest and wrapping my upper arm around him.

I realize then that I might be in shock. My missing feather is like a black spot in my mind, an empty hole. The only feather that the Valkyrie or Keres ever shed naturally is our birth feather. It falls out when we're one month old.

Mom told me that some Valkyrie used to keep their birth feather to give to their bonded partner—it would allow their human love to live a longer life than normal. But she also told me that too often, birth feathers were stolen like the Keres feather had been.

She'd burned mine to ash just like her mother had burned hers.

I sigh against Slade's chest, finding his regular breathing comforting. On impulse, I rise from the bed again and remove the borrowed shirt and my jeans, needing the press of his skin on mine. He has the same effect on me that a cold shower usually does, triggering the well of power deep inside me, making me calm. So calm.

Also... not calm.

I laugh at myself. Most people would require a cold shower

to get through what I'm feeling right now, but I soak it up, the kick to my heart triggered by his skin and his scent.

I curl around him and within moments, I'm asleep.

~

I wake up feeling peaceful for the first time in a long time.

I fell asleep with my arm and leg hooked over Slade's body, but sometime in the night, our positions have reversed so that I'm plastered up against his chest, his upper leg hooked over mine, his upper arm wrapped around my back while mine curls around his waist and our lower arms are squished between us.

He's still fast asleep.

After carefully untangling myself, I head to the bathroom, and then, sensing movement out in the hallway, I throw on the overlarge shirt and pop my head out the door.

William pauses in the middle of placing something on the floor outside my room across the way. "I thought Slade might need some clothes," he says. "How is he this morning?"

"Still asleep." I take the offered clothing—a pair of jeans and a shirt—with a nod of gratitude. I have no idea if they'll fit him, but it's worth a try.

William gives me a gentle smile. "I'm going to check on Tansy. I'll be back in a couple of hours to open the bookshop. There's fresh bread in the kitchen if you're hungry."

"Thank you, William. I appreciate you letting us stay here until Slade's healed."

He smiles. "I appreciate the company."

He strides away along the hallway but stops before he disappears down the stairs. "I almost forgot. Briar left this note for you. She was here earlier this morning, but I didn't want to wake you."

I thank him and take the note, which is written on the back of one of the bookshop flyers. The note says:

F collected a package from the Family. He continues to meet with their representatives. Will continue to watch.

B.

I asked Briar to watch Fallon's movements and report on his connections with the Tirelli Family. If I read between the lines, Briar's note confirms that Fallon collected the book from them and now has the *Valkyrie Vade*, as we feared.

William has already left, so I'll have to give him the bad news later. Closing the bedroom door behind me, I return to bed, curling up against Slade again, pulling his arm around me.

His voice rumbles against my ear. "Did I die?"

I stiffen in surprise that he's awake. Gathering myself together, I tip my head back to see him, to check that he's not still unfocused.

His eyes are deep wells. His focus is gentle but clear. "Where am I?"

I break into a slow smile, happy that he looks so much better than last night. "You're in a place I lived when I was a girl. We're safe here. And no, I made sure you didn't die."

A slight crease forms in his forehead. "What does that mean?"

"It means I kept you alive."

"I don't have any wounds." He must have checked while I was gone. His gaze is questioning. "How is that possible?"

I grin. "Magic." *It's not a lie.*

"Hmm." He gives me a skeptical look, but it fades as his gaze drops to my lips. "Whatever you did, thank you."

"You're welcome," I say, and it's the most natural thing in the world when I scoot forward a little and drop a kiss on his lips. It's a soft touch, intended to be fleeting, but he responds, chasing my lips as I withdraw, coaxing me back to him so he can kiss me fully. When his arms capture me, his hands stroke up my back and tangle in my hair.

My heartbeats speed up in response, but I place both hands on his chest so I can draw a firm breath. "As much as I want to kiss you, I really can't handle another close encounter with you, Slade Baines. So I think we should probably—"

He growls. "Boot."

"Mmm?"

"Please tell me my boots are in this room."

"Uh… yeah… Let me…" I disentangle myself for the second time this morning, not really sure why it's so important that I find his footwear. Although it gives me breathing space. Snuggling up to him while he's asleep is very different to when he's awake. If I'd known he'd regained consciousness, I wouldn't have been so quick to slide back into bed with him.

I sigh inwardly. I want too many things that I can't have with Slade.

I retrieve his tall boots from the floor at the base of the bed, turning to find him on his feet beside me. He moves so quietly. And he's wearing nothing more than he was on the day I first met him.

I hold up the boots between us, but I'm confused when he doesn't take them.

"Right boot," he says. "It has a concealed pocket inside it."

I check the pocket that's located inside the boot at calf height. It's made of the same protective material as the suit and designed to conceal weapons.

I pull out a string of foil packets. My mouth drops open. "How did you…?"

He looks guilty. "I swiped them from a store while I was blurred. It wasn't my finest moment. But I put some money on the counter when the shop assistant wasn't looking, so it wasn't technically stealing."

I don't quite succeed in smothering a laugh. "You carried these in your boot instead of a weapon? While you were being shot at with machine guns?"

"It was good motivation to stay alive." His grin fades. "Hunter..."

He crosses the distance to me as I allow his boots to slide to the floor with two soft thuds. He stops before he touches me, his focus zeroed in on me, his nearness an intense force that makes me want to lean into him.

His gaze caresses my cheeks and lips, that almost-physical touch as his focus follows the line of my eyelashes to my chin and slowly back again.

He lowers his voice to a husky rumble. "Only if you want to."

CHAPTER FORTY-NINE

y breathing increases. My throat is suddenly dry. "I wanted to the moment you woke up."

I close the gap between Slade and me, knowing that I'm completely prepared for the consequences, for the very real possibility that I will bond with him. I've given him a feather already. I can't kill him. The only other consequence will be that I'll always have to tell him the truth. Well... I'm already doing that. And other than that... never loving anyone else... Right now, I'll take that consequence.

I reach up on tiptoes and press my lips to his. He wraps his arms around me in response, pulling me closer, the intense desire in his eyes making my body heat. I unlock my inhibitions the moment his hand tangles in my hair, his fingertips stroking my neck, sensations running the length of my spine, the shivers a thousand times more intense than before.

Is it because he carries part of me with him now? I stop wondering. I don't care why. I just want more.

His hungry lips find my neck and shoulders, the space between my breasts, and then my stomach. I drag my shirt off my head and he follows the hemline upward, his lips following his hands all the way up the center of my chest from my stomach to my mouth.

As his hands stroke down my back, unclasping my bra, I arch into him. He takes his time, sliding my bra off, stroking and kissing each part of me that's revealed with every infinitesimal shift of the material.

By the time my bra falls to the floor, I'm shivering uncontrollably. My body is ready, but I can't find the words to tell him that. My brain won't connect with my mouth, except to make me moan when he lifts me off my feet and guides my legs around his hips in the middle of the room. But we're both still wearing underwear.

"Slade." I force my vocal chords to function, deeply accusing. *"Clothes."*

A lazy smile breaks across his face. "I don't intend to rush this, Hunter."

True to his word, he holds me against him, stroking the backs of my thighs while he kisses me, tasting every part of my mouth and lips, exploring my neck and the sensitive skin beneath my earlobes. I use the opportunity to trace the muscles of his back, my fingers flexing against his skin, loving the way his breathing increases when I touch him.

He guides me down to the bed, not quite lowering himself over me, taking his time removing my only remaining clothing. As he slides my underpants off, he gives them the same treatment as my bra, every tiny square inch of me kissed and stroked until my head spins and my breathing is out of control. I can't reach him from here; all I can do is run my hands through his hair.

He guides my legs around his hips as he returns to my mouth, remaining a little above me. *Damn.* He's still wearing underwear. His lips part, his pale blue eyes a piercing glint as I press upward, wanting all of him against all of me. He drops his mouth to mine, the lightest kiss, not giving me what I want, making me growl at him.

I wrap my legs around his hips and drag him down to me, giving him a haughty glare when the corner of his mouth rises in a smile that makes my heart hammer.

Then... *damn him...* he starts all over again, his hands and mouth finding every part of me, tracing along my neck, my collarbone, my arms, even paying attention to my tattoo and all of its swirls as his tongue tastes every part of my increasingly hot skin.

The more he kisses me, the more his body warms, a silvery glint growing in his eyes. His satisfied smile grows with every second that I shiver beneath him.

I gasp as the light catches the muscles of his arms and torso, the harsh lines of his face, the slight cleft in his chin. The silvery power that was contained in my feather—now contained in his body—must be responding to my body, to my power. It's the power I've been keeping tightly controlled, but I won't be able to control it much longer.

It shocks me to realize I'll lose control with the next stroke of his hand. No matter where he touches me.

Right then, he lifts himself off me, but I follow him upward, reach for a foil packet, and slap it against his chest. "Now."

To my relief, he doesn't take his time, standing and removing his underwear and taking care of the protection before swiftly returning to me. He's breathing as hard as me and it's all the permission I need to do what I want.

I don't wait for him to make it back to the bed.

I can't.

I rise upward to meet him, drawing him down and inside me in the same movement as we fall back onto the bed. I wrap my legs around his hips, arching into him, drawing him deeper, not caring that we're half off the bed and half on it.

His breath wrenches as he pauses, eyes widening, but only for a moment. "Hunter..."

He gathers me into his arms as our bodies settle into each other, repositioning me farther up the bed. I sigh out the relief I feel to finally be part of him, but it's quickly replaced with the most intense need I've ever felt in my life, through my back and chest, right down into my center. The worst... *best*... burn...

I reach up to brace my palms against the head of the bed, my back arching, needing him to move. His chest is heaving, his lips parted, one hand on either side of my torso. He balances on one hand to run his fingers down my cheek and neck, dropping his lips to mine, drawing my tongue inside his mouth, a fierce kiss.

Shivers hit me so hard that my body rocks against him. He responds by stopping our kiss so he can draw back just far enough to see me, to remain focused on me as he begins to move, slowly at first. The glide of his body against mine sends the need inside me into overdrive.

My body rises to meet his, matching his rhythm as it increases, pleasure washing through me. With every stroke it feels like... flying. Like the moment I lift from the ground and my wings stretch out, the wind beneath them.

Slade's eyes become molten silver as his breathing increases, telling me he's close to the edge. It's an edge I need to leap off, to let go, to let my wings out. Fiery sensation builds inside me, burning through my center up into my chest until I'm gasping for breath, matching his powerful movements. Until...

The orgasm breaks across me. Like glass shattering, splintering every single part of me. I grip Slade's back, holding on, as the crash sends all of me spiraling up and outward, an uncontrollable force so powerful, I rise up off the bed, pressing against him, pressing my mouth against his, crying out against his lips.

He crashes against me, but I know he's close to the edge and not quite there with me, even as pleasure spirals like a windstorm inside me. But it's only getting stronger... so much stronger that I can't bear it.

My back needs to open. My wings need to unfurl.

Why haven't they? *Why?*

Sobs rip from me. "I need… please…" I'm begging my own body, but Slade is listening for what I want. His eyes glow with a light that he shouldn't control and my own eyes widen as I focus on the silver glint that's brighter now than I anticipated.

His voice is a deep growl as he says, "Tell me what you need, Hunter."

I whisper, "You."

His jaw clenches. He draws backward, dragging my lower half up toward his, one big hand gripping either side of my hips, pulling me as close as we can get. The burn explodes inside me, a million times stronger than before.

I forget my wings.

I forget everything.

As the glow in his eyes increases and his own need takes over, Slade drives into me, and I take him with me into the crash.

CHAPTER FIFTY

Slade lifts me upward so I'm straddling him, resting on his kneeling legs on the bed on either side of his hips while our bodies remain connected.

His chest presses against mine with every indrawn breath. The silver light flickers in his eyes, dimming now, but unmistakable.

His arms sweep around my back, keeping me close as he kisses me and strokes my hair, gentle kisses, his big palms coming to rest against my shoulder blades—shoulder blades that should have shifted to let my wings out but didn't.

I didn't bond.

I don't understand how this is possible. Everything inside me tells me that Slade is my match. That I'm *his*. I've never felt anything like what I felt with him just now.

I should have bonded.

Is it because I gave him my feather?

Did I break myself?

I tilt my head back, my loose hair cascading down my back, staring at him wide-eyed, trying to find the answers in the set of his jaw, the part of his lips, the way he's searching my eyes as hard as I'm searching his.

"Hunter?"

I'm certain I look scared right now. I also know it's not an expression he's used to seeing on my face when I look at him. "Slade… ask me something you think I'm afraid to answer."

He shakes his head, as if he's going to refuse. "Why?"

"Because I need to tell you the truth."

He hesitates, a deep crease forming in his forehead, concern etched in every part of his body. "How did your mom die?"

I focus hard. *I won't tell him… I can't tell him…*

"Gareth killed her."

I freeze. Deadly cold. I couldn't lie to him, which means I should have bonded with him, but I didn't.

Something's broken. Something isn't right.

His eyes shoot wide as his arms lock around me. Shock ripples through him so hard that it rocks through me too. "Gareth killed her? But assassins aren't allowed to kill each other."

"He found a way around the Code."

"Does he know that you know?"

"Yes."

Slade is frozen before he speaks in a rush. "Then you're in danger. You have to get out of the Realm, get as far away from him as—"

"No. I can't." My hand shoots to Slade's chest before he can protest. "Please! Don't ask me why."

I disentangle myself from his body. He quickly deals with the protection while I slip on my underwear. He doesn't bother with his clothing, catching me in his arms again.

"Hunter, you're scared right now. After what we just did… after how intense that was… I don't want you to feel like you're alone. Because you're not."

Do I really believe that I'm not alone? Something William said repeats on me. It was at the moment before I healed Slade.

Your mother did everything she could to make sure you would never be weak like she was.

Mom must have done something to my wings. She wanted to stop me having the same weakness she did. She bonded with Gareth and it was the most dangerous thing she ever did. She didn't want the same thing to happen to me.

But it obviously didn't work because I still tell Slade the truth.

And… I know in my heart that Slade won't hurt me.

I make a decision. I may not have bonded with him in the usual sense. My wings didn't reveal themselves. But there is no way in hell we could have sex like that and not be each other's match. And this way, he doesn't know what I am. My secret is safe. Maybe that's what Mom wanted to protect me from: the danger of revealing that I'm not human. I don't know what she did to make this happen. Actually, I don't even know for sure that it was because of her. But I need to stop fighting what I feel for him.

I exhale my panic and fear. Slowly.

"I'm here, Hunter. Tell me what you need."

I relax against his chest. "I need you in my life."

His arms are warm around me and the tension seeps out of him as he relaxes against me too. His voice takes on a fierce edge when he says, "I'm not letting you sleep alone in the Realm."

I allow a smile to creep onto my face. "Don't get all protective on me, Slade. You know I don't need it."

An answering smile lifts the corners of his lips while his gaze caresses me again. "I know you don't, but once was not enough."

His body is already reacting to mine. He drops a kiss on my mouth, a tentative query that sends shivers down my spine.

I answer him by kissing him back.

He murmurs against my mouth, "I'm glad you put some of your clothes back on. I'm going to enjoy taking them off again."

With a laugh, I nudge him backward and quickly rip off my underwear.

"Or not," he says, reaching for a foil packet before lifting me up against the wall, guiding my legs around his hips, and joining our bodies.

This time, I don't fight the burn as we both tip over the edge.

A long time later, we shower and dress. The jeans that William loaned Slade fit him, although he's definitely going for the skinny-jeans look with them and he's in danger of busting open the shirt with his broad chest. I have to bite my lip to keep from laughing about it.

He kisses the lip I bit, taking his time to explore my mouth before I lead him out to the kitchen to make toast. Afterward, we wash up quietly, but my movements slow as I realize we have to go back to the Realm. Slade seems to realize it too.

"You have to be careful," he says. "I know you can look after yourself, but Gareth is shrewd. We both know he doesn't want to choose a new Master. You're a liability for him. He'll have a plan."

I agree, but I can't allow my fear to overwhelm me again. "He has no choice but to make you Master of the Legion now, Slade."

Slade doesn't answer, his expression becoming shadowed. I already told him I can't stay in the Realm forever, but I also told him I want him in my life. I don't know how I can have both, and he's smart enough to know those two things don't fit together.

He pauses before I descend the stairs ahead of him, tugging on my hand. "You should wear your mom's assassin's ring."

"You saw it?"

"The glass case was hard to miss."

I don't hesitate. "You're right. It's mine."

I head back to the bedroom to retrieve the ring, pausing in front of the set of drawers to place the ring on my finger for the first time, amazed at how the magic in it adjusts the size to fit me perfectly.

It may not be a true assassin's ring, but it's spelled to behave like one and I sense the strength in it. For a glass ring to be this strong, it had to have been created by a very powerful sorcerer. I feel an affinity with it, as if it matches my power instead of fighting with it.

Slade watches me from the doorway with an expression on his face that I can't read. "Hunter… you're…"

As I shift on the spot, I catch a glimpse of myself in the mirror on top of the dressing table. My eyes are a deeper green and my shoulders are thrown back. I am… strong.

There's a lot I might question about Mom's decisions, but this ring is perfect.

I whisper. "Let's go back."

Halfway up the street, we meet William and Tansy walking in the opposite direction. William appears relaxed as usual, but Tansy is quiet, her head down. She only looks up when we're a few paces away and William nudges her.

I don't have time to introduce Slade before Tansy takes a deep breath and begins to speak. "Hunter, I want to apolo—"

She stops mid-sentence, taking a quick step backward, and I'm not sure why until Slade angles in front of me, his hand shooting to my arm, drawing me back in a protective gesture, giving Tansy the full force of his fierce rage.

He isn't wearing his assassin's ring and he has no weapons, but Slade doesn't need magic to hurt someone if he thinks they're a threat.

I whisper, urgently, "Slade, it's okay. This is Tansy. She's my friend."

Slade's glower is unforgiving. "She's a witch. I can sense it."

I say, firmly, "She's a good witch."

He doesn't look convinced. "Is there such a thing?"

For the first time, I have sympathy for the fear Tansy revealed last night. Assassins are trained to treat magical beings as enemies. We're taught every possible way to kill them. Only one of my targets in the last week was human. The other two were magical.

When I first came to Saber Lane, I assumed Tansy was a dark witch too. I would have even taken a shot at Dean, if he as much as looked at me the wrong way.

"Of course there's such a thing. What a person is doesn't define who they are." Then I add with a smile, trying to bring the tension down a notch and emphasize my point, "Mr. Assassin."

Slade considers me and then Tansy. The tension eases from his shoulders, but I can tell that he's forcing himself to relax.

Worry settles in my stomach. I've never seen Slade around a non-human before. Well, a non-human that he can detect, that is. His reaction to Tansy was stronger than I would have thought, even for an assassin.

I take his arm. *Let's start this again...* "Slade, this is William. He owns the bookshop where we stayed last night. He looked after Mom and me when I was a girl and kept us both safe. I owe him a lot. And this is Tansy, a good witch who helps the people on this street when they need it."

Slade gives them both a cautious nod. Tansy's lips are sealed shut. I have a feeling that whatever apology she was going to make has long sailed away.

William steps up, defusing the remaining tension with his calm manner. He speaks carefully, and I'm grateful that he doesn't make any assumptions about how much Slade knows about me. "Hunter, be careful in the Realm. Remember that you can come back here anytime you need help." He glances at Tansy. "We will all help you."

Despite her obvious fear of Slade, she gives me a quick nod and I have to respect that she's trying really hard right now, especially standing face to face with a couple of killers. And offering them help, no less.

"Thank you both," I say. "I'll remember that."

CHAPTER FIFTY-ONE

As soon as we gain entrance to the Realm, we pull up short, the press of Slade's hand against my lower back signaling a warning.

Ridley paces back and forth at the entrance just inside the Realm's wooden door, rounding on us as soon as we appear. He doesn't seem to miss the way Slade touches me, his eyes narrowing, more angry than I've seen him before.

He demands to know, "Where have you been?"

I take a step back. "We went out for breakfast to… celebrate Slade's mission." I glare back at Ridley. "You gave me permission to come and go as I please."

His eyes narrow. For a moment, I think he's going to call me out on the lie, but instead, he glares at Slade. "You lost *this*."

He holds out his palm, revealing Slade's training ring resting on it.

"I found it in a place it shouldn't have been," Ridley grinds out. "Next to a pillow that was in bad shape. But it looks like I was worried sick for no reason."

I search Ridley's face, suddenly realizing… He's angry because he was afraid. I left my room with the door open,

Slade's assassin's ring lying on the floor beside a bloody pillow, and I didn't tell anyone where I was going.

I give Slade a quick shake of my head when he shoots me a questioning look. He was unconscious for all of it and doesn't know what Ridley's talking about.

Before I can muster the right words for an apology, Slade reaches for the ring but quickly withdraws his hand with a sharp indrawn breath.

Ridley's forehead creases. "Slade?"

Slade swallows visibly but speaks carefully. "That ring is not for me anymore."

Where I stand beside Slade, I'm a ball of confusion. It hurts me to touch that ring. Now it looks like it hurts Slade too—but only since I healed him with my feather.

Ridley closes his fist around the ring. "Very well, come with me."

Concerned about where he might be taking us, I ask, "Where?"

The corners of Ridley's mouth turn down and now my stomach churns with worry.

"Gareth wants to see you both," he says, his jaw clenching. "Immediately. In his office."

I exchange a look with Slade. "Okay."

We both step in the direction of the administration building, but Ridley barks. "Not that office. The Cathedral."

"What?" Slade is as surprised as I am. "Why there?"

"And how are we supposed to enter that building?" I demand to know. "Since we're still technically Novices."

"You will enter it because a choice has to be made." Ridley spins and strides away from us without any further explanation.

I don't like the sound of that. What choice? Why does Gareth want to see us both at the same time?

We were allowed to enter the Cathedral when Cain Carter visited and it seems the protections have been lifted once again.

I'm certain Ridley wouldn't be leading us there otherwise. He and I haven't seen eye to eye but he wants a new Master appointed and he wouldn't allow Slade to be hurt.

We reach the Cathedral within minutes and I'm surprised to find the other Novices waiting outside too. They all wear guarded expressions, but each one checks me over in their own way. Brandon's consideration is casual, Rowan's is sharp, and Lutz… Well, a dark grin grows on his face as he looks between Slade and me, as if he sees more than I want him to.

Ridley gestures us all inside with a grunt. As we stride through the hallways, I realize that Slade is no longer hiding his strength. He walks tall, powerful at my side. Brandon might have called me a stone-cold assassin, but Slade is a red-hot one.

Lutz brushes past me, murmuring. "I guess you won't need me after all, sweetheart."

I give him a scowl, and he winces as if my failure to understand him actually hurts.

"You're glowing, Hunter. It's hard to miss."

He walks on without a backward glance, joining the others and Ridley ahead of us.

When I catch Slade's eye, he gives me a quiet nod. "Be careful. We don't know what Gareth has planned."

A few minutes later, Ridley gestures us inside a lavish meeting room. Gareth stands on the far side, but he isn't alone. To my surprise, the Guardian stands beside him, regal in a flowing dress that sways around her when she moves. Fallon and Lincoln are positioned off to the side of the room and Ridley takes up position with them.

Even more surprising, Cain Carter stands on Gareth's other side, a lock of his nearly-black hair falling over one eye. I can't read his expression. It's blank and a far cry from what it was the night of the charity ball.

In fact, I can't read this situation at all.

I check briefly in case the Clave is anywhere in sight, but it isn't. Returning my attention to Gareth, I consider him warily as the other Novices gather around behind us. Seats line the back of the room, but nobody's using them.

I try to relax, but I sense the tension in Slade's body reacting to the tension in mine. He reads me too well. Gareth can't be trusted. Even with all of these observers around us.

Master Gareth jumps right in. "I've called you both here because after Slade's successful mission last night, I now have a problem. One of you must be named Master, but the question is which one."

I glance around the room. "There's no competition. I'm not a candidate."

"Well, unfortunately, you are."

Where she stands beside Gareth, the Guardian's brow furrows deeply. Maybe it's his use of the word "unfortunately."

She speaks up. "Hunter, you were the first Novice to be declared a Superior," she says. "This ranks you above all others."

I can only blink at her. "I'm not a Superior."

Now, she glares at Gareth. "You didn't tell her?"

He shrugs, his gray eyes glinting. "I didn't think she needed to know."

The Guardian folds her arms across her chest, her lips pressing into an unhappy line, but she takes a breath before she speaks once more to me. "Hunter, you became a Superior from the moment I granted you a ledger. The fact that a client requested you by name sealed your status."

What? Many emotions wash through me, but disbelief is the strongest. If what she's saying is true, then it means I could have entered the Cathedral already and stolen the Clave.

I've had a whole week to take back what belongs to me and I didn't know it.

"However," Gareth interjects, unperturbed by my clenched fists. "The mission Slade carried out last night has no match in the history of assassins. The past record was five kills in one night." He inclines his head at Cain with a smile that doesn't reach his eyes. "A formidable record previously held by Cain Carter."

Slade's was seven. He knocked Cain's record out of the ballpark. Cain doesn't look perturbed about it and I respect his reaction to Slade's achievement. Any true leader knows that records are made to be broken. If possible, they break them themselves.

Gareth continues. "This ranks you both equally. Which is why I've called the Guardian and the Heir Apparent of the Horde here as witnesses. I propose a test to determine which one of you should take over the role of Legion Master."

I can't hide the tension in my body now. Whatever he proposes, it's bound to be something that will get both Slade and me killed. On top of that, I don't want to be Master. Now that I know I can come and go inside the Cathedral without harm, I have to steal the Clave as soon as I can and get out of here.

And... leave Slade behind...

I exhale slowly, trying to push aside the sudden pain that pierces my chest.

Gareth continues. "As you know, there is a poison that all assassins covet and have been trying to find for many years."

My thoughts of leaving stop. *Poison? Not verdan... Don't say verdan...*

It's the poison that can remove the resin from around the Clave and reveal the weapon it hides.

"Fortunately for the Legion," Gareth says, with a growing smile, "we have identified that the verdan plant is being harbored by three Furies within the Legion's borders on Mount Greylock. That gives us the right to claim the plant."

My stomach plummets so fast that I sway on the spot. The Guardian gives me an alarmed look. Slade reaches out to steady me but stops himself just in time.

Opposite me, Gareth is triumphant. He knows exactly what this means. He must have decoded the *Valkyrie Vade* already and knows the verdan will remove the resin from the feather. Now he's sending us to fight the Furies and bring it back for him.

"Whichever one of you retrieves the verdan plant will become Master of the Legion."

A whirlwind of thoughts threatens to swamp me, but I push them away. I have to stay clear and focused. Gareth is trying to pit Slade and me against each other. He will count on me not telling Slade what the verdan plant is and what it does. He will count on me fighting Slade to stop Slade bringing the plant back.

And if we don't kill each other, he'll count on the Furies to do it for us.

But he clearly doesn't know me well enough if he thinks this plan is going to work. And he definitely doesn't know Slade.

"You have until lunchtime to prepare yourselves," Gareth says. "Then you will travel to Mount Greylock by helicopter. The journey will be easy. Taking the verdan from the Furies will not be."

Gareth's cruel eyes sparkle at me. The light from his assassin's ring glints as he folds his hands in front of him. "One more thing. You will each now receive your Superior rings. Guardian?"

She retrieves a tray from the table behind her and steps forward with it.

Two rings rest on the tray's surface, one copper and the other silver.

Holding it out to Slade first, she balances it one-handed to point to the copper ring. "Slade Baines," she says, her voice formal. "I've chosen this ring for you to represent your skill and strength."

Slade reaches for it, but his fist hovers, stopping above its surface, descending and then recoiling. His gaze flashes to me.

He turns back to the Guardian and shakes his head. "Not that one."

She blinks at him, appearing taken aback. "But… this is the ring I've chosen based on your current ring. This one is powerful beyond imagination, Slade. It's yours if you want it."

His response is firm. "That is not the one for me."

I consider the other ring—a solid silver ring with fine etchings around each edge and a row of black diamonds set into the center.

I allow myself to smile for the first time since we entered the room as I ask, "How powerful is the one that is intended for me, Guardian?"

She swallows visibly and the admission seems to pain her. "Even more powerful than Slade's. It will allow you to accomplish magic never before seen, Hunter."

I meet Slade's eyes as my smile continues to grow. "Then I believe Slade should have it."

The Guardian gasps. "But, Hunter…"

I hold up my hand to silence her, revealing the ring I've kept hidden in my clasped hands until now. "I already have my own."

Off to the side, Superior Fallon almost jumps out of his skin. "The glass ring! But that is the most powerful—"

"And it's mine," I say firmly. "Left to me by my mother."

Fallon immediately looks to Gareth for a solution.

Gareth's expression is pinched and unhappy, but when it comes to the rings, he doesn't get the final say. "Guardian, what is your ruling?"

"All assassin's rings are supposed to return to me when their owner dies," she says. "However, it is a Superior's right to choose the ring that matches them. Provided I sanction it."

She purses her lips, contemplating me. For a moment, I think she's going to deny me. Then the smallest smile appears on her delicate features, a hint of defiance glowing in her regal eyes. "The glass ring belongs to Hunter Cassidy."

She returns to Slade before Gareth and Fallon can object, holding out the tray again. "Slade? Which ring is your choice?"

He immediately reaches for the silver ring, slipping it onto his finger, allowing it to seal around his skin. The effect is instantaneous. His eyes take on the same silver sheen I saw earlier, the dark gray rims around them even darker and sharper.

My power responds to his, leaping out from me with surprising speed, the air glowing between us.

The Guardian gasps, Cain's eyes widen, and Gareth's confidence fades.

He rallies, a hiss in his voice. "Let the mission begin."

We don't wait to be dismissed. Slade and I spin and stride from the room in unison.

Halfway down the corridor, he murmurs to me. "We can't talk here. Meet me at the dorm once you've gotten your things together."

His voice becomes a growl, echoing in my ears, reminding me of his body against mine. "Gareth isn't going to win."

CHAPTER FIFTY-TWO

I pack as quickly as I can, changing into a protective suit and sturdy boots.

Then I hurry to the food hall to retrieve a small amount of dried food and bottled water. I'm not sure where the helicopter will drop us. Staying hydrated could be the biggest challenge during the trek up the mountain.

My boots pound a determined beat wherever I walk. The other assassins avoid me on the footpath and inside the hall, cautiously watching my movements. I guess news travels fast. They must be wondering if I'll be their next Master. A woman, no less.

Quickly, I return to my room and pack everything I want to take with me: every weapon I have, along with my ledger, finally slinging Mom's sword—*my* sword—over my back. It fits neatly beside my backpack, which is made of slash-proof material.

I need to meet Slade in the dorm, but first...

I need to steal the Clave.

No matter what plan Slade has, I can't come back here after today. I have to get the Clave as far away from Gareth as I can.

I also need to find the *Valkyrie Vade*, defeat the Furies, and destroy the verdan plant. I can't leave any loose ends. Then—and only then—Mom won't have died for nothing.

My hands suddenly shake. There's only so much of my plan that I can share with Slade. There's too much I can't tell him.

One step at a time, Hunter. You can do this.

I stride from the room, ready to implement a full blur on my way to the Cathedral, but I freeze when I bump straight into Ridley outside my door.

He clears his throat. "Hunter."

"Dad."

He flinches, but it's out there and I can't unsay it. I tell myself I'll never seen him again after today, so I may as well say what I'm feeling while I can.

He pulls himself together faster than I expected, staying focused. "Gareth will do everything he can to make sure you die today."

Even if it's the truth, I wasn't expecting Ridley to be quite so forthright about it.

His lips compress into an angry line. "We all know this quest is intended to get rid of you."

Well, Gareth might succeed a little too well. I'll disappear, but not in the way he wants.

Ridley places his hand on the doorframe, leaning up against it. "I know I haven't been much of a..."

"Father?"

He nods. "But I don't want you to get hurt. Which is why I've told Slade who you are to me."

My eyes widen in surprise. "You told him...?"

"That I'm your father. And that if anything happens to you on this quest, it won't matter if he's Master, I'll kill him and hang the consequences."

My mouth drops open.

Ridley's hand clenches around the doorframe. He pauses

before he speaks, chewing his words in a way that tells me I'm not going to like what he's about to say.

"That night Anna gave me her sword, she told me that Gareth was closing in. She asked for my help. But I didn't want to believe what she was trying to tell me."

He swallows. Looks away.

My heart squeezes. My voice is a bare whisper as pain wrenches through me. "You didn't help her."

He shakes his head, looking me in the eye. "As soon as I said *no*, she told me that you were my daughter. Then she looked at me exactly like you're looking at me now."

Rage follows my pain. Mom never asked anyone for help. Never. But she asked Ridley, and he turned her down.

I take a step right up into his chest, trying to control my anger. "And how is that, *Dad?*"

"Like I'm the scum of the Earth."

My hands turn into fists. "She would be alive if you'd listened to her."

"Yes." Raw pain burns at the back of his eyes. "I have no excuses. But I'm not going to fail you the same way I failed her. Which is why I'm telling you... I'm ordering you... don't try this mission alone. You won't get past the Furies by yourself. You need to work with Slade. Once you've got the verdan, then the two of you can decide who's going to bring it back—"

"It's not that simple." I haven't retreated. I'm still in his face. Anger clouds my judgment and makes me take a risk I wouldn't normally take, but I'm about to test his vow that he won't fail me. "Do you know why Gareth killed her?"

He answers me with a quick shake of his head. "No."

"To get the Keres feather," I say.

His forehead creases. "That one he showed us at the celebration? But he said he bought it."

"Mom had it. He wanted it. Badly enough to kill her."

Ridley's forehead is creased, a wary look. "What has this got to do with the verdan?"

"It removes the resin off the feather."

He inhales sharply. "Gareth wants to release the feather and whatever Keres power lives in it."

"I can't let that happen," I say. "Mom died protecting that feather. I need to get it back."

Ridley catches on fast, giving me the information I need. "The feather is in his personal quarters on the third floor. There's a sitting room outside his bedroom where he keeps his most prized possessions. But you'll never get in there undetected—"

I hold up my hand with the assassin's ring on it. I'm not supposed to blur inside the Realm. It's breaking the rules. But I'm about to challenge my father's assertion that he doesn't want me to die.

"Watch me," I say. "Or rather… don't."

I implement a full blur before his eyes and he jolts backward at the space I leave behind. Superior Fallon must have told the other teachers what I did in class, blurring and holding a blade to his throat, but no doubt they thought he was exaggerating.

I pull away from Ridley as he searches the space for me, not finding me even when he taps into his own power. He's wearing his ring today. Giving up, he finally runs his hand over his eyes.

I guess he assumes I'm gone when he says aloud, "I hope she listened to me."

Backing away from him, I run the distance to the Cathedral, my backpack and sword firmly tied to my back.

I pause on the doorstep. I waited nearly six months to infiltrate this building, paid my dues in bruises and almost-broken bones. Finally, I can step inside it without an invitation.

I don't waste any more time.

It takes me only a minute to make it to the third floor and creep along it. I'm completely invisible, but I can't assume there aren't extra protective spells around Gareth's room, so I tread carefully, using my senses to detect any magical boundaries—the usual magical tripwires—and maneuver around them.

Pausing at the door to determine that his room is empty, I enter quietly.

The Clave sits right in the middle of the room, displayed in the same glass case and on the same pedestal as it was the night of the dinner. I check the remainder of my surroundings—a desk, scattered chairs, coffee table, and lots of paintings—before I creep forward the three paces it takes to reach the glass case.

There aren't any protective spells around it. He's too arrogant.

With deft fingers, I remove the lid and lift the feather from its internal pedestal within the case.

I've been through so much pain for this moment. And now the feather rests in my palm, much smaller than it looked inside the case. It's the length of my hand, a brilliant copper color, every part of it perfect and delicate, preserved inside the resin.

Inside Mom's death blood.

I close my fist around it and slip it into my pack.

In its place, I position the tin feather I bought from the homewares store that I visited on the day of the charity ball. It isn't a great decoy; it won't survive close inspection—not by a long shot—but it will trick Gareth's eye if he glances in this direction.

I take a moment to look quickly through his desk, hoping to locate the *Valkyrie Vade* too. I *want* that book. But I'm forced to step back fast when the door opens behind me.

Gareth enters the room, smiling to himself as he walks to the desk and places something inside it that I can't see.

Despite the aura of power and triumph around him, I don't hesitate. I round the furniture, prowling toward him, ready to wipe that self-satisfied smile off his face.

We're alone for the very first time. It will be easy to kill him. Hang the assassin's code. He broke it first. I wasn't expecting to have this opportunity, but now that I do, I'm not letting it go.

I reach for his throat, preparing to let my wings out…

The door opens again and Fallon strides into the room.

I step back quickly, plastering myself against the wall as he walks right up to my location.

"Master Gareth," he says. "We've pinpointed the Furies' location on the eastern side of Mount Greylock."

"I want that plant!" Gareth snarls. "I promised Lady Tirelli she would have her prize." He taps his fingers on his thigh. "Maybe I should go and get it myself."

Fallon takes on a placating tone. "Master, you are powerful, but only Hunter can defeat the Furies. I wish you'd told me sooner that she was Valkyrie. I could have found a way to hurt her. But now you can use her. Send her to do your work for you. Then you can destroy her and Slade."

Gareth clicks his tongue, clearly undecided. "I have the means to kill Hunter now, but it won't be that easy. Slade will try to protect her. You know how powerful he has become. He has an affinity with assassin's magic that I've never seen before, especially now that he has that damn silver ring. Curse the Guardian for letting him take it."

Fallon shakes his head. "Lady Tirelli won't be happy. She was hoping to control him."

Gareth exhales. His lip curls. "I will kill Slade too."

"And who will be Master?"

"I will ask the other Faction leaders to choose. Cain Carter will never agree with the Dominion's choice, no matter what it is. The distrust between him and the Heir Apparent of the Dominion is well-known. Which will lead to a deadlock."

Fallon nods. "Leaving you as Master."

Gareth grins. "Precisely. And once I have the verdan, the feather's secret will be revealed to me."

"Very well." Fallon heads to the door, opening it but pausing there. "I'll make sure everything is in place."

I've heard enough and delayed too long already. The open door is my escape so I slide through it as soon as Fallon swings it wide.

My mind is racing.

Gareth said he has the means to kill me now, but I don't see how that's possible. Is there a way he thinks he can force me to choose my own death? I shudder hard. He did it to Mom. I can't discount the possibility that he will do it to me too.

I force myself to focus on the positives.

I have the Clave. I don't have the Valkyrie book, but I'll have to accept that. Now I need to get to Mount Greylock and destroy the verdan *and* make sure that Slade stays alive. And, dammit, get Slade back here as Master. If I don't get the chance to kill Gareth, I sure as hell don't want Gareth to continue in his position of power in the Legion.

Can I really succeed? I panic-laugh inside. Probably not, but I'm going to try.

I slip along the corridor, down the stairs, then I exit the building and head for a shadowy spot beside it, checking for observers before I exit my blur.

Hurrying to the dorm, I take the steps two at a time, to find the doors wide open.

The room falls quiet when I enter.

Slade stands at the head of the room, dressed in a new protective suit, weapons layered about his body in the same way as they were when he took out that gang. He clips a final dagger to his belt. The other Novices are scattered around him, randomly sitting or standing. I'm surprised to see that Thomas and Matthew are here too.

As I move to Slade's side, he turns to the others. "I think you all know that Gareth doesn't want to be replaced. He'll do everything he can to make sure neither of us comes back alive."

Lutz shocks me by stepping up first, but his question is directed to me. "How can we help, sweetheart?"

Wow, he actually sounds sincere.

I take a deep breath. "Slade and I will do everything we can to keep each other alive. If we survive the Furies, Gareth will come after us as soon as we call it in—as soon as he knows the Furies aren't a threat anymore." I look around at the others. "You need to be on the lookout back here. Delay him. Stop him if you can. When one of us returns, no matter which one it is, you need to do everything you can to keep that person alive."

I swallow, sensing Slade's focus on me. I'm talking about one of us returning, not both, and I don't have to look at him to know he doesn't like the sound of that.

I finish with, "Gareth will fight to the bitter end to stay on as Master for as long as possible."

Rowan says, "You have our word we'll do what you ask."

Brandon, Thomas, and Matthew also nod.

Lutz assumes his usual drawl once more. "Sure, sweetheart."

Slade gives him a nod. There's never been any love lost between them. This is the most amicable I've ever seen them.

Before we leave, Thomas gives Slade a bear hug, thumping him on the back. "Stay alive, cousin. I'll never be able to face your parents if you don't."

Outside the dorm, Slade murmurs to me. "This isn't how I wanted today to turn out. You deserve much more than this."

I miss a step. Just this morning… I close my eyes briefly. He promised that he would sleep in my room tonight but that won't happen now. I open my eyes to find Slade looking at me. The pull toward him is so strong that I have to fight it.

I whisper, "I'm sorry it turned out this way."

I don't want to leave you.

The helicopter is already waiting for us, its blades whirring, the billowing wind buffeting us as soon as we step onto the courtyard.

The Guardian stands beside Cain at the courtyard's outer rim. Gareth and the Superiors are also present to see us off.

Ridley watches me with an eagle eye, but for the very first time, I allow myself to believe that he cares about what happens to me. That he might possibly be willing to fight for me as his daughter.

Cain hasn't said much and he remains a quiet force while the Guardian shouts to us, her voice whipping away in the wind, "We will be here to witness the results and ensure the outcome is certain when you return. Good luck."

Luck isn't going to keep us alive.

CHAPTER FIFTY-THREE

It takes a little over an hour to reach Mount Greylock. The helicopter drops us in a clearing halfway up the mountain, which is covered in fiery orange leaves as the trees change color with the oncoming winter.

There are hiking trails as well as skiing facilities, but we'll have to stay off the well-used tracks. I'd love to implement a full blur, but I'm not sure if I can maintain it for the full trip. I need to conserve my energy for when we arrive at the top.

The Furies are located deep within the forest to the east of the War Memorial Tower on the summit. Their hut is closer to the tourist buildings than I would have expected.

The helicopter's copilot hands us maps as well as radios. In his words: Whichever one of us is still alive can call it in. The pilot and copilot are both Superiors—ones we've never met before. As soon as we disembark, they lift off again.

I lead the way through the trees, following the slope upward while Slade watches our backs. We keep up a quick pace and I'm glad my boots are supple and comfortable for the trek. I've got to hand it to Ridley. He really knows how to choose our clothing for us. We stop regularly to keep up our fluids, navigating through the fiery trees.

Finally, Slade breaks the silence. "I couldn't ask this back in the Realm and I don't know if it's safe to talk even now, but this mission isn't only about killing us, is it?"

"It isn't."

When I don't elaborate, he persists. "The verdan is a powerful poison. It's worth a lot to anyone who has it, but there's more."

He's way too smart. My heart skips a beat, but he didn't ask me a question, so I don't have to answer.

I turn to him, placing a hand on his chest, sensing the beat of his heart like it's my own. The power from his assassin's ring calls me. Unlike every other assassin's ring I've come across, this one is almost a mirror to my soul. The Guardian certainly chose it well, even if she meant it for me.

"The verdan does a lot more than most people know," I say. "All I can tell you is that we can't let Gareth get his hands on it. But I can't tell you more, and I need you to not ask."

His expression softens. "I know you have secrets, Hunter. We all do. I want to know yours more than anything else, but I won't ask you for anything you don't want to give."

He shifts his attention to the task ahead of us, his boots crunching softly in the leafy forest bed. "What do you know about the Furies?"

Glad for the change of subject, I supplement the information we learned in class with what I know from Mom. "There are three of them. Hellbent on vengeance. Their power is to inflict pain and disease. I guess that's why they have the verdan. They seek vengeance on men who've committed crimes and they especially don't like liars."

Which means they won't like me at all.

What I don't say is that they're going to know what I am. Mom warned me about that.

I can hide my true identity from many magical beings, but the Furies can see into your soul and every terrible thing you've done, every lie you've ever told. For me, well, that's a lot of hate that's going to come crashing down on me.

Slade adds, "They carry whips and wear poisonous snakes around their bodies. We'll need to be careful of those."

"Do they sleep?" I ask, not knowing the answer.

Slade purses his lips. "I don't know. We should assume they don't. But it's still our best plan to attack at night."

"Slade… I appreciate that you haven't asked me why I'm here," I say. "I've done everything I can to make sure you become Master. Anyone else might think I'm here because I want to claim that right for myself."

He pulls me to a halt, his hand light on my arm, gentle. A smile tugs at the corners of his mouth. His eyes twinkle in a rare show of humor. "You're here to protect me."

I laugh. "Because you won't survive without me."

His smile fades as he fixates on my mouth and eyes. I remember Lutz telling me that I'm beautiful when I smile. I don't do it very often. I'm not sure that I've smiled at Slade very much at all.

He looks shell-shocked.

He swallows. "That might be true."

He resumes walking, but he's not done talking. "You said we can't let Gareth get hold of the verdan. I won't ask you why. I trust there are reasons. But I assume that means we can't take it back to the Realm, even if we defeat the Furies. Do you intend to destroy it?"

"Yes." I close my eyes. *Curse this truth-telling business.*

"Okay. But we can't let Gareth continue as Master. How are we going to beat him?"

I say, simply, "You will go back alive."

Slade stops walking, swinging to me, his blue eyes questioning.

"This test is only because there are two of us," I hurry to say. "If one of us goes back alive, the Guardian and Cain Carter will force Gareth to choose that one, whether or not that person has the plant."

He searches my eyes. "You're not coming back."

"I will keep you alive, Slade. I will destroy the plant. And then I'll send you back to the Legion to claim your place. That's all there is to it."

"Without you."

"Without me," I say.

"No." He takes a sudden, deep breath and it makes me think he didn't intend to speak his denial out loud. It was too raw, too filled with feeling. It wasn't a command, not a wish, not even a request, just pure emotion trying to stop something that can't be stopped. "I don't want to lose you."

My hands start to tremble because he's breaking my heart. "One of us goes back. The other one destroys the plant. The one who destroys the plant will have to run far and fast for depriving the Legion of this prize. That's me. That's what I need to do."

"There has to be another way," he says.

My silence is his answer. I continue walking, stepping through the shafts of sunlight falling between the trees.

It's peaceful around us, far too calm for my pounding heart. I have to focus on my plan and not my feelings. If I keep Slade alive... if I destroy the plant and escape with the Clave... then I will have beaten Gareth.

I will have done what Mom couldn't.

CHAPTER FIFTY-FOUR

We approach the Furies' location at sunset.

There's still enough light to see without lamps, but not enough that our approach is easily detected.

Along the way, we decide that our best plan of attack is to approach by the front door. They will sense us coming, no matter what we do. We can't conceal ourselves and their power will allow them to discern our intentions immediately. Our only option is to draw them out into the open, where we have a chance of fighting them.

The hut is a small log cabin with a shallow porch at the front. It looks like an abandoned settlers hut, old but sturdy, no doubt cold, but the Furies won't mind.

Firelight spills from the cabin windows and lamps light the porch at intervals. It almost looks warm and inviting. But that's what the Furies do best—lure in their prey.

We drop our backpacks at the edge of the clearing, concealing them behind a tree.

I unsheathe my sword and Slade grips two daggers. Neither of us carries guns. The Furies are self-healing. Bullets will simply fly straight through them, whereas a blade can be used to do more significant damage that will take longer to heal.

It doesn't take the Furies long to glide out of the building. They have olive skin and deep brown eyes, long legs and graceful necks. They are perfectly identical in looks, triplets, except for the colors of their hair: red, black, and gold.

It doesn't take them long to size us up.

As they line up along the porch, they talk in unison, their voices a sibilant hiss, their question directed at me. "Vulture Woman, we have no quarrel with your kind. Why have you darkened our door this night?"

My gaze flicks to Slade. His brow is furrowed, most likely because of what they called me, but I hope he'll interpret their name for me as an alternative for "assassin woman."

"You have something we want," I say.

A malevolent smile grows across the face of the first Fury, the one with golden hair. Her head swings from side to side like the snake that slithers around her waist.

I have no doubt that she has already read my intentions—she will know I want the verdan—but she asks anyway, "What could you possibly want from us? We have nothing to give but pain and torment."

My lips stretch in a challenging grin. "Perhaps that's what we want."

She glides down the stairs toward me, her feet barely touching the ground. She doesn't have wings, but she can float. She will be able to move fast, to dart with the speed of the snakes she carries.

I stand my ground, not starting a fight as she circles around me, her hands inches above my shoulders, the snakes writhing close to my neck and ribs. Their hisses make my skin crawl, but I remain completely still.

She pauses, her hands above my back. A gasp on her lips, she leans close and speaks so quietly that I doubt Slade can hear her, even while wearing his ring. "You have given away one of your feathers. But why would you risk such a thing?"

My brow furrows, since I wasn't expecting her to comment on that at all, and certainly not with so much shock in her voice.

Without waiting for a response, she makes her way to Slade, who remains tense but still as she circles around him at a snail's pace, assessing him from his boots to his hair, her gaze following the droplet of sweat that slides down his exposed neck, until she returns to face him.

He seems to be a puzzle for her. I expected her to detect that he was the one to whom I gave my feather, but a deeper crease settles across her forehead.

Her lips part. "You are… a mystery…"

He remains where he is, his hand on his weapon, no doubt ready to draw it at a moment's notice.

Her hand snakes out as if to grab him and he reacts, his assassin's ring lighting up and the magic igniting around him, silver light glowing from every angle of his body. His dagger flashes. The snakes around her body barely miss being decapitated.

The Fury leaps back just in time.

But instead of displaying fear, she smiles at him. It lights up her face and for a moment, she is beautiful, alluring, her hair a golden wash down to her waist, her inhale a gentle pull.

Alarm shoots through me as Slade's hand relaxes on his weapon. The Fury exhales and so do her sisters. The scent of flowers from their mouths fills the space around us and dulls my thoughts.

Or at least… it's supposed to.

Their lulling voices reach me across the distance, all three Furies speaking in unison again. "This man will be a worthy kill."

I'm already running toward Slade when the snake at the golden-haired Fury's waist darts out, quick as lightning, and sinks its teeth into Slade's neck. I scream with rage as black fluid streaks straight up the veins in his neck and face, filling his eyes.

He jolts, gasps, and drops his weapon. The paralysis is instant. He will still be able to hear us, but he won't be able to see anything and he won't be able to move.

I ram into the Fury, my sword swinging, slicing through the snake's neck in one clean sweep. The reptile drops away from Slade, but the damage is done.

Mentally, I rebuke myself. I shouldn't have let them get this close to him.

The golden-haired Fury leaps out of my way, cackling at me as the remainder of the snake's body around her waist heals before my eyes. It swings around, a new head forming on what used to be its tail.

Her two sisters float around me, circling me.

They speak one after the other so seamlessly that it's no longer clear which one of them is talking. "Why try to save him, Vulture Woman?"

"What is he to you?"

"Join us in the kill."

"You know you want to."

"It's what you are."

I shut them up with a snarl. "You just made me your enemy. The next one who touches him dies."

The Valkyries have never been enemies with the Furies. Our goals have always aligned: vengeance and justice. But now that they've attacked Slade, all bets are off.

The women recoil at the intensity of my declaration, but only for a moment.

The one with the golden hair gleams at me. "Challenge accepted."

She launches herself at Slade, hands outstretched, teeth bared, aiming to drive her fingernails into the bitemarks that the snake left behind.

Slade's eyes are pure black with poison now, his body convulsing as he drops to his knees but remains upright.

I barrel into her, knocking her off course, my blade sliding through her chest at the same time. I spin and deflect a snakebite from the redhead, following through by slicing at the clawed hands of the brunette. She spins out of my way just as I would have cut her hands off.

The one I stabbed is already on her feet, healing quickly. My katana flashes in the lamplight, back and forth, deflecting blows, cutting snakes into pieces so quickly, they can't grow back fast enough.

One of the Furies manages to grab my hand, using her strength to push me aside, just far enough away from Slade for the brunette to dart at him.

"No!" I'm too far away to stop her.

Her long fingernails sink into his neck. I can't see it, but she'll be drawing out his soul before she injects disease into his body.

I fight my way back to him, allowing the burn to spread across my back, preparing to reveal my wings so I can take their lives and save him.

I'm certain he won't see my wings because his sight is clouded. I can hide them again before he regains his sight. His life is worth the risk. He's worth any risk...

Just as I reach her, the Fury wrenches away from Slade, clutching her hand and clawing at the fingers that had connected with Slade's neck. She screams and spits blood and the snakes around her body writhe in pain as she clutches her stomach. Doubling over, she clambers backward.

She shoves her sisters away from Slade, screaming, "Poisoned soul! He is not human!"

Her accusing eyes meet mine as I skid to a protective halt in front of him.

She points at me while her sisters' fingers also rise to me. Accusing. "He. Is. An. Abomination."

The three Furies begin to scream, their wails cutting the air, wild shrieks filling my ears as they spiral around each other.

They whoosh right past me, hissing into my ears, "Not human!"

Their bodies, snakes, and wispy dresses form a flying mass that disappears into the trees.

I return my katana to its scabbard on my back, scanning the sky in case the Furies circle back, but within moments, they're gone.

I spin to Slade, catching him before he falls backward, supporting him and holding his head in my hand. Without hesitation, I place my lips against his wound where the snake bit him and I suck as hard as I can, spitting out the poison it injected into him. I repeat the motion twice more until he finally sucks in a sharp breath, his eyes clearing.

He shocks me by leaping out of my arms and to his feet, forcing me to open my arms and let him go.

He spins to me, half-crouched. I'm not sure if he realizes that he has snatched up his weapon from the ground and is now pointing it at me.

"What the hell were they talking about?" he asks.

"I..."

"They said I wasn't human. But, Hunter, I swear to you, I'm not a magical being. I *hunt* magical beings. I *kill* magical beings. I'm not one of them."

Hunt... kill...

I flinch, but he doesn't seem to see it. I've never heard him speak with so much anger about non-humans. The fury in his eyes scares me.

It's the same force he showed when he met Tansy, when he

336

asked if there was any such thing as a good magical creature. It's so intense that it can't be a product of our training. It has to be something more…

I'm full of fear now as I ask, "Slade, what haven't you told me?"

CHAPTER FIFTY-FIVE

*S*lade's expression darkens, harsher and sharper than I've ever seen it. "My older brother was killed by a woman with feathered wings."

I'm doused in ice. Frozen. My arms, legs, heart, blood—all as cold as death.

A woman with silver wings... My heart pounds like a hammer in my chest and it won't stop. *Not Mom. It couldn't be Mom.* But what other winged women are there? The Keres are all dead, and even then, their wings were copper. Angels don't kill humans. And dragon shifters have leathery wings, not feathers. Maybe a harpy or a hawk shifter... but with silver wings?

I try to think. There has to be someone else. *Anyone* else.

Please... Not my mother...

Slade's voice is raw, his breathing sharp. "I saw it happen. She sucked my brother's life right out of his body. That's when my rage began. That's when I decided to become an assassin. That's when I began pushing myself beyond my limits. To be stronger, faster, more brutal."

He advances on me. "Now they're telling me that I'm not

human?" He drops his weapon to the bed of leaves at our feet, his gaze like a knife across me. He takes my shoulders in his hands. "I'm human, Hunter. I swear to you."

But he's not. Not since the moment I gave him my feather.

A little bit of Valkyrie power now lives within him. That's what the Furies must have tasted and it was poison to them. It would have killed them if they'd drunk more of it. To my shame, I wanted them to because it would hurt them more than Slade. He was going to be fine. It would have taken a little while, but the Valkyrie power would have expelled the snake poison from him.

I can't reassure him that he's human because I can't lie to him. I can't tell him I believe him because I don't. I feel like the blood has drained from my body, leaving me weak and fragile.

I say the only thing that's true: "I hear you."

"I don't want you to think I'm something that I'm not because of what they said. I don't want you to look at me and wonder if I'm…"

He lets me go and I wobble, but he's almost begging me now. He must think I'll hate him or maybe fear him because of what the Furies said.

He has no idea the opposite is true.

My own cruel voice inside my mind finishes his sentence for him, mentally placing the words in his mouth that he doesn't say but I'm afraid to hear: *A monster like me. A monster who killed his brother.*

Because that's all he knows of magical creatures—that they are violent and commit unspeakable acts of cruelty and need to be killed.

I regain my voice, knowing that what I say in this moment could break us.

All I can speak is the truth. "It doesn't make any difference to me whether you're human or not. I will protect you with my life. No matter what the Furies said. You could be human or not human and I would feel the same way about you."

Astonishment floods his features. "It wouldn't matter to you?"

"Not at all. Not every magical creature is an enemy. Some are gentle and kind. Many are harmless. Yes, some are violent, but so are some humans."

He's searching my face again, but his voice lowers, his tone and expression shifting rapidly to concern. "Hunter, you're hurting." His hands cup my cheeks, forcing me to meet his eyes. "I don't know why, but I've hurt you. Tell me what's—"

No, no, no... I can't tell him what's wrong. I can never tell him what I am. I'm grateful now that I didn't reveal my wings to him this morning. I can only imagine what would have happened if I had.

The chances that Mom killed his brother are very high, but she would have had a reason. His death would have been sanctioned, but her ledger can't be read by anyone else, so the Guardian is the only one who knows the truth and she will never say a word.

All I know right now is that it had a significant impact on Slade. He's made it clear that his brother's death made him who he is today, and now he has a natural distrust of all magical beings—especially women like me.

I can't answer his question. I have to stop him asking it.

I crash into him and kiss him before he can finish speaking. His lips are soft beneath mine, surprised, but his arms slip around me, drawing me closer as he deepens our kiss. I link my hands around his shoulders, taking what I need from the taste of his mouth and the sensation of his lips on mine.

My body moves without thought, pulling him back to the cabin, not allowing our lips to part. The Furies won't return for days. Gareth won't descend on us until we call it in.

I tug at Slade's suit and he kisses me back with the same

ferocity. We make it to the porch without drawing breath before crashing through the door into the cabin, slamming it shut behind us.

It's surprisingly homely for a Fury hut. I navigate toward the rug on the floor next to the fireplace, registering the ruby-red plant sitting innocently in a pot on the nearby table: the verdan plant. I know it from the pictures Superior Lincoln showed us in poisons class. It resembles a red orchid: a single short stem filled with bright flowers.

Slade demands my attention, deftly disconnecting the clasps at the side of my suit, his focus zeroed in on me.

I don't know if he even saw the plant. It feels like all he sees is me.

I return to undoing his suit, peeling it off his arms and chest and finally his legs. He tugs off his boots and tips them up to reveal the necessities with a grin. "I'm never going anywhere without these boots."

A laugh tears out of me, but it's almost a sob and he hears it, spinning back to me with concern written all over his features. I kiss him before he can try to ask me again what's wrong, distracting him by urging the last of his clothing off and slipping out of mine.

He doesn't slow us down until we're connected. Then he takes his time exploring my body, sending all of my senses into overdrive.

I take what I can, fearing it will be the last time I do.

CHAPTER FIFTY-SIX

*R*ising up from the rug, I don't put my suit back on.

Instead, I take one of the Furies' dresses. It's soft and sleeveless and will allow my wings to unfold easily, even if it will ride up in the wind.

The idea of flying in a dress is romantic and all, but not so much when the breeze whooshes up your butt. I'll have to tie the material around my waist to keep it from billowing up around my face.

"Hunter."

I can't turn around. This moment is already ripping my heart into ribbons.

This is when I have to say goodbye.

He drops tantalizing kisses along my shoulders as he says, "Promise me you'll come back to the Legion as soon as Gareth loses command."

The idea of belonging somewhere is so alluring. I'm shocked to realize that I want it. The other Novices aren't a threat to me anymore. They might even be my allies now.

But it's all too late. Slade doesn't know about the Clave, which is still hiding in my backpack, and he doesn't know that

I'm Valkyrie. No matter what happens, I have to keep it that way.

I've already delayed too long. "Gareth will continue to hunt me."

"He can't hurt you, Hunter. You're an assassin."

"The Furies are just the beginning," I say. "He'll find another way."

Slade takes hold of my shoulders and turns me to face him. "Don't make me beg, Hunter. Destroy the plant, wait until I'm Master, and then come back to the Legion. Please."

I need to put a stop to this conversation before he asks me anything I don't want to answer. "Slade, you don't want me in your life. You think you do, but you really don't."

His gaze deepens. "Hunter, I lov—"

Our heads snap up as the whir of helicopter blades whooshes overhead.

Slade's alarmed eyes meet mine. "I didn't call it in yet."

"It's Gareth." My heart sinks. If he's taking the chance of arriving before he knows the Furies are gone, it has to be because he discovered the Clave is missing.

Damn. I should have found a way to leave sooner.

Slade launches into action. He grabs my backpack and sheathed sword, helping me put them on before he whirls to the table, grabs the plant, and throws it straight into the fire.

He spins back to me. "Blur now, Hunter. Get out of here. I'll lead him away."

My gaze is fixated on the plant. It sits in the fire, the flames licking *away* from it in a safe sphere that doesn't touch the pot or the flowers. It isn't burning.

I was hoping that destroying it would be as simple as chopping it up or throwing it in the flames like Slade did, but apparently not.

Slade regroups quickly, crossing the distance to the fireplace, reaching right into the flames, and pulling out the plant.

"Okay, same plan." He offers it to me, wrapping my hands around its cool surface. "Blur. Take it with you. Get as far from here as you can. I'll take care of Gareth."

I find myself saying, "Blur with me."

He shakes his head, "You can't blur all the way back to the Realm. We have to split up. If this plant is as important as you say it is, then you need to take it somewhere safe."

He's talking at a million miles an hour. I steal a moment to study the planes of his face, the firelight reflecting across his chest, his hands that will never touch me again.

I whisper, "Okay."

Then I do as he says, blurring myself, watching as his focus shifts from the space where I was to the empty space I leave behind. He must know I'm still here because I will have to open a door to leave, but it's clear he no longer sees me.

I lean forward to kiss him, not pulling him into the blur with me, knowing that he won't see, hear, or feel me. "Goodbye, Slade."

He steps back, his expression changing, becoming resolute, determined.

After he checks his weapons, his hand lingers on the silver ring around his forefinger. I sense him drawing on its power to strengthen him even more than the force he already wields in his body alone.

He steps out of the hut into the darkness beyond, leaving the door wide open behind him.

I follow him out, keeping to the side of the building as the helicopter hovers above the treeline and a single figure fast-ropes to the ground, sliding the length of the thick rope to the leafy forest floor before the helicopter flies away again.

I take a moment to hide the plant in my backpack. Just like it looked in the flames, it appears to have an invisible shield around it that stops it breaking against anything else in my bag.

I zip it up to the sound of Gareth's demand for answers.

"Where is Hunter?"

"She's long gone."

Gareth's mouth twists into a cruel line. "Let's see if that's true."

His hand shoots out. He's wearing not one, but two assassin's rings. One of them is the copper ring that Slade refused to accept, the one that was like his training ring, the one that hurt me.

The one that hurt him.

A blast of light streams across the space between them.

I swallow a scream as Slade evades the blow, darting out of its path. He implements a partial blur, silver light streaming around his body, making him faster and more agile.

Gareth spins and blurs too, copper light filling the space around him. He throws off his cloak and moves faster than I expected. The breath stops in my throat at how fast he moves. There's a reason he became Master.

I swallow a scream as the two men collide, power streaming around them.

They trade blows at lightning speed, the force of their magic shifting the forest bed, lifting the leaves with every thud of their boots or impact of their bodies.

Silver and copper light encompasses them and creates an eerie glow up into the trees and the dark sky.

Slade is faster, leaner, more agile, but despite that... Gareth is winning.

While Slade's blows knock Gareth around physically, every time Gareth uses the copper ring's power, dark light shoots through Slade and it's draining him, hurting him. Finally, Gareth locks his hands around Slade's neck. The copper ring presses right up against Slade's skin, driving Slade to his knees.

Gareth roars into the forest around him.

"You gave him part of yourself, Hunter! You thought it

would make him strong, but it made him vulnerable. Show yourself or I will kill him."

Gareth waits for me to react. I take a step forward, but I can't believe him. He's trying to trick me. Any moment now, I'm certain that Slade will free himself...

Gareth shouts again. "You think I can't kill him. You think your power will protect him. But I have a secret to share, Hunter. The awful secret about assassin's magic."

Slade tries again to free himself, slamming his fist into Gareth's thigh and sending burning silver light through him. In response, the light from Gareth's ring shoots down his body to meet the invading force, forcing it away. Copper light bursts outward, striking into Slade, knocking his head to the side while Gareth holds him.

My shout is concealed within my blur. "Slade!"

He groans, appearing barely conscious.

My eyes widen as fear consumes me. I take another step forward, indecision raging within my mind.

Gareth shouts, "The rings weren't created by some mythical warlock. They were made from stolen feathers."

He pauses. "Yes, Hunter. Stolen feathers."

My knees wobble. Slade once told me he thought there was more to assassin's magic. He said he didn't believe the story that a warlock created five hundred rings for assassins to wear.

My heart burns at what Gareth is telling me. Five hundred rings means five hundred stolen feathers. No wonder I hated wearing my training ring. If it was powered by a stolen feather —by another Valkyrie's power—then I had no business controlling it. It pushed back at me, and now I realize, it must have been trying to make me stop using it. Humans wouldn't be able to sense it like I could.

Gareth continues. "The ring that Slade now wears was made from a stolen Valkyrie feather. That's why he can wear it without pain. Your ring, Hunter, was not made from a feather at all. It is the only ring that was actually fashioned from powerful magic."

His lips curl into a smile as he asks me the question I fear. "Guess what kind of feather was used to make this copper ring?"

My heart has stopped beating within my chest. I carefully place the bag with the verdan and the Clave inside it onto the ground and then I exit my blur, stepping into the open, the dress swishing around my legs as I move toward Gareth.

I whisper, "A Keres feather."

It's the only power that can kill me. And now it can also kill Slade.

"There you are." Gareth smiles. "I have to thank you, Hunter. It's almost impossible to know which feather was used for which ring. They were created so long ago that nobody knows anymore. Even a copper-colored ring can be made from a Valkyrie feather. My old ring, as it turns out, is one of those. But when Slade returned this morning with his wounds magically healed and suddenly refused to touch this ring, it was obvious it was from a Keres. Finally, I have the power to destroy you."

Slade is trying to speak, his gaze becoming more focused as he fights the concussion. "Wh… at?"

Gareth laughs. "We're going to play a little game now, Hunter. Slade is going to ask you questions and you're going to answer them. Truthfully. Like you have to."

Slade finds his voice, stronger than I expected. "I'm not asking her anything."

"Oh, I think you'll want to." Gareth licks his lips. "Why don't we start by asking her what she is?"

CHAPTER FIFTY-SEVEN

My hand shoots out, trying to stop the question rising to Slade's lips. The perfectly normal question that anyone would ask.

"What is he talking about?"

I slump. *No.*

Gareth gleams as he tightens his hold around Slade's neck, driving him closer to the ground. "There we go. Question number one. Such an innocent one, too. You have no idea what you just did to her, Slade."

My mouth is already opening, the compulsion too strong to deny. "I... am..."

Not human. Not human. Not human.

I gasp. Inhale. Exhale.

I fight it with everything I have inside me. Pain wrenches up from my stomach, biting and clawing at my insides. I can't tell Slade what I am. I *won't* tell him what I am. If I do, he'll never trust me again.

I scream out the pain, doubling over, shrieking it out.

This compulsion killed Mom. I have to fight it with everything I have.

The force of my scream blasts across the clearing like a physical force, buffeting Gareth and Slade, sending leaves whirling into the air.

Slade shouts my name, ramming his fists into Gareth's chest this time, streaming power into him as hard as he can. "Hunter!"

Gareth shoves the copper ring flat against Slade's temple, making him roar with pain, making him shudder and shake. "Ask her what she is!"

"No!"

"Ask her where the Clave is!"

Slade's eyes water, pain ripping across his features as he tries to fight back. "I don't know what that is!"

My pain eases as soon as Slade's attention leaves me. The compulsion lifts. But Slade's pain is getting worse and it's hurting me too. The connection between us is too strong for me to deny the pain he feels.

"If you don't do what I want, Slade, you're no use to me," Gareth says. "If you're no use to me, then I *will* kill you."

Slade rasps, "Go to hell."

Gareth's eyes meet mine across the distance. "So be it," he says.

I shoot forward, ramming into Gareth, knocking Slade out of his grip. The Keres power that Gareth was about to unleash into Slade's body sizzles past me, barely missing my chest. The deathly force makes my blood run cold.

I have one focus now and moments to get it: the ring. Somehow, I have to remove it from Gareth's finger.

I punch a fist into his face, forcing him down, grabbing his hand at the same time, screaming out the pain as I take hold of his finger in my fist.

The ring won't kill me until he wills it to and it will take him a moment to recover from the blow to his head.

I pull at the ring, trying to tear it off his hand, searing pain burning me because of the contact. It doesn't budge. The malevolent force inside the ring knows what I am.

I am its enemy. Its purpose is to kill me.

Gareth rallies, his cold eyes meeting mine. He struggles for a moment before he realizes… I'm right where he wants me. I'm touching him, and all he has to do is unleash the Keres power into me where I crouch over him.

I have mere seconds. I have to act. Right now. There's only one way I'm going to get this ring from him in that time. Even reaching for my sword will take too long.

There's only one way to save myself. Only one way to save Slade.

Gareth's cold eyes dare me to take that chance, knowing what it will cost me.

At the same time, the Keres power bursts from his hand, a burning flame that shoots across my palm, up my arm, to my shoulder…

Tears of pain stream down my cheeks and sizzle in the Keres flames.

I have no time.

I meet Slade's eyes where he has fallen back against the ground. He jumps to his feet, darting forward to help me.

More fear than I've ever felt streams through me in that moment. Fear of what I'll see in his face. But I have no choice.

My power bursts through me. My back shifts and my wings surge open, shining and powerful, spreading across the clearing like silver bullets.

Slade skids to a stop, his eyes shooting wide. He jolts and falls backward, away from me. His blue eyes sharpen, his body more tense than I've ever seen it, his power leaping outward, no doubt triggered by the intensity of my own power.

He is consumed by shock. Pure shock. I feel it like a physical force that knocks into me and I know that right now he won't see me. He will only see his brother dying.

He will only see the woman who tore his life apart.

My heart rips into two, splitting so painfully that I have no chance against it. My only defense is to switch my feelings off completely because if I don't, I'll collapse. If I want to stop Gareth, I can't feel anything now. Not pain, not fear, not sadness.

Not loss.

I turn back to the old Master. The Keres power has almost reached my heart. I take hold of Gareth's finger, my body burning brightly.

His skin smokes beneath my hand.

He screams as I snap his dead finger right off. I drop it to the ground and the copper ring with it. The Keres power fades, its poisonous force draining from my body, as if I'm emerging from a deep pool of water.

I stare at the ground where the ring lies as Gareth continues to scream, clutching his hand, his power gone. The wound is cauterized, so he won't bleed. Other than losing his finger, he is unharmed.

I haven't broken the first rule of the Assassin's Code.

He scrambles to grab the ring, but I rest my boot over it so he can't reach it.

Using my full strength, I take hold of him and wrench him off the ground, beating my wings as he continues to shout and struggle. Then I knock him into the nearest tree trunk—a sturdy pine—whacking his head against it.

He goes limp in my arms, unconscious.

I float there, holding him, the silence behind me deafening.

Slade's emotions beat at me like hot flames. I sense them all with my heightened power. I've shown him who I am—*what* I am—and the pain and shock that rises off him is excruciating.

I close my heart, kill my feelings, and fly Gareth's unconscious body to Slade, dropping him at Slade's feet like an offering. I hover in the air beyond him, my wings beating gently, maintaining my height just a little above the ground. Eye height with Slade.

I meet his gaze and he is… shattered. In pieces. Barely holding himself together.

My presence must be triggering unwanted memories, images of his brother's death that he's pushed away for years. The longer I stay, the more pain I'll cause him.

My voice doesn't sound like my own. My speech is disjointed. "Tie him up with your power. He can't hurt you now. I'm sorry, Slade. You're not entirely human anymore. I healed you last night in a way that changed you. You were going to die. I had no choice."

His eyes are like stormy pools. His voice is raw. "The bullet wounds. That's why they were gone."

I lower myself to the ground, my feet settling into the leaves so that I can curl my wing in front of me and accentuate the feathers, revealing the empty spot at the base of them. "I used a feather to save you."

His gaze rises from my wing. I thought that he would stop searching my eyes now. That he would have the answer he was always looking for, but still… he searches.

He asks, "What did Gareth mean when he said you have to answer me truthfully?"

"It's the only weakness a Valkyrie has. Bonding with a man means I can never lie to him."

"You bonded with me?"

"Yes."

"You have to tell me the truth?"

"Yes." I swallow and try to focus. "You need to call it in now. Tell Ridley you don't trust the helicopter pilots. He'll make sure you make it home safely. You will be Master of the Legion."

Slade doesn't move. He's perfectly still. His voice tears out of his throat. "Do you love me?"

"Yes."

Tiny pieces of my heart spiral away from me. I beat my wings, backing away from him, and retrieve the Keres ring. Without touching it, I scoop it up with the nearest large leaf. I don't intend to take the deadly weapon with me.

If there's nothing else I can do, I need Slade to know that he doesn't have to fear me.

I tuck my wings into my sides and walk back to him, holding out the ring to him. "If… one day… you feel you must kill me… then this is the weapon to use."

He stares at the copper ring, his face ashen, pale, and every muscle in his body tense. "I never understood before why you looked at me as if I could destroy you."

His gaze shoots to mine. Pain flares in every angle of his features, every taut muscle in his jaw, the set of his shoulders, the press of his fingers into his palms, curled up like fists.

His eyes become deep pools and there's nothing but aching in them.

He curses softly and a bitter exhalation escapes his lips. "All I do is hurt you."

He holds my gaze for a final moment. A moment that destroys me.

Shaking his head, a single movement, he steps away from the ring and away from me, refusing to take the weapon. His emotions shut down and his expression becomes a perfect mask. A perfect assassin's mask, revealing nothing.

I want to see anger, distrust, hatred. Anything. *Anything.* Not the emptiness I find in his face.

"Go, Hunter," he says. "Don't look back."

I step away from him, my wings held tightly to my sides, silver feathers glistening in the moonlight. Striding through the bed of leaves, I bend to pick up my backpack, dropping the copper ring inside it.

My knees buckle. I almost fall but reach out to right myself against the nearest tree. I need to scream out my pain, but I can't do it here.

Everything I needed to retrieve from the Legion is either in this bag or on my back: the Clave, my mother's sword. I even have the verdan, and now a copper ring that can kill me.

But I found a lot more than that in the Realm.

I found my father. And I found love.

Then I lost it.

I turn back only once to see Slade binding Gareth from head to foot with magic, immobilizing him in glistening silver ropes. Slade's movements are focused, angry, and brutal as he drags the binding around Gareth's body with ruthless force.

He is the Master Assassin now.

Seeming satisfied that Gareth can't move a muscle, he retrieves the radio, gripping it in his fist so hard that his knuckles turn white. His chest rises and falls with sharp indrawn breaths.

He presses the button and speaks. "Come and get me."

There's a pause.

Ridley's voice answers. "Where's Hunter? Is she safe?"

Slade doesn't look up as he grips the radio. Doesn't look at me. "She's gone."

I back away from the pool of light outside the cabin, needing to fly, to leave this heartache behind. To escape it.

I protected the Clave. I did what Mom couldn't.

But I paid the price.

I start running, beating my wings.

Mom gave her life to safeguard the secret that the Clave hides. But... I'm not her.

I'll be damned if I don't find out what the weapon is. And then I'm going to destroy it. Because until it's gone, I won't be safe.

Until it's gone, I won't be free.

It's time for this secret to be unearthed.

I soar up over the tops of the dark trees, away from Slade, away from everything I want, leaving fragments of my heart behind with every beat.

Continue Hunter and Slade's story in Assassin's Mask.

ASSASSIN'S MASK

(ASSASSIN'S MAGIC BOOK 2)

I am an assassin. Bonded to my enemy.

Love could be my end.

I fought beside Slade Baines in a battle for our lives, only for his secret to tear us apart.

Determined to ignore the broken pieces of my heart, I vow to destroy the deadly weapon that my mother died to protect.

But my enemies are gathering, targeting everyone I love in their quest to find the weapon.

I'm forced to make a deal with one of the Legion's most formidable assassins—a deal that throws me right back into Slade's path.

It's a dangerous place to be.

Slade's power is growing. Cold. Ruthless. Irresistible.

As undeniable as the connection between us.

One thing, I know for certain:

Rejecting our bond could destroy my heart.

Content information: Assassin's Mask is dark urban fantasy romance, the second in the Assassin's Magic series. Recommended reading age is 17+ for sex scenes, mature themes, and violence. Ends on a cliffhanger.

ASSASSIN'S MENACE
(ASSASSIN'S MAGIC BOOK 3)

**I am a villain's daughter. Trying to escape my past.
Love can never be mine.**

I've mastered the art of hiding in plain sight.

My only goal is to bury the violent secrets of my past. A past
that was forced on me, not chosen.

But my fate is turned when I unwittingly step between an
assassin and his prey, an act that provokes the fury of the
Assassin's Legion.

Now, my only ally is a stranger. Cain Carter. A man whose
touch heats my body and soul.

I literally fall into his arms, and he is…

Kind. Compassionate. Terrifyingly sexy.

He offers me everything I've never had: pleasure, safety, and hope.

Until I discover that he has violent secrets too.

That's when I'm forced to make a choice.

A choice that will destroy my heart.

Content information: Assassin's Menace is dark urban fantasy romance, the third in the Assassin's Magic series. Recommended reading age is 17+ for sex scenes, mature themes, and violence. Ends on a cliffhanger.

ALSO BY EVERLY FROST

ASSASSIN'S MAGIC

(Dark Urban Fantasy Romance)

1. Assassin's Magic

2. Assassin's Mask

3. Assassin's Menace

4. Assassin's Maze

5. Rebels

6. Revenge

7. Rogue

8. Assassin's Match

SOUL BITTEN SHIFTER - COMPLETE

(Dark Urban Fantasy Romance)

1. This Dark Wolf

2. This Broken Wolf

3. This Caged Wolf

4. This Cruel Blood

SUPERNATURAL LEGACY - COMPLETE

(Angels and Dragon Shifters)

1. Hunt the Night

2. Chase the Shadows

3. Slay the Dawn

4. Claim the Light

DARK MAGIC SHIFTERS

(Dark Urban Fantasy Romance)

1. Wolf of Ashes

2. Bond of Flames

3. Crown of Fate

KINGDOM OF BETRAYAL

(Fantasy Romance)

1. A Sky Like Blood

2. A Sin Like Fire

3. A Storm Like Iron

4. A Soul Like Glass

BRIGHT WICKED - COMPLETE

(Fantasy Romance)

1. Bright Wicked

2. Radiant Fierce

3. Infernal Dark

STORM PRINCESS - COMPLETE

(Fantasy Romance)

1. Book 1

2. Book 2

3. Book 3

DEMON PACK - COMPLETE

(Dark Paranormal Romance)

1. Demon Pack

2. Demon Pack: Elimination

3. Demon Pack: Eternal

MORTALITY - COMPLETE

(Science-Fantasy Romance)

Mortality Complete Set: Books 1 to 4

1. Beyond the Ever Reach

2. Beneath the Guarding Stars

3. By the Icy Wild

4. Before the Raging Lion

<u>Stand-alone fiction - dark romance</u>

Corrupt Me: Immortal Vices and Virtues

ABOUT THE AUTHOR

Everly Frost is the USA Today Bestselling author of fantasy romance, urban fantasy and paranormal romance novels. She spent her childhood dreaming of other worlds and scribbling stories on the leftover blank pages at the back of school notebooks. She lives in Brisbane, Australia with her husband and two children.

- amazon.com/author/everlyfrost
- facebook.com/everlyfrost
- instagram.com/everlyfrost
- bookbub.com/authors/everly-frost
- goodreads.com/everlyfrost